The Dutchman

By Susan Eddy

With illustrations also by Susan Eddy

Chapter One The Arrival

November 5, 1839. Canterbury Connecticut

Down a lane of little shade, between two great stone walls and beneath an archway, a wagon pulled by two giant black horses neared the end of its journey. The gentleman driver let out a breath as he approached a red clapboard manor home, passing between rose gardens still showing hints of color. He brought his horses to a stop in a large circle between home and barn where a man with a badge was holding two saddle horses. "What is this about?"

Two work men were there. Behind them, three women in aprons hurried out from the house.

"You must be Van der Kellen's son. That makes this man your problem now," the constable said.

"Excuse me?" Robin Van der Kellen removed deer skin gloves one finger at a time.

"I didn't do nothing he says," the workman insisted.

"You were too drunk to know what the hell you did." The constable watched Robin climb down from his wagon. "I brung your man back. He owes the tavern $10 for that window he busted, unless you want to pay it now."

Van der Kellen's mouth came open. He looked down, extracted his leather purse and counted out the coins. "I will deduct it from his wages." He handed it to the constable.

"Constable Poole. Welcome home." Poole pocketed the money and mounted his horse. He rode off, pulling the second horse with him.

 Van der Kellen looked at the two stockmen and three maids before him, speechlessly. He was dressed rather finely for a man on the road, in a black three-piece suit and a wide brimmed black leather hat. His vest had 5 shiny buttons. A pistol on his hip was revealed through his open jacket. The brass trim of it caught the light.

"I'll tend these horses for you," the other stockman said. Van der Kellen's horses had long curly manes and equally long curly tails. Their hooves were hidden within plumes of fur that grew down from their ankles. Their tack was also fancy, dressed with silver buckles on the bridles and silver brow bands. In fact, gold trim on the browbands glimmered against the pure black horses. "We will need to unload your belongings first. Did you drive these all the way from Boston yourself, sir? Fancy horses for this sort of work. What do you call these?"

"Friesians. They're a draught horse originating in the Netherlands. Very powerful and nimble. Headstrong. Stopped four nights along the way instead of three. Check their hooves." The gentleman's accent was foreign. He took in the estate, the burgundy red painted home, the barn, the servant's quarters and the five employees standing around him. He removed his leather hat, freeing a bell of light brown shoulder-length hair. "Good evening. I am Robin Lodewijk Van der Kellen, second eldest son of Willem Van der Kellen. I am a barrister, a lawyer, like my father. I am not a farmer. And there will no doubt be some changes necessary around here, for myself most of all. But I thank you for staying on following his passing."

Marie stepped forward, a pretty, dark-haired maid. "Sorry for your loss, sir. You must be exhausted from your travel. Can I serve you hot supper and offer you some tea or water?"

"Thank you, miss. I would appreciate that very much. I confess I'm starving. The one thing I do need unloaded here tonight is this bed. I would have that brought inside and established in the master bedroom. That is where I'm sleeping tonight. If that means the rest is unloaded tomorrow, fine with me. But I am sleeping in my own bed tonight even if I am not in Boston any longer. Slept three of the last four nights on the ground."

"No wife beside him." Marta tugged onto both of the maid's aprons.

"Yes, sir. We'll get right to that," the elder stockman said.

"If there is anything of my fathers in that room, I would have it removed before I walk in there. Tonight anyway, I would not see any of it," Van der Kellen said.

"Yes, sir," June said. "I'll see to that."

"Thank you. I appreciate it." Robin looked over his horses briefly, before collecting his rifle off the footbed. He walked around the back of the wagon, pulling up the canvas to indicate the parts of the bed he wanted. His put his rifle strap over his shoulder. His feather mattress was on its side with pieces of a mahogany bed against it, two trunks, two leather saddles, and a number of crates of belongings.

"I'll water these horses straight away." The troublesome stockman leaned in for a look at the rifle. "Had any trouble on the road? That's a short barrel."

Robin met eyes with him. "I had no trouble at all."

The man still stared at him, taller than him, bigger. Neither stockmen went to work.

"Am I having another problem with you?" Robin asked. "I only just arrived."

"Nope." The man broke off his stare and stepped round the back of the wagon where Albert shook his head.

"McKinney." Marie scolded him. "Behave yourself. This is his farm now."

"Get back in your kitchen, woman!" McKinney shouted back.

"Never raise your voice to a female." The gentleman warned with a fist on his hip, holding the jacket behind his pistol. "I see everyone seems to know their place here except you. Allow me to explain it to you. Carry my bed in the house. Assemble it. Unhitch these horses and bed them down for the night. Is that clear enough?"

"Yes, sir." McKinney lowered his eyes.

June walked back to observe the bedding. "He has his own mattress with this. Let's get the other out of his room and get his bed made up when they bring this in. We'll move the other down the hall. This bed's much nicer."

"Thank you," Robin said to her. "Stockmen, what are the livestock on hand?"

"Six cattle. Two milking cows. One pig. A dozen or so chickens. Two riding horses," Albert said.

"Is there room in the barn for my two Friesians?" Robin asked.

"Of course, sir. We can get your wagon unloaded tonight for you."

"Thank you. Mind this one on the left." Robin patted the horse. Then he turned to look at the three women with his hands on his hips. "Any pressing concerns of the estate I must know about?"

"Just that supper is ready for you." Marie gave him a bit of a courtesy.

"Your names, please. You first, the girl with authority."

Robin Van der Kellen entered his new home by way of the kitchen door. The kitchen had a large hearth, simple dining table, working tables along the back walls and the room smelled of wood fire and fresh baked bread. The warmth hit his cold face. Behind the door were empty wooden hooks on the wall, and he hung his hat there. From the ceiling above his head there were candles hanging, baskets, and bundles of dried herbs.

Marta hung Robin's overcoat on the hook beside his hat and gave it a quick caress disguised as straightening. She followed June upstairs to work on the bedroom. They both carried his pillows and quilts up. They had previously made the master bed up with the best linens of the house, which they would now pull off and store away.

He watched them go by and waited there in the kitchen, looking about and letting his eyes adjust to the darkness. The room had wide planked flooring, post and beam ceiling, grey painted wooden walls. There were pots and pans hanging from the ceiling in the work area. Light came from the fireplace, two windows on either side of the door and two oil lamps in the room.

Marie, the young dark-haired woman, stepped behind the worktables in the kitchen. She filled a bowl with water and collected a small towel and bar of soap. She brought these to the kitchen table. "If you'd like to wash your hands, sir. Then I will show you to the dining room while they bring your bed up the stairs."

Robin just nodded and laid his rifle on the table with a thud. He washed his hands and face too over the bowl and used the towel to dry up, letting out a surprisingly long sigh. When he stood upright, he stretched. Then he looked around and set his rifle up on the broad mantel of the kitchen fireplace. "If you don't mind, this is where I prefer to keep this. Will it be in your way?"

"No sir. I can hardly reach the mantel. That's why it's empty."

That made Robin smile a bit. "Indeed. Yes miss."

"Longuiel. Miss Longuiel. This way." She led him to the hallway, where the grand stairway wound up toward the second floor. A parlor and grand front entrance of the house were at the base of the stairs. To the right was a hallway. The first room was the formal dining room where a place was set for him with white cloth, blue flowered china, glassware, and biscuits. A fire was crackling the fireplace on one side of the table. The setting for him was with his back to the fire and facing the hallway. "I thought you might be cold from the ride here or would you prefer to sit on the end?"

"This is wonderful. Thank you, Miss Longuiel." Robin took his seat. He drank the water and sat back in a bit of exhaustion. "Your name is French. Your accent American."

They could hear the parts of the bed being carried up the stairs.

"Yes, it is. Would that be your middle name on the archway out front?" Marie asked.

"Yes, though more likely named for my maternal grandfather." He was looking up at the sideboard along the wall, and the tapestry hanging beside it. The tapestry was a map of New England.

"If you'll excuse me, I'll fetch your supper." The girl left the room.

In the kitchen, Marie Longuiel dished out the pork roast, carrots, potatoes, gravy onto a plate, set the plate on a tray.

The two other maids came in from outside carrying bags and crates. Marta commented to her, "Found the bedroll he slept on out there. His back could use a comforting, and that beautiful little backside of his."

"Wouldn't mind that occupation, would you? June, what did his father say about him?" Marie cut a slice of warm apple pie to add to her tray. "Tell those two to keep it down while he's eating. You don't want him to think they're killing each other with his bed posts."

June grumbled, "Fine thing when horses wear more gold than I ever will."

Marta whispered back, "No wife. I thought he had a wife."

"I don't know where you got that idea," June said. "Did he stop to polish them boots up the road?"

"Keep it down you two," Marie urged.

"What's wrong with him that he doesn't have a wife?" Marta said.

"Not a thing," Marie whispered.

"Yeah, well his father didn't think much of him," June whispered very quietly.

"What did he say?" Marie asked.

"I just hope they don't put a bed post through the wall. Doesn't sound like he wants to lay his body anyplace his father did. Wait till you see the embroidery on these." June had arms full of fine bedding. "His father wrote him a number of times and never heard back, and he only lived in Boston."

"Might as well be the moon from here. What else did he say?" Marie picked up the tray. "Don't forget to make sure we removed all of his father's things from that room. Probably afraid he passed in that other bed."

"All gone. Just complained that he never did a thing he was told."

"Like why you don't run a hay farm when you're a lawyer?" Marie carried the tray across to the dining room and the other women carried more of Robin's belongings up the stairs.

Robin was standing up in front of that tapestry, studying it, as Marie carried the tray in. His jacket was off and it was her first sight of him in trousers, vest, and shirt. He was quite slender, though his rear end and thighs had a nice musculature, evident through wool trousers. His hands were on his hips. She served his meal, finding his holster and pistol lying on the table. "Will you be needing anything else, sir?"

Robin turned around. "Ahm, no thank you. That smells wonderful, Miss Longuiel."

"I will check back with you shortly."

She left the room and Robin was alone. He sat down with a cup of tea and looked down at his place setting of plate, a fork, a spoon, and a knife. Slice of pie. Two candlesticks were on either side of him, candles lit. He unfolded a simple napkin and laid it out on his lap. And soon the food melted in his hungry mouth. The corn biscuits were delicious. The pork was so tender. The roasted carrots could use pepper and then they would be perfect. No black pepper on the table.

In the kitchen, the two stockmen paused on their way out for more bed rails. "That's his rifle?" McKinney pointed at the mantel.

"Leave it. It's his house now," Marie scolded.

"Never seen one so short. I have to look." He took it down to examine it.

"Baker Rifle Company. Put it back." Albert looked over his shoulder.

"That's British. Ain't it?" McKinney put the rifle back as it was, arranging the strap as Van der Kellen had. "Never saw a British gun before."

"I have. Better this way than aimed at you," Albert said. "Get that bed put together. Move on."

"Why is it so short?"

"Close combat maybe. Place for a bayonet on it. See that pistol on his hip, did you?"

"Suppose mister fancy knows what a bayonet is for? Shaving his whiskers maybe? Opening letters?"

"Shut up, you two fools." Marie put her hands on her hips. "And get out of my kitchen."

"Oh, it's her kitchen but his house. We'll see how that works out."

Marie ate her supper standing up in the kitchen.

"Carrying money, I don't blame a gentleman for wearing a gun on him." June sat across from Marta at the table. "Stupid not to. He doesn't look poor."

"But his pistol on the table in there, like he doesn't trust us," Marta said.

"I don't trust some of us," June remarked.

The two stockmen looked at her.

"Well, you have to admit he knows horses," Albert said. "I'll tell him tomorrow one hoof on the ornery one is a bit cracked. Shoe lost a nail. Might have given him some grief on so long a journey. Caused by the road, no doubt. Handled him well to get it here without laming the animal."

"I'm not telling him shit. That horse knocked me down four times going into his stall. Finally, he took the other ones' stall and pushed that horse right out. So fine. I shut them in the opposite of how they road in here. Bloody insane they are."

"I'll tell him I put a little salve on the front left and we let them rest in the stall for a night. Turn them out tomorrow."

"Can't picture him sleeping on that bedroll for three nights. I'll bet she can." McKinney pointed at Marie, laughing. "She's trying to imagine it least ways."

"Are you finished eating? You can bring me your plates," Marie said.

June and Marta gathered up their dishes. "Upstairs is all ready for him."

"I'll tell him," Marta offered.

"I'm telling him. Be glad I'm not telling him about your incantation over his pillows, or the dance it involved." June turned and walked down the hallway, leaving behind the laughter in the kitchen.

Her new landowner appeared to be a bit younger than she was. He'd eaten all of his meal, including the apple pie. And his head was in his hands, elbows on the table.

"Excuse me, sir." June said from the doorway, with a knock or two on the wood.

He raised his head and sat up properly.

"Sir? Your room is ready," June just said.

Robin pushed out his chair and stood up. "Thank you. Please show me the way to my father's office and his books and give my apologies to everyone else for being exhausted." He collected his jacket and holster.

"You had a long journey. No need to apologize, sir." June led him into the next room. "What did you eat on the road?"

"Oh, you don't want to know. Jerky and apples and such. I did find a nice inn in Providence for one night and they packed me some salted pork and bread to bring along for today." Robin saw the desk and the journal on the top. He sneezed at the cigar smoke when he opened the journal. He took the book under his arm. "Show me my room, if you would please."

Down the hall toward the stairway, Robin noticed closed double doors beside the stairs. He followed her up and round the landing. On the second floor was another set of closed double doors directly above the others. Half the house seemed to be closed off.

"Well, a hot meal must have done you well, sir." June led him down the hall to the very end and to a set of open double doors. "I hope this will suit you. Is there anything else we can do for you?"

Robin looked into the master suite and saw his bed made up and fireplace going. "Wonderful. Thank you, no. Would you be the one who wrote me the letter?"

"Yes. June Taylor." She nodded. "I apologize for going through his papers to find an address for you. Appreciate you writing back so soon."

Van der Kellen turned in the room to look at the maid in the doorway.

June smiled a bit. "We'll be leaving the house for the night, but you can be sure, if you fire off a shot we'll come running."

Robin almost laughed as he looked down at his pistol and holster in his hand. "That's quite funny, ma'am. Might it come to that?"

"Good night, Mr. Van der Kellen, and welcome." June left down the hallway, smiling.

Robin shut the double oak doors. He set his pistol on the nightstand, left side of the bed, beside a lit oil lamp. He laid the journal on the bed. There was a seating area to his left and a large stone fireplace ahead to the foot of the bed. A nice big fire was crackling in it. The wood floor had planking over a foot wide running from door to hearth. Smaller boards surrounded the stone hearth and fireplace. This fireplace must be directly above the one in the kitchen, sharing the chimney, and the warmth. It made his, the warmest room in the house.

There was a closed door to an outdoor balcony. When he looked out the window beside it, he could see a covered balcony with a view of the entire valley below the house. The estate sat on top a very huge hill with river valley below and cultivated fields all belonging to him. The balcony could be a summer bedroom for him, he thought. Unbearably hot here in the summer. Even worse than Boston. He suffered in the heat.

He heard some laughter downstairs and the kitchen door closing loudly beneath him. When he glanced out the window, he saw the two men walking toward the servant's quarters with a lamp. Two wooden buildings on the other side of the barn, across the courtyard, appeared to be where they lived. Leaving the house for the night.

At his home in Boston, he always went to bed hearing the staff cleaning up in the dining room and then climbing the stairs to the top floor. Of course, some nights he came home late after court. In the predawn hours of the morning, he'd hear them walking down the stairs and beginning their day before he rose. The valet used to wake him when he needed to get to work early and lay a pressed suit over the foot of the bed for him.

Robin turned down the blankets to find his Boston sheets on the feather bed and his four down pillows. His trunk was at the foot of the bed. He made his way around to the trunk, stooped to unlock it with a brass key from his pocket. He pushed the lid back and set aside two swords. Then several rolled up maps were set aside. From beneath, he removed a special bottle of brandy. And there were a few of them inside, beneath his neatly folded uniforms. Then he locked the trunk again. The bed roll he'd used in his travels lay on the two cases of books with his other trunk and bags. His two canteens were there. His saddle bags. His briefcase. All that he owned and it was only one trunk more than he had returned with from India. He lowered his chin. Still no more baggage than a gypsy.

No gaslights outside to light the windows at night. The only light came from the whale oil lamp near the bed and the flickering fireplace. It was a darker night outside than any he'd imagined. At least sleeping on the ground offered him the stars overhead for study. It was too quiet. No carriages bobbing over cobblestones and brick ways for listening.

The mantel above the fireplace displayed only a vase and a Dutch windmill clock. The dressing table had only a pitcher of water and bowl, with some neatly folded towels. He opened an armoire to find it empty. Drawers were empty.

A room to the far-right side was the water closet, with the chamber pot, a large copper bathing tub, and table of folded towels. Beside the tub were pails of cold water. He would have to hang them over the fire himself if he wanted to clean up, or use it cold.

He looked at that brandy on the nightstand and let out a long slow breath. He could go downstairs for a glass. The house should be empty except for the maids washing dishware. He could barely hear female laughter down there. Out the window, he could see light from the men's and women's quarters, across the turn around.

But no, he just sat down on the edge of the bed and ran a hand up through his hair. He pulled off his boots and stood them up them beside the bed. He pulled a chair over beside his night table so that when he undressed, he had a place to lay his clothing. Then he sat cross legged on the left side of the bed with that journal open in front of him. Beside him, he reached the bottle of brandy and pulled out the cork. He took a drink from the bottle. Then he opened his father's bookkeeping journal to read in his hand the state of the accounts.

Chapter Two First Morning in Connecticut

November 6, 1839

Robin Van der Kellen came downstairs dressed in a finely tailored dark charcoal wool suit, with fold marks in a few places. With this he wore a white shirt and matching gray vest. The shirt was more wrinkled than anything but the jacket hid that fact. He wore a green silk ascot within the top two buttons of his shirt. He wore short ankle boots of shiny black leather. His shirt cuffs were adorned with gold cufflinks. He entered the kitchen where three maids were working and the two stockmen were sitting at the kitchen table. He slid a gold pocket watch back into his vest pocket. "My apologies for being a bit late. It is highly unusual for me. I will get right to the day's business. I regret to inform you that I cannot employ all of you."

The two stockmen got up from the table then. "You're not serious? You expect us to do this work with only one of us?"

"If you will let me finish, please," Robin said firmly. "I would have you tie the cattle and one cow up to the back of my wagon. They're going to town to be sold off. The two saddle horses as well. The pig is going to be put down and slaughtered tomorrow. The chickens will stay. Having done all of that I will be left with only my two Friesians and one milk cow. I will not need stockmen any longer. You will both be paid for what my father owed you as well as for two weeks ahead for the inconvenience and lack of notice."

"We're both out of a job," Albert said to the others.

McKinney lunged at Robin. "Why you...."

Albert held his friend back at the same instant Robin drew a pistol from his holster and pointed it at him. And then he cocked it, to their surprise. He held it steady, with his elbow at his hip. It was a finely polished wooden pistol with brass trim and iron stock.

"You can stay and tie up the animals as I instructed and receive your wages, or you can get the fuck out of here now," Robin said firmly and calmly. "Your choice, stockmen."

Both men stepped back and put their hands up, shocked almost equally at the gun and the profanity.

McKinney made a glance at the rifle on the mantel not far from him. "Be careful where you point that fancy pistol, Mister Van der Kellen. I find most gentlemen don't know which end is the dangerous one."

"Get to work or get walking. Your choice." Van der Kellen stepped in between the men and the fireplace. "You can still leave later today with wages and good reference. Or can you take one step toward me... and learn a whole lot more about me. I'd like to think you're just angry about losing your employment. Is that the way of it?"

"Yes, sir," Albert said.

Reluctantly and with tugging from Albert, McKinney nodded. "Yes, sir."

Robin uncocked but didn't lower the weapon, not yet anyway. His dark eyes studied the men and that pistol remained steady. His left hand remained a second away from pulling the hammer back on it again.

"Hitch up the drafts too, I reckon?" Albert said. "You might rather rest those a day or two."

"Hitch them up, please." Robin kept watching them.

"You want that pig slaughtered too? I'm really good with a knife," McKinney said.

"You have enough work to do. Leave that to me. I can give you a ride to town when I bring the stock in to sell." Robin only lowered the weapon when the angrier one turned away and walked out the door.

Albert followed him out. "Yes sir."

Robin walked to the window and verified where the men were going. Only then did Robin return the gun to his holster and turn toward the three women. He found them all gaping at him. "I apologize for my language, ladies. I understand only one of you does the cooking?"

"Yes, sir," Marie said, gravely. "That would be me."

"I would ask you to stay on, if my behavior hasn't turned you off. The other two of you I must also end your employment. I am terribly sorry. I will also pay you the wages and take you to town with the stockmen. You best pack your things. I would prepare a very fine reference for wherever you find work," Robin said.

June grabbed hands with Marta and they walked out the door together, Marta starting to cry.

Marie would have lowered her eyes from Van der Kellen, but she couldn't. She was breathing hard.

"Miss Longuiel, you can do some house cleaning as well as the cooking? There will be a lot less of either with just you and I here, of course."

"Yes, sir," Marie said.

"I can't afford to keep the others but I can afford to pay you, if you stay," Robin said. "Will you?"

She nodded, smoothing her hands down her apron. "Happy to, sir. Would you take some breakfast in the dining room then? I set a place for you."

Robin shook his head and picked up a coffee cup. He used a towel to pick up the coffee pot and poured himself a cup. "Thank you. I couldn't possibly eat after firing four people, especially two women."

"I'll pack something for you to eat, just in case, sir. There's no restaurant in town, except the tavern. It won't open until supper."

"Thank you. I'll be in the office."

November 6, 1839 Later that morning

"Mr. Van der Kellen, the cattle are all tied to the wagon. That's going to be a slow walk to town. You know that, right?" Albert said.

McKinney was standing near the wagon with his arms folded.

"Yes. I'm sure it will be." Robin handed a folded piece of paper to each of them, containing a reference and the money they were due. The paper was sealed with RVK stamped into the wax. Robin buttoned up his coat, surveying the line of animals behind his wagon. He laid a hand on one of the riding horses that was also tied on.

"Are you sure you wouldn't rather I stayed and butchered that pig for you tomorrow?" Albert asked while the other stockman counted out his Connecticut paper money.

Robin shook his head. "I'll do it. I'd rather you spent your time in town finding employment. I don't wish to take up any more of your time."

"You shorted me ten dollars," McKinney said.

"For the tavern window," Robin reminded.

"Well, I'm walking." McKinney picked up his bag and walked off down the driveway. "Bastard."

"Mr. Van der Kellen, I mean you no disrespect. I worked for your pa for two years. One man alone cannot work this property, not even if you get rid of the stock," Albert said. "Are you sure you wouldn't rather I stayed on? Even the wood I chopped will not get you through the winter. There is more to working this property than a man from the city can know. No offence."

"I'm certain there will be more work than I imagine. But I imagine a lot. The simple fact is I can't pay you. So, you must move on," Robin told him.

"Well, I appreciate your honesty. I'm going to be honest too. You can't work this place alone. You're a skinny lawman from Boston. Those hands have never done work before. They'll be bleeding before you chop a cord of wood. What are you going to do with that cow? Marie don't know nothing about cows. And what are you going to do when the hay fields need harvesting? When you hit the bottom, I only hope I'm still around to come back. But it will cost you."

"Mister, you don't know me. And you will not be hired back."

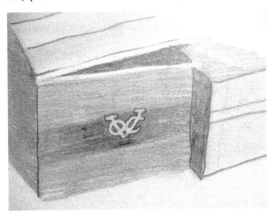

When the wagon returned just before sunset, Marie pulled on her shawl and hurried out across the courtyard toward the barn. The horses and wagon had stopped inside the barn, in the center of the two rows of stalls.

Van der Kellen was unhitching the left-hand horse. He noticed her standing nearby. "Hello Miss Longuiel. Please give these some room. Stand back if you will." A few more straps to undo and the horse pounded the barn floor and shook his mane as he stepped free of the wagon. It snorted loudly at him.

Marie hopped back, startled.

Robin held onto the bridle hard in a fist and scolded the horse in Dutch such that the animal allowed Robin to walk him directly into the first stall. Robin shut him in there and returned to the second horse.

"Mr. Van der Kellen, Albert said one of the hooves on that horse was cracked. Said he put something on it," Marie spoke up. "I'm not sure if he told you."

"He did. And I had it mended at the livery in town, a new shoe. Thank you," Robin said. "Is everything all right?"

"Yes. I made supper. I was just...afraid you would stay in town tonight, is all." Marie folded her arms tight, holding her shawl closed about her.

Robin continued unstrapping the second horse. "Of course not. This is where I live now."

The maid still stood there.

This horse was free to move but didn't. It just stood in place though Robin tugged onto the bridle. The horse was looking at the girl.

She stood there.

Nobody seemed willing to move.

In frustration, Robin said, "Miss? Are you wanting to quit? Tell me now."

"No. Oh no sir."

"What is it then?"

"Nothing. Nothing to do with you anyway." Marie looked at him. "It's terrifying here all alone."

"Oh? Well, I thought it more frightening with two stockmen who hated my guts," Robin admitted. "Alone, I'm fine with." He commanded the horse to move in Dutch. He led it into its stall.

Marie watched him hang a bucket of grain inside each stall and divided a bale of hay between the two of them. "I must tell you, I never saw a gentleman tending horses before. Do you know what you're getting into? No offence, sir."

"I'm not offended. I know horses. Do not worry. Mind you, nothing else about farming do I know." Robin closed up the stalls and collected his rifle from the wagon. "I'm willing to do the work. It just may take me a while to learn what exactly the work is. If you need anything, if you see anything I need to be doing, please say so."

"That cow needs milking twice a day. It only had once," Marie blurted out.

Robin stopped walking. "Oh. Do you know how to do that?"

"I've seen it done. I've never done it," Marie said.

Robin thought a moment. "Come and talk me through it." Robin walked deeper into the barn, looking at the horse stalls, his father's carriage, a plow, a hay rake. Up above, it was full to the peak with hay. A couple chickens wandered about on the floor. There was a cat draped over one of the rafters, watching him below. Robin continued walking toward the lone cow at the other end.

Marie grabbed a pail off the wall on her way behind him.

Robin leaned his rifle against the wall and picked up a stool. He entered the cow's stall.

"You might want to hand me your jacket, sir," Marie said. "And roll up your sleeves."

Robin looked down at himself. He turned away from her and quickly unbuttoned his jacket. He laid it over the door of the stall. He removed his gold cufflinks and pocketed them into his trousers. Then he rolled up his white sleeves.

"Have you...you've never done this before either?" Marie asked.

"What happens if I don't do this twice a day?" Robin moved the stool down closer to the back end of the cow where the udders were.

"Cow dies and we won't have milk, butter, or cheese," Marie said.

"I would imagine the milk comes from there." Robin sat down on the stool and leaned to take one udder into his hand. He grimaced.

"Pail, sir." Marie held it up in her hand. "Catch?"

"Yes, toss it here." Robin caught the tin pail by the handle. Then he set it beneath the udders and tried again. Nothing happened. "When does it start?"

"I...I think you have to push up. Push your hand up and sort of grab the milk down," Marie said.

Two barn cats squeezed past Marie and beneath the cow's stall door. They moved in beneath the cow, looking up at Robin.

Robin tried again. Nothing. "They're laughing at me."

"Keep trying. Push up, grab milk down and kind of squeeze the milk out into the bucket," Marie suggested.

Robin tried that, slipped off the stool, and squirted milk all over the cats as he fell over into straw.

Marie burst out laughing and then caught herself. "Oh, I'm so sorry. Are you all right, sir?"

Robin sat up laughing and set up the stool again. "I've never touched a cow in my life. Disgusting, it is." He got into position again and set up the bucket. The two cats were licking milk off themselves and each other. "Now I see what they were waiting for. I should try to get some in the pot, this time."

"I'm so sorry." Marie stifled her giggling.

"It is quite all right. Look. It's working!" Robin was squirting hot milk into the pot. "Do I have to do all four?"

Robin entered the dining room, fastening the cuffs of a clean shirt and wearing his black trousers from the day before.

Marie served his dinner, the same pork loin, carrots, and potatoes as the night before. Slice of pie too. She poured him a glass of apple cider.

And then, after he finished his meal, he carried his plate, silverware, and empty glass back into the kitchen. He set them on the table near her wash bin.

"Oh my. You needn't go to all that trouble. I can collect those." Marie was ladling cream off the milk into a separate ceramic jar.

"It's no trouble," Robin said. "Are you all right walking back to your place alone in the dark?"

"Oh. Yes. I'll just take this lamp with me. I need it to light the fireplace anyway," Marie said.

"Might I inquire, where do you keep the glasses?" Robin asked.

"Right here, sir." Marie opened a cabinet. "What can I get you?"

"Just one of those short glasses will do." Robin held out his hand.

Marie said to him, "I placed one beside your brandy for you, sir. If that is what you wanted it for."

"Oh. Thank you. Exactly what I intended it for."

"Good night, Mr. Van der Kellen."

"Thank you. Good night, Miss Longuiel." He turned and went up the stairs, looking again at those closed doors to the other half of the house.

November 7, 1839

That morning, as Marie left her small building, she noticed Van der Kellen standing out on his balcony. He was leaning on the railing, his woolen robe wrapped around him. A couple roosters were crowing.

Against the red siding of the house, the morning sun was warm enough that he could stand there, bare foot, and survey his property in the distance.

Marie opened the barn door, releasing chickens.

He watched her cross the driveway. And she made an obvious effort not to look up at him.

Inside, Marie set a place for him on the grand dining room table, with white cloth and napkins again. She set his place near the fire, looking toward the tapestry, and nine empty chairs around the table. This time she used the fancy plates from the sideboard.

Robin sat down and immediately picked up his porcelain plate to examine it.

"I'm so sorry. Is that not clean? I'll get you...." Marie stammered.

"No, miss. It's just that…these dishes came from India." He turned it over to look at the back. Then he set it down in front of him. The center of the blue design had a VOC incorporated into it. "Dutch East India Company. Are there more of these?"

"There are a few place settings to match that one. Not enough for the whole table. There are also a few very pretty ones." Marie opened a sideboard along the wall and showed him a teacup.

"May I examine that please?" Robin held out his hand.

Marie gave it to him gently.

"Incredible. My mother saved these all these years. I sent her that almost fifteen years ago. It traveled all the way from India to Amsterdam and all the way here without breaking," Robin said.

"There are only a few pieces to match that cup, a few saucers, a few cups. The tea pot itself is lovely but has a crack in it, so it just sits here looking lovely." Marie returned the cup to its place beside the teapot when Robin set it down.

Robin let out a breath and just looked down at the VOC on his plate.

"I'll be right back with your breakfast, sir."

When she returned, she served him eggs, ham, biscuits and coffee with cream.

He asked, "Without sounding insensitive, would you happen to know what became of my father's watch?"

"Oh. No sir. I'm sure he had one. Did you check the safe?" Marie poured the coffee into his cup. "I'm terribly sorry."

"How did he die?"

"Very sudden. His heart, we believe. Climbing the stairs one day," Marie said gently. "We put all of his things in the larger room beside yours. I don't recall June saying anything about a watch. All of his things are there and in the library. His desk is there. His safe. I'm afraid none of us know how to get into it. I would look in there if I were you, sir."

Robin nodded. "Thank you."

"Were you very close to him?"

He looked up at her. "Ahm, no. I was not."

"June found your name and address in the desk. Some bankers came, and we had to give them your name and address as well," Marie said.

"Yes. I know," Robin said.

"It was good that you wrote us back. We didn't know what to do. Some wanted to leave. The Reverend came from town and we buried your father in the family plot out back, with your mother. I'm sorry I never met her," Marie explained.

Van der Kellen put down his fork and cup.

"Can I get you anything else?" Marie asked.

"Would you have any black pepper?"

"Oh certainly. I'll bring that right away."

Robin passed through the kitchen, finding Marie preparing some baking. Saying nothing, he took his coat and went out to the barn. When he returned, about an hour later, he set another pail of milk on Marie's worktable.

"How did it go today?" she asked him.

"Better. Six cats today." Robin demonstrated the milk all over his jacket and sleeve. "You were right about removing this."

"Oh, I can get that out for you. Leave the jacket on the chair. I'll get to the washing this afternoon."

"I'm sorry to make extra work for you, Miss Longuiel." Robin turned his back to her to unbutton his suit jacket and pull it back off his shoulders.

"No trouble at all, sir." Marie glimpsed him again in just vest, trousers, and shirt. She saw the glint of gold on his cuffs again. "You best stop wearing those around here, those gold jewels on your cuffs, sir."

"Oh. But I must use them to close the cuff," Robin explained.

"No buttons?" Marie asked. "Let me see."

Robin moved closer to her and held out his wrist.

"I've never seen such a fancy shirt. You should wear some of your fathers for work outside. He has simple ones with buttons and buttonholes. You don't want to lose any of that gold in the manure, do you?"

Robin laughed. "I thought shoveling it was bad enough. No. I guess I can get cleaned up until the next time I have to milk that thing again. You really make butter and cheese from that milk?"

"And cream for your coffee." Marie indicated the cheeses up on the shelf above her worktable.

Robin nodded. "Very well then."

Marie hadn't seen him for hours, so she looked about the lower floor of the house for him, the parlor, the dining room, and finally the library. Van der Kellen was in there with books pulled off the shelves and in stacks on the floor.

He was kneeling on the floor between the stacks with one of the books open and his hair tucked back behind his right ear. His dark eyes turned up at her as she stood in the doorway.

Marie wrapped her arms in front of her. "Would you be thinking about lunch by any chance?"

"Oh. Yes, I suppose so." Robin stood up and dropped the book into one of the piles.

"They are not in English or French," Marie commented.

"Dutch," Robin commented. "Law books. They were not in order. I can't stand that." Then he sneezed. "Forgive me. They're also covered in dust and cigar smoke."

Marie turned away to hide a smile.

He wiped dust off his hands onto his trousers.

"Let me get you a towel," she offered. "You do not smoke then?"

"He was told the cigars were killing him," Robin said. "Horrible habit I'm fortunate to have never begun."

Robin followed her down the hall to the kitchen. He waited beside the table while she poured water into the bowl for him again and offered him a towel.

"What did you do for a living, sir? I heard you took over his business in Boston. It was a law firm, wasn't it?" Marie retreated to her work area and started to serve out a bean and pork soup.

Robin washed his hands and used the towel. "You call it a lawyer in this country. I argued cases in court and did most of the research."

"I thought maybe you were a scientist, by that instrument on your mantel."

"The sextant. I would have liked that, to be a scientist. But there's no money in that." Robin went into the pantry to look around. When he came out, he said, "Are you all right doing this work by yourself, Miss Longuiel?"

"Yes, sir. Easy enough to cook for two people, and keep the house, the parts you use."

"When you have the time, could you show me how to use the iron? Some of my things got very crumpled with my packing them," Robin said.

"Oh, I was going to tell you just leave them on a couch in your room and I'll get them ironed."

"It seems simple enough to do," Robin said.

"Not with those collars and pockets. I wouldn't want you to burn them. You best let an expert do it. Leave them on the couch," Marie told him.

"There's no hurry. Whenever you have the time. I had better go turn out those horses before lunch. I'll be back inside shortly."

November 8, 1839 Sunday

Robin walked out of the barn to find a wagon coming up the drive. Wearing brown trousers he disliked, and a baggy shirt of his fathers, he brushed some straw off his trousers self-consciously. He strolled into the center of the turnaround. The wagon came to a stop between him and the house. A man, woman, and three children were on board, all dressed well.

"Good afternoon," said the man.

"Good afternoon indeed," Robin said. "Wonderful Belgians, sir."

"The young Mr. Van der Kellen knows his horses. I thought we might see you in church but since we did not, I thought we'd best come by and say hello." The man tipped his hat. "We are the Lee's from next door that way."

"Could I invite you in for tea?" Robin asked.

"No thank you. We have to be going. You would be Willem's son from the city then?"

"Robin Van der Kellen, at your service." Robin gave a slight bow.

"How is it you have such knowledge in horse breeds, sir?" Mr. Lee asked.

"We used to raise all manner of warm bloods on the farm back home in the Netherlands. Belgians, Dutch, and Danish horses," Robin said.

"And how are you getting on, sir?" Mrs. Lee asked.

"Very well, as far as I can tell. Just arrived a few days ago. I'm afraid you caught me working in the barn. I apologize for my appearance," Robin said.

"Is that you a mess? You must be something cleaned up," Mrs. Lee said.

Her husband shot her a look. The children laughed. There was a boy of about 16, another maybe six years old and a girl of 13.

Robin's leather gloves were dirty and shards of straw were clinging to his trousers. A bit of hay was in his hair. That baggy shirt plumed out at his elbows and waist.

"Well, my boy hires out occasionally. If he can do any work for you, just come on over," Mr. Lee said. "Winters are bad in these parts. You'd better lay in more firewood than that. Do you have any help here at all, given that your stockman came by my place looking for work?"

"Just a maid. I'll manage," Robin said. "Thank you."

"Did you bring the maid with you from Boston, then?" Mrs. Lee questioned.

"Ahm, no, Ma'am. Kept her on here and let the others go. Brought them to town," Robin said.

"You can meet everyone in town if you come to church," Mr. Lee said. "It would be advisable. Dispel any rumors going about."

"Rumors about me?" Robin asked. "I only just arrived."

By Susan Eddy

"You're not English, are you? Your pa was Dutch. That's what I told them anyway," Mr. Lee said. "Some don't know there's any difference. Is it just the two horses then?"

"Two." Robin put his hands on his hips. "And a cow."

"Got plenty of hay laid in? Silage?"

"It is full to the rafters," Robin replied. "Excuse me, what is silage?"

"Green fodder, fermented to be fed to that cow and the horses especially in the winter. He's got a silage crib in there." Lee pointed toward the barn.

"Oh yes. Kuilvoer," Robin said. "Forgive me. I did not know the English word. Yes, of course, there is plenty of kuilvoer in the barn."

"Well, you'll be all right then. Like I said, come on over if you need help. Good day, Mr. Van der Kellen." He took the carriage around the roundabout and out the driveway. The girl waved at Robin.

"Do please come round for supper some time?" Mrs. Lee said.

He was still standing there with his hands on his hips, ruffled a bit. "That would please me. Just send word when."

"I'll send someone round to invite you," Mrs. Lee told him.

"Thank you very much."

November 11, 1839

"I beg your pardon, sir. I thought you were outside." Marie backed out of his bedroom.

"Miss Longuiel, it is quite all right. I left the door open. Would you come in for a moment?" Robin stood up from sorting the clothing in one of his trunks.

She stood in the doorway with her arms wrapped tightly around folded towels. "Did you not like the ironing I did?"

"It was wonderful. Thank you. I'm afraid I've found more for you. What I need to say is, ahm, there is an armoire in the corner full of women's clothing." Robin leaned his head toward the oak furniture in the corner. It was a tall piece of craftmanship far too heavy to be moved.

"Yes. I know that one."

"I wonder, if there is anything inside that you could use, would you mind taking it?" Robin said.

"Oh, I couldn't, sir. I believe those were your mother's," Marie said.

Robin paused. "Well. Sat there for five years. May not fit you but perhaps with alteration they could be of use to you. Anything in there you like, please take them or give them away. I would like it emptied. Here is an idea. I will take all of it and place it on the bed across the hall. I don't know any of it. I have no attachment to anything in that cabinet."

That made her look at him.

"What I mean is, she had sent to me the keepsakes that I wanted," Robin said. "I doubt I saw her in anything I would remember."

"Oh. I meant no...."

"Miss Longuiel." Robin set his hands on his hips. "We must work together. We should verbalize some rules. I do not like assumptions. First rule, do your job. Second rule, anything I can do to make your job easier, you must tell me. Third rule, I suppose since we live alone, we must establish privacy. If my bedroom doors are shut, do not enter. Open, come and go as you need. I will never enter your building out there unless you need something fixed. What rules would you have for me?"

"For you, sir?"

Robin shrugged. "Of course. Pay you every month, probably. I saw my father's bookkeeping. What else?"

"May I...may I make a suggestion?" Marie asked timidly.

"Of course."

"You are going to ruin those boots in the barn. There are some old boots of your fathers that would fit you. Mind you, he never worked in the barn like you do," Marie said.

"I suppose he didn't. I might give that a try next time I shovel stalls." Robin smiled. "I know where they are. The boots that is."

Marie almost laughed. "Another thing. You don't eat enough. Except for your first meal here, you eat hardly anything. Is there something wrong with my cooking?"

"Oh no. Of course not." Robin's eyes searched the floor for a moment. "I'm still...not sleeping well. Not eating. I do not think I am ill. I just...am not adjusting to being here. I miss my life, I suppose."

"What can I do to help? Do you have a favorite food? Would you like another apple pie?"

Robin turned his eyes to the formal suits he was unpacking. "You made an excellent apple pie. One of the best I ever had."

"I would be happy to make another. We have several sacks of apples to use up," Marie said.

"You did not give me any rules to follow." He looked at her plainly.

"You put your laundry in the basket there. You keep your own vanity room so clean there is nothing for me to do except bring you towels. You make your bed every morning. I am finding it very hard to lodge a complaint."

That made him laugh. "Trained by a nanny, I suppose. And beat up by little sisters if I didn't bathe."

Marie smiled, blushing. "May I make one more suggestion?"

"Please."

"Those are such fine suits. You wanted all of your father's removed but we put them all across the hall. You might find something in there to wear for shoveling horse stalls or hauling firewood besides those fine trousers," Marie said.

"You are right, of course. I'm a lot thinner than he was. Don't know if I could keep his pants up." Robin grinned. "Tight belt, I suppose. But that way, if I'm covered with manure, I can just bury the pants with the manure."

Marie stifled a laugh in the towels she held. "I can take some of the pants in. I can sew."

Robin smiled and nodded. "You must want to put those towels some place. I will just start carrying these women's clothes across the hall. Why is half of this house closed off? That is driving me crazy at night to think about."

Marie stopped and looked at him.

"The whole wing over there, why is it closed off?"

"I don't know. It has been the whole time I've been here."

Robin opened the closed double doors on the second floor. Because of the high ceiling of the ballroom, the upper level was up another half set of stairs higher than the second floor of the home and it bypassed the area with the grand entrance down below. The ceiling was lower there, just above Robin's head. There were six smaller bedrooms in that hallway, rather obviously rooms for maids or butlers. They were furnished, though not as luxuriously as the bedrooms near Robin's. Van der Kellen exited the hall and closed up the doors again.

He went down the stairs to open those closed doors also, and wandered into a grand hallway. To one side was the main entrance hall with open ceiling all the way up to the roof top and doors to the turnaround drive. He wandered further to find butler's room for coats and hats. Then there was a lady's salon with couches of pink silk and a gentleman's smoking room. And beyond that a grand ball room.

Robin walked out on checkerboard floor of black and white marble, looking at mirrored panels on the walls and chandeliers with dangling cobwebs. As he looked at himself in a mirror, he could see his breath in this room. Huge marble fireplaces at either end of the room were as cold as rock ledge outside.

November 20, 1839

Robin Van der Kellen walked up the path from the family cemetery at the overlook of the property, rifle strap over his shoulder, his long black coat billowing unbuttoned. The day was overcast and evening was coming on. His boots kicked up the fallen leaves and he rustled right through them. Red maple leaves. Red and brown leaves from the apple trees. His expression was...sad.

Marie glanced at him as she was taking down laundry from the lines outside. She rapidly folded up the pantalettes in her hands and dropped them into the basket. Then she took down a skirt and folded it to cover the others.

Van der Kellen suddenly spun about, looking back the way he had come. He cocked his rifle, brought it up to his shoulder, and fired.

Marie dropped her laundry into the basket and ran toward him. "Oh my God."

Robin trotted into the long grass. Then he ducked down out of sight.

She still ran toward him.

Suddenly he stood up with the legs of a turkey in his fist. The hen was hanging down and he was examining it. The wings spread out limp.

Marie came to a stop just in front of him. "Oh my. What a great shot you are, sir!"

Robin laughed. "Ahm, I am guessing we can cook this."

"Oh yes. I have just the roaster for it."

"You may wish to look away. I plan to bleed it." Robin held the bird in his left hand and with surprising balance, reached for a knife inside his right boot.

"I've done chickens, sir. Maybe I can hold it for you." Marie took the feet from him in both hands.

Robin slit the turkey's throat precisely on each side. "Watch your skirts there. Pass it back to me. I'll carry it up to the house."

Marie gave him the turkey. "I can take your gun for you. You don't want to just take off the head?"

"I can't dull this knife." He held the bird out. "Ahm, this is a bigger creature than I thought." He passed the rifle to the girl. Then he laughed. "It weighs quite a lot."

"Does it? Well, I can make a soup out of the rest of it. Was that your first turkey, sir?" Marie walked along with him, carrying his rifle with the strap over her shoulder.

He reached over and pushed the rifle barrel down. "This is a turkey?"

"Sorry sir."

"The gun was fired already, but always point the barrel down at the dirt when outdoors. Keep your hands away from the trigger. Hold it here. You'd best get your laundry in before you cook this. It looks like rain tonight," Robin said. "We have a similar bird in the Netherlands. My brother and I went hunting when we were young. Will you need help cleaning this?"

"Oh no, sir. I can take it from here. If you just set it on the table for me." Marie looked up at him. "Did you find the family plot out back? I put the flowers there for your mother so you would find her."

"Thank you. Yes. That was very kind of you," Van der Kellen said.

A teenage boy came riding up the drive, alone on a horse.

Robin stopped in the turnaround, turkey hanging from his fist.

"Mr. Van der Kellen, I'm Jonathan Lee. My ma sent me to invite you to Thanksgiving supper tomorrow. Two o-clock. Please come and your maid is welcome to dine with ours," Jonathan said.

"Two o-clock tomorrow. Thank you. We'll be delighted to dine with you."

Chapter Three Settling into Country Life

November 21, 1839

They arrived at the Lee's white Colonial home, where a stockman was quick to take hold of the horse harness. "I'll tend this fine horse for you, sir."

"Thank you." Robin stood up and collected the bottle of brandy off the floor. He climbed down while the stockman held Marie's hand to assist her down.

"Welcome Miss Marie. Delighted to see you again."

"Hello Luke."

Robin looked to see Marie have to shake her hand from Luke's as she stepped away from the carriage. He waited to see that Luke stepped back. Then he turned toward the front stairs.

Mr. Lee emerged from the house. "Ah, Mr. Van der Kellen, welcome."

Robin climbed the steps and extended his right hand. The two gentlemen shook hands.

"Good day, Mr. Lee." Robin offered him the brandy. "For you sir. I hope that it does not offend you on a Sunday. So kind of you to invite us. This is my maid and chef, Miss Longuiel."

"Thank you. We shall enjoy this after dinner together. Miss Longuiel, please join my maids as my guest as well. Don't let them talk you into helping."

"Oh thank you, sir," Marie said.

Luke said something to her, from behind her. Robin could not make it out. Marie hurried up the stairs from him.

Inside the grand entrance hall one of the Lee's maids met Marie and scurried her away toward the back of the house. Another maid took Robin's hat and coat for him.

Robin entered dressed in his fine black 3 piece suit, crisp white shirt, and blue silk ascot this time tucked in at his neck and tied elegantly. Mr. Lee was also dressed in a 3 piece suit as the family had just come from church. "Right this way, Mr. Van der Kellen."

"Please call me Robin."

"Robin. And please call me Joseph. This is my wife Jennifer, daughter Jane, and sons Jonathan and Jeremiah." Joseph Lee introduced them around the dining table.

"Everyone's names begin with a J," Robin noted.

"Makes initials on the handkerciefs easy," Jane blurted out.

"Please have a seat Robin and tell us about yourself. We know absolutely nothing about you save your lineage," Jennifer said.

Robin sat down where she indicated, across from the eldest son with the parents at either end of the grand table set with fine china, candlesticks, and etched glasses. He unbuttoned the bottom button of his jacket. The daughter Jane was watching from beside him. "My father did not talk about me. I take that as a blessing. Ahm, tell you about myself? I am a lawyer in the Netherlands and the state of Massachusetts. I took over my father's firm in Boston until his passing and I needed to come here to settle his affairs and wrap up his last case. Before Boston I served in the Dutch cavalry for six years."

"Are you married, Robin?" Jennifer asked.

"Ah...no. I was once." Robin unfolded a napkin into his lap.

Jennifer and Joseph exchanged a glance.

One maid poured glasses of wine and another served biscuits.

"A cavalryman then? Surprised your father never mentioned that. He said one son was a doctor. There was another son and some daughters," Joseph said.

Robin smiled. "Ah well that was officially my name. The other son." The raising of his eyebrows made the family laugh. "He never approved of my enlistment or that I shipped off to the Dutch colony of India. He wanted me to partner with him in the law firm." Robin realised the children were all riveted on what he was saying. "I was not much older than you, Jonathan, and I wanted to see the world not a bunch of law books. Then I saw too much of the world in the service and was happy to take up studying books."

That made everyone laugh again.

"Will you tell us of India, sir?" Jonathan asked.

"Yes, please. Tell us anything with your accent," the girl said.

When Mrs. Lee raised her wine glass, Robin proposed, "Proost. To your health in Dutch."

"Proost."

"To your health. Proost. You're not married then? I know all the unmarried females in the county, Robin," Jennifer said, to more laughter.

"Next to Constable Poole's wife, the dress maker, she's the biggest match maker in eastern Connecticut," Joseph said.

Robin blushed, looking down at the napkin in his lap. "I'm rather a recluse and quite shy. You might find that difficult to market."

"Not with your charm and looks, my dear," Jennifer said.

"How old are you, Robin?" Jane asked.

"Jane. Jennifer. Don't make the young man uncomfortable. Let him dine in peace," Joseph encouraged. "Besides, what do you plan to do with the hay fields come summer? Or do you plan to sell the estate?"

"I did plan to sell it and move back to Boston. That may take me a while," Robin said.

"You sold off all your stock I see. Your angry stockman told me his side of it," Joseph said. "Said you pulled a pistol on him."

Everyone fell silent.

Robin set down his wine glass and made simple eye contact with Joseph Lee. He wet his lips.

"I'm hoping he did not injure you at all in the course of the firing," Joseph added.

Robin averted his dark eyes to the napkin again. "Did you hire him?"

"Even if I did not know the character of the man, the firing by a gentleman neighbor of mine would be enough for me to let him pass. And I do know the man. He's nothing but trouble," Lee said. "You just kept the one girl?"

"Well..." Robin began. "I can't cook."

Mrs. Lee giggled a bit. "It's quite propper, I'm certain. Call us over if you need a chaperone."

Robin smiled and then the family laughed.

"Would your accent be a bit Irish, Joseph?" Robin asked.

"Why yes it is. Nice change of subject. I was born here but both parents came from Ireland. That does not make me sympathetic to the British," Joseph said.

"Of course not. The Irish make no friends in England." Robin tasted his first course when Jennifer Lee began to eat hers.

"And where do the Dutch stand?" Joseph asked.

"I fought the British for six years, if that answers your question," Robin said.

"Indeed. To the war hero then."

"Interestingly, my family descends from Scotland as Van der Kellen means of the Gaels or Gaelic," Robin said. "Given the circumstances,

I've never visited Scotland. Hopefully I didn't fight any distant realitives in India, but that's why I wouldn't take a post in Western Europe."

"Fascinating. Why the cavalry, Mr. Van der Kellen?" Jonathan asked.

"Grew up on a horse farm. We bred warmbloods and harness horses. I was always working in the barn. I had some success as a competition rider as a teenager. Anything to anger my father. He burned the ribbons I won when I was seventeen and threatening to leave home. The minute I turned eighteen I enlisted."

"Knowing your father," Mr. Lee began. "He wanted you to take on intellectual pursuits instead."

Robin nodded. "Indeed. I was a very good student. It was just more fun to jump a hedge in the fox hunt. Did not want to spend my life facing my father across a partners desk."

"I see then why you enlisted," Joseph said. "You still joined the law profession to spite your father's urging."

"I very much enjoy defending the less fortunate. The daily routine can be a bit dull in the court house. But the case once in a while where I can really make a difference in the lives of the poor, is my motivation," Robin said.

"Admirable. You'll find no shortage of the less fortunate around here. Most of the wealthy like yourself live in the hills surrounding Norwich, among the ship captains and factory owners," Joseph said.

That made Robin look at him. He wet his lips as he thought a moment. "And what is it Norwich is known for?"

"Norwich is a sea port, a major one in New England. Factories building everything from furniture to guns to textiles can be found there. We had to start making it ourselves, cut off from England by the war," Joseph told him. "And now that the railroad runs all the way from Boston to Worchester, and New Haven to New York, all that freight will no longer have to go by sea. Soon they will get a bridge across the

Thames River and the train will go all the way from Boston to New York directly."

"Is that how you arrived here? By train?" Jane asked him.

"I wanted to bring my horses so I just loaded up a wagon and drove them from Boston," Robin said. "My horses would not have enjoyed two days on a train. They would rather walk it, as evidenced by the number of barn stalls one of them has destroyed. I'm working to double the size of their stalls in the barn. They will like it better when they can turn around easily."

Robin was served a three course supper on fine china, with six pieces of silverware, a white cloth napkin, glass of wine and glass of cider. Dessert was warm peach pie with melted butter on top, and another glass of wine.

"Tell us about India, would you?" Jonathan said.

"Very well. Since I don't wish to talk about war I will tell you about India itself. Do you know about elephants? I've ridden on an elephant many times. Fascinating creatures although not very pleasant smelling. The hairs on their backs are so prickly they can pass through any number of blankets and rugs and stick you where you don't want to be stuck, right in the backside. Four of us road on the back of one elephant with a native driver to lead the animal. We often scouted on the backs of elephants rather than horses. The mangrove forests were too wet for horses to get through and many of them got broken legs in the attempt. The thing about an elephant is, it can weigh 8,000 pounds and yet walk absolutley silently through the brush."

"You actually road on an elephant, sir?" Six-year-old Jeremiah looked up at him from across the table.

The girl, Jane, touched one finger to Robin's golden coin cufflink, making him look down at her hand near his on the edge of the table. He pulled his hand into his lap.

"Many times. Got so used to it we'd take turns sleeping across the spine of it. Three of us scouting and one catching a nap," Robin said.

"What did it smell like?" Jonathan asked. "Was it awful? Like the worst giant boar?"

"Like nothing you have here," Robin said. "I can picture it in my mind but I can't describe it. The young ones which are more agreeable to riding, smell a bit like raw honey. To this day, I can't stand the scent of honey. It was like honey mixed with...with elephant."

The kids laughed.

"Shall we retreat to the parlor for some brandy then?" Joseph said, after dessert.

"Children, get your school work done," Jennifer said.

"But mother, can't we come along and hear more stories?" Jeremiah asked.

"Only adults in the parlor. You have a math test tomorrow. Go do your studies while you still have day light."

Robin rose, set his napkin beside his plate, and followed Joseph Lee into the next room. Only Mrs. Lee joined them and closed the double doors. Joseph opened the brandy and poured three glasses.

"Cigar, Robin?"

"No thank you. I do not smoke. But go ahead if you enjoy them," Robin said. "Thank you for a fine supper. And so kind of you to invite my maid, as well. It has been wonderful to get to know you."

"And you as well," Joseph said. "I would like to press you on something. If you do come to sell your estate, you best be told that you have some of the finest hay fields in Connecticut. Much of the state is so rocky but you have all the flood plains of the river. I'd be looking to buy a few acres off you, if you do come to sell."

"Thank you. I will bear that in mind," Robin said. "I do plan to walk my property line. Is there a marking between yours and mine?"

"Rock wall all the way down to the Quineboug river. And then on the other side, your land goes all the way beyond the tree line to the intersecting brook," Lee said. "You have many, many acres. Mine ends at the river."

"So many fine hay fields and yet my father's bookkeeping reflects so little income, if I may say," Robin mused aloud. "I don't understand it."

"It's a quandry. I can tell you some. Your father wouldn't hire Mohegans to harvest the hay. Brought men in from the mill in Norwich. Probably had to pay the mill too. I would look there," Joseph said.

"Mohegans?"

"Local Indian tribe. They come round from farm to farm to help with the harvesting. Good workers and cheaper than others. We don't allow any slavery in this state," Joseph said. "Voting to abolished it soon officially."

"Oh. Years ago my father had some indentured servants," Robin said.

"White servants. Worked off their time, no doubt. Your father never had darkies. They're free men aroud here," Joseph explained. "Occasionally we get some that escaped from down South. You encounter any, you let me know. We help them get up North."

Robin swirled his brandy thoughtfully. "I never quite understood the American concept of slavery. I do believe you got it from the British."

"I wish you would come to church some times," Jennifer said. "It would give you a chance to meet available females or it is sure to be a long winter in that big house alone."

"It always is a long winter alone," Robin said quietly.

"You were married once?" Jennifer asked. "Annulment? Did your family not approve?"

"Do not press him for what he does not wish to talk about. He's only just met us," Joseph said. "Well you certainly made an impression on my boys. Anytime you need help over there, I'm sure they would oblidge."

"Thank you. That is most kind. I'm sure I will be most grateful for help at some point," Robin said.

"I won't mention the impression you made on our daughter." Jennifer grinned.

"Ahm, a sweet little girl, whom I promice to stay away from." Robin held his hands close to his vest.

The Lees burst out laughing.

Mr. Lee walked Robin out to his carriage and Marie was already estabished inside it. The stockman held the bridle. Lee said, "Find your way home then?"

Robin laughed. "I can see the red peak from here."

Joseph Lee laughed heartily. "Goodnight Mr. Van der Kellen."

Robin climbed up into the seat and picked up the reins. "Goodnight Mr. Lee. Thank you again."

The stockman stepped back, calling out, "Good night, Marie."

"Lopen op." Robin tapped the reins on the horse's back and drove him out the driveway.

Marie sat in the back, holding a pie on her lap.

They arrived back at the Van der Kellen estate and the carriage came to a stop outside the barn. Robin hopped down and walked around to hold up a hand for Marie but she had climbed down already, with the pie in her left hand.

"Forgive me. I came to assist you," Robin told her.

"I'm quite able. Mrs. Lee has sent another peach pie home with you," Marie said.

"Ahm. No need to make any sort of dinner for me. I'm quite full from all that for the evening," Robin said.

"Perhaps a piece of pie before bedtime then. Just let me know when," Marie said.

"Did you have a pleasant meal with the girls?" Robin asked.

"Very pleasant. And did you enjoy your meal as well?"

"Very much."

"I will get this pie to the kitchen then." Marie gave him a bit of a curtsy and walked off.

November 22, 1839

Marie saw movement out the kitchen window. Robin dropped an armful of firewood, ripped off his coat and tossed it to the ground. He jumped back from it.

She moved closer to the window.

He searched the ground and stomped on something. Then he picked up his coat to shake it and examine it inside and out before pulling it back on.

She laughed inside the kitchen.

He kicked over the split logs before picking them back up and carried them toward the kitchen door.

Marie hurried from the window to pour a cup of coffee from the heavy pot, using a towel around her hand.

Robin entered and dropped all the wood near the hearth. Then he began to pile them neatly for her. "Will this be enough for the night? I sure hope."

Marie pointed at the wood. "Missed one."

Robin jolted back from the pile and stood upright.

She stepped on a spider on the floor.

"Mijn hemel!" Robin collected himself. "If they were any bigger in this country one could shoot them."

"Well, you're welcome to try." Marie kicked the remains of the spider into the hearth. "I thought you were about to strip all your clothing off out there."

"One tickle and I would have. Are they poisonous?"

Marie busied herself with bringing him the cup of coffee. "I don't believe so. The bite just hurts."

"Is there anything poisonous here?" Robin accepted the cup. "Thank you."

"Just that ivy you were walking through out there." Marie smiled and turned away.

"I do believe you are making fun of me," Robin said lightly.

"The wood spiders did a pretty good job of that."

Robin laughed. "Bastards."

"Kick the wood pile before picking them up, or toss them down first. Either way," Marie said. "Only the rattlesnakes here will kill you. And some of the mushrooms. Not these of course. I don't think. Maybe this one."

He laughed. "I'll see you eat that soup first then."

Robin drove the wagon into the little town of Canterbury. Marie watched his eyes go to the tavern next to the mercantile. He stopped them in front of the store and pulled back on the brake.

"You know, I can get what we need in the store, sir." Marie stood up.

Robin picked up his rifle off the floor and climbed down. "Are you certain? Will five dollars cover it?"

"More than enough. I'll bring you back what's left." Marie climbed into the front where he'd been sitting and turned around to step one boot out feeling for the step he'd used.

Robin pushed her foot to the right spot. Then he withdrew quickly, realizing he was beneath her skirt. "I do beg your pardon."

"Thank you for not letting me fall." She reached out a hand to him.

Robin took her hand firmly and guided it onto his shoulder. "Big jump. Can you do it?"

Marie hopped down before him, looking at his full red lips so close to her mouth.

He stepped back from her.

Marie smoothed out her skirt. When she raised her eyes, way behind Robin, Marta and June were walking toward her.

Robin took out his leather pocketbook and put some coins into her open hand. "I'll meet you inside in a few minutes. Thirty minutes, perhaps."

"Yes sir. Take as long as you like," Marie said.

Robin disappeared into the tavern. It was dark inside and took his eyes a moment to adjust. Several men at the bar and at tables had a good look at him. One of the men was the constable with a badge on his coat. Robin opened the scarf at his neck and adjusted his rifle strap over his shoulder, holding the barrel up. His boots sounded on the wood flooring as he walked to an empty side of the bar. His posture set him apart from all the men leaning over the bar or on elbows on tables. Van der Kellen stood upright and proper until the bartender came to him.

"You're that new Dutchman with the hay farm, aren't you?"

"Indeed."

"What'll it be, then, Dutchman?"

"Whiskey, please."

The bartender reached beneath the bar to set a glass in front of Robin. Then he opened a bottle and poured.

"Would you have any brandy?" Robin asked.

"I can get you some. Take me a week maybe. You'll have to buy it by the bottle. Nobody around here drinks it," the bartender said.

"Get me a case." Robin set a five-dollar coin down beside his glass. "And two bottles of this for now."

The bartender looked him in the eyes and then picked up the money. "Will two bottles get you through 'til the brandy comes?"

Robin put back his shot of whiskey. "If it is watered down as much as this, I doubt it."

The bartender glanced down the bar at the other patrons who started laughing. "Oh, you want the un-watered-down whiskey? Why didn't you say so?" He set two bottles of whiskey on the bar for Robin.

Robin picked up one of his bottles and opened it for a taste in his glass. "Better."

The men at the bar broke up laughing.

Marie was followed into the mercantile by Marta and June, who swept her off to the corner to ask, "Marie, how is he?"

"How is the magnificent Mr. Van der Kellen?" Marta insisted.

"What's he like? What does he do?"

Marie held onto her heart with both hands, still clutching his coins. "He's an absolute dream."

"What did he give you to shop with?" June pawed at her hands. "I thought he was broke."

Marie opened her hand to show the five silver dollars.

"Can't afford us, I see. What has he sent you to purchase?" June asked. "A golden calf?"

"He went in the tavern." Marta looked out the window. "What is he like? Oh my, he makes my hands sweat, he does. What does he do in the evenings? Does he chat with you?"

Marie laughed. "Be quiet. It's his first time to town. Once he figures out that's nothing like a drinking establishment in Boston, he'll be in here looking to go home. I used all the salt on that pork. I have to get a few things. He wants coffee. Can you believe that?"

"He doesn't drink tea?"

"He does but he likes coffee in the morning, nice and strong."

"Has he found his way out to your bed yet?" June questioned.

"June!" Marie swatted her. "He would never."

"He's only been here a week. He's smart enough to find his way," June remarked. "Gentleman like that is going to be bored here with no company. You think he loved your cooking that much? You'll spend the summer in your confinement."

"Who would mind?" Marta blurted out. "I just love his accent. Never did I love being fired so much. And him standing there with that shiny pistol. My hands are sweating again."

"That's just what men like. Sweaty females," Marie snapped.

"What did he send you here to buy with five dollars? Not just salt. Does he know he won't find much in here?" June went on.

Marie looked about. "Go get me that jar of honey over there. And pepper. He likes his soup with black pepper ground in it. His eggs too in the morning."

"Is that so? Likes it hot, does he?" June teased. "What does he like the honey on? Your lips?"

"How are you two doing?" Marie put her hand on her hips.

"We found work at the Inn. We're okay for now," June said. "Staying there and trying to work off our keep."

"He's still in there," Marta said from the window. "That's his flaw. He's a drinker, but beautiful when he does it."

"He hasn't had nothing but a small bottle of brandy since he arrived." Marie gathered up her supplies, black pepper, cumin, salt, flour.

"What does he do in the evenings when you're all alone in the house together?" June asked.

"He reads books, draws a map of the property, sorts through his father's office. He reorganized all of the books because he said they were not in the right order. Law books those are," Marie said.

"He reads books? Is that what a gentleman does with all that leisure time?" Marta questioned.

"He hasn't had all that leisure time. He works in the barn a lot. He's been walking the property, drawing pictures of it. The Lee's had him over to Thanksgiving supper yesterday," Marie said.

"Were you invited?"

"I was. I ate in the kitchen with Rachel and Louise while they served the dining room. At least they didn't ask me to help," Marie said.

"How did that go?" June asked.

"They made him a fancy meal. Three courses and dessert. I wanted to crawl under the table," Marie said. "I'm sure that's what he's used to. We don't eat like that, can't eat like that."

"Lees don't eat that way everyday honey," June said. "That was special for him. Trust me."

"After the dinner he went into the parlor with Mr. and Mrs. Lee for brandy. The children went to do their schoolwork or chores. I could hear them having a good time in the parlor, some laughter. That Mrs. Lee is so fond of him," Marie said. "Only so obvious, we're not allowed in that parlor."

"Except to clean it," June said. "Did he actually butcher that pig all by himself? Or did you have to do it?"

"As if I could. He did it just fine. Didn't even get any on his pretty boots," Marie said. "Didn't even flinch and yet dances like a marionette with a spider on him."

"A dandy like that? Has he paid you yet?" June asked.

"Spiders?" Marta asked. "Has he seen the ones in the quarters? Even the cats don't eat them."

"Same as he paid you two. And they're the same spiders in the woodpile," Marie said.

"And when does he pay you again?"

"End of the month, I assume. First of the next perhaps."

"We'll see about that."

"You're so sure he's a swindler. Just because he's handsome?" Marie asked.

"Right. Because he's broke," June said. "Heard in town his father left him with debt. That's what that banker was calling for. This one had to sell his home in Boston to pay it all. Will he now have to give this house to his older brother? That's what I want to know. He's not the eldest son, you know?"

"He's coming. He's coming." Marta rushed over from the window. "I think I need to loosen my stays. Am I showing enough bosom?"

"Maybe he can sell that golden horse tiara to buy you a ring," June commented.

"I'm out of this." Jonesy put his hands up.

"I don't know you two." Marie moved away from them to the jars of tomatoes and made a collection of her things on the counter.

June and Marta hid behind the shelf of bolts of cloth, peeking through it.

Robin didn't enter right away. He set down a package of two bottles of whiskey and laid down his rifle into the wagon behind his seat.

"Where is he?" June asked.

Marie continued her shopping and asked the shop keep, "What has this come to so far?"

"Three dollars and twenty-five cents, Marie. You got that on you?"

"Of course."

"So that's the old Willem Van der Kellen's son, is it? I hear he's from overseas. Likes the spices, does he?" the shop keep said. "Is he paying with our money?"

"He gave me five US dollars. So be nice to him, Jonesy," Marie snapped. "Is there any way you can get me sheets of large paper? Very large?"

"What? Roll paper. Like butcher paper?" Jonesy asked.

"Yes. Maybe. What would that cost?"

The man laughed. "Better behave yourselves, ladies. The Dutchman is coming."

"Don't mention the paper," Marie cautioned. "Just get me some."

The door opened and they heard his boots clunk lightly on the floorboards. He glanced about the shop, taking in crockery and medicines. Finally, his eyes settled on Marie.

The shop keep hurried around from behind the counter, extending his hand. "Mr. Van der Kellen, so good to finally meet you. I run the shop. I'm Ennis Jones. They call me Jonesy."

Robin shook his hand. "A pleasure, sir."

"Will you be needing anything else here, sir?" Jonesy asked. "I run to New London once a week for supplies. I can find anything there. Just give me a head's up that you be needing it."

Marie started putting her supplies into a crate. "I have everything from the list."

"No, thank you."

Jonesy went to Marie and she handed him the coins. "Before you go, I've got some letters for you. For your father, if you don't mind. My deepest condolences, sir." He went behind the counter to get their change.

"I suppose I will take them. Thank you," Robin said.

Three letters were handed to Robin. He glanced quickly at the addresses on them and then pocketed them.

Marie collected the seventy-five cents and returned the dollar seventy-five to Robin. Their hands touched briefly and electrically. He pocketed the money and picked up the crate for her.

"I can bring that out for you," Jonesy said.

"I have it. Have a good day, sir." Robin carried the crate out and held the door for Marie.

She gave a quick glance at Marta and June in the store before walking out past Robin at the door. She smelled whiskey on him as she squeezed her skirt past him.

Robin took his bottles of whiskey and a glass into the library to sit down at the desk and laid his father's letters out on the desk. As his hands worked the cork out of the bottle, his eyes sorted the letters. All were single sheets of paper, written on inside and folded closed with a wax seal on one side and addressee on the other. Willem Van der Kellen, Canterbury, Connecticut.

Mr. Van der Kellen,

I regret to inform you that all records for the East Street Bank were destroyed in the fire. While I deeply sympathize with the people who lost money in the tragedy, I can offer no means of verifying who they were. Hundreds of them have come to my office, but I find only five of them could prove they had accounts at the bank by presenting promissory notes. I promptly refunded their money using funds from the bonds we held for the bank. The amount totaled only $55. I had to turn away all of the others and close business until they stop lining up at my door.

Best of success in your case, sir.

Sincerely,

James McCoy

McCoy Insurance Company

Mr. Van der Kellen,

Please appear in court for the trial of Christian Pascal, ten o-clock in the morning, October 4th, 1839. Be prepared to provide the prosecution. The court appointed defender shall be Attorney Thomas Albertson of New York.

Thank you, Sir.

Miss Andrews, East Side Court House, New
York Manhattan Island

October 1, 1839

Mr. Van der Kellen,

This is the third notice of payment due I have sent you.
Please be aware, if I do not receive your payment of
twenty dollars, next month I must call in your loan
and demand payment in full of $230. If this
payment is not received, I shall be forced to claim the
estate you have mortgaged. With your reputation as a
lawyer, I find it hard to understand why you do not
keep your debts paid. Forgive me for being blunt, sir.
My patience has grown thin.

Sincerely,

John Bradford, Norwich Central Bank

Robin refilled his glass of whiskey and sat back in the chair. He read the
last letter once again. He pulled his father's ledger from the drawer and

flipped to the most recent entries again. He found a blank sheet of paper, ink well and quill. He began jotting down some figures. And he began going back further into the ledger, doing the same.

It was with a particularly foul curse in Dutch that he opened the safe in one try, using his older brother's birthday as the combination. Inside he found a cigar box of Treasury notes and coins, two pair of gold cuff links, a ceramic bowl containing Dutch coins, and a mysterious brass key. A quick rummage through the cigar box did not reveal his father's gold pocket watch, however.

Hours had passed before Marie appeared in the doorway. By then Robin had four sheets of paper filled with neat rows of figures and circled conclusions on them. He looked up at her.

"Sorry to interrupt. I was going for the night. Would there be anything else you need tonight?" Marie asked.

"Ahm… no, miss. Thank you."

"Is everything all right?" she asked. "Any trouble in those letters?"

"No. Related to his case, is all." Robin let out a tired breath and closed the ledger. He rose from the chair and collected the whiskey bottle and his empty glass. "I'll get back to this in the morning."

"That's the idea. You must be tired." Marie moved back from the doorway and into the hall.

On his way up the stairs, he tried that brass key in the doors that closed off half of the house, but it didn't fit, and wasn't locked.

December 5, 1839

On the day of their first snowfall, Robin carried a ladder through the kitchen, into the closed off wing of the home, down the hall, and into the ballroom. Marie followed him, confused. She watched him stand the ladder against the wall and climb up with a length of clothesline.

He tied one end of clothesline to a nail in the wood trim, a nail once used for the hanging of party decorations. When he climbed down, he met eyes with Marie in the doorway.

"For the winter you may hang your washing in here. I know it is insane, but who's going to see it except you." Robin carried the ladder across the width of the room and set it up there. He climbed and tied the other end of clothesline to a nail there, extending it tightly across the room at what he thought would be Marie's eye level. "Would you please stand beside this so I get the right height for you?"

Marie wandered inside onto the checkerboard floor and weighted down his line with one finger. "I can hand the line to you."

While standing on the ladder, Robin pulled a knife out of his boot to cut the line. "How many do you need?"

"Three should do," Marie said.

Robin hopped down and moved the ladder again. He climbed up to set the next one. "I find, in life in general, there are women who always ask for more than they need and there are women who always need more than they ask for."

She handed the line up to him.

"And then there is you, Miss Longuiel."

"Which kind am I then?" Marie smiled.

"You have three lines outside. You need exactly three. You ask for three. You are unique among females. Therefore, I'm making you four." Robin climbed down and moved the ladder again. "With pleasure. What else can I do to make your work easier?"

"I don't suppose you can fix things?"

"Generally. What needs to be fixed?"

"Well, let me show you. The baking oven won't latch closed. Everything takes longer to bake when the door won't latch."

"Show me." He followed her to the kitchen and had not previously noticed that one side of the hearth had a built-in iron oven while the other side had the open fire and hooks from which to hang pots over the fire.

"Look at this." She gestured him to come closer. "If you would, sir."

He had to stand shoulder to shoulder with her and observe how the latch was not tightening the door closed. "Oh. Yes. I see. Let me get some tools. I can try to tighten that up."

She turned to look at him, almost with her nose in his hair. "Well. Then I'll have to remember how to bake bread regular again." Bergamot and lemon oil.

December 25, 1839

"As it is Christmas, would you join me for dinner?" Robin asked.

"You wish me to sit in the dining room with you, sir?"

"I'm… I am asking if I may join you in here, actually," Robin said. "It's getting really very cold in there. Your hearth is already so nice and warm."

"Of course. You've been working outside. You must be freezing," Marie said. "I'll fetch a nice hot cup of tea for you."

"Thank you. And I apologize for not thinking ahead to a gift for you. But this is a holiday bonus for you." Robin set a little cloth packet of coins down on the table. "Do you have family you would rather be with? I would understand. Friends in town? Time off, perhaps?"

"Thank you, Mr. Van der Kellen. But you did think ahead. A Christmas bonus? I don't think I've ever had one." Marie accepted the packet of coins but did not look inside to count them. She pocketed it. "I have nowhere else to be. You wish me to set the table in here then? For us both?"

"Yes please. I would like to take meals out here with you from now on. If you don't mind," Robin said. "I don't want to have to chop wood for another fireplace all winter. You made another apple pie?"

"I hope you meant that you liked apple pie. I um, got you a present. It isn't much." Marie moved behind the worktables and pulled out a long roll of paper tied with a red ribbon. She brought it to the table and laid it across before him. "I remembered that day you showed me how to use your compass and the drawings, the maps you were trying to make. I know this isn't fine white paper. But I thought maybe you could use it to practice. It's just a roll of butcher paper."

Robin smoothed his hands on the roll and toyed with the ribbon a bit. Suddenly he rose from the chair and hurried for the parlor. "Excuse me a moment." He disappeared into the dark room beyond.

Marie's hand went to her mouth. She moved quietly around the table and toward the doorway. He was standing in the dark parlor, his back to her. She could see the white of his handkerchief pulled from his pocket.

Marie moved quietly into the room to stand behind the sofa, her hands on the back of it. "Forgive me, sir. I..." She saw his hand go up so she remained standing quietly. "I shall leave you at once."

"No. Please. Thank you so much, Miss Longuiel. This means very much to me, for my map making."

"Really?"

"It touches my heart so that you listened to me and you remembered. Especially given...how very far I am from my family at this time of year." He turned to look at her. "It's just that...not a soul on earth has paid so much attention to me in so many years."

"Oh. You are missing your family. Of course, you are. Some company for dinner would be good for you then. I'll set the table there for us both. You come along when you are ready."

January 13, 1840

The handsome Dutchman made his way toward the blacksmith shop. The cold wind almost took his hat off, and yet he had two more blocks to go, down the road, past homes, toward the livery. Beside it was the blacksmith shop and the banging sound rang from inside. Robin opened the door and loosened the scarf about his neck. The blistering heat of the kiln was a shocking contrast to the below freezing conditions outside.

The smithy looked over at him and howled, "One minute." He continued banging out a horseshoe for a few moments. The man had enormous bare brown arms.

Robin looked about at wares for sale along the walls. Harnesses. Tack. Saddlebags. Iron pots and pans. He had to unbutton his coat as he looked around.

Finally, the blacksmith stopped his banging and wiped his hands on a rag. "You're that Dutchman, aren't you?"

"Robin Van der Kellen, sir."

"I ain't no sir."

Robin lowered his chin.

In the silence that followed, only the fire crackled.

"If you came in just for the heat, I can get back to working," the man said. "If not, is there something you need?"

Robin pulled out a hinge from his pocket, looking at it.

"Well speak up, would you? When that kiln is hot, I have to get my work done."

"Would you be able to make a new hinge for a baking oven door?" Robin held out the one in his deer skin glove.

The man took it and held it up to the light. "I've got a basket of these over here. I have some that will work."

Robin followed him toward the side wall where other items for sale caught his eye.

"This one. Same size and stronger because I made it. Cost you two bits though," the blacksmith said. "Cost you more to have me fix that one."

"Very well. I'll take it and these." Robin selected three tin items from hooks on the wall.

"Fifty cents, then."

Robin removed his gloves to extract the coins from his pocketbook while the man put the three tin items and the hinge into a small sack.

They traded coins for the sack.

"When you go to put that on the oven, remember to let the fire die down over night and the iron cool off. And still, you best wear them leather gloves," the blacksmith said.

"Thank you, sir."

"Like I said. I ain't no gentleman. Don't be calling me sir."

"You gave me no alternative name by which to call you," Robin explained.

The blacksmith pushed him back a step. "Are you getting on airs with me?"

Robin's rifle strap slid down to his elbow, but he caught it. He moved back toward the door and began closing up his coat. "No, I was not."

"Get out. And the next time you need a shoe on those giant horses of yours you can take them to Norwich."

At that Robin just exited the building. His hat was blowing from the tether about his throat. His coat was half open. He walked back into the wind, toward the store where his saddled Friesian was tied to the post. He ducked beside the horse to tie the sack to the saddle, secure his hat on his head, and buttoned his coat. He put one boot into a stirrup and hoisted himself up into the wind. "Genie, lopen op. Goddammit."

It was a long ride back home through sideways snow. Down one entire road he bent down against the horse's neck for warmth, wrapping his arms along the neck. Finally, he passed the Lee's. And at long last entered through the stone walls of his driveway. He rode up to the barn door and then dismounted to get it open.

Genie entered and waited beside his stall. Robin spent some time unsaddling him and brushing the wet off of him, before he put him into the stall. Then he fed both horses, blew out the lamp in the barn, and carried his purchase toward the house. The sun was red on the horizon.

Marie hurried over to take his hat and scarf. "I was so worried you wouldn't make it back before dark."

"It's awful out there," Robin admitted.

"You're soaked through." Marie took his coat off him and hung it up.

Robin made his way to the table and clunked his package down, and his rifle. For a moment he just leaned there with both hands on the table and his backside toward the fire.

"Are you all right?" Marie asked him. "What is that?"

"I'll show you tomorrow. I'm in no mood right now."

"Get into some dry clothes and get warm then. I have soup and tea for you. I could make coffee if you like."

He remained leaning there, head down.

Marie retreated behind her worktable. "Something happened in town?"

"I'll go change. In the morning I'll fix your oven door. If you would please, let the fire die out tonight and go cold so that I can do it." Robin took out the new hinge and set it on the mantel with his rifle. Then he took the sack upstairs with him.

January 14, 1840

Marie came in the back door and closed it quickly against the snow. She found the lantern lit on the hook over the cold ashes of the hearth, where she usually hung her stew pot. And Van der Kellen was already fastening her new hinge onto the baking oven door.

"Good morning, sir. How goes it?"

"Ow. Still fucking hot. But...I think I've got it." Robin tried the door, open, and closed. Open again.

"I'm so sorry. Are you burned?" Marie asked.

"Starting off the day well, huh?" Robin looked at his left hand. His little finger was red.

Marie grabbed him by the wrist. "Hurry. Right over here." She pulled him toward the window where ice rimmed the bottom. "Get that on the ice, now."

"Ow! That's worse than burning it." Robin leaned his head to the shutter and let her press his hand against the ice.

"Keep it there. As long as you can. I've done that myself a hundred times. You'll be grateful that this is winter when you've done it," Marie said.

Robin was facing the wall. Into the shutter he said, "It's fixed. You can start the fire again."

"You hold that to the ice." She stepped back from him. "And tell me what happened in town."

"He was mean to me."

"He was mean to you? Who?" She put her hands on her hips.

"The blacksmith told me I had to take my horses to Norwich from now on. He shoved me. What did I do to him?" Robin blurted out.

"The blacksmith? Oh! That had nothing to do with you." Marie suddenly laughed.

"Pardon?" Robin turned.

"Back on the ice." Marie pushed his hand back to the windowsill. "I heard from Jonesy that your Klootzak knocked that blacksmith down when he shoe'd him. The whole town was laughing about it. He's afraid of your big horse. That's all."

"He's afraid of my...." Robin stammered. "He wouldn't tell me his name."

"It's Mahomet. He's half Indian. Doesn't like to tell anybody his name."

"Is that right?"

"Twice your size and he can't handle your horse. And you road to town on one of them," Marie said. "You sure made him look cowardly to the whole town."

"Well, I...I wish he'd just said so. How am I supposed to know what my horse did when he shoe'd him?" Robin exasperated. "Please start your fire and start some coffee, would you?"

"Did he hurt you? You said he shoved you."

"No. Please do not ask." Robin stepped away from the window ice and examined his hand.

"Does that hurt?"

"Burns incredibly."

"Back on the ice then."

That evening Robin brought down the sack from the blacksmith's and opened it on Marie's worktable. "I have something for you. I hope at least that you will accept this as the late Christmas gift I intended."

He set out for her three tin cookie cutters. One in the shape of a circle, a tree, and a star.

Marie smoothed her fingers along the tree and picked it up. "For me? Oh Mr. Van der Kellen. These are so wonderful. I'm going to try them out tomorrow."

"I hope you don't think that was my intention. A rather self-serving gift it would have been," Robin said. "To get myself cookies."

"No one would consider your actions to be self-serving," Marie told him. "Let me see your burned finger. I feel terrible you got hurt fixing my oven door."

Robin looked down at his hand but he stepped back from her.

"You don't want me to see it."

"Ahm. It's fine."

"No, it isn't. I know oven burns well enough."

Timidly, Robin finally conceded and held his left hand out over the table. He turned his elbow out to reveal the burn down the left edge of his little finger.

"Did you put anything on it? I have some salve." Marie went to her pantry to hunt for it.

"No. It's all right. I think," Robin said.

She came out with a small jar and some length of bandage. "You can't even bend it. Sit down at the table." She found her scissors.

"Do you have any honey?" Robin took his seat near the fire. He extended his hands out across the table.

Marie looked at him. "Honey?"

"If you don't mind, I prefer honey on burns."

Confused, Marie brought the jar from the pantry and sat across from him. She cut a length of bandage and another small strip to use as a tie. Then she opened the jar. "This might hurt for a moment."

"Yes, I know."

"Pardon me." Marie dabbed a spoon into the honey and then swiftly smoothed it down the length of his pinky. "I never heard of this. Are you certain?"

That made him shut his eyes and nod. Before he looked again, he felt her ease the bandaging on and around his finger. Her hand brushed the top of his. Her fingers touched his left ring finger as she tied a knot to hold the bandage on. Before she took her hand away, he lifted his to feel her palm with the backs of his other fingers.

She withdrew and closed up her jar of honey.

January continued, cold and dark. Van der Kellen perfected his map of the estate on the large butcher paper, weighted down flat with pottery on each corner on the kitchen table. Marie made him oatmeal or sugar cookies in the three shapes of the cookie cutters.

February came on with more snow and blowing wind. Robin began teaching her astronomy. Marie let him help her dip candles.

March 5, 1840

A sudden knock on the door had Marie run to open it. "Mr. Lee. Please come in."

"Is Mr. Van der Kellen about? I urgently need him."

From the library, Van der Kellen emerged. "Mr. Lee. What brings you out in this cold?"

"Sir, you once said in conversation that you grew up on a horse farm. Would you have any knowledge of their birthing concerns?" Mr. Lee held his hat in both hands and stood, dripping with snow by the back door.

"Quite a lot. What is the problem?" Robin asked.

"I have a foal not coming. The mare has been laboring for hours, hard, all day. She's wearing out. And I see barely a back hoof showing," Mr. Lee said.

"Back hoof? It's supposed to be a nose and front hooves." Robin began pulling on his coat and hat. "Is the mare down?"

"Since sunset."

"Mijn God. You should have got me sooner. " Robin buttoned up the coat.

"I brought you a ride," Mr. Lee said. "If there is anything you can do, for the foal or the mare, sir."

"There is everything I can do, if I'm in time. Marie, I don't know when I'll be back. Don't wait up." Robin opened the door for Mr. Lee.

By Susan Eddy

Chapter Four Influenza

March 10, 1840

"Mr. Van der Kellen, it is inappropriate for you to live out here on this estate alone with the girl." Doctor Johnson drew from his bag a small bottle containing a tincture of opium. He poured some into the teacup and set it on the nightstand.

"I had to let everyone else go. She's all I can afford. She's not a servant." Robin coughed and began trying to rebutton his shirt. "Feel as if my skin hurts wherever the clothes are."

"Your fever will get worse before it betters. For now, you're breathing all right. Does your chest hurt?"

Van der Kellen shook his head. "No."

"Head hurt?"

Van der Kellen nodded. "Awful."

"Coughing up blood?"

"No."

"You can't keep doing it all by yourself. You've gone and made yourself sick. Now if you don't stay in bed, you'll lend yourself to consumption, and don't think a gentleman like yourself can't catch that. Believe me you can. It has nothing to do with status and it's in almost every farm around here. One of the Lees next door to you, even sicker than you are. The younger boy."

At that Van der Kellen looked up, frightened. "Jeremiah? It was his foal I just birthed."

"Haven't you any family I can send for? Friends in Boston perhaps?"

"No. My family are all in the Netherlands. They could not be here for months if I sent word now."

From the hall, Marie listened in, her back to his bedroom wall.

"Best send them a letter. Tell them how sick you are. Drink that right now. I will instruct the girl to keep this fireplace going, give you one spoon of laudanum every six hours, keep you watered, and you are not to get out of that bed until that cough is better. And you're to eat this." He set a jar of peaches down on the bedside table. "My wife sent you that. Saw you in town once, apparently. Scurvy is the next thing you'll get. I'll come back to see you in two days. Send the girl to the Lees if you need me sooner. Stay in bed, Van der Kellen. Rest. Water. And take that laudanum for the fever."

By Susan Eddy

Marie Longuiel hurried down the stairs to the kitchen.

The doctor came down behind her and set his bag on the table. "Miss, that fever of his will worsen fast. If you don't take care of him..."

"I certainly will, sir."

"Very well then. One spoon of laudanum in water or tea every 6 hours. I just gave him two. If you have to, just give it to him straight on the spoon. Set the bottle down though, out of his reach. I've seen patients knock the bottle to the floor in their struggle. And then there is nothing to control that fever."

Marie nodded.

"Make him drink all the water you can. Get soup into him if you can. You have some honey? Put some in his tea for his cough. You cannot leave him alone up there all night. When that fever hits, he won't know where he is. He could fall down the stairs. Keep him in that bed. Tuck him in, tie him down, if you have to," the doctor said. "You're not going to get much sleep the next few nights. Don't leave him alone any longer than you absolutely must."

"Yes, Doctor."

"You are the only one here? He's got horses out there, doesn't he?"

"Yes, two of them. A cow and chickens," Marie said.

"That's it? Has he been doing all that by himself?"

"Yes, Doctor. He takes care of the animals in the barn. But I can do all that for him."

"You cannot. You can't leave him that long. If he's sick for a week and those horses die, he won't be happy. You know what those things are worth. You know the way to the Lees, next farm over?"

"Yes. And to town."

"I'll tell Mr. Lee that Van der Kellen's horses need tending. If he needs me you go to the Lees and have their older boy fetch me, if I'm not there already. Keep making him drink water even if he resists. And you know what he's going to need to do if he's drinking water?"

"Oh!" The girl averted her eyes quickly to the floor.

"I'm going to be blunt here, young girl. He'll be too dizzy to get out of bed. Bring him the chamber pot in the bed. Beneath the covers, the gentleman can urinate into the pot, then slide it out to you. He's not eating so he won't have need to do the other. If he's sweating badly, he won't need to urinate. But then you have to keep dry sheets on him. Keep his head up on pillows. Now you know what you're getting into. If he's coughing up blood, come get me. If he struggles to breathe, come get me. Don't mean to frighten you. You are the one keeping him alive the next few days."

"I have tended some sick before. I will do as you say." Marie gave a bit of a bow to him. She met his eyes then.

"I'll try to come tomorrow, or the next day for certain. People dying of fever in farms all around here. He's strong and healthy. The very old and very young come first."

In a few moments Marie came right into the master bedroom, struggling with a bundle of firewood, eventually spilling it uncontrollably to the floor. She tossed a number of logs onto the fire and stacked the others on the hearth. When she turned and stood up, brushing her hands down her apron, she met eyes with her employer in the bed. "I'm so sorry, sir."

"I'm terribly sorry about this, Miss Longuiel." He pulled the top of his night shirt closed and pulled up his blankets. His knees were up beneath the blankets. Then he coughed as if in such pain.

"It's quite all right, sir. I spoke with the doctor at length before he left. I have my instructions," she said, looking down. "My mother died of consumption. That's how I came to be working here. Pardon me." She walked closer to the bed to pick up the jar of peaches beside his bottle of laudanum. "Doctor said you're to eat one of these each day. I'll get you a bowl and a spoon."

"Ahm, Miss Longuiel," he said. "I am terribly sorry."

"Nothing to be sorry for, sir." She left the room. "You're sick, is all."

Marie was startled to find him sitting up in the chair by the fireplace. She immediately brought the fresh hot tea to him. "What are you doing out of bed, sir?"

"I couldn't breathe. And I was so cold. Wait a moment. I want you...I would have you sit down here and we would talk about some things." He gratefully drank in the hot liquid, finding bit of honey in it. That was different. "Sit, please."

Reluctantly, Miss Longuiel sat in the chair opposite him. The two high back chairs sat facing each other by the hearth, as if for man and wife. The bottoms of her skirt were wet to her knees and dripping onto the floor. Seeing him look at that she quickly said, "I'm sorry sir. I'll clean that right up."

"Don't care about that. You must choose a room and move into the house. I can't have you walking out there in the snow, and taking care of me," he said. "And now livestock too."

"I couldn't, sir."

"Who's going to know out here? And I swear to you I will never, ever, enter your room," he said. "Besides, it's one less fire to keep up. I'm sorry about the horses. How can I teach you they need grain and hay?"

"The doctor said he would tell the Lees to look after your animals," she said. "There's still plenty of firewood from the last time you chopped it. I just have to bring more in for the night."

"Oh, this is awful."

"You stay in bed as the doctor said to. What happens to me if you die? I guess I'll be living out there." She pointed at the window.

"I didn't think of it that way." He lowered his eyes to his hands wrapped in the blanket.

"Oh, my sir. I'm so sorry for my tone. I can't believe I just yelled at you, and you not feeling well."

He wet his lips and pushed down his blanket, feeling too hot now. His shirt fell open revealing the hair in the middle of his chest. "Miss Longuiel, do you think when we are alone that you could call me Robin? And I could call you by your given name? What is it?"

"I couldn't, sir. But you may call me Marie," she said.

"Marie. That's very lovely." He swallowed as if it hurt. "I must say something difficult. Sit for another moment please."

Marie sat with her best posture and waited.

"There is a key to my trunk in the drawer." He gave her intense eye contact. "Whatever money is in my pocketbook and that trunk you take it. Combination to the safe is in there too. Send the trunk to my sister. You'll find letters from her."

Marie cleared her throat. "The doctor has scared you. You're going to be just fine. You'll see."

"I'll do my part."

"And I'll do mine. I'll get you something to eat if you'll get back into bed, sir. Please. If you pass out here, I can't get you into the bed by myself."

He nodded. "That makes very good sense."

"Can you walk to the bed by yourself?" Marie asked.

"Of course."

When Marie returned, she found him face down on top of the bed, in that blanket, up on his elbows. "Sir? Mr. Van der Kellen?"

He just held his head in his hands and moaned.

"Oh oh. Doctor warned me you might get this way from the fever. We need to get this medicine into you, now."

He was shivering. He said that he hurt all over, in Dutch.

"Sir?" She pulled down the covers and reached for his arm. "I do beg your pardon but you must get under these covers now, sir." She pulled hard to get him to slide toward her so that she could tuck his feet and bare legs beneath the blankets. His head tucked into her shoulder. As she pulled the covers up over him, he clung to her, his head sinking to her chest. His whole body shook. "It's all right. It's all right. Let's get you to drink this water. Let go, just a little. I can't get you to eat anything this way. I'm going to make you some broth."

When he leaned his head back against the headrest, she brought the cup to his mouth. His cheek was so hot. He tried to turn his mouth away from the cup but she pinned him back with her knee on his chest and held onto his chin. She got the full cup into him and she wiped off his lip with her thumb. "Is that staying in you? The medicine?"

"Wie ben jij?" He said softly. Who are you?

"You're very feverish. Just rest."

"Ik wil je." He grabbed her hand. I want you.

Marie sat on the edge of his bed and held his hand.

Robin Van der Kellen laid down onto his side, facing her. He shoved his covers down.

She pulled them back up and tucked them in around him. She waited and watched to be sure he'd stay that way. Yes, he was asleep again. That would buy her a little while to get some things done for him, but no telling how long.

Just before sunset there was a knock on the kitchen door and a young voice called, "Hello in the house?"

Marie hurried down the stairs to the kitchen. Around the corner she saw a teenage boy.

"Hello Miss. I'm Jonathon Lee. My pa sent me to tend to Mr. Van der Kellen's horses."

"Thank you. How are your brother and sister?" Marie asked.

"A little better today, miss. I shoveled the stalls out and refilled the water and fed them. Cow and chickens too," Jonathon said. "They're all set for the night. I'll come by tomorrow midday to do the same."

"Thank you. I can't leave him long. His fever is bad," Marie said.

The boy pointed to the kitchen table. "Milk there from the cow. She's running dry. There's hot soup my ma sent you. I'll tell the doctor to come by here when he can."

"Thank you, Jonathon. Please thank your folks for this."

That night Robin could not stop coughing and it was probably 2AM. Typically alone in the house at that time, no one would have known to help him, but that night Marie came in with a lamp lit and set it beside his bed. "I'll be right back with some tea. Just hold on, sir." She tossed some more logs onto the fire and went downstairs in her robe and slippers.

Robin sat up in the bed, against the pillows, coughing and with feverish headache.

Marie now had a crock and cup. But the first thing she did was put a spoon of laudanum into his teacup. Then she poured in chicken broth from Mrs. Lee's soup. "It's not that hot yet. But this way you can drink it right now."

His hands were shaking when he held them out of the covers.

Marie sat down on the bed with him and held his hands down. She pulled the blankets up over his hands. "Keep them warm under there. I'll see to it." She held the cup to his mouth gently and let him take a drink. "Try again. It has your medicine in it so you can sleep. That's it. Keep going."

Half the cup gone he nudged her arm. "Wait. I must breathe."

She set the cup on the nightstand. And boldly she felt his forehead beneath his bangs. His dark eyes closed as she did. His head leaned into her hand. He was normally neatly shaven, but now had half a week's beard that she stroked a finger along. "You're quite feverish. I'm sure the medicine will help. Are you hungry? I can get you more soup."

"No. No, please find her. You must find her." He met her eyes as she helped him drink the rest of the broth.

"Find who?"

"My wife Adrianna. I can't see her face anymore."

"You have a wife? You told the doctor all your family was overseas." She saw that the broth and medicine had gotten into him so she set the cup down and pulled his covers up higher on him. "Get down in there and back to sleep now."

"Where is she?" He said more in Dutch.

A beautiful language, she thought.

He threw back the covers again and his neck was shiny in the lamplight. He popped off two buttons while tugging on his shirt.

"I can't believe she didn't come with you. Oh my God." Marie covered him up again and leaned down over him to hold him down. He rocked against her for a while, coughing into the quilts. Marie grasped another pillow and pressed it up against him. "I'm right here, darling. Just sleep. Just go back to sleep."

Marie had a short nap in the high-backed chair by the fire before Van der Kellen stirred again. The dawn light was just turning pink outside on the snow. She went to the bedside and felt her employer's forehead and cheek, horrified to find him burning hot with fever. His curls were wet to his forehead and cheek. She pulled the covers off his shoulder to find his shirt soaked through. He was sweating and shivering so hard that he couldn't lie still. It had only been two hours since giving more laudanum to him.

"Well. No choice except to change these." She crawled onto the bed with him and unbuttoned his shirt. "I do hope you don't awaken in the middle of this. If you don't mind, I'm just going to talk my way. Look at the embroidery. These buttons look like seashell, maybe. I'm glad I found those two you broke off. I'm always afraid to lose a button in the washing. Oh my. I suppose a man has hair on his chest. We will just not be surprised by that."

She pulled the tunic up and over his head. She slipped it off his arms and for a moment she was stunned by how beautiful he was. His skin was fair and he was lean but muscular. The hair on his chest and arms was a bit darker than that on his head, more like that of his beard. She wiped him dry with a towel. "Well let's get this on before you catch your death of cold." She had to lift his head to slide the clean shirt over it and feed his arms into the sleeves.

He clung to her. Marie just held him, kneeling with him, rocking him gently. She stroked his hair and that seemed to calm him. "Oh my. How wonderful it would be to hold you like this all night. Oh, to be your wife comforting you. What sort of woman wouldn't come with you? And you, I mean, only the most beautiful man I've ever seen. Kind. Gentle. Decent. I've never been married. At this rate I never will be. Keep sleeping, please." She put a little kiss on his hot forehead as she slid away from him.

She slid off the bed and around to the other side to pull the covers down. She pulled the top sheet out completely and unfolded a clean one into the bed as best she could.

His undergarment? How was she going to do that? He sweated through that too. It must go.

With a deep breath she just reached beneath the blankets to slide his underwear down past his hips and down, down to his knees and off. Her heart was pounding as she picked up the clean one and fed his feet into it. She had to fold back the covers to pull the under shorts up his thighs. "Well, I sure hope I am making this comfortable for you because I really don't know what I am doing. I've never been married before. Of course, I told you that already and it's just as true now. I think that's right. Looks maybe right. Oh God I've only done diapers. Well so that is a man." At last, the shorts were on. Not buttoned, but on. His shirt was down in place. And she rolled him to the other side of the bed so that she could change the bottom sheet. He took to the cold side of the bed anyway, seeming to want it. "What kind of wife wouldn't be here to look after him?"

Finally, she rolled him to the clean dry side, buried him the blankets, tucked him in, and took a bundle of laundry downstairs. She cried all the way down and did the laundry. The wet sheets and clothing she hung to dry on lines drawn across the old ball room. The only dance going on in there was the one that got sheets across the lines.

Through the windows she saw Jonathan Lee ride a horse up the driveway toward the barn again.

When Jonathan finished, he knocked on the kitchen door and leaned inside. "All set again today, miss. There's the milk. How is he?"

"Terrible fever. How is your brother?"

"Better. What do you need, miss?"

She almost sobbed. "I need his fever to break."

"Don't worry, miss. He's a war hero. If anyone can do it…"

Deciding it was only an hour before he could have more medicine, she poured some onto a spoon and held it to his mouth to deliver it. He didn't fight her, but his eyes closed as he held onto her.

For two hours all he did was moan. Every breath that left him was with a moan and sometimes a cough. Marie sat in the bed with him, his head in her lap. If she tried to get up, he would throw off his covers again. So, she held him there, petting back his damp curls. He rocked against her as if he hurt so all over. And this went on until he exhausted himself and slept. Marie slept also, sitting up against his headboard.

It was another evening before he awoke in bed. He rolled to his side and moaned, looking about.

Marie awoke in the chair, startled, and came right to him. "Are you all right, sir?"

"O mijn God." He held his head for a moment. "Mijn hoofd doet pijn." Oh my God. I feel like I died.

"Can you hear me, sir?" She felt his forehead. "Good heavens. Your fever broke. Finally."

"How long was I out?" He said in English.

"Two days," Marie said. "We must get you out of this bed and into dry clothing again. Let me change these sheets. You sweat right through everything last night, twice now. You don't want to know how we changed everything. I didn't know you are married, sir."

Robin looked up at her, alarmed.

"Forgive me."

"I said things?" he asked.

"Things I will never repeat. You have my word on that," Marie said. "I'll lay out fresh clothing for you. And then I will get some hot soup up here. For now, you drink this water, all of it."

Weak as a kitten, Robin made his way into the kitchen with a hand on the table all the way along it. He reached for the arm of the kitchen chair nearest her cook fire, and lowered himself into it.

Marie set down her cooking in alarm.

"I...I thought it would be proper for me to sit down here while you do the bedding. I can't believe how wet my pillows are. Like I dumped a pitcher all over the bed. I am so sorry." Robin wrapped his arms tightly to him. He had not shaved but dressed himself in the trousers, underclothing, and shirt she had left for him. He had his short boots on. "Forgive my appearance."

"No need for all that. You could have sat in the chair, any of the dozen chairs up there in your room." Marie picked up a bowl and spooned chicken soup from a pot on the fire. She set this before him with a spoon and napkin. "Are you okay, sir?"

He nodded. "Thank you, Marie, ever so much."

She reached forward and felt his forehead again. "No fever. Sorry. I won't have to touch you again. I promise."

That made him look at her. "You...."

She turned quickly away. "You certainly grow a beard quickly." She picked up a blanket from the clean laundry and wrapped it about his shoulders, easing his hair out on top of it. "How do you feel?"

Robin felt her touch and had some sense of lying against her. "So tired. Sort of in pain all over. A little hungry."

"Well good then. Eat that and I'll give you more. Don't go anywhere. You're too weak to go about on your own."

"Wait. The horses...."

"The Lee's older boy come by every day to shovel and feed them. He says they're fine. He's been milking the cow too."

"Did he say how Jeremiah was?"

"He's better. Jane too."

As she went to the stairway, she looked back at him. He was blowing on his spoon before trying the soup. His hands were long and slender. The firelight behind him made his face impossible to see. She went up to his bedroom, thinking about that picture frame lying face down on his dresser. Before she carried out the sheets for washing, she lifted that small frame to look on the painted likeness of a young blonde woman wearing a locket. She laid it back down beside that very locket from the painting.

Marie opened the locket to find a coiled clipping of brown hair. Robin's, she thought immediately. She put it back as it was beside his gold pocket watch. Marie hurried down the stairs. He has a wife.

Robin's forehead was in his hand, as he sat curled up in the chair beside the cook fire. His shoulder length hair flattened by the pillows, looked dark against the fire light. His feet were up on the next chair, his knees up to his chest and all wrapped in the blanket up to his chin.

The empty bowl was beside him on the table.

Marie set the laundry down and approached him. "Are you all right?"

Robin looked up at her.

"Can you hear me? Robin?"

He nodded.

"Will you drink some water or milk?"

He nodded.

Marie brought him a glass of milk and as it passed from her hands into his, the feeling of his fingers on hers was electric. She shyly went back to work in the kitchen, watching to see if he could drink that.

The sound of her pots and pans made him look over. And they looked at each other at length.

"You must be quite lonely here, having lived in Boston," Marie said. "If you'd like to write to your family now that you are all right, I will get it to town for you."

"How did you get the doctor?"

"I ran to the Lees. Their older boy fetched him," Marie said.

"But that's almost a mile from here, in the snow."

"I hated to leave you alone that long but there was no other choice. If the doctor hadn't told me what to do for you, I would not have known," Marie said. "Never saw anyone that sick who lived."

Robin lowered his chin so sadly.

"I'm sorry. But you recovered. You're all right now," Marie assured him.

"Would you mind coming here?" Robin asked. "I have no voice."

Marie set her things down. She pulled out a kitchen chair to sit across from him.

"What did I say last night?" Robin whispered.

"It was the fever. I don't know how much of it was real or not," Marie told him. "Quite a lot of it was in Dutch. It's a beautiful language but I don't understand any of it."

"What did I say that you did understand?"

"It's just, you were calling for her. Your wife. I'm afraid I had to tell you I was her just to calm you down. I just wanted to keep you in the bed where you were safe," Marie said. "I do beg your pardon, and hers."

"I was trying to get up?"

"To look for her," Marie said.

At that the Dutchman teared up. He put his forehead down in his hands.

"I'm so sorry, sir. Can I get you anything?"

"A little brandy, if you don't mind." He wiped his eyes.

"Of course." Marie went to pour him a small glass of brandy and brought it to him. His hands were cool on the table. She sat down across from him, studying him closely. "Why do we not send for your wife? Didn't she come with you to America?"

He drank his brandy for a moment. It was with a soft pillowtop voice that he told her, "She became ill on the voyage from Amsterdam. Terribly sick when we reached the new world. Died not long after in our new home on Beacon Hill."

"I'm so sorry. She was lovely," Marie said. "Oh my God. You're a widower."

He looked away from her and nodded.

"How long ago?"

"It was five years ago, though it seems a lifetime and yesterday all at once."

"Surprised a lawyer like yourself didn't remarry," Marie said.

"For many of those years I still loved her," he said.

"Of course, sir."

"I couldn't love anyone now," he said. "I've lost everything. To save my father's name I had to pay off his debt. Sell my practice, my home, though I could hardly stand to even live in it. Come out to Connecticut to settle his affairs. Just couldn't let that bank take an estate worth over three thousand dollars for a ridiculous $200 debt. I do not have employment. I have nothing to offer anyone."

"You are still young, sir. You'll get back to your life in the summer. I'm sure. This is a low point, because you are not feeling well. It will pass."

She looked around. "I suppose I have work to catch up on. While I still have a job."

"Marie, I can afford to pay you. Just so you are aware. You deserve a fortune for last night. When I sell this place, you'll get it."

"Just grateful to be here last night. A man all alone like that. I don't know what I would have found by morning if you'd been left alone."

Robin felt at his shirt buttons as he looked at her. "Did you say you changed my clothing? All...all of it?"

Marie dropped a ladle on the kitchen floor. She picked it up and turned her back to him. "Did I say that?"

She heard him stifle a laugh but she could not look at him.

He made his way back up the stairs to the upper level of the manor home, looking into each bedroom as he leaned on the wall. The bed that was his fathers was in the room on the right. On the left, the other fireplace room with a sitting area. Another bedroom and another. As he made his way toward his open bedroom doorway and the light of his fireplace inside, he looked into the last door and Marie was coming up the stairs behind him.

She stopped.

Inside this very small room next to the master suite, the blankets were turned down and some skirts lay over a chair. A pair of slippers were on the floor.

"Why did you choose this one? The others are nicer." Robin leaned in the doorway and catching his breath. "I was only wondering."

"If you were coughing, I couldn't hear you from down the hall," she said.

He put his hands up. "I said I would never enter and I won't. Keep it." He went into his bedroom, pausing there. "Good night, Marie. And thank you again. You need not move back out there in the cold. Get a good rest tonight. You can have any room you like." He shut his bedroom door.

"No, I can't," she whispered.

March 14, 1840

Thunder struck then and heavier rain followed. "I can make you a nice hot bath if you'd like, later." Marie put the pot of soup heating over the fire again. Then she brought him biscuits and coffee.

"Thank you." Robin held onto her forearm. "Marie, wait."

She just stood there, looking away as he restrained her gently, his fingers and thumb about her forearm.

"I know exactly what to say. Thank you for saving my life." At her looking away, he released her. "I'm sorry to hold you. I didn't mean anything except gratitude. I should not have done that."

"Oh no. That was very kind of you." Marie put her hand on her arm where his had just been. "I could wash your hair in a bowl here at the table, if you can lean your head down over it."

"No valet in months. My hair has never been so long."

"I wash mine that way all the time and it's much longer than yours," Marie said.

"Is it?" Robin looked at her shyly.

"Very well then. After you eat." Marie used a flat spoon to stir the soup. "Almost ready."

Robin drank his coffee and warmed his hand on it. "It was just snowing the other day and today it is rain. Why is that?"

"You are in Connecticut. That's why." Marie dished out the soup into a bowl for him. "I'm going to fill that cast iron pot with water for your hair next."

"Embarrassing. But given what you've already done for me, I suppose this is simple enough to endure," Robin said.

"Don't be silly. Think of how great you are going to feel when you're all clean and dry and in your nice clothing again." Marie went to pour water into that kettle. Then she pulled out the two big pots and tin cup she usually used to wash her own hair. She then brought two kettles of water up the stairs to his room. She hung those in his fireplace, tossing more wood on his fire. She collected his hairbrush, a towel, and his Boston soap.

More thunder rang out, as Robin ate his lunch. He watched her set his things down on the other end of the kitchen table.

"I put water heating upstairs for you."

Robin nodded. "Do you think me vain?"

"You?" Marie picked up his empty bowl. "Absolutely."

Robin gave her a doubletake.

She smiled, bringing warm water in one of her pots to the table. "Ready? Just duck your head over this empty pot and I will pour the water onto your hair to wash it. It won't take long at all. Hands on the table."

Robin quietly went to her and let her do this for him.

She slid the towel beneath his chin. "Use this if you get water in your eyes." She leaned in beside him and smoothed his hair down over the pot. "Hands on the table."

"What? Why?"

"So I know where your hands are." She used the cup to wet his hair and used fragrant soap with bergamot and lemon oil in it. Once his hair was sudsy, she began to rinse. Her hip was against his side. Several cups of clear warm water rinsed his hair very well. "Okay towel up and around. Let's get you sitting in a chair again. Are you all right?"

"Yes, miss."

Marie wrapped the towel around his head, keeping water from running down his neck as he sat down. Then she padded the towel to dry the water from his long shoulder length hair. She padded his cheek and neck, finding his eyes closed. She continued to dry his hair in the towel. "Do you feel dizzy?"

"No." He was still gripping onto the table edge with one hand and the chair arm with the other.

Marie patted his hand on the table then. "Easy now. Let me brush your hair and then you can go up and take your bath. Water is heating. You're holding on. You can't be dizzy if you are going to have a bath, you know?"

"You told me to."

"Told you what?" She pulled a second dry towel for his shoulders and laid the wet one aside. Gently she brushed out his hair, lock by lock in her hands.

His chin was down. "Hands on the table."

Finally, Marie moved around the table to see his face.

Van der Kellen wet his lips. He took a moment to translate first. "I am not accustomed to a woman's care." His eyes searched the floor. "I confess, I forgot…how tender it was."

Marie put her hands on her hips. "That awful, huh?"

He looked at her and found her smiling. Then he smiled sheepishly.

Marie carried up two more buckets of hot water, following Robin up the stairs.

"I should be helping you," he said.

"Can you pick out your clothes?" She carried the water to his vanity room and poured buckets into the copper tub. Then she went to get other two from the fireplace.

Robin was anchored at the foot of the bed by an arm wrapped around a bed post.

Marie used a towel to lift the iron pots off the hooks in his fireplace. Then she carried the two to the tub. She set the iron pots down in the water already there. It was about six inches deep and the sides would be ice cold. She laid a towel over the back of the tub to lean against. And she set two more towels close by on a table with his nice smelling soap.

He was now sitting on the edge of the bed, holding onto that bed post, watching her.

"Those pots are heating up the water nicely. Just give it a few moments before pulling them out. Then just leave them beside the tub. I'll collect them later." Marie picked out his trousers, underclothes, shirt and stockings and laid them on the bed.

In his mind he heard himself asking her to stay and help him, and how that sounded. "Would you…."

Marie rounded the bed with some distance, added logs to the fire, and then made her way to the door. "Be careful. Open this door when you're through."

She closed the doors as she left and bounded downstairs.

March 15, 1840

"Van der Kellen's here. Van der Kellen's here," the girl called from the window.

Joseph Lee hurried out the front door. His wife and children followed.

The giant Friesian horse, saddled, with Mr. Van der Kellen hunched on top, came to a stop at their front entrance. Robin leaned over the neck of the horse, and swung one leg down, the other foot in the stirrup. Then with both boots on the ground, he clung hard onto the horse.

"Are you well, sir?" Joseph grabbed the bridle of the horse and Robin by the forearm too.

"Mr. Lee. Thank you. I'm better. How is Jeremiah?"

"I'm well, sir," Jeremiah spoke up.

Robin settled eyes on him and forced a bit of a smile.

"And you sir?" Jeremiah asked.

"I'm...over the worst." Robin looked at all of them, leaning on the horse. "I don't wish to get too close to anyone. But I did want to thank you for Jonathan keeping my horses alive. And the cow. And thank you for the food you sent."

Luke looked kindly on the gentleman, as he took the horse's reins and held it still.

Joseph drew Robin's arm around his shoulders. "You're about to drop. You should not be riding yet. Come inside and rest. We'll carriage you home, sir."

"I could not expose you to…"

The two maids appeared on the porch too, taking this in. Rachel had a hand to her mouth.

"Nonsense. You and Jeremiah had the same thing. We've all had it. Come inside and rest before you drop, sir. And how did you saddle that draught horse?"

Robin dipped at the knees a bit. "I've ridden him before. I was fine until I got up there. My balance is gone. It must be the sickness. Never lost my balance on a horse before. Not even when shot."

"We'll be getting you back to Marie. She'll be frantic about you missing," Mrs. Lee said.

"Luke, get the carriage hitched up. Tie his horse to it," Mr. Lee said. "And you two, send some supper home with him. Get moving everyone."

"I don't know how to thank you. Without you and Marie I would not have survived." Robin staggered along with Mr. Lee.

Mr. Lee helped him up the steps to the house. "I suspect you owe most of that to Marie then. She's the one you best make it up to."

Robin sat in the parlor, crossed his legs and wrapped his arms to his stomach.

"Could Marie use some help so you can get back to resting?" Mrs. Lee said.

"I think Marie has everything handled at home. But we appreciate the food very much," Robin said. "I should have asked her. She's probably done nothing but tend me for days now."

"I'm sending Rachel and Louise home with you for a day to do work about the house, get the laundry caught up, let Marie get some sleep lest she catches all this," Mrs. Lee said to the maids. "We'll come back and get you before bedtime tonight. Now go pack up some food to bring over there."

"Yes, ma'am. Delighted to." The maids left the room.

"How is the foal?" Robin asked.

"He's wonderful. We named him after you," Jeremiah said. "Mr. Robin."

The thirteen-year-old daughter blurted out, "Are you sweet on your maid Marie now?"

"Don't you ask him such a thing," Joseph said.

"You shouldn't ask a gentleman such a question," Jennifer Lee said and then added with a warm smile, "Well, are you?"

The family laughed and Robin smiled shyly. "I'm sure that would be as inappropriate here as it is in Amsterdam."

"Don't you be so sure. You're in a free country now," Jennifer said. "And you're a gentleman. It's all up to you. Drink your tea and let's get you home to Marie."

Mr. Lee helped Robin into the carriage with the two maids. Rachel and Louise had baskets of food. They sat facing him, backwards in the carriage. Both women were in their twenties, like Marie, and younger than him. The carriage moved on with Genie tied to the back.

Robin held his coat closed at the neck. He was shivering such that the girls unfolded a blanket over his lap.

"If I may say so, sir, so glad that nothing happened to you on the way over. You still look very pale," Rachel said.

"And don't worry. We'll take care of everything," Louise said.

"Thank you." Robin only nodded and road silently back to his own place.

Marie came running out with her shawl wrapped around her. "Is he all right?" She called to the stockman driving the carriage.

"Yes, Miss Marie. Got him right in the back." Luke pulled on the brake.

Robin was already opening the door and extracting himself from the carriage.

Marie hurried to grab his arm. "Are you crazy? Riding off like that?"

"Yes. Apparently."

It was then that Marie saw the two maids.

"Mrs. Lee sent them," Robin said.

"Hello Marie. We brung you food. And we're put to work over here for the day," Rachel said.

"We'll take care of everything," Louise added. "Mr. Van der Kellen is not to worry about a thing."

Robin walked toward the door, pausing to see the stockman leading Genie to the barn. "Wait. I must warn him about…"

"Luke can handle the horse. Let's get you inside." Marie opened the door and urged Robin inside by the arm.

The two maids carried the food in and set up on the kitchen work tables. They quickly looked around and divided up tasks.

"Are you hungry, Mr. Van der Kellen? I can prepare you some lunch," Rachel said.

"I'll take this laundry. Get these sheets washed," Louise said.

"Robin, you should get up to bed," Marie said.

The two maids shot her a look then.

"I need to sit in the parlor for a bit. I am actually very hungry," Robin said.

"Very well then, sir. I will get lunch ready. Go ahead and get some sleep, Marie. We have everything under control," Rachel said.

Robin met eyes with Marie and the two of them went into the parlor.

Robin sat on a sofa and Marie pulled a blanket over him, whispering, "They're going to know I'm living in the house. What do I do?"

"You're doing nothing improper here. You must be exhausted. You've been up with me for days. Go ahead up and take a rest," Robin encouraged her. "It's okay, Marie. Let them work."

Marie tapped on his knee and strolled back into the kitchen. "Bring Mr. Van der Kellen a cup of tea to warm him up. The laundry, you'll think this is crazy, but you can hang it in the ball room down the hall to the left. I have clothesline in there. He has clothing there that needs ironing and brought upstairs. He needs firewood brought up stairs too."

"Yes, Marie. We'll take care of all of that," Rachel said. "Go get some sleep. We'll find things all right."

"I'll just take a little nap, I think. You're certain?" Marie said.

Louise looked over with arms full of sheets. "We'll take care of everything, Marie."

Marie finally consented and just walked up the stairs.

Rachel and Louise looked at each other, but not for too long before Robin entered with his blanket around him.

Rachel quickly pulled out the kitchen chair nearest the hearth. "Sit right here, Mr. Van der Kellen. Get nice and warm and here is some hot tea for you. Lunch will be heated up soon."

Robin sat in the chair, pulling his blanket about him.

"Here is fresh cream and biscuits, sir." Rachel set them before him on the table.

"Thank you."

"Shall I set you up for lunch in the dining room or would you rather..."

"Right here, please," Robin said.

Louise put the sheets soaking in the wash tub and gave Robin a bit of a courtesy as she passed to assess the ball room situation.

Robin poured cream into his tea and savored the taste of it. This was different tea.

Rachel put the iron heating up on the oven while she warmed chicken breast and drumstick, potatoes and a serving of apples. Then she went to work washing pots and pans. She glanced at Robin and made eye contact with him, nervously. "Are you all right, sir? What else can I get you?"

"I'm better. Thank you." He ate one of the biscuits with his tea.

There was a knock on the door and Luke entered. "Mr. Van der Kellen, I have fed and shoveled out your horses for you. Milked that cow though it ain't got much left. Fed the chickens too. I'll bring in some firewood before I head back home. Is there anything else you'll be needing, sir?"

"Thank you, very much. No, thank you. I appreciate it," Robin said.

"Yes, sir. My pleasure. Rachel, I'll be back for you two at about eight tonight."

"All right. We'll be caught up by then," Rachel said.

The stockman brought in a cart full of firewood and stacked it by the hearth before leaving.

Rachel served Robin's lunch to him, with napkin and silverware.

Louise stopped in the doorway then with arms full of clean sheets. "I will make your bed, Mr. Van der Kellen, if you will be wanting to take a rest after your meal. I'll just be a few moments upstairs."

"Thank you. Very kind of you."

Louise nodded and went up the stairs. She found the rooms by the top of the stairs to be open and empty bedrooms. Having never been in the house before, she looked into each room along the hall, heading toward the obvious master suite at the far end.

In the bedroom right beside Robin's, Marie was asleep in the small bed.

Louise left the door open and continued into the master suite. She laid the clean sheets down on a sofa near the fireplace and stoked up the fire with more wood. There were two swords crossed over the fireplace. She took in Robin's four poster Mahogany bed, the trunk at the foot with the golden VOC, and let out a good long breath before she went to work.

She peeled back the woolen blankets to get the sheets off. On the nightstand was Robin's pistol, bottle of laudanum, spoon, two used teacups. The oil lamp was almost empty. She would make the bed, gather up the laundry basket of Robin's clothing, and carry the lamp downstairs to refill it.

Robin was eating his apples as she entered the kitchen.

Louise and Rachel whispered in the pantry for a bit.

Robin watched them both emerge. "May I have a word with you both please?"

"Yes, sir."

"Yes, Mr. Van der Kellen."

They both came to stand beside the table.

"Is everything all right?" Robin asked.

"Of course, sir. We were just dividing up the chores between us."

"Are you certain? Is there something you wish to ask me?"

"Oh, no sir," Louise said.

"Marie has been taking care of me all day and all night for days. Let her sleep. And then she's in charge when she comes back down," Robin said.

"Of course, Mr. Van der Kellen. We're going to get Marie all caught up here today." Rachel gave him a nod and so did Louise.

"Thank you. I appreciate your help very much," Robin said.

Robin rose from his bed, folded his blanket and pulled on his suit coat. He brushed his hair and noticed day light still coming through the windows. Dressed appropriately, he entered the hallway to find Marie's door still open. He lingered to look inside, seeing her asleep in her small bed. He could hear the two women talking downstairs in the kitchen, couldn't make out what they were saying but heard some female laughter.

He smoothed his suit coat down and made his way to the stairs, and down. He held onto the rail.

The conversation in the kitchen stopped.

He looked in from the hall.

"Mr. Van der Kellen? Are you well, sir?" Rachel wiped flour from her hands with a kitchen towel.

"I am fine. Thank you." Robin entered the kitchen and sat down at the table where he always did.

Louise was ironing his shirts in the back of the kitchen, using one iron and heating another on the oven. She moved to trade them, studying the Dutchman. "What can we get you, sir?"

Robin looked down and reached to the inner pocket of his suit coat. "Would a cup of tea be much trouble?"

"No trouble at all, sir." Rachel filled a teapot and hung it over the fire. "Won't be long. How would you like some cookies?" She brought a plate of them over and put them on the table before him.

Robin put two silver dollars down beside the cookies. "Would you allow me to pay you for your work today?"

"Mrs. Lee is paying us our regular wages, sir." Rachel watched him.

"Please. I insist. You'll have to work twice as hard when you get back to your own house," Robin said.

Rachel picked up the coins and brought one to Louise.

Louise giggled. "She sent us to spy on you, Mr. Van der Kellen."

Rachel giggled too and prepared a teacup and saucer on a tray with a spoon and tin of cream.

"How...how so?" Robin questioned.

"She hasn't been inside this home in years. Wanted to know what you've done with it," Rachel said.

"Oh." Robin picked up a sugar cookie and took a bite. "You must tell her I apologize for not inviting the family over for dinner. I'm not really set up for entertaining. Miss Longuiel has her hands full with all the cooking and cleaning as it is."

"Anytime you want to have them over, Louise and I will be happy to help Miss Longuiel," Rachel offered.

"Happy to," Louise put his shirt over a chair and started ironing another.

Rachel poured the tea into his cup and brought it to him on a tray. She placed the saucer and cup before him. Placed the spoon on a napkin and a tin of sugar with the tin of cream before him. "What else can I get you, sir?"

"You are not afraid of catching this sickness from me? I'm so fearful that Miss Longuiel will come down with it," Robin said.

"We both had it. Everybody in the Lee's house had it, two or three of us at a time." Rachel returned to the kitchen worktable to making two loaves of bread. "You'd best send for our help if Marie gets sick. You'll need a cook and someone to clean up. Besides, you can't be tending to her in her bedroom."

"I suppose not. No." Robin put sugar and cream into his tea and had a sip. He savored the cookie and ate another.

"We'll have her all caught up with the washing and ahead in the baking before we leave today," Rachel said. "Is there anything else we can do for you? Oh, and Luke took care of your stock out there today."

"How did you saddle and ride that huge animal? Luke said he hardly got him into a stall," Louise said.

"Oh." Robin smiled. "I'm afraid my horses are used to my commands in Dutch. I hope your fellow Luke wasn't injured."

Louise and Rachel laughed.

"Luke? No. He just said how on earth did that skinny Dutchman get these beasts to do anything?" Louise said, making them all laugh. "No offence, Mr. Van der Kellen."

"None taken. I am a skinny Dutchman," Robin said, brightening a little.

The girls giggled.

"Oh. I owe Luke some payment as well when he comes back tonight," Robin said.

"Not Luke. He's happy any chance to see Marie again," Rachel blurted out.

Robin's eyebrows rose. "He...he has an interest in Miss Longuiel?"

"He's been sweet on her since she arrived. Her mother used to work for the Lee's you know?" Rachel said. "When the Lees lived in Bridgeport. So, when your father Mr. Van der Kellen was hiring a cook, Marie's mother was sent for. But she had passed on. Marie came instead."

"I did not know that," Robin admitted. "Do you happen to know…. Has this Luke ever…ever asked for her hand?" He looked down and broke a cookie in half, and then just looked at the pieces as he laid them down on the plate. Two broken pieces.

Louise and Rachel watched him, and glanced at each other.

"What sort of fellow is he?"

"I don't believe your Miss Longuiel has ever noticed Luke," Louise said.

"Doesn't like him at all," Rachel added.

"Did he ever take her to town on Saturdays?" Robin asked.

"He went to town for drinking on Saturdays. She may have gotten a ride with him," Rachel said.

Robin just stirred his tea. The broken cookie just lay there.

They noticed his cheeks flush pink and his nose a bit.

"Luke and Hank couldn't believe what you did with the foal. They thought the mare was dead for certain. And for a gentleman to get that dirty to save a horse, was…" Rachel said.

"Hard to watch, it was," Louise admitted.

"The birthing or Mr. Van der Kellen with the baby horse slopped in his lap?" Rachel teased her.

Louise laughed. "The birthing of course. Where did you learn such a thing?"

"Oh. I grew up on a horse farm. To be honest, I had seen that done. I just did not realize how hard it was to pull the foal out, back feet first," Robin said. "Did you know June and Marta well?"

"Knew June well. She'd worked here for ten years," Rachel said. "Went to church with us every Sunday. I saw her in town a week or so ago. She asked about you, how you were."

"I wouldn't be surprised if she hated me. I didn't want to fire anybody when I came here. Had to let ten people go in Boston as it was," Robin said.

"Doesn't hate you at all, sir. June and Marta would be happy to come back if situations allow." Rachel put two loaves of bread into the oven and set the sand timer.

"About this Luke again. Has he worked for the Lees very long?" Robin held up one finger.

"Um, yes. Longer than I have," Rachel said.

Robin pushed the cookie pieces together. "How...how do you know he has an interest in Miss Longuiel, if you don't mind?"

"Well, McKinney said she's the prettiest girl around," Rachel said. "He and Luke got into a fist fight over her once. Broke up the tavern."

Robin looked at her then.

"Mr. Lee banned Luke from town for two weekends after that," Louise said. "We heard McKinney spent a night in the constable's for what he done in the tavern."

"You really fired McKinney at gun point?" Rachel asked. "I was serving the table and overheard. Sorry."

"What you overheard was not for your ears," Robin said.

"Of course not, sir," Rachel said. "It's just that, it's a good thing you did. He would have hit you."

"Robin, how are you now?"

"I'm better. Just going to lay down again." Robin met Marie in the hall that evening. "Would you...would you give this to Luke when he returns? For tending my horses and the cow. I already gave one to each of the maids."

Marie accepted a silver dollar into her hand. "Of course. You look so flushed. Are you feverish again?" She reached for his forehead.

Robin withdrew from her hand. "No. I don't think so. I'm just needing to lay down. I'll be fine."

"Well, I'll go see what those girls have done to the place."

Robin closed his bedroom door and he retrieved a bottle of brandy from his trunk. He heard a carriage arrive to pick up the maids. Robin stood by the bedroom window to watch the man with the carriage below and he took a drink right from the bottle.

Chapter Five   A Very Fine Man

March 16, 1840

As Marie worked in the kitchen, Robin sat at the table, near the fire, with papers, pen, and inkwell. He'd been writing for some time. He had a small stack of letters folded perfectly and addressed in a very neat little pile. The tip of his tongue seemed to help guide his quill.

"You have beautiful writing, sir." Marie set down a cup of tea for him.

Robin glanced up at her.

"I've always heard that was the mark of a gentleman," she said. "Are you writing your family?"

Robin set down his quill and wiped the black ink off his fingertips on a small rag. "Sending inquiries for employment to some of the lawyers in Boston and New York. Although...I really beat some of these men quite badly in court. I expect they may hold a grudge. Humility is something I'm not swallowing well."

"Perhaps this will help it go down." She opened a jar of apples and spooned some into a bowl and set it beside his papers with a spoon.

"You should have some yourself, you know?" Robin said to her. "Can't have you getting sick as well. Come on. I want to see you sit down here with me and eat some fruit."

"I couldn't. You don't mean that."

"I mean everything I say. Come on," Robin encouraged. "Join me."

She sat down across from him with hers.

"Where is your family, Marie?"

"Don't have any, except for some cousins in Bridgeport," Marie said.

"You said your mother passed on. What about your father?"

"I never knew my father. Mother said he was a French soldier. Said he would marry her but he didn't. Then we heard he was killed in the war," Marie explained. "Maybe he did or he went back to France. We'll never know."

"I'm terribly sorry. Did your mother give you his name?"

Marie nodded. "She took his name too. But they were never married. She was treated better if they thought she had a husband. Mother always visited the Norwichtown graveyard once a year to put flowers on the French soldier's graves. I figure just in case my father was one of them. I do think she loved him."

"I'm so sorry. I fully understand," he said. "Can you read, Marie?"

She shook her head. "Only in French. A little. It's all my mother could teach me."

His eyebrows rose. He said to her in French, "Your mother was French too? It has been so very long since I visited Paris."

"You speak three languages then?"

Robin sat back watching her. Prettiest girl around. Two stockmen fought over her. "Four, actually. My mother was French and father Dutch. Both languages were spoke in the home as I grew up with one older brother and two younger sisters. But at the same time, I was educated in English, always with the plans that the family would travel to America."

"Did your brother and sisters make the voyage too?"

"No. They had married and stayed in Amsterdam. My father and mother came here first, after 1828, established a foot hold in Boston. Father started out a very successful barrister. Then he became ill, let things slide. He was told he must move away from the pollution of the city. I was sent for, to take over the practice. By then I had fallen in love with a young lady and she was very excited about America. She thought it would be so glamorous." His smile faded and he lowered his chin. "Mother passed away before I got to America and Adrianna...just two weeks after. I was alone in a strange country and very low. Very low in spirit."

"Well, I'm so glad you are feeling better. It is very nice to have you working in here rather than the library," Marie said.

"This tastes a bit like your apple pie," Robin said.

"Yes. It's the cinnamon," Marie said. "There's something else too. I'll have to ask them. Nutmeg maybe. I don't want you going over to the Lees again."

Robin shot her a look. "You think I will take ill again?"

"No. I think those two maids want to get into your bed," Marie said. "With you in it."

Robin smiled and shook his head. "I don't think so."

"They brought you two jars of apple preserves. And a chicken. And soup. And cookies. Did you see these cookies?" Marie said. "They're heart shaped."

"They were ordered to." Robin looked down and grinned.

Marie shook her head. "There's a heart split in the top of the bread. I don't think that was for me."

"If you get sick, they offered to come and take care of us," Robin said. "You know I would have to do that."

"Well. You can't cook," Marie said to him.

"I haven't tried, actually," Robin declared. "The little girl over there is sweet on me. Now that frightens me. She's twelve or something. She put one finger on my cuff at the dining table. I moved my hand away like it was on fire."

Marie laughed.

"I do think I shall go lay down for a while." Robin gathered his letters and rose to set them up on the mantel beside his rifle. He found Marie still watching him. He reached in and gently laid his hand on her forehead. "Just checking."

Marie giggled.

He carried his ink and pen across the hall and into the library, returning them to the desktop, in his father's office. Robin exited and started up the grand stairway. He held onto the railing and climbed each shallow step more and more slowly. By the time he got to the landing, halfway up, he realized he couldn't get enough air and felt light-headed.

Marie hurried up to him and held out her arm. "Don't stop here. Get on back to bed."

Robin hesitated to touch her.

"Don't be silly." Marie just took his left arm around her shoulders. "Hold the railing. One step at a time. Let's go."

He did that, struggling to breathe on the last few steps, but sucking in the fragrance of her hair. "Your hair smells like vanilla."

Marie said, "You can smell that?"

"You smell wonderful," Robin said. "Sorry. I am not supposed to ever know that. Am I? I should not be able to tell from the other side of the room. Sadly, that means never enjoying again how lovely a woman smells."

"What do you mean never? I'm sure you'll marry again."

At his bedroom door, she tried to release him but he held onto her. Afraid to look up at him, she kept her chin down. Robin pulled her into his embrace, wrapping both arms about her shoulders very gently. And he hugged her. Marie found herself in his arms, her mouth against his shoulder, her chest against his.

"Thank you, Marie." He opened his arms, releasing her.

For a moment she did not move back from him, but she felt obligated to.

Robin made his way to his grand four poster mahogany bed. He reached both hands onto the quilt and crawled onto the bed.

Marie pulled up another quilt from the foot of the bed and covered him with it.

"But my boots," he said, into the pillow.

"I'll get them. Just rest." Marie folded the quilt up to reveal his short ankle boots. She unbuttoned and removed both of them and then covered up his stockings.

"How is it you are not sick?" Robin asked her.

"Everybody in Bridgeport was sick just like this. I've already had it three or four times."

The next morning, coming back from the root cellar off the kitchen was when she noticed Mr. Van der Kellen's coat and hat were gone. "Oh no. Not again." She looked out the window to see blinding white snow and it appeared that there was a rope leading out from the door toward the barn. She opened the door, blasted back a step by snow. And there was a rope tied to the hitching post near the door, going off into the white toward the barn. Halfway to the barn, Robin was a figure in black against the snow, making his way back to the house by way of the rope.

Once she got him into the house and shut the door, she just blurted out, "Are you insane, sir?"

Robin laughed. "Obviously." He dropped a sack of firewood beside the cook fire.

"You're supposed to be in bed." Marie began collecting snowy wet scarf, hat and gloves from him. His face was red from the cold. His hands were like ice. "Get out of everything wet immediately. Just drop them on the floor and get back into bed."

"I'm fine. I'm just a bit frozen. Be careful, there are eggs in the..."

She took his coat from him and hung it over a kitchen chair by the fire.

"This weather is crazy." He sat down in the same chair, holding his hands toward the flames. His hair was wet as the snow in it melted and he shook it out. "I feel like a took a bath in the snow. I am wet right through."

She grabbed the tea pot from the fireplace and poured a cup for him. "This should help. You're feeling fine?"

"Yes. Thank you. I woke up much better," Robin said. "Your pot is at the door. I brought the hot water out to the horses to thaw out their water. They were very thirsty."

"I was about to do that," Marie said.

"I don't want you out there. It's too dangerous until this storm is past. The horses are fed and watered for now," Robin said. "Chickens too. Oh, you'd better get the eggs out of my pockets before I forget and sit on them."

"And the milk? Did you forget to milk the cow?" Marie asked.

"Oh. I confess I gave it all to the cats," Robin admitted sheepishly.

Marie laughed.

"I'm sorry. They surrounded me with their big eyes, purring. What was I supposed to do?" Robin said.

"You are a softie for those cats. You are all wet. You'd better get out of these. Immediately." Marie picked up a blanket from the clean laundry and brought it to him, holding it up like a barrier. "Just take this blanket and get upstairs when you drop the wet clothing."

Behind the blanket and in front of the fire, he removed his trousers, his shirt, and well his undergarments were soaked through too. He removed it all and took the blanket from her to wrap about himself.

"Now go on, before you catch another sickness. Go on," Marie ordered.

Robin left in the blanket. "Don't forget the eggs."

Marie picked up his things realizing that all of his clothing were in this pile. She rummaged into his coat pockets and found two eggs. "Surprised he didn't give these to the cats."

"This snow continues I don't know how we'll get out the door." Robin looked out the kitchen window with a book in his hand. "I can't see the barn."

"Where did you get the idea for the rope? That was quite smart." Marie was chopping carrots and potatoes into a pot.

"Ahm, used that before, in a monsoon, a blinding heavy rain."

"Rain so heavy you can't see through?" Marie asked.

"Oh yes."

The wind shook the house at that point. Even the fire in the fireplace shuddered as cold air blasted down the chimney. Robin put more wood on the fire. "Better keep this going. I think the storm tonight will be very bad. I don't know if the chickens will survive the cold tonight."

"I hope they do," Marie said.

"I'm not going out there again to bring them in here. They have plenty of straw. If they're smart, they will cuddle together like the cats do." Robin looked at Marie. "Well. If it comes to it, there are a lot of Dutch law books in there that we can definitely burn."

Marie laughed.

"And I would take great pleasure in tearing them apart. Had to memorize so many of them," Robin said.

"Well, if it would make you feel better, go right ahead," Marie said. "I'm sorry I am always making vegetable soup. We have so many carrots and potatoes to use up."

"I very much like your vegetable soup. Especially if you have onion," Robin said.

"Oh. I do. I would be happy to put some in," Marie said. "I should make cookies more often. I have ingredients. I have the cookie cutters you brought me."

Robin poured himself a cup of tea and sat down by the fire with his book. "Too busy being practical? Sounds like someone else I know."

Marie continued to chop ingredients into her pot and then she brought it to the fire, close beside him to hang it from the hook directly over the fire. "Well, I'm going to have to make you cookies before those harlots, I mean maids, across the field make you some more."

He lifted his eyes from the book onto her right beside him and he laughed out loud.

She stood up and glimpsed his open book. "One of those Dutch law books?"

Robin smiled. "The science of cartography. That is map making. I have always loved studying maps."

"Maps? Is it because you want to travel?" Marie asked.

"Yes, in part. I would like to improve my own map of this property and its relationship to town. It must come down to mathematics."

"You can read it to me in Dutch." Marie listened to the wind hitting the house. She folded her arms and remained standing near the fire for the warmth and to look over his shoulder at a map. "I should like to hear your voice. I mean your language. Is that the Netherlands?"

"Yes. Here is Amsterdam. I grew up here. Lived here for a while." Robin pointed his slender finger on the map in the book.

"And where is France from there?"

"Over here," Robin said. "Do you…care for that man, Luke?"

"Luke Collins? He's a pig," Marie said.

That made Robin laugh. "That is a relief." He laughed again. "Why…why is he a pig?"

"Stares at me all the time. Waggles his tongue at me when nobody's looking," Marie said.

"What? I won't allow him to behave that way around here," Robin insisted. "No one treats a female that way, especially when trying to...to court her."

Marie looked at him.

Robin looked down at his plate. "You know, Marie, if there was someone that you wanted to court, I would... I would...."

"There isn't," Marie cut him off.

Upstairs it was bitter cold. The only fireplace up there was in Robin's room or the other one on the opposite end. Marie's room beside Robin's had none. Robin paused in the hall. "Marie, it will be so cold in your room, even if I leave my door open."

"I have many quilts to get beneath with my bed warmer."

"Marie, just consider this..."

"Oh, I couldn't." She put her hand to her mouth and stepped back against the wall.

Robin put his hands up. "Not that. I swear. But...couldn't you sleep on a couch in my room near the fire? I could pull it over. Would that be nice?"

Marie still had her hand over her mouth.

"Miss, it's cold enough to freeze a water bowl in your room. In survival situations one must forego silly conventions," Robin said. "This is the coldest night I can remember in this country. I have endured the hottest hell of India and this is the exact opposite, the coldest of arctic winters. Have I moved to the North Pole? I struggle to choose which is worse." Robin walked into his room and dragged the couch from the other side of the room to face the fireplace. He moved one of the chairs aside.

Then he added plenty more wood to the embers of his fire. He stepped away, back to the far side of his bed before saying to her, "It will be the warmest place in the house. A shame to let it go to waste."

Marie couldn't help but look at the inviting couch.

Robin pulled back the covers of his bed. "Bring your pillow and quilts. I swear to you I won't cross the room. Give me a moment to…get into bed."

Marie went into her room and stood there with her arms folded tightly, for a moment. Her room was dark and bitter cold. Her window was frozen with ice.

Robin removed his boots and his trousers. He slid into his cold bed with his shirt and sweater on. He laid down with his back to the door and gripped the blankets in his fists as the sheets were so cold. He heard the door close. He lifted his head to look.

Marie hurried with pillow and blankets in her arms, to the couch she'd seen him napping on occasionally. As she laid her head on a pillow where he once had, she listened for any sound from him in the bed behind her.

Robin put his head back down. The thought of that vanilla fragrance hit him and he ached.

In a few moments she heard him blow out the lamp beside his bed.

March 18, 1840

Marie awoke and looked over at the bed. All she could see was the mound of blankets up over Robin in the middle. She wrapped up in her blanket and reached to place more wood into Robin's fireplace quietly. She wished him a warm place to get dressed when he got up. But for herself, she would cross to her cold bedroom after a lingering look into Robin's bed. His blankets were up to his ear. He was facing her, still sleeping with long lashes closed over fair skin. His head was on two pillows and the other two he'd pulled down to either side of him beneath the sheets. Cocooned in there, she thought with a smile. She quickly dressed and went down the stairs.

In the kitchen, she stacked up more firewood in the embers of the hearth, and heard the wind outside. While there was sunlight upstairs, down here the windows were dark and covered with snow. She had to light the oil lamps. She prepared a pot of coffee to brew over the fire once it got going. She could see her breath in the room.

For the first time she was wearing some of Robin's mother's clothing. She had on a heavy wool skirt and knit sweater on over her blouse. Hopefully he wouldn't notice.

The fire needed some kindling added to hurry things along but finally there were flames licking up toward the coffee pot. She thought about the eggs for breakfast but decided to heat up a pot of the vegetable soup instead.

"Oh my," said Robin from the doorway.

Marie looked at him. He had a scarf around his neck, tucked into his jacket, and hands in his jacket pockets.

"I think we're snowed in." Robin walked toward the door and unbolted it. He grabbed the handle and pulled but the door did not open inward. He tried harder. "Frozen shut."

"Wind was coming from that way," Marie said.

Robin bolted the door again. "I don't know why I did that. I can't open it and I'm bolting it closed. I wonder what condition the front door is in."

"It will be a while before coffee is hot, I'm afraid."

"It will get there." Robin left the room.

Marie heard him try the front door. Then he made a walk through the house before returning to sit beside her fire at the kitchen table.

"The rest of the house seems to be intact. I could see the barn from upstairs. It looked okay," Robin said. "I'll have to get out there somehow to tend the animals."

"How are you going to do that?"

Robin shrugged. "Window somewhere. One of them will have to open. After that heats up get some water to boil so I can water the animals."

"Yes. I just...wish you didn't have to risk going out there. Our water is frozen." She indicated the barrel in the corner. "I had some in a pot over here for coffee that wasn't frozen yet."

"Oh. I can't move that barrel or I would bring it near the fire. But you know what?" Robin said. "When I get a window open, I can hand you some pots of snow to melt over the fire."

"I'll get those ready. I was going to heat up soup this morning. Unless you want eggs instead."

"Hot soup would be perfect. Were you warm enough last night?" Robin asked.

"It was so nice. Yes," Marie said. "And you?"

"Alright once I stopped shivering," Robin said. "Please, feel welcome to that couch for the next several nights when it is so cold."

Robin managed to open a window in the parlor, opposite the side of the house, the East side. First, he filled six pots with snow and handed them to Marie inside the window. Then he waited for the snow to melt over the fire.

Once a pot had boiling water ready, he bundled up in coats, two pairs of trousers, boots, hat, scarf, leather gloves, and climbed out. Then he took a pot of boiling water from her and began making his way through two feet of snow toward the barn.

After an hour Marie heard him digging from outside at the kitchen door. She had melted more pots of snow into a nice big pot of fresh water for cooking, drinking, and cleaning plates. The sounds of digging went on for the entire length of time it took for a loaf of bread to bake and then some. Finally, she heard a pounding on the door.

She hurried to it, unbolted it and knocked on it in return. Then she stepped aside.

Another knock and the door burst inward, spilling Robin in the snow onto the kitchen floor.

"Oh my. Are you alright?" Marie hurried to him.

He was on one knee and managed to get up, laughing. "Got the door open."

"I see that. Are you hurt?"

"Bruised knee. I'm fine. But this chicken is not." He reached back outside and picked up a dead chicken from the snow and then shut the door. "What do we do with this? The others are fine and the horses are fine."

"We cook it, of course." Marie took the bird from him. It was frozen stiff.

"I wasn't sure about that. If it were summer, I don't think we would eat it," Robin said.

"No. Absolutely not if you found a dead chicken in the barnyard. Is that what happened to this one? Froze last night?" Marie asked.

Robin was breathing hard, unwrapping his scarf from about his head and neck. "Apparently too proud to press in with the others. Sadly, it was by itself alone in the barn. The cats are burrowed into the hay together. I'm sorry. I gave them the milk again."

"Well, don't think about it. I will make roast chicken now."

Robin removed his wet coat and hung it on the hook with his hat and scarf. He sat down at the table.

Marie put hot coffee in front of him. "Don't ask for cream."

"I suppose I had that coming. Is that the soup on the fire?"

"Yes. Would you like some more?" Marie asked.

"Yes please."

She dished out a bowl of soup for him. "I'm glad it is you here. I can't imagine living alone here with your father. He wouldn't even talk to me."

"Well, he wouldn't have talked to me either," Robin remarked. "Would have sat here smoking cigars that were killing him and said I told you so. Told you that you would regret choices you made in your life. Never have your own practice. Never be as accomplished as your brother. Never marry as well. Always chasing skirts and not using your brain."

Marie burst out laughing. She set down the soup in front of him with spoon and napkin. "Chasing skirts? I thought you were shy."

"My father and I differed in our definitions of skirt chasing." Robin raised his eyebrows. "And many other things."

"Go on then."

Robin got some hot soup into himself first.

Marie went to work on the chicken on the worktable, her back to him. Just when she thought he would say no more he began again.

"I was about to visit him out here when a letter arrived. After reading his words in that letter I knew I would never see him again. It was only a year since Adrianna died. I should have married as Robert did, a woman of a notable family that could bear many children. Adrianna wasn't wealthy. My father never met her. But he knew me well and what I would choose at that age."

Marie looked at him as he gazed into her vegetable soup. She drew in a deep breath and didn't realize Robin could hear that. He was looking at her now.

"I apologize," he said. "I did run on."

"You married for love," Marie blurted out.

"A foolish idea to my father who left his estate to Robert and married off his daughters to wealthy men. I would have to earn my own living or, as he intended, marry a wealthy woman," Robin said. "The ones he and mother had arranged for me...unacceptable. So, I left home. Enlisted."

"I will never understand that tradition of the wealthy to pass everything down to the eldest son and nothing to the other children." Marie went back to preparing the chicken for roasting. "At least if you're poor there is nothing to fight over. You don't have to give this place to your older brother, do you?"

"Ha! He can come and collect it! And pay me back for my house and practice in Boston," Robin declared. "He'll never take a boat for six weeks. Amsterdam as a society would collapse without the good Doctor Van der Kellen."

"So, these women you were supposed to marry, what was wrong with them?"

Robin looked at her.

Marie smiled. "Come on. Too fat?"

Robin lowered his chin. "That is improper to say."

"Homely? Plain?"

Robin laughed.

"Very homely?" Marie pressed.

"And fat," Robin said. "Nobody fighting over those women."

That night Robin was pouring two small glasses of brandy on the nightstand. "You're taking the couch tonight, aren't you? It's just as cold as last if not even colder."

Marie paused in the hallway. "Um. Yes. If you don't mind."

"Of course, I don't mind. I brought you a glass."

"You mean for me to…. You won't tell anyone?" Marie said.

"Of course not. Pick it up on your way to the couch." Robin sat down on the bed to pull off his riding boots. When he stood up, he began to open his belt and Marie burst out with a giggle and ducked into her room across the hall, her hands over her eyes.

Robin laughed. "No! I'm just taking off the belt. Not the trousers."

"How was I to know that?" Marie called from her bedroom.

Robin pulled back the covers and crawled into his bed wearing his trousers, shirt, and a wool scarf about his neck, laughing. He sat back against the pillows, shivering and pulling one pillow down beneath the covers along each side of him.

In a moment, Marie came into the room, in her dress, socks, sweater, and mittens. She stopped when she saw him sitting there, watching her with a grin.

"You didn't take anything off," Robin said.

"I did. Not telling you what." She picked up one brandy and handed it to Robin.

"Corset?" He asked.

"Not telling you what." She picked up the other glass of brandy.

"So, I was right then."

She hurried to her couch and sat with her back to him, arranging her pillow and quilts. "You're not supposed to know about such things."

"I know a great deal about such things." Robin sipped his brandy. "How do you get it tied on behind your back anyway?"

"Are you offering your services?"

Robin laughed. "No. I just…You called my bluff. I'm terrible at doing up corsets. Banished for life, really."

"Are you blushing?" She turned to look at him.

He pulled his scarf up over his nose.

"Yes, you are."

He sipped his brandy. "I love the natural shape of a woman without the corset."

March 21, 1840

She heard the wood chopping and wandered around the corner of the house to look.

Robin brought the ax down and split the log in front of him. Though it was cool out, he had no coat on. She could see his breath in the air. His shirt was becoming untucked. His hair was tied it back at the base of his neck. It looked very smart that way. He had a graceful way of bringing that ax down. His legs had a nice shape to them, his thighs had muscle. And though his hips were narrow, his backside had a nice shape. She didn't know his athleticism came from years of horseback riding, and it wasn't from sitting in the saddle, but crouching in the stirrups.

Marie walked up behind him, silently in the snow, admiring all of his features.

His back was to her and he set up another log on the stump. He lined up the ax and brought it down with a bang. The log split and fell to either side.

"Can I help?" Marie asked.

Robin jolted and jumped.

Marie burst out laughing.

He dropped the ax and brought both hands to his throat. "You just scared the fuck out of me."

She almost went to her knees laughing.

Robin doubled over laughing finally.

"I'm so sorry." Marie laughed heartily. She laughed so hard she cried.

He laughed for some time. He paced around the stump and picked up his ax. He laughed such that he was wiping his eyes as well.

She started to pile up the split wood onto his cart, still giggling.

"Never heard you laugh like that before." Robin looked at her for a while. He finally set up another log. "If my heart can endure it, you should...laugh more often."

She picked up more wood and carried it to the cart. "Your hair is different. I quite like it this way."

He nodded rather formally. He returned to wood chopping and she filled up the cart.

"I can drag this to the house, if you like?" Marie said.

"You cannot. That's too heavy." Robin set a hand on his hip.

"Watch me." Marie picked up the handle and pulled the cart away from him, using her legs beneath her skirt.

Robin leaned on his ax handle, watching her.

She looked back and waved at him. She heard him laugh and go back to his work.

Chapter Six   The Marksman

Robin was rummaging around in the pantry and came out with honey, a few small towels and a bar of lye soap. "Marie, are you afraid of horses at all?"

"No, sir. Not that I know of."

"Will you assist me for a moment?" He poured the hot water from the teapot into a small pail and gestured for her to get the door. "Grab your coat."

Marie pulled on her coat and opened the door for him.

She followed him out to the barn and up to one of the stalls.

Robin looked at the horse and then indicated its right front leg. "He's injured himself on the stall, I believe. It will go septic if I don't get him to hold still and let me work on it."

"Aren't you going to fetch the farrier?"

"I can't wait for a farrier. And I can't afford for this horse to go lame. Besides, there's nothing he would do that I cannot." Robin opened the stall and set his pail down in the corner. "What I need you to do is hold this towel over his eyes tightly. Not over his nose. But just hold him there."

Marie stepped inside the stall and closed them inside. "You can do this, sir?" She had only inches to stand in between the wall and the giant black horse, and she shared that space with Robin.

He gave her one of the towels and soaped up the other with hot water, ducking down to the pail on the floor. "Not all gentlemen are useless. Some of us have skills." He rose and looked up at the horse's head. "Over the eyes please."

Marie tossed the towel up over the head, covering the eyes.

Robin stood up shoulder to shoulder with her and grabbed the ends of the towel beneath the jaw and tugged the horse's head down with it. "Hold him right here."

Marie gripped the towel with both hands. "Isn't this the horse you don't get along with?"

Robin was down at those hooves beside her. "Ah he'll make that obvious shortly." He soaped down the wounded knee of the horse and the animal grunted. It couldn't back up any further as its rump was against the back wall.

"Easy now," Marie said to the horse. The hind feet stomped. "Easy. You don't want to step on him."

"That's good. If he knows you're in here too maybe he won't kill me." Robin dried the clean wound and then used the last of their honey to wipe onto it. Then he bound it firmly with bandaging. He stood up and met eyes with Marie as they were trapped between the horse and the wall. "Let him go now."

"Oh. Yes." She released the towel and the horse looked at her with one brown eye. "You have such a pretty mane and pretty fur about your ankles."

"Feathers, they're called. He likes you considerably better than he likes me. Let me out."

Marie opened the stall and stepped out.

Robin grabbed his pail and squeezed out too, closing the horse inside. He shook out his left hand and examined it.

"He kicked you?" Marie asked.

"Knocked me down fourteen times in there," Robin said hotly. "That's when I decided I needed you."

"Should have asked me after the first time."

Robin said to the horse, "Klootzak!"

Marie laughed a bit.

He looked at her.

She laughed more.

Finally, Robin laughed too and said more things in Dutch.

"What did you call him?" Marie asked.

"Ahm, politely translated to giant back end of horse. But my words were not so polite."

As they walked back to the house, she picked up a snowball and wrapped it in the towel. Inside the kitchen, she offered it to Robin. "For your hand."

He took it and sat down at the table, icing his hand in the snow. "The next time we are in town would you see if there is another jar of honey at the mercantile?"

"Of course. Why did you put it on the horse, sir?" Marie asked.

"Same reason you put it in my tea I suppose. It has healing properties. Ancient Egyptians used it on wounds a thousand years ago," Robin explained.

"There was plenty last time we were in town. I'll be sure to get more." Marie looked at him.

Robin stood up. "Thank you. I have too much to do to sit here all day." He walked out and Marie watched through the kitchen window as he walked back to the barn. He let the snowball fall from his hand as he walked.

Robin Van der Kellen stared into the horse stall, leaning both arms on the top board of the gate. The horse continued to chew. Robin paced the length of the barn, up the middle of the stalls, toward the wall of hay bales and back toward the corn crib. Back and forth until he exhausted himself and finally climbed the hay to sit where he could see the heads of both horses.

He wrapped his scarf up over his head and pulled on his gloves. He lowered his head into his gloves, his elbows on his knees. The cold dark of the barn set in. His breath he could see in the air, even by the light of the one lantern. The chickens were huddled down.

And then the horse he'd mended grunted.

Van der Kellen raised his head.

The horse thumped against his stall.

That evening, after dark, he still had not returned to the house. Marie could see a dim light on in the barn. She donned her coat and walked slowly across the yard. The doors were shut. On her toe tips, she peeked through a window. There was the other horse.

She opened the small door beside the carriage doors and looked inside. It appeared that only one oil lamp was lit and hung beside the horse stalls. A number of chickens ran about. "Sir? Sir Robin?" She entered and closed the door against the wind. "Are you in here?"

She found the stalls all clean, the horses munching on hay and small sacks of grain. She wandered further inside, looking about. The horse Robin had worked on still had his leg bandaged. She ducked and looked into the stall.

"Marie."

By Susan Eddy

She jumped in surprise. Behind her, seated halfway up the stack of hay bales, there was Robin Van der Kellen. She looked up at him. He had his arms wrapped around his knees.

"Did you need something?" he asked.

"I...I was afraid the horse knocked you out in here."

He unbound the scarf from about his head and began to climb down. "I didn't mean to alarm you." His voice did not sound like his own. Gravely.

"Were you keeping an eye on him? You must be hungry. You skipped lunch. You've worked so hard all day, sir." Marie straightened up. "I was hoping you would come inside to supper."

He reached the barn floor and folded his arms tightly to him. "I don't mind a day's work, really. The barn is spotless."

"Yes, it certainly is. And so are the horses," Marie said. "You certainly do keep a fine barn."

She watched his mouth as he blew out the lamp, dropping the barn into utter darkness. Marie did not move and when he did, he ran into her, collecting her into his hands. "I beg your pardon. Stay right here." He passed her and opened the door. What little moon light pierced the barn and revealed the small distance between their bodies. "After you, Miss Longuiel."

Sadly, she exited the barn.

And silently he followed her back to the house.

Inside the kitchen door, he hung his coat on the hook. Marie moved behind the worktables.

"I will take my supper in the dining room, if you don't mind. From now on."

"I will set a place for you."

Robin went to wash his hands in the bowl behind her.

She lit lamps in the formal dining room and set his place and his supper in there. She added details she hadn't thought of in weeks. Tablecloth. Cloth napkin. Gold rimmed china charger to set the plate on. Cut crystal glass for his water. And that tea pot of his mother's that he sent her from India.

He walked in and set a bottle of brandy down beside his plate. He didn't even bring a glass.

Marie saw him take a drink right from the bottle. She drew a small cut glass piece of stem ware from the sideboard, looked it over for dust, and then set it on the table for him.

She remained in the kitchen as he dined alone in the next room, taking her own meal standing up and pacing. She heard him on the steps.

She heard his bedroom door close.

Marie cleaned up his plates and put the teapot back on the shelf. The glassware had not been used and the bottle of brandy was gone. She blew out the lamps. From now on...

March 22, 1840

The following morning, he didn't come down until nearly ten o-clock, when normally he arose at dawn. Marie was aggressively scrubbing pots, but she paused, wiped her hands on a towel and brought him a cup of coffee at the kitchen table, where he had pulled out a chair and sat with his head in his hand.

"I apologize for last night," he said softly.

"Nothing to be sorry for," Marie said. "I set the table for your breakfast."

"I couldn't possibly eat anything."

"I suppose not if you drank that entire bottle," Marie said, not exactly scolding him.

He shook his head. "It won't happen again. I must look at that horse."

"You're worried about the horse?"

He said into his coffee. "Not only."

"What may I do?"

"If you could just distract him." Robin drank his coffee. "I have to see what I'm dealing with out there. If it's any worse I must cauterize it. And he will try to murder me, when I do."

"Where did you learn to doctor horses?"

Robin downed his coffee quickly. "Pulicat, India. War against England. They took a seaport from us. And more."

Robin had his supper alone in the dining room that night. Though not a grand place setting with several pieces of silverware, glasses, plates, cups, embroidered napkins, it was the best she could do. There was no butler standing behind him to take away each empty plate. Nobody wore white gloves. There was no wine to drink and no dessert to enjoy. After a few bites, he picked up his plate, fork, and glass of cider. He carried them back into the kitchen and sat down at the table right across from her, not at the end. And neither of them said anything about it.

April 20, 1840

130　　The Dutchman　　　　　　　　　　　　By Susan Eddy

When the weather improved and a month had passed since Robin had been sick, Robin had hired a young man named Paul Stuart to care for the horses, chop wood and such. He was to live out in the servants' quarters and work only three days a week. The other two days he would work on the Lee's farm.

Robin Van der Kellen entered the kitchen one day to find the man had Marie pinned flat on the floor and her dress was up. He was between her bare legs and boots. She screamed desperately and grasped for a frying pan amidst the broken dishware on the floor. He slapped her across the face and she let him have it with the frying pan over the head.

Robin rushed in and grabbed the man by the arm. "Get off her! Get up!" Robin pulled him up and threw him tumbling toward the door.

"I didn't do nothing she didn't want." The man said, getting to his feet, closing up his pants.

"Get your things and get off this property right now!" Robin yelled at him. He lunged for the rifle above the fireplace and cocked it. "Now! Get out."

"You can't work this place alone. Want her for yourself, do you? I understand." The man put his hands up.

Robin aimed the single shot rifle at him. "I'll never see you around here, and furthermore, I'll tell everyone around you're a rapist. You won't find any work here. Get moving."

"We'll see about that." The man left angrily slamming the door behind him.

Robin spun. "He's getting a weapon." His hands scrambled onto the mantel for reloading supplies.

The girl was sitting up on the floor, crying, pulling her skirt down and discovering her broken buttons and her exposed breast.

"Marie, are you all right?"

She was still crying on the floor, closing up her clothing. Robin went near her, without touching her, and knelt on the floor. In his softest voice he said, "Marie, I am well within my rights to shoot him now if he violated you. You must tell me."

She scrambled to Robin and threw her arms about his neck. "Almost. Oh God, if you hadn't come in."

"All right. Stay here. *Right here*. Don't move." Robin deposited her into the chair by the fire and he went outside with that rifle.

Marie heard a shot fired immediately and she ran to the window, fearing for Robin.

Robin Van der Kellen dropped the smoking front loader and pulled his pistol. He closed the distance to Stuart before he could pick up his bag. Marie saw Robin kick him in the chest, pound him in the mouth with his pistol and grab the bag away.

Robin backed off a bit to crouch and rummage through the bag, coming up with Stuart's pistol, which he tossed away into the grass by the kitchen door. He backed away from the duffel bag, still aiming his own handgun at the man.

Stuart picked up a bag off the ground and trotted down the driveway ahead of him.

It was a long time before that kitchen door opened again, and Marie shrieked when it did.

Robin entered, shut it, bolted it. "It is just me."

She ran to him and wrapped her arms about his neck tightly.

Robin still had his rifle in one hand and pistol in the other. "I had no idea he was that sort. He was never to come in the house when I'm out. What happened?"

"I thought he was hungry. I just offered to feed him." Marie was shaking against him.

"Did he hurt you? It's all right. Oh, he won't be back," Robin said.

She stepped back, crying. She wrapped her arms tightly to her and shook.

After setting his weapons on the kitchen table, Robin pulled out another pistol from his pocket and examined it. "Lefaucheux. Old. Shit for a weapon." He set it down. "He hit you. Are you injured?"

"He grabbed my arms so hard."

Robin looked at the weapons on the table. "Marie, did he violate you?"

"No. Not that."

"Do you know what I mean?" Robin looked at her.

"I think so," she admitted. "No, he didn't."

"You think you know what I mean? When I represent a case to court, I must be perfectly clear." Robin walked around the table to stand in front of her. "Forgive me. Are you a virgin?"

Marie flushed and nodded.

"Still? After that?" He pointed toward the kitchen floor where she'd been pinned down.

She nodded again.

"All right. Sit down." He invited her back into the chair and walked toward the cabinets. He found the brandy and poured two glasses. One he gave to her. One he set on the table. "This will brace you. You're all right, Marie. Not all men are violent like that. I do apologize for hiring him. I shall be more careful."

Robin stood at the end of the table with his hands on his hips, his eyes down on the floor.

"Did...did you pay him?" she whispered.

Robin picked up his brandy and took a deep breath. "Of course not. After I trimmed his ear with a lead ball, he didn't want to be paid anymore. He seemed to want to run."

"I can't believe you defended me that way. No one ever has. I do admire you so."

He downed his brandy. "Surprised my attack wasn't just as repulsive. You didn't look out the window."

"Have you been with any woman since your wife?"

Robin almost shuddered, and lowered his chin such that only chin, pout, and nose were visible beneath his bangs.

"Forgive me. That was too personal. I don't know why I would be so out of line."

"Today, you can say anything you wish," Robin said. "And I must respond."

"What was she like? Aren't you so lonely...for a woman's company?"

Robin looked down at the floor. "She had the most lovely voice. Played the pianoforte and sang to me. A bit afraid of me, I think. A very timid girl, but so pretty I could hardly stand it. We wanted to move to America where I could have my own practice. My father was getting older. He would retire soon. No. The answer to your question. No. I have not been with any woman since my wife."

"It must be terribly lonely."

"No more than it must be for you."

"But you're not even in your home country. You don't even have friends here," Marie said.

"No, I don't." Robin set about reloading his Baker rifle on the kitchen table. And he downed that brandy, not watching her. His cheeks were as flushed as hers. From the pouch he set out the lead balls, punch, powder flask, and tiny blue patches of shirt.

She had to hold the top of her dress closed, watching him. "Did you say your...wife was afraid of you?" Marie whispered. "I never thought that possible until you went after Stuart like that."

Robin blinked. "I made the mistake of marrying her in my uniform. Then she was frightened by all of the weapons I had. I have. Sword on my belt, you know, and... She wasn't strong like you."

"Uniform?" Marie asked. "War hero..."

"I'll tell you some time." He stood the rifle on its butt on a chair and poured powder into the muzzle from a small tin flask. Then he set a blue patch over the muzzle opening. Then he placed a lead ball on top of the patch and used the punch to drive the ball and patch down into the opening. He then removed the rod from its position along the barrel and held it up to then ram the ball all the way down into the gun, being mindful not to hit the ceiling with the rod.

She had finished her brandy and set the glass on the kitchen table. "I will get changed and then start supper."

His back was to her, as he leaned over the table to lay the rifle down. He started a similar process on the pistol. "I'm sorry about that. If I knew my way around a kitchen, I surely would do the cooking tonight. I'd probably poison us both."

Marie paused and barely whispered, "Did you kill him?"

Robin looked at her. "No. If I see him again, he knows I will."

Marie came back to the kitchen, taking in Robin's guns on the table, the bolted kitchen door, and Robin loading wood into the cook fire. Robin stood up and turned. "If you...give me an occupation I'm happy to see it done."

"You...really can just have a seat and let me do my cooking, if you don't mind." Marie moved past him toward the work area. "I'd rather be busy right now." She tied on an apron, looking away from him. She picked up that iron frying pan from the floor. Then she picked up the broken dishware.

Robin returned to sitting at the table.

Marie began preparing some carrots and potatoes to be roasted. She had some pork left from earlier that day she would add to the pot and place on the hook over the fire. Then she sprinkled some salt and pepper into the pot. "I'm so embarrassed for my behavior earlier, for panicking like that."

"Actually, you held yourself together far better than many men in combat their first time. Your reaction was honest. Smart, really. No need to be embarrassed with me," Robin said. "I know it's not a good comparison, but I remember being so surprised the first time I found myself in a fight. And then I had the benefit of training to kick in. You had no such training. Though I dare say, you are no defenseless female with a frying pan in hand. If not for his shoulder in the way, you'd have knocked him out."

Marie stood behind the worktable and just shook for a moment.

"Ahm..." Robin stood up at the table.

At the movement of his chair, she jolted.

"Alright, please, I believe I know a remedy for this," Robin said. "The food is cooking. You can sit down now. Take a rest. I'll get you another drink of brandy."

"I don't know what is wrong with me."

"Well, I do." Robin got up and moved past her into the kitchen to fetch the brandy and their two glasses. "You were attacked. Your first time, I'd imagine." Which glass was hers and which was his, he didn't know. He didn't care.

Marie made her way to the kitchen table and sat facing the door with her back to the safety of the cooking area. The table was between her and the door and Robin's guns lay right in front of her.

Robin returned to the end of the table and poured two shots of brandy. He set one before her. "Do the guns frighten you? I could move them."

"No. Please don't move them. Would you close the shutters?"

"On the windows? I would except that I could see muzzle flash out there in the dark and know where it came from," Robin said. "Then I know where to fire back. Ever since India, I can't bear a closed shutter in battle."

Marie held a hand to her heart. "I'm sure you know what is best."

Robin sat on the other side of the table, closest to the door and the fire. He could watch the windows from there. "Have you had brandy before me?"

Marie looked down at the glass. "No. I have had whiskey, though women are not supposed to."

"Why not?"

She sat down and picked up her glass. "Not lady like."

"My mother enjoyed a nice glass of brandy on a cold winter evening," Robin said. "I think a lady can have a drink as long as she is not drinking alone."

"Are...are you any good with these?" Marie indicated the guns. She took a sip and winced as it burned and warmed her throat and stomach.

"Extremely...good with these. It's almost a curse. If there is one innate talent I do possess, it is killing with these." Robin's tone was so chilling that even he heard how it sounded in the room. "You'll be safe tonight. It is very normal to be frightened right now. It will pass. If I may do anything, I am at your service."

"Have you ever been? Attacked?"

"Attacked, oh yes. Raped? No." Robin made her smile. "Never give up hope, though."

Robin heard his bedroom door open and raised his head off the pillow. She closed the door again. In the firelight, Marie walked to his bed in her night gown. Robin could see her silhouette through the gown.

He quickly threw back the covers for her, scooting back to the cold center of his bed, the cold center of his universe.

"I'm not here for my employer tonight, but for the man who saved me so bravely." She looked at a sword leaning against the nightstand and the pistol on top.

"And I... will only comfort you tonight. You see the pistol there. You're safe." Robin pulled another pistol out from beneath one of the pillows and set it on the other nightstand.

"You can have anything you wish." She sat down on his bed, her back to him at first, and then she turned.

"Well, a million men would take you tonight. I'll have you when it's the boring little barrister you want," Robin said, welcoming her into his arms. "You need not sleep with me to get my protection. You have it."

Marie slid her feet beneath his covers and laid back with her head on his pillow. The bed was warm from his body and his warmth engulfed her. "It is so much more than protection I want."

Robin pulled the covers up over her and wrapped his arms around her shoulders. Only his upper chest was against her. His chin was against her temple on the pillows.

Marie cried, and he held her. He kissed her temple. His forearms were crossed over her. And she wrapped her hands about his forearms, clinging to him.

"Sleep. You are safe, Marie."

"I put you in danger. What if something happens to you? It's all my fault," Marie cried.

"I am in control here. All right? And none of this was your fault," Robin assured her.

"What if he comes back?"

"I have four weapons I can reach from this bed. I'll be listening all night. You can rest, sleep this off. It's all right, Marie. The dawn will come. Trust me. Even the darkest of evil nights will end."

Chapter Seven   Spent Lover

April 21, 1840

The fireplace had burned down to just embers and the pink light of sunrise came in through the windows of the master suite. This room extended all the way across the west end of the house, with windows on the three sides.

Robin had fallen asleep and rolled to the other side of the bed with his back to her.

Marie raised her head from her pillow. She reached one hand to gently stroke his hair on his pillow.

Throughout that night he had held her so lightly, so gentlemanly. He'd even kissed her forehead a number of times. His hands never wandered, never explored the woman in his arms.

When Robin rolled to his back, Marie slid out of the covers and fled the room for her own.

"Marie..." He sat up alone in the bed.

Robin got dressed, shaved his whiskers, and brushed his hair. He pulled on his riding boots, tucking his trousers down into them. And then he belted on his holster about his hips. He slipped the pistol into it and verified the pouches of the holster contained the lead balls, powder flask, punch, and wadding he needed to reload. As an afterthought, he strapped on another holster about his waist and sheathed that sword into it.

He entered the kitchen, leaning in and looking about. Then he fully entered to stand by the table.

Marie stopped slicing bread to meekly make eye contact with him.

"Are you all right today? Sore?" Robin questioned.

She nodded.

"I have need to go to town. You'll have to come with me. Can you manage a ride in the wagon?" Robin asked.

"Yes, of course. Have something to eat first?" Marie said.

"Yes. Please. Is there much time before it is ready?"

"Not long at all. Coffee is ready."

"Oh. Then I will hitch up a horse after we eat." Robin sat down at the end of the table, near the fireplace. He had to lay his sword along the edge of the table.

Marie set a cup of coffee in front of him and Robin caught hold of her wrist, gently. Then he released her. "Forgive me. Are you hurt from yesterday?"

"A bruise on my arm, is all. Thank you, again." Marie turned and finished preparing his breakfast of eggs, fried potatoes and onions, and bread. She had smaller portions of the same for herself and sat at the table a few chairs down from him.

Robin ate some of his meal before leaning forward and sliding some coins beside her plate. "This is just for you. Replace that dress."

"What? That's too much. You paid me last month."

"Not nearly enough," Robin said.

"What is that for?" Marie indicated the sword.

Robin had another bite. "I think you know."

Robin hitched one Friesian to his father's carriage. "You'll ride up front with me."

"I couldn't do that, sir."

"Come on. We need to talk. I won't be talking over my shoulder." Robin took her hand and helped her up to the seat. Then he climbed up and took off the brake. He took the reins and got them moving. She threw a blanket over both of their laps.

She looked at Robin beside her, in his wide brimmed black leather hat and wool scarf wrapped up about his neck, over his black overcoat.

"First I need to speak to Mr. Lee." Robin turned the horse into the driveway of the next farm over.

Lee and his eldest son were hitching a horse to a plough beside their barn. Two stockmen were moving some cows in the background.

Robin pulled his carriage in and turned it around between the house and the barn. The eldest daughter waved at him from their garden. She started to hurry over.

Mr. Lee and son Jonathon waited as Robin set his brake and climbed down.

"Mr. Van der Kellen. What can I do for you?" Lee said.

Robin removed his hat. "Mr. Lee, may I have a word with you in private please?"

"Boy, finish hitching this horse up," Lee told his son. "Tea, Mr. Van der Kellen?"

"No, thank you. I'm on my way to town," Robin said, walking with Lee into the barn.

Marie shivered beneath the blanket as she waited in the wagon. The girl came over to talk with her beneath the dogwood tree that was starting to bloom.

Inside the barn, Lee turned to look at the Dutchman and waited.

Robin straightened himself. "You could say I fired Mr. Stuart yesterday. You haven't seen him, have you?"

"No, I have not."

"I apologize. He will not be working for you either."

"And the circumstances of this firing?" Lee asked.

"Forgive me for being blunt. I caught him attacking my maid. I ran him off at gunpoint evening last," Robin said.

Lee had to clear his throat. "You're certain?"

"Oh yes. Do not allow that animal on your property."

"Absolutely not, sir," Lee said. "I thank you for this information. Is the girl all right?"

Robin replaced his hat on his head. "Just frightened."

"Understandably. Did he um...?" Lee said.

"No. I got there just in time," Robin said. "Had her pinned down on the floor."

"Well, Mr. Van der Kellen, Robin, you have my gratitude and admiration, sir."

"I appreciate that, Mr. Lee. I do apologize for depriving you of your help. But I could not allow that man on my property or yours, around your wife and daughter, if you know what I mean."

"Thank you, sir."

"Good day, Mr. Lee. I must report this to the constable."

Mr. Lee held a hand to his throat as he watched the Dutchman leave the barn.

It would be just a half hour ride to town and still very cold, just above forty degrees perhaps. Road conditions were muddy and Robin let the horse make his own pace. Marie moved closer to him. His knee was against hers, though his right hand held the reigns on his right knee between them. His holster was also between them, beneath his coat. That sword was on his other side. His rifle lay behind their feet.

Down the road a while, looking straight ahead, he asked, "Marie, did I do anything wrong last night?"

"No, sir. Of course not."

"You ran out in a hurry. Please don't be offended or think that I...did not find you...desirable." Robin looked down at the reigns in his gloves.

"Oh, and do not think that I assumed you were the sort to take advantage."

"Of course not," Robin said. "Many...many other nights I would have been so delighted by your...manner of company."

That made Marie laugh.

And they glanced at each other and each quickly looked away.

Robin was smiling. "I was on guard all night. I apologize. Such an offer has never been extended to me before."

"Surely it happens everywhere you lie down."

"No. Surely not." Robin laughed. "I'm glad you're laughing again. You must stay close to me for a while. Don't go off alone anywhere. Let us make certain Stuart has left the area."

"You're wearing your holster. You haven't since you first arrived here," Marie commented. "You never wore a sword before. Oh my."

After a few moments Robin said, "I'll be wearing them for a while now."

"I'm sorry to bring you trouble."

Robin laid his gloved hand down on hers. "You are no trouble at all."

As they neared the first of the houses, she slid away from him on the seat.

"I have to talk to some men first. I want you to get what we need from the mercantile. I will meet you there to pay for it," Robin told her. "Stay with the people there, that shop keep you know. And see about fabric for a dress or something."

"But I could pay our bill with what you gave me," she said.

"No. That's yours. I'll pay our account at the mercantile, always. There is a dress maker somewhere. You should inquire." He parked the carriage in front of the store, set the brake and hopped down. He held a hand up to help her down. He saw her safely into the mercantile. Then he adjusted his hat and coat, picked up his rifle, and walked toward the constable's office.

"Mr. Van der Kellen. The Dutchman. What can I do for you?"

Robin looked about at three men gathered with the constable in his office. He held his hat in his hand. "I have business with the constable."

"My friends are your friends. This is John Kinley, owns the bank in town. This is Edward Jansen from Fort Griswold, South of here. And Mathew Keen. He does trade for the Mohegans." The constable got up from where he was seated on the corner of his desk. Then he took in all of Robin's weapons. He extended a hand toward Robin. "I'm Michael Poole. Constable."

Robin passed his hat to the left hand with the rifle. He shook hands. "Robin Van der Kellen. I hired a man, Paul Stuart, a few days ago. Caught him attacking Marie Longuiel, my house maid. Have you seen that man since?"

"Paul Stuart. Don't know him. Did you shoot him?" The constable sat back down on top of his desk.

"No. He only tried to rape her. He's about as successful at that as he was at tending horses. I injured him as I ran him off," Robin said. "I would have you make certain he's run out of this territory. He is not to work for anyone else in town."

"On just your word, sir?"

"You have a daughter? You want him in your house?" Van der Kellen said forcefully, making eye contact with each of them.

"The maid all right?" the constable asked. "Spoiled?"

"No. Not injured," Robin said.

"And yourself? Injured?"

"No."

"You fight him?" Poole asked.

Robin shrugged. "Had him at gun point."

"Well, you sure have trouble with your stockmen," Poole remarked.

"Are you a Federalist, sir? Where do you stand between the English and us Americans?" Edward Janssen said.

"What is your rank, if you please?" Robin asked the man in American uniform.

"Ensign," Janssen said. "What's with the sword? Was he a pirate?" He laughed.

Robin glared at him.

"What is your profession, sir?" Janssen asked. "Or you just inherited that estate with the best hay fields around and no need for work?"

"I am a barrister, a lawyer. I am wrapping up my father's cases," Robin said.

"Where do you stand between the English and the French, given the French maid?" the banker said.

"Decidedly, northeast of it all. I'm Dutch, not English or American." Robin donned his hat and reached for the door, keeping his rifle in his left hand. "You'll see to it?" He made eye contact with the constable.

"I will. Good day, Mr. Van der Kellen. Don't come in my office with three weapons again."

Robin pulled open the door. "Think I've only got three?"

Poole and the others rushed to the window to watch the Dutchman cross the street.

Marie hid one package behind her back as she waited at the counter for Robin to pay for their supplies. Robin also had a package from the tavern next door. Crated up were sacks of flour, tea, container of butter, beans, jars of tomatoes, a jar of honey, and beside the crate were four sacks of grain for the horses. Marie slipped her package into one of the crates. It was all carried out to the carriage by Jonesy and Robin.

Robin came in from the barn and stopped in his tracks in the kitchen. "Marie, what are you cooking?"

"It's a surprise," she said.

"But it…it smells like beef."

"It is beef. Pot roast."

"But we didn't buy any beef."

"No, we didn't. But I did, sir," she said.

"But that would have been all your wages. You spent it on…." He leaned over to see into the iron pot over the fire and back to her peeling carrots.

"You haven't got your strength back fully and I could really use a great supper for a change." She continued peeling potatoes.

He smiled just a little. "Well, it so happens that I got us something to go with it." He pulled a bottle of wine and a bottle of brandy out of his bag. He put the wine on the table. "Alike in minds, it seems, yet again." He walked to the cabinets to put the brandy away.

"Don't get too hungry yet. It will take hours," Marie said.

"You could have bought yourself fabric for a new dress or something. May I?" Robin stole a carrot to munch on.

"Who's going to see it out here." She smiled. "There are some biscuits there for you."

He smiled. "It will all be gone in one night, two maybe."

"But how wonderful it will be while it lasts."

Robin stole a biscuit too and poured himself a cup of tea. "Hours?"

Robin returned to the kitchen to find she had set the table with a white cloth, candlesticks, and the gold rimmed china. The candles were flickering on the dishware and glasses.

Marie had changed into a dark green velvet dress she had altered herself from that collection of his mothers. "Try this." She had a bit of roast beef on a fork and offered it to Robin.

Instead of taking the fork from her, he let her feed it to him. And then he stepped back with his hand to his mouth. He muttered something in Dutch.

"Too hot?"

He sighed. "So wonderful. Magnifique. There is a Yankee pot roast like this in Boston."

"You must not speak French around here."

"Yes, I'm well aware of that. Three men almost flattened me in town for being neutral on the whole matter." He strolled toward the table and began to open the wine bottle using a fancy silver bottle screw.

Marie served out two plates of roast beef, potatoes and carrots, with spoons of beef broth on top. She set one down for him and then one for her across the table from him.

Robin poured two glasses of red wine. And he waited until she sat, before he did.

"I feel like a proper lady," Marie said.

"I thank you for sharing this with me." Robin raised his wine glass. "To a new start."

"To your new start." She raised her glass as he did and then tasted it when he did.

"Isn't it your new start as well?" Robin asked.

"How so, sir?" Marie asked. "This is wonderful. I've never had wine before."

"Marie, won't you call me Robin?" he said. "I would love to hear you speak my name with your American accent. I've only heard you say my name once or twice perhaps."

She met his dark eyes across the table. "Robin."

He smiled warmly. "How old are you, Marie?"

"Almost twenty-five."

"Really? You're 24?"

"Old maid." She sipped wine and smiled.

Robin laughed. "Definitely not. You're beautiful. I do wonder what you would look like with your hair down."

And then they ate. He refilled the wine. The glasses were small.

"How old are you then, sir? I mean, Robin?"

He slid his hair behind his ear and squirmed a bit. "I'll be thirty-five in May. May 25th."

"You don't even look thirty. We thought you were in your twenties. But I don't think it matters for a man," Marie said. "As long as you're handsome."

"Do you think me so?"

"Well, everyone does." Marie shrugged.

"Everyone?"

"All the women in town turn to watch you," Marie told him.

"Still? And what do you think?" He met her eyes.

Her cheeks were blushing from the wine, but she was also emboldened by it. "I love to watch you chopping wood. A very fine man, I think. Every bit."

They continued to eat.

Marie picked up the bottle screw. "How does this work?"

"Twist off the silver sheath. There. Careful. The bottle screw is sharp," Robin said. "It is rather dear to me. A gift when I graduated law school, from the Orde Van Advocaten, the Dutch lawyer's association."

"It is beautiful silver."

"This is extraordinary. You really outdid yourself," Robin said. "You are a chef."

"Thank you."

"You know, I really don't know how to end this night. That would really depend on you. Whatever you decide is quite all right with me." Robin lowered his eyes briefly. "I don't know what your expectations are but if this supper was anything more than a thank you or just a celebration as you said, ahm… perhaps I should stop rambling and let you say something."

They were quickly finishing the meal and the wine.

"If you promise not to laugh, I'll show you," she blurted out.

"Show me what exactly?"

"My hair."

He laughed. "Oh." Then he said, "May I? I love to undo a woman's hair." He rose from his chair and walked around to behind her. He removed one hair comb and then another. He set them on the table. He had to discover how her hair was twisted around and found more combs to remove. And then her long almost black hair was released into long ringlets that unfolded down to her waist. At first, he used his fingers to loosen locks of her hair. And then he picked up one of the combs and began to comb her hair from the ends up to the back of her head.

Marie's chin was down when he stepped around her, looking at her closely.

"Marie, you're stunning. Beautiful." Robin sat down, not in his chair on the other side, but in the chair on the end, closer to her, very close to her. His knee was against hers. He stroked slowly her hair back from her cheek. "Have I just crossed the line? I figured we were a long way past the line after last night. But you give me hope that I may."

Marie looked at his long slender hand on the table and then she touched his fingers. She pushed his sleeve up, touching his wrist, and the light hairs on his forearm. She then unbuttoned his cuff, two shell buttons, to slide her fingers deeper into his sleeve.

Robin was drawn closer to her. His forehead was near hers. His fingers caressed the underside of her wrist until they nervously linked fingers together. Robin leaned in and kissed her mouth boldly. And then after meeting her eyes, he supported the back of her neck to continue kissing her. His tongue touched her lip and she could not resist touching hers to his. With this encouragement, he kissed her more deeply, enchantingly teaching her how he liked for them to kiss, a deeper kiss than she'd ever known.

Her hands did not block him but rather, one curiously felt his collar and warm neck beneath it, and the other gathered a handful of his hair up.

After this kiss, his mouth was wet with hers. He searched her eyes. "Does your... invitation still stand?"

Marie nodded. "Even more so."

"Are you certain? It's not the wine talking?" Robin asked.

She urged him to stand up.

"I shall require verbal consent," he said. "Forgive me. Such a romantic. I sound like I'm in court again."

Marie looked up at him and he kissed her again. She wrapped her arms around his slim waist, inside his jacket. She felt him breathing harder as he folded around her. His hands held her hips to his.

"Marie," he whispered. "Are you coming to bed with me?"

In the softest and boldest voice a young woman could manage, she kissed his ear and then said into it, "Yes, Robin. I give myself to you."

To quell the shivers that shot down his neck, he downed the last of his glass of wine. He slipped his pistol into his pocket. They both blew out the candles on the table. Then he took her upstairs by her hand.

On the landing they looked at each other. In the hall, they kissed. She entered his bedroom first with Robin close behind her. He shut the bedroom door with the thought that it would stay warmer inside by the fireplace. He set his weapon on the nightstand.

Robin kissed her again. Marie embraced him about his waist inside his jacket, feeling each breath he took. He held her up against him and backed toward the bed. His kiss was entrancing to her. She did not want her mouth parted from his. The gentle touch of his tongue, the softness of his full lower lip, even the accidental touch of her teeth on his was more intoxicating than wine.

He was backed against the bed. He opened and pulled back his jacket. Marie helped him off with it. He tossed it onto the trunk at the end of the bed. And then he had to study this green velvet dress of hers. "I've never seen you in this before. Rich colors suit you." He unbuttoned the back of the dress and let it drop to the floor. She stood there in corset and pantalettes.

They both sat down on the bed to pull off his boots and her shoes. Most of her bosom was revealed above her corset.

Robin took her cheek into his warm hand, looking down her corset, watching her breathe. "Am I frightening you?"

"No. I could do anything with you. I want to keep kissing you."

"I will kiss you all night, darlin. Get under these covers. Just like this, okay? Let's get you warm." Robin pulled down the covers behind her. He opened his belt and his trousers. While Marie slid into the bed, he removed his pants and threw them onto his jacket, tossed her dress there as well. The tails of his shirt came down over his undergarment.

Marie held back the covers for him to slide in with her. He rolled over, taking her into his arms and kissed her deeply again. And this time he pressed his body against hers all the way down to their toes. He felt her curves, her hip, her thighs. He followed the stays of her corset up to fill his hand with her breast.

With the warmth of wine, they rolled into the bed together. He kissed her mouth hungrily and she kissed back. Her hand felt up inside the back of his shirt and warm skin of his lower back. Her fingertips traced his spine downward. She encountered the top of his undergarment and slid her hand down over his backside. They moved together. They breathed in time. His hips were narrower than hers. His shoulders were broader. Her skin was so soft. His thighs had light hair on them.

"What do I do?" she whispered.

"You stop me any time if you are frightened. Yes? Otherwise, I'm going to make love to you," Robin whispered. "Please let me make love to you." His hand was loosening her ties in the back. "You know, there is a bit more to it than this?" He opened her corset.

"I've never done this before. I don't know at all."

"We will just take it slow." Robin sighed, feeling her hand slide down the back of his hip and she slid his undergarment down. "Curious? You can touch me, anywhere."

"So can you," Marie invited him.

"Yes?" He pressed his hand between her thighs. "Take these off? I would touch you there."

"Why?" Marie squirmed out of her pantalettes.

Robin lowered his chin and smiled. "I'll show you." He untied her corset, tossed it aside, and filled his hands with her breasts. They kissed deeply again. He let her unbutton his shirt before he slid fingertips up her thighs.

"I mean, how do I know what to do?" Marie whispered.

"I've always had a way with women. I'll show you…pleasure." He soon felt the comfort of her warm skin against his, the taste of her mouth, the feel of her breasts in his hands, in his mouth. He sighed at the feel of her hands on his bare chest. His long slender hand felt her where no one ever had before. And she ached inside for him. "You want me. You see? So sweet…."

And he felt her curiously slide his undergarment down in front. She whispered to him, "I saw you when you were sick. All of you. I had to change your clothing. You weren't like this then. Does it hurt?"

"Quite the opposite. Your hand is ecstasy to me." His breathing had changed. Her hand stroked the length of him and made him moan. He closed her hand around him and his eyes clenched shut. For a moment he didn't even breathe.

He urged her onto her back.

Marie yielded to him.

Robin spread her legs with his knees, getting on top of her. He kissed her mouth, her cheek, her throat, as he pressed his body against her. "Trust me. Just relax." He looked into her eyes, until he couldn't resist any longer. "I want you so, Marie. Are you all right?" He waited, letting her relax, all the while knowing that he hadn't felt anything like that in so many years that his need was unimaginable.

"I think so."

"I think I am not," he told her, getting up onto her. "This...can become as pleasurable to you as you are to me. You will not be so shy the next time. I need you now." He got up on his arms and thrust a few more times. He moaned something in Dutch, soon unable to translate anymore. He held her down and couldn't hold off climaxing hard any longer. He moaned as if he were dying, into the pillow beside her head. And immediately afterwards, he knew he shouldn't have done it that way. He trembled. His body trembled. "Marie, I will make you my wife, you know."

Robin, moments after promising to hold her all night, laid his head on the pillow beside her and dosed off to sleep. Marie looked at him in the flicker of the firelight. She rolled to face him and watch him sleeping. His dark eyelashes lay against fair skin. He had sideburns down to his jaw line. And the shape of his ear was nice. At last, she could touch him, kiss him, snuggle in his arms and all he could do was sleep in the contentedness of a spent lover.

She sat up in his bed, looking about the master suite with different eyes.

Would the gentleman still want to marry his maid when morning came?

April 22, 1840

He rolled over when he felt her getting out of the bed. "Marie? Are you all right?"

"Yes. I'm just getting dressed. Do you want tea or coffee?"

"Wait. I want to talk to you," Robin said.

"Oh no."

"Marie. Are you okay, sweetheart?" Robin sat up nude in the bed and looked at her standing in just her dress from the night before. "Marie, I love you. I do."

"Oh Robin. I was bleeding. I have to…."

"I know. It's all right," Robin said. "Sit here. Come here."

"I'm sorry." She sat on the edge of the bed.

"For what? Being so wonderful? Being so sweet and innocent? For letting me take that from you?" Robin asked, his hand moved from her wrist to link fingers with hers. "What can I do?"

Marie wiped her eyes. "I'm okay, I think."

Robin slid closer to her and wrapped his arms around her waist. His head was at her hip. Her back was to him. "It is not time for your monthly? Then I caused it. You're all right. I'm sorry about that. It was your first."

She nodded.

"Your mother or another woman never told you what it would be like to be with a man?" Robin asked. "I'm sorry. I should have told you first then. It would have sounded awful coming from a lawyer and not a poet. You would have never agreed. You were wonderful, Marie."

"I was? I didn't do anything."

"Oh. Yes, you did. You gave up something for me. Please tell me you did not do this because I protected you. Please Marie. I have been falling in love with you for so long. Please tell me you feel something for me?" Robin leaned up behind her, his chest against her back.

She leaned back and held onto his arms about her. "I was so afraid you changed your mind about me. I love you so. I have since you arrived."

Robin pulled her to him. They held each other in silence for a very long time. He kissed her temple and cheek. He stroked her hair. He whispered to her, "Lay down. I'll make love to you again."

"In the daylight? In the morning?" Marie whispered.

"What does time of day matter?" Robin whispered into her ear, making her giggle. "When we're in love?"

"I was going to make some coffee," Marie said. "I...I need some coffee."

"Are you shy? Are you squirming away from me?" Robin asked.

"Shy. Yes. I can't even look at you. You're not wearing anything." Marie giggled.

"I know I'm not wearing anything. You weren't either a minute ago," Robin whispered. "I love your body, every curve and your beautiful long hair. I love your soft skin and the taste of you."

Robin looked at her across the kitchen worktable that morning, she in her simple gray broadcloth tying on an apron. He was in fine wool trousers, button up shirt, and finely tailored suitcoat. The tablecloth and candlesticks of last evening were gone. Marie picked up his silver bottle screw from the worktable and placed it on the dining table for him.

With his chin down and eyes round, he asked, "Marie, are you all right?"

She looked up at him and smiled meekly.

Robin straightened up his posture quite formally. He entered the room a bit. "Marie, ahm, I remember Adrianna was a bit sore the next day. I am sorry about that. I don't think it's me. I think it just is that way...the first," Robin said in a soft voice. "But it will pass. Just a day after that man attacked you and I... I should have waited. I'm afraid the thought of another man having you and... I had to make you mine."

"I'm all right. I wouldn't exactly want to do it again right now," Marie said with a bit of a smirk.

Robin smiled. He lowered his chin. "Well, that's one of us." He moved around the table to her side and took her so gently into his arms. "Marie, when I return to Boston, you will come with me as my wife. We have a wonderful time together. We laugh and work well together. No one in Boston will ever know that you once worked for me."

"You're serious?" She said into his shoulder.

"I want us to go into town and be married," Robin said.

Marie dropped her fork. "Here? You don't want to do that here."

He reached for her hand. "Why not?"

"Robin, they know I'm your maid. They'll talk you out of it. Humiliate you if they have to," Marie said. "I couldn't bear that."

"Impossible. They won't talk me out of it and I have nothing to hide. Neither do you," Robin said.

"Robin, I... I can't pass for a lady. You must be joking."

"I know I am ten years older than you, and that's a lot. But you're not a little girl. You are far more mature than your age. You were running this place before I arrived. Authority like that wasn't given. You took it. And though I may have to work for some of my former colleagues at first before I can open my own practice again, I can make a good life for us in Boston, here, or wherever. I have money saved. I am not so broke as they say. I am just smart with my funds. I think Marie Van der Kellen would be a very nice name." Robin embraced her. "Marie Frances Longuiel, will you marry me?"

"Yes, Robin. Yes!"

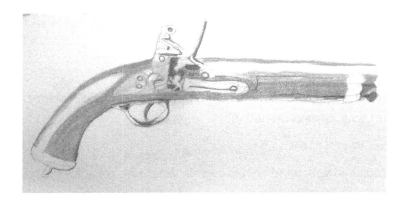

Chapter Eight Prancing Lion

April 22, 1840

For the first time ever, when Marie hopped down from Robin's carriage, he held out his arm for her. She looked up at him and smiled as she wrapped her hand about his forearm. Her heart was pounding. She feared he could feel how she shook inside.

Robin patted her hand. Then he picked up his rifle and lead Marie into the mercantile. Marie had to open the door, unwilling to release his arm until the two of them were visibly inside the store. Then she separated from Robin to purchase a few items.

Robin stepped up to the counter and Jonesy behind it. "May I post these letters, sir?"

Jonesy tore his eyes from Marie and looked at the letters on the counter. "New York for these and Boston for these? Certainly. That'll be ten cents each, Mr. Van der Kellen."

Robin pulled out the coins from his leather purse. "Really? I'm not buying the horse that carries them. Where can I find the reverend?"

"Mid-afternoon on a Saturday? Tavern most likely." Jonesy accepted the coins but didn't bother to count them. He was studying Robin. "The stage sets the postage. I just collect it."

"Marie, wait in here just a moment. I won't be long," Robin said to her. "Get whatever you like."

"Yes, Robin."

Jonesy stepped around the counter after Robin exited. "Marie? Did you hurt your ankle or something?"

"No. Why?" Marie said.

"You...had your hand on him and all. What's he going for the reverend for?"

"Jonesy." Marie gleamed and grabbed onto Jonesy's forearms. "We are getting married."

He grabbed onto her hands then. "Marie? You're marrying the gentleman? Mrs. Van der Kellen, then? I'm so excited for you. I can't wait to spread the word."

Robin entered the tavern to everyone looking at him. The line of men standing at the bar turned to take him in. One of them was the man of the cloth, one was Constable Poole. Robin stepped closer to the men. "Reverend, might I speak with you?"

"Seems you already are. You're that Dutchman, aren't you?" the Reverend said. "Big hay farm to the North?"

"Indeed. Robin Van der Kellen."

"What can I do for you?" The Reverend took another drink of whiskey.

The men all looked at him.

Robin straightened up and said, "You can marry me and Marie Longuiel. Now, if you don't mind."

"Who?"

"That's his maid," the banker blurted out.

The bar remained quiet as all the men listened.

"Mr. Van der Kellen, I don't know how things are done in Amsterdam, but here in the new world, a gentleman like yourself really doesn't need to marry beneath his station just because he is…fond of creeping down into the pantry in the middle of the night."

The men laughed.

"I'll do without your council. I merely request that you marry us," Robin said to the reverend firmly.

"With child, is she? What's the urgency? You'll regret these choices you made in your life," the reverend said. "I won't do it to you, sir."

"Are you refusing to marry us? It's not as if you are busy, reverend. Sorry to interrupt your drinking. There are other churches in this new country." Robin put his hand on his hip and held his rifle by the barrel. "And I won't have you or anyone talking of my future wife that way."

"All right. No need to raise your voice, Dutchman. But you're going to wait about it for one week and think on it well. Next Sunday, if you bring her to service with you, afterwards I'll go ahead and marry the two of you," the reverend said.

"Sunday?"

"Then you can be just as miserable as the rest of these chaps." The reverend indicated the men at the bar, who burst out laughing.

"We won't be seeing him in town next week," John Kinley, the banker said, laughing.

Robin rapped the banker on the chest. "Yes, you will and you'll be our witness. Bring your wife to stand up for Marie."

"Your maid? She must give it to you good, Dutchman."

That made the bar laugh.

Robin shoved him back a step. "Perhaps I can do better than a pig to stand up for us."

The men around really burst out laughing.

"All right. Listen up." The constable strolled over from the end of the bar. "Dutchman, you've got brass ones. I'll stand up for you, if only for the amusement of it. Kinley is a giant pig." He made the men laugh. "By the way, that Stuart you ran off a few days ago, wanted for murder in New York. I just heard. You did well to run off a murderer. You probably should have just shot him in the head. Though I don't suppose you ever killed a man before."

Robin looked him in the eyes. "You would be wrong."

"Well…you'd best tell me about that then." The constable took Robin firmly by the arm. "Next door in my office."

Marie, meanwhile, was standing with Jonesy in front of the mercantile, looking wistfully at the dressmaker's shop across the way, wondering if Robin was having a drink.

Robin was ushered out of the tavern by the law man, most ungentlemanly, out onto the street. Marie looked on in shock. Poole had Robin's arm behind his back. She hurried toward him.

"Is this her?" Constable Poole asked.

Robin jerked his arm free. "Marie, I believe you know Constable Poole, at least by badge if not by ill manners."

"Don't leave her standing out here in the cold. Get on over to the dress makers. That's my wife in there. She'll set you up with a dress for your wedding." Poole looked from Marie to Robin. "I know you're good for it."

"Marie, of course. Please do. Anything you want." Robin kissed her hand and she walked off shaking her head at Jonesy.

"My office, Van der Kellen. You know the way."

Robin walked with him in the cold to the next wooden building. It was a family home, with the parlor converted to an office. Inside was a desk and a wood stove badly in need of more tending. It was where Robin had spoken to him about Paul Stuart.

Poole threw more wood into the stove. "Sit down. You need to stay out of sight. I have something to tell you about your pa."

"My father? I've been here six months. What is it you've been in such a hurry to tell me?" Robin asked.

Poole took a seat on the corner of the desk. "That wit must run in your family. Insulting, it is. Sit down. Set your rifle on the desk or you make a law man very nervous. You especially. And keep your hand away from that pistol."

Robin sat in a chair and laid his rifle down, pointing away from them both. "What do you mean, stay out of sight?"

Poole poured two whiskeys on his desk and slid one toward Robin. "You're in danger. And I wasn't certain of it until I talked to the traders who told me about Paul Stuart killing a man in New York. Does the name Thomas Albertson mean anything to you?"

"A business associate of my fathers, I believe, in New York." Robin looked up at him.

"Drink that." Poole indicated the whiskey while he leaned to see the iron stock of Robin's British-made Baker rifle. His hands were folded in his lap.

Robin picked up the shot of whiskey. Without blinking, he downed the whole thing and set the empty glass down.

"Nervous?" Poole asked.

Robin's brow furrowed. "Furious."

"Where did you learn to shoot like that? Military? Overseas?"

Robin nodded. "My father told you that?"

He shook his head. "I saw Paul Stuart's shot off ear."

"He was here?" Robin put hands on the arms of the chair as if to get up.

Poole indicated for him to stay seated. "Complaining about you, right after you left town. Said at thirty yards you shot off his ear and then you knocked out his front teeth. You refused to pay him for his work, he said. You disarmed him and you ran him off. That's military." Poole drank his shot of whiskey. "You'd have paid him if he didn't try to rape your girl. Relax, I told him to start hiking and don't ever come back. That was before I knew he killed this Thomas Albertson in New York."

"He killed my father's business associate? He knew who I was then?"

"You give him that bruise on the forehead?"

Robin wet his lips. "Marie did. She was fighting him off as I entered."

Poole laughed. "Really?"

"Frying pan."

Poole laughed for a moment. "That little woman out there? You've got your hands full with her. Have you been through your father's papers? All of them yet?" Poole asked as Robin shook his head. "Well do something a lawyer would do, rather than just getting on top of your pa's kitchen help. Even if she is damn pretty and half your age..."

"That's not funny. She's not that young. And just what is it you're implying?" Robin grabbed the whiskey and poured himself a second shot.

Poole watched him with the whiskey and laughed. "That settles it right there. I like you, Robin Van der Kellen. And I sure didn't at first."

Robin downed the second drink and cleared his throat a bit after. "Well, it's not mutual. Except for the immediate dislike."

"Your father didn't leave you with tons of debt. He left you with tons of money he and Albertson walked away with after all those bank robbery cases. There was even a recently dead bank robber they prosecuted. His pile of money disappeared. If Albertson didn't have it, some think your pa did. You just have to find it. And you're about to have more company like Stuart, trying to beat you to it."

Robin stared at him.

"I thought you'd need that drink."

"What makes you think my father hid money out there in the house?" Robin said. "He would have paid off the banker he owed two hundred US dollars to in Norwich and I wouldn't have had to sell my home and my practice and move out here to the middle of Goddamn nowhere."

"It's my town you're talking about. You'd better look at documents from the Albertson firm. In the meantime, do you mind if I take a look about the property?" Poole asked. "Maybe he had no other way to get you to come out here from Boston. You never did before."

"What's your interest in this?" Robin asked.

"I just can't figure you out, really. But I don't trust any man who can't down a shot of whiskey like you just did, twice. And this ain't watered down."

The tilt of Robin's head changed. "What did these gentlemen, these traders say exactly?"

"Now you're sounding like a lawyer."

"It's getting near dark. You best stay at the inn for the night." Constable Poole walked out to Marie at the carriage with Robin. "It's not safe for you on the road after dark."

"And leave my fortune unguarded?" Robin put a hand on his hip as he turned to look at Poole.

"Still don't believe me, do you?" Poole said. "All right. Dammit. Let me get my horse. I'll be riding out there with you."

"I don't need your escort," Robin shot back. "And why would I trust you?"

"Trust me." Poole got in his face to say. "If I wanted all the money, not just a share, I would let Stuart kill you and go find it myself."

Marie looked up at Robin then, clinging to his arm. "Stuart?"

Robin stared him down.

"Badge, remember?" Poole stepped back from him. "This ain't no broach."

"Marie, get into the back, get down right behind me, and bundle up in the blanket. The temperature is dropping," Robin told her.

"What is it? What money? Stuart is after you now? Oh, it's all my fault."

"No. It's my father who got us into this. I'll tell you it all later. I think we'll have company for a few days. Unpleasant company." Robin helped her up into the wagon. He climbed up front and handed her the blanket. He set his rifle across his lap. His hands verified his pistol and reloading supplies on his holster in an automatic fashion. They verified the sword was handy.

"Robin?"

"If there's any trouble, I want you to get down back there and hold on tight. I know this horse can't run hard for very long but they do run powerfully," Robin said. "I need to teach you to reload for me."

"What sort of trouble?"

"My father's sort. Apparently. I just found out everyone thinks he kept all the money from a bank robber he prosecuted. And Stuart killed a lawyer in New York before coming here for that money."

"Robin, are we getting married?"

"Did you get a dress?"

"She's making it quickly."

"We're getting married next Sunday. I just... have to stay alive until then."

She reached up and tugged on his coat between the seat and seat back. "Not funny."

"Did you get any other dresses?"

"No."

"We need to get you more. And we will. I have a feeling we must go to New York soon."

"New York?" Marie curled up right behind Robin, her back to Robin's but below him. She wrapped the blanket up around her and pinned her package from the mercantile up beside her.

In a few moments the constable came riding up beside them and Robin got his horse moving. "Lopen op." He tapped the reins. Robin and Poole looked at each other.

Almost in sight of Robin's estate, a shot was fired that hit the buckboard beside Robin's feet. Marie shrieked, "Robin, are you all right?"

"Get down. Hold on." Robin aimed his rifle and fired back, then he howled at the horse and slapped the reins to get it to bolt up hill. No doubt the crack of the rifle had something to do with how hard it bounded ahead. The power of the giant Friesian was surprisingly explosive.

Constable Poole drew his rifle as well, but it was Robin's shot that gave them clear passage over and down the hill. Soon they were out of range inside Robin's gates. He drove the carriage up the drive, between two stone walls, and into the courtyard between the manor house, barn, and servants' quarters.

Poole drew up alongside him. "Order and Rank?"

"Cavalry, Captain of the Royal Netherland Guard," Robin said.

"And they thought you were such a dandy when you came to town." Poole circled on his horse. "Sweep the house fully before you let your guard down in there. I'll make a sweep around it, checking windows."

Robin reached up for Marie.

She set both hands on his shoulders.

He grabbed her beneath her arms and swung her down to him. "Stay close to me." He handed Marie the rifle and drew his pistol from his pocket. His kitchen door he unlocked with a key. Inside the house it was dark. "Get a lamp lit." He laid the rifle on the table. He ripped off his coat though it was cold enough in the house to see his breath. He drew his sword and kept it in his left hand.

She lit the oil lamp with a stick from the fireplace.

"Grab hold of my belt and follow me. With your lamp, I need to see the corners. Stay behind me and duck if there is any trouble. Don't drop the lamp."

Marie did as he said.

Robin led her through the house. All clear.

When he brought her down the stairs, he still had that pistol drawn. "Can you get a fire going, love? Big one? We need the light. And make some strong coffee for a long night."

"Got it." Marie nodded and added kindling to the embers in the cook fire. She stacked firewood over it as it got going.

Robin got set up on the table to reload his rifle.

There was a knock on the door and still, when Poole opened it, he met Robin's pistol. He put hands and guns up. "Just be me."

Robin lowered the weapon and uncocked it.

Poole indicated the sword on the table. "What are you doing with that?"

Robin grabbed the sword and flicked it to Poole's throat. "Any other questions?" He withdrew and re-sheathed the sword.

"Nope." Poole entered and bolted the door. "I unhitched your horse and put it up. Put my horse in your barn." He set Marie's package from the store down on the table. "Horse on the left is an asshole."

"That's his name, actually," Robin said. "Klootzak."

Poole looked at him and laughed. "Well, happy to meet you, Marie Longuiel. I thought you were marrying a fop until I realized Captain Van der Kellen is actually a marksman. Extremely good one, that is. Maybe the best I've ever seen, demonstrated right here tonight. That shot from a moving carriage at a moving horseman, and you nailed him in the head."

"Not too much detail for her, if you don't mind." Robin brushed out and primed the rifle with gun powder. Then he poured powder down the barrel, set a patch on top and a lead ball on top. He started the ball in with the punch and then rammed it down with the rod.

"Didn't make my identification job very easy," Poole grumbled.

"Captain?" Marie stood up from the hearth. She thought about what he said about a uniform, a war hero, and that sword so swiftly utilized just then. "I'll get some coffee and some supper started." She collected her package and unwrapped fresh coffee and a jar of preserves.

"Thank you, Marie. Poole and I have a lot of paperwork to go through," Robin said. "You can read, can't you?"

"English?"

Robin nodded. "If my father wrote anything in Dutch, give it to me. That will be the good stuff."

Poole looked at him.

"Unless you'd rather guard the house from outside in the cold," Robin told him.

Poole shrugged. "Why would he write anything in English?"

"Anything that the court might order to see, he would write in the language of the court," Robin clarified.

"I went up the hill to have a look. Probably Paul Stuart there. You finished him, all right. I brought his musket. His horse ran off. Probably turn up at a farm around here tomorrow. I'll check around and search for the horse. I'll know that saddle when I see it. I imagine, if that horse belongs to anybody, it would be Marie."

Robin picked up his coat off the floor and hung it up on the hook behind the door. "Where is that musket? What sort?" Then he unwrapped his scarf.

"It's old. French. Used around here in the war. Accurate up to 20 yards or a bit more. Have a look." Poole laid the musket and his own down on the kitchen table. He opened his coat, comparing his gun's length to Robin's. He glanced from Marie to Robin and back. "Don't look at me. I could be home with my own wife right now. So...carry on you two." Poole finally lowered his chin with a smile.

Robin let out a long breath but finally did give Marie a wink.

"No need to sleep in separate rooms tonight because I know you are not," Poole said.

"Enough." Robin walked toward him and pulled out the chair at the end of the table. "Don't be vulgar in front of her."

"You don't have a dog or anything? How do you know if anyone's breaking in?" Poole sat down.

"I just saved your life, as slow as you ride. Is there anything else you want to complain about?" Robin asked.

"You sure have a short rifle, Captain."

"Cavalry," Robin snapped back. "You can't reload yours on the back of a horse, now can you?"

"Is that what I think it is?" Poole pointed at Robin's rifle.

"I don't know what you think at all, much less what you think you're getting out of this, Constable. There isn't any fortune hidden here to share with you," Robin said to him. "If my father had money from a bank robbery, he would have returned it to the bank."

"You sure?" Poole grabbed a loaf of bread on the table and began to cut a slice off of it. "It is what I thought. Baker Rifle Company. England. Ten percent. That's all I want. Got any butter? You need some security here. I'm starving."

Robin walked to the pantry and pulled out the butter. He brought it and set it down rather loudly on the table. "Are you ever going to fire that Enfield or you carry it for ballast? You must need the extra foot for accuracy."

Poole buttered his slice of bread and sat back. "Baking some of your last bread, darling. Soon you'll have a staff to do it for you. You eat in here, do you? There's a dining room over there, you know? You really are fond of the kitchen, Dutchman."

Robin walked around the table into the kitchen to stand near Marie. "Are you all right? That must have been frightening." He opened his arms to her and didn't quite know how to put hands on her.

Marie set down the coffee tin and wrapped her arms around his waist. "You killed Paul Stuart?"

Feeling her hug, Robin placed his hands gently on her upper back. "Don't waste another thought to him."

"Captain? You must tell me," she said softly into his lapel. "You've said a few things that…"

"Yes. Do tell," Poole said from the table. "Six months here and you never told her you were a captain of the Dutch calvary? Where did you fight? Against the British? Or with them?"

Robin kissed her forehead and walked back toward the table. "What I went through was so awful I passed up promotion, retired, finished law school and left Europe. Do you think I'll just chat lightly with you about it?"

Poole pulled a flask from his pocket and set it on the table. "Maybe you'll have few drinks and tell me. I know how you like whiskey."

Robin reached across the table and picked up the flask. He set it on the fireplace mantel. "You're not touching that. If somebody's shooting at us I insist you stay sharp."

Poole gave in with hands in the air. "You do sound like a captain."

"What is your background?" Robin asked him with furrowed brow and fist on his hip.

"Connecticut militia. Sargent." Poole watched him sit down. "That's how I knew you were a marksman." He noticed the empty wine bottle on the kitchen worktable and grinned. "Oh? A bottle of wine last night, huh? I see why you had to get married today."

Robin involuntarily blushed and looked away from Marie.

That made Poole laugh out loud. He glanced from Marie and back to Robin. "It's all right. It's all right with me, Dutchman. If you can shoot like that, you can bed anybody you want."

Robin set his rifle up on the fireplace mantle. "You will not be vulgar in front of her or you will sleep in the barn. That is, if you can charm Klootzak."

Marie turned last of their pot roast into a stew as Robin brought out two of the desk drawers full of papers and he was going through them with Poole in the light of the cook fire. They were both drinking coffee.

Poole was still staring at Robin's pistol on the far end of the table. When Robin went back to the library for more paperwork, Poole picked up the pistol to examine the imprint in the steel near the trigger.

That made Robin stop short but then eventually enter and set down an armful of journals.

Poole put the weapon down. "Prancing Lion. How did you come by this?"

"Former owner gave it to me," Robin said.

"That, along with your Baker rifle makes you quite a man of suspicion around here," the constable said.

Marie looked over.

"Why exactly do you have British guns?"

"They're the best in the world. They're better than your crude American weapons," Robin replied. "Better than German."

"You don't carry Dutch weapons?"

"They get most of their muskets and pistols from German manufacturers," Robin explained.

Poole pointed at the pistol. "Where did you get that British East India Company pistol? You know that thing can get you killed around here."

Robin glanced at Marie.

Poole looked at her too. He turned and walked into the library down the hall and waited for Robin to join him where he collected Robin by the collar roughly. "Tell me right now if you're a British spy."

"If I was, you'd be dead." Robin just straightened his posture and waited to be released. Then he said, "I fought the British in India. They took a colony from us. That pistol was aimed at my face. I had fired both guns already. I cut his throat with my bayonet and took that pistol out of his hand, making sure he didn't bleed out on my boots. Fine weapon. The very latest technology. Only their officers had that model. The Baker was issued to me in the Cavalry. There's no easier rifle to reload in the saddle. Don't ever grab me in that manner again. Twice you've done it. The next time, I don't know if I can stop myself."

A study of Robin Van der Kellen

When Robin reentered the kitchen, Marie had a worried look on her face. Robin seemed unruffled and went back to examining the paperwork on the table.

Poole entered more slowly and just refilled his coffee, not making eye contact with anyone.

Robin took down a pistol from the mantel and set it on the table in front of Poole.

Poole picked it up to turn the iron toward the firelight. "Stuart's? Lefaucheux?"

Robin nodded. "Is that unusual for this territory?"

Poole shrugged. "I've seen a few. It's old. Could have traded for it. Flintlock. Ugly damn thing, compared to yours. Maybe he came from up north, French country in the war." He slid it on the table to Robin, handle first. "Maybe he even served on their side. War of 1812. Against me."

Robin took it and put it back on the mantel. "Where is the nearest French fort to us?"

"Along the St. Laurence River up there. Montreal territory. Or west all the way to the big lakes. Buffalo," Poole said. "How did you take that from him?"

"Shall I show you?" Robin said.

Poole just raised eyebrows. "I'm good."

The two men just quietly began sorting through papers until the stew was done and served to them on what little clear space remained on the kitchen table.

Marie sat down across from Poole to eat her bowl of stew. Robin was on the end of the table.

Robin met eyes with her and said, "See, now you frightened her. You can't discuss such matters in front of females."

"You're not a British spy. Fine. I'm convinced." Poole looked to Marie. "He's not. Relax, girl."

"I know he's not," Marie said. "I don't want you to hurt him."

Poole raised his eyebrows and looked at Robin down the table. "Don't worry. That ain't easy."

"Don't frighten her. She's the lady of the house. You're just a guest," Robin said firmly. "Uninvited guest."

"Fine beef stew here, young miss. You are a fine cook," Poole then said to Marie.

"Better," Robin said. Then he had to soften his tone. "Marie, how long did you work for my father?"

"Not long. A few months before he died," Marie said.

"Did you overhear anything about Thomas Albertson or New York or the East Fourteenth Street bank?" Robin asked.

"No. He never stopped in the kitchen. I never went upstairs when he was up there," Marie said.

"I guess you did when this one was home," Poole said. "Does he look like his father?"

"No. Not much," Marie said. "The nose maybe."

Robin shot Poole a look. "But you said you knew my father."

"I was just checking to see if she did. No, you don't look like him," Poole said. "I guess your ma was pretty."

Robin let out a long breath. "I'm getting very tired of your games. I want you to be straight with me and especially with Marie. Or I'm seeing little use in having you around."

"Albertson said on his deathbed the money was here. He gave it all to Pascal's prosecutor, a Mr. Willem Van der Kellen. That's what the bank robbers believe."

Marie lay in Robin's bed that night, hearing male voices downstairs. They were talking about the robbery for hours. She snuggled in the midst of his pillows, inhaling the scent of his hair on them, hearing his sighs. She wrapped her arms around one of the pillows and laid her head on another. She hoped he would come up to bed with her and she would awaken in his arms, but it was not to be.

April 23, 1840

In the morning when Marie came downstairs, she found Poole asleep on a couch in the parlor. Robin was asleep at the table, with his head in his arms.

There was a pile of journals beside Robin's head. Marie opened the cover of the top one and observed the Dutch writing. She very lightly stroked Robin's hair as he slept, but she did not want to wake him. Beside him was that pistol in question. She did take a moment to look at the polished brass and fine wood. But she looked for this prancing lion, Poole mentioned. It was an imprint in the iron of the gun. The mark of the British East India Company. This gun could get him killed here.

She went into the kitchen to get some fresh coffee started. Flour and eggs busied her hands but in her mind, she heard his sighs, and as her eyes looked on him she felt his curls through her fingers and the muscles in his shoulders, his weight on her hips. How fascinating he was when he reached a point of no control, overrun with passion and ecstasy. He'd dosed off after, so relaxed was he. She could cuddle him then as she'd dreamed of for months.

By the time bread and coffee were cooked and smelling fantastic, Robin lifted his head and looked about. He rubbed his eyes and sat up. His eyes took in Marie cracking eggs into a bowl. And he smiled. He stretched and got up from the chair.

Marie watched him stand in front of the fire and try to rub at his sore neck. He stretched his slim body, leaning with a hand on the mantel.

When he turned around he said, "Where did Michael go?"

"Who?"

"Poole."

"Oh. Parlor to sleep. I'm making you some eggs."

"And I adore you for it, darling." He used a kitchen towel to pick up the coffee pot and fill a cup for himself. "Would you like some?"

"Yes please. Oh but you can't do that." Marie started to reach for the pot.

"Certainly, I can. When we're married, I'll be working for you," Robin said.

Marie giggled, wiping off her hands on the towel.

He set the hot pot down on a trivet and wrapped his arms around Marie from behind.

"Did you find out anything last night?" she asked him, wrapping her arms about his and leaning her head back on his shoulder.

"Yes. I miss sleeping with you." He kissed her temple. "Well, I found out his handwriting has turned awful. What was that you said about the mark of a gentleman? I suspect in this case it was his failing eyesight or nervous hand. Found out we have lots more to go through. He kept records of everything, it seems. Every case. Every witness." Robin held her body to his, folding about her and whispered, "I want you so."

"I think since we will be married Sunday, you should wait until then."

Robin hugged her harder. "I think since we will be married Sunday, I should have you all I want until then."

Poole had awakened with footsteps on the wooden staircase and came back to the kitchen table. It was Van der Kellen's return down the stairs that had awakened him.

"Still don't believe it's here, do you?" Poole said to him.

"I will tenaciously continue to search these records if only to prove to you that I'm poor," Robin told him.

"Well at least you know she agreed to marry you while you're a poor landed gentleman," Poole said. "Before you're filthy rich. Unless you plan to give all the money back to the bank or something."

"If it was stolen from a bank of course I intend to return it. I swore an oath to uphold the law. Didn't you have to when you got that tin broach?"

"Silver broach. Those people are all dead. Stuart and his gang saw to that," Poole said. "Look here, the owners of that bank right here." He handed documents across the table to Robin.

"Just keep looking. What else was with these documents? Is there a date?" Robin picked up the journals. "His notes are organized by date."

"April 12, 1839."

"Hmm. I know where I was that day. Cross examination in a Boston court." Robin dug down into the pile and pulled out a different journal. He flipped through the pages back to April. "Interviewed Pascal in his cell April 30th. Had two bullet wounds in him. Almost incoherent."

"Almost what?"

"Hard to understand. Pascal was dying in jail." Robin read further. "Said he told everything to his defending barrister Mr. Albertson. Wouldn't tell my father anything without Albertson there."

"Says here the bank had 85,000 stolen, a mix of US dollars and continental currency." Poole handed another piece of paper to Robin. "That's what Pascal was charged with stealing. Continentals are worthless."

"85? But here it says only $18,000," Robin said of the journal. "Michael, these are two different banks."

"The guy got around," Poole said.

"East Fourteenth Street Bank in New York on March 4, 1839 and Norwich Bank February 15 of the same year. Norwich isn't that far from here. I wonder if they have any records," Robin said.

"Norwich, Connecticut?" Poole said. "Bout a half day ride from here. I suppose he could have gone from Norwich to New York city in two week's travel. Could have taken a train even, or steamer."

"Well with $18,000 from the Norwich bank he could have bought any travel he wanted out of town," Robin said. "There were no wanted posters for him yet. I need Albertson's notes. And Stuart killed Albertson. Great. Now I need to interview Stuart and I had him right here. He spent all that morning in the barn."

"Was he looking for money or shoveling out stalls?"

"Definitely not shoveling. But I searched the barn thoroughly. Marie, that day I fixed the horse's leg. I cleaned every inch of the barn. If anything had been buried or hidden I would have found it before Stuart was ever here."

"Are you sure he was in the barn?"

"Not entirely. He attacked Marie in the kitchen."

"I found him in the root cellar," Marie said. "He was coming out of there. I thought he was hungry."

"Hungry? For a sack of potatoes?" Poole said. "Suppose he was looking for the loot, ran into Marie, and decided to attack her as a distraction?"

"His trousers were undone. It wasn't just a distraction," Robin said.

"You think robbers don't branch out into rape occasionally?" Poole said. "No offence, Marie."

Robin stood up and used a piece of kindling from the fire to light an oil lamp. And then he carried the lamp down into the root cellar.

Michael Poole got up and followed him.

"Root cellar indeed." Robin looked up, holding the lamp away from the roots above his head and ducking.

Poole grabbed his arm and said into his ear, "You didn't just agree to marry her because she was raped and possibly with child, did you?"

"No." Robin withdrew from him.

"How do you know she wasn't?"

"Because I know."

"How?"

Robin said quietly, "Because I took her virginity night before last."

Michael stared him in the eyes. "Oh. After the wine?"

Robin almost smiled and shoved him back a step. "Shut up."

"All right." Michael turned and began to look around in the root cellar but he laughed. He began moving a bushel of carrots and sacks of potatoes to look beneath them. But he laughed more. "I just assumed you were doing it out here for months with the girl."

"That's not the behavior of a gentleman," Robin said.

"Well, you were a hell of a gentleman after a bottle of wine, my friend." Poole had to sit down on the potatoes laughing.

"Poole, get up," Robin said seriously.

"What? Oh come on. Nobody expects you to be a monk."

"Get up." Robin pulled him up by the arm and picked up a piece of gold off the floor. It was just peeking out from beneath a sack of potatoes. He turned it over in his fingertips and Poole leaned in to study it.

"That's not a US dollar or continental," Poole said. "What is it?"

"This is a French franc," Robin said.

"Your maid is French."

"She was born here, in America. Her father was a French soldier." Robin knelt down and began searching the area of the coin. There was a small hole in the potato sack and Robin reached his finger into it, pulling out more gold coins.

Robin tore the hole larger and coins came pouring out of it. There were only a few potatoes on top. "French weapons and now French gold."

Poole picked up a handful of them. "These are all French gold."

"Yes." Robin stopped pouring them out. "That sack was on the bottom." He walked over toward the stairway up and called up to the kitchen. "Marie, are you there?"

She came to the door.

"How long have these potatoes been down here?"

"I'm sorry. Have some of them gone bad?" Marie asked.

"The sack on the bottom. How long was it here?" Robin asked.

"I believe they were all harvested in the fall."

Robin reached up and handed her the first gold franc that he found.

Marie took it and looked at him in surprise.

"The sack was full of these," Robin said.

"All this time it was full of gold coins?" Marie gasped.

"French gold." Robin looked at Poole who was piling the coins up on the floor like a boy making a snowman. He said to Marie, "How long was Stuart down here?"

"I don't know. Not long I don't think," Marie told him.

Poole stood up. "There's no way Stuart left his stolen gold down here. He was looking for Pascal's. And I think we just found some of it. Pascal probably got shot for telling somebody where this was before he got arrested."

"Neither bank robbery listed French currency," Robin said.

"So there were more banks robbed than the two we know about." Poole pointed at the pile of gold on the floor. "Well I know who 10% of that belongs to. I can tell you that."

"Just hold off. It's not going anywhere until we figure out where it came from. There weren't any potatoes harvested since I got here," Robin said.

"No. It was all pulled up in September," Marie said from the stairway. "You arrived November 5th."

"Anyone else work in the kitchen before I arrived?" Robin asked.

Marie shook her head. "Just Marta and June. They didn't do any cooking. And then the two stockmen. You let them go when you sold off the cows and the riding horses."

"You never saw this gold before, obviously," Robin said.

"Are you joking? I would be shopping in Boston right now," Marie said, making them laugh. "There's been a sack of gold down there all this time? Oh my God."

"Can't I just separate out one tenth of it? Just to see how much it is?" Poole said.

"No." Robin put his hand on his hip. "Let's finish searching in here and put all those coins in this flour sack. We have to figure out a safe place to keep it. Can't believe my father thought that was a place."

"Well, it was pretty safe here for six months or more." Poole began filing the flour sack with coins.

"Well now it is not because all three of us know it is here," Robin said.

"Don't even suggest you're going to put it someplace only you know about. Not unless you want to give me my cut right now. Then you can put yours wherever the hell you want to. Sprinkle it all over your bed if that's what you want to do with it," Poole said. "Return your 90 percent to some bank in New Haven. I don't care."

Robin put his forehead in his hand for a moment. "I would have sold this property in a few months and never known this was here. Fine. Sort out your cut and take it."

Happily, Poole prepared to take the bag up to the kitchen table for sorting.

Robin grabbed him by the arm. "Right here. And you're not to spend it until we leave town. Once word of this gold gets out this property won't be safe anymore, not with an army to guard it."

"Fine. I won't spend it yet. Don't even know where to change in French money for ours anyhow. You're already thinking about where to go for that. New York or Boston, I'd imagine. But not here," Poole said. "I'll be a lot happier with that buried in my own back yard."

"Are you sure you trust him?" Marie asked quietly.

"No, I don't trust him. That's why I agreed he can take his portion now," Robin admitted.

"Well thank you very much," Poole said. "Go back to calling you the Dutchman, then. How was he, sweetheart? How much wine did she have that night before yielding to your skinny ass?"

Robin just glared at him.

"You sold off riding horses and kept those two draughts? As a cavalryman that must have hurt," Poole went on to say.

"Just don't you talk for a while," Robin warned him. "If you value your teeth."

Poole put up his hands and backed up.

Robin drew Marie into his bedroom that night and shut the door.

Marie looked up at him and wrapped her arms around his waist. "You must be so tired."

Robin kissed her forehead and embraced her warmly. For a moment they just held each other, feeling so intimate and yet so new to each other that their hearts raced. "What do you want me to do with this money?"

She kissed his throat. "It is not for me to say."

"Of course, it is. You know I may not find who this money actually belongs to and be forced to keep it," Robin whispered, smelling her hair. Then he smoothed his hand over the bun of black hair at the back of her head. He sighed and began pulling out combs.

"Perhaps you should stop reading then." Marie shook her head and collected the combs from him.

"Ahm, but there is still $103,000 to be found. I may find that by reading," Robin said.

"Robin, I can't tell you what to do with it when you are certainly rescuing me from a life of poverty just by marrying me as you are." Marie kissed his throat again, more warmly than before. "You hid this money well from Constable Poole then?"

"Not yet," Robin said, kissing her temple and returning to undoing her hair. "No not at all well yet. It's right here." He indicated the nightstand where his pistol was resting.

"You must find a better place than that," Marie said. "I know a place."

"Where? Pray tell."

Marie separated from him and went to the fireplace where she pulled up a loose floorboard near the hearth.

"How did you find that?" Robin looked into the opening.

"Got my skirt caught in it once cleaning the ashes out."

"Well. Whatever would we do without a woman's skirts? Hiding all the treasures." Robin collected the bag of gold coins and was about to insert it down into the floor beneath the plank when he laid his head down on the floor to look inside. He reached in and had to insert his arm almost up to the shoulder. His legs pushed out behind him until he lay flat. He pulled out a wooden cigar box.

Marie knelt beside him, petting her hand down his back. "What is that?"

"Shhh. It's not the only one in there." He used the fireplace poker to retrieve two other boxes. He opened the lid of one, revealing stacks of $10 Treasury notes.

"Are those money?" Marie asked.

"Treasury Notes," Robin told her.

"Are those worth anything?" Marie whispered.

"They're promissory notes from the US Government. Yes I believe they are still good. Banks pass them from one to another. They're just not used as currency for goods or services." Robin opened another box to find US dollars in gold and silver coins and a folded piece of paper. Robin opened the paper while Marie picked up one of the $10 paper notes to examine. "There's more. He's hidden it in other places of the estate. Out along the rock wall. In the ball room mirror. In the root cellar. He was planning to move that to a better hiding place. Why would he...why wouldn't he leave reference to it for me to find and send shares home to my brother and sisters? And if it had to be returned to the banks, was he tempted to keep it?"

Marie put the bank note back into its box. "If these are from the Norwich Bank, why do they not say so?"

"Norwich Bank issues bank notes for depositors to use, based on what they have in their vault. They invest some of it. They lose some of it. If they go out of business those Norwich Bank Notes are worthless. That's why the robbers stole the gold and silver, and these Treasury notes." Robin retained the handwritten note inside his coat pocket.

"All those people with Norwich Bank Notes have lost all their money?" Marie asked.

"I can give them the gold and silver if they bring me their bank notes. Then I become a banker." Robin took twenty US dollars in gold coins out of the box. He handed them to Marie. Then he closed up the boxes and began to slide them back into place. Finally, he slid in with them the bag of French gold. He perfectly replaced the floorboard and dusted over it with some of the surrounding fireplace ash so that it matched the rest of the flooring.

"What is this for?" Marie asked.

"For your wedding dress and any other clothing you need. And another beef roast, if you don't mind, for Sunday. I'm sorry about your roast becoming stew today. We'll make it up to us next Sunday."

"This money, does it not go against your own conscience?" Marie asked him. "I've never held so much money in my hand at one time."

Robin leaned his forehead to hers as they sat on the floor there. "If I must return it to the bank, I'll repay it out of my own pocketbook. If anything should happen to me, you take this money and run away to Boston quickly. Sell this estate. Once we're married, it's yours. I'll write out a will first thing in the morning."

"Don't speak of such things," Marie begged him. "Won't Poole suspect if I spend most of this at his wife the dressmaker's?"

Robin shook his head. "He thinks I'm good for it. Twenty dollars won't raise suspicion."

"But what do I buy for you?" Marie asked him. "A new shirt for the wedding? A new vest?"

"If you wish. But I'd rather find beneath your wedding dress something extraordinary that takes a very long time to unbutton or unlace. It will slow me down."

Marie giggled and he smiled so warmly. She slid closer to him and kissed his mouth. Robin kissed her lovingly, his tongue sliding softly over hers. He was breathing hard by the time she separated to look at him in the firelight.

"Is this all so fast for you?" Robin asked. "I should have courted you for a while. But we went straight to bed together. Now we must get married. I mean, I want very much to marry you. Have we missed our courtship?"

Marie smoothed her hand on his cheek to his sideburns. "How would you court a woman?"

"I...I can't ask your father's permission. Or I would. Dine with you and your parents. I'm so sorry we cannot do that." He looked into her eyes.

"I hope to meet your family."

"What about your family in Bridgeport?" Robin asked.

"My cousins? I would love to show you off to them someday. You're so handsome and a landowner, a gentleman. I should write them," Marie said. "Are you going to invite me into your bed tonight?"

"I thought you wished me to wait."

"I think I'd rather give Poole reason to tease you and make you blush again in the morning."

Robin smiled and started to scoop her up into his arms, collecting her knees over one arm and her arm about his neck. "You don't think he'll hear me, do you?"

"I will do my best to make certain he does."

Robin stood up with her. "I think I should make you abstain for a week then, Miss Longuiel."

She whispered into his ear. "Then you should not have shown me where to touch you that way."

Chapter Nine Norwichtown

April 24, 1840

Marie did up Robin's buttons as he pulled a vest on over his white shirt. Then she buttoned the vest for him as he held her by the waist of her dress and the corset he'd tied. "You dress me like a doll," he said.

Marie looked up at him and smiled. "For months I've ironed your shirts and jackets and trousers. At last, I get to dress you up in them. You're my doll, yes."

Robin kissed her forehead. "Funny. For months I've thought of getting you out of your clothing not dressing you up in them."

Poole was sitting at the kitchen table with a cup of tea when Robin and Marie came down the stairs.

"If I wanted to make my own tea I would have stayed with my own wife last night," Poole said. "You're going to wear the girl out before your wedding."

"Quite the contrary. She's ruining an old Captain of the Guard." Robin poured Marie a cup of tea. "Perhaps we can persuade Poole to make breakfast."

Marie laughed.

Robin sat down at the table with a smile and set his pistol down on the table. He picked up the next journal he needed to examine.

Marie brought Robin a cup of tea and took hers into the kitchen.

"Norwich. Norwich again, I'm telling you, we need to see if they have any records there at the bank, at the county clerk's office, and the town council," Robin said.

"Then we leave tomorrow," Poole said. "I'll have you back by Sunday."

"I cannot leave Marie here alone, given circumstances."

"Pack her up and she can stay with my wife. Maybe she can teach Alice how to make me wail as if I'm dying that way," Poole said.

Marie burst out laughing.

Robin just raised an eyebrow and waited for Marie to collect herself. "You're going to loan me a horse?"

"Can't expect you to ride one of those buffalos you have in the barn," Poole said.

"Not for that distance. Norwich it is. I will board the buffalos, as you called them, at the livery in town. They won't eat much." Robin rolled his eyes. "Klootzak might destroy the livery and eat the farrier. Marie, you don't mind? You can do that shopping we were discussing."

"Of course. I'll get you that new vest." Marie winked at him.

"I'll bring you a present from Norwich, though it pains me to be parted from you for a few days," Robin said.

"Or inches, apparently," Poole commented.

Robin packed for a trip on horseback, in saddlebags with a bedroll, rifle, pistol and a package of salted pork and bread. He hitched up the carriage and then brought out Marie's packed bag. He drew her alongside the carriage to whisper to her, "Stay in town with the dressmaker and say nothing about the money. And do take care." He put a letter into her hand.

"Be ever so careful on the road, my love. You're still in danger," Marie whispered, on her toes to have her mouth so close to his. "What is this?"

Robin stroked her cheek, looking into her eyes. "Deeding this estate to you, should anything happen to me. Poole witnessed it. It's legal. Now, don't worry about me. Curse, remember?"

Poole had his horse saddled and closed the barn behind him. He mounted and road over to the carriage.

Robin assisted Marie to climb up to the front seat. He climbed up beside her, took off the brake, and got the team moving.

Marie was standing with Alice Poole, in front of their home, when Robin Van der Kellen strolled back toward them from the livery. He had a long black coat on, black wide brimmed leather hat, and his Baker cavalry rifle over his shoulder. Beneath his open coat he wore a pistol on his hip. In riding boots to his knees, he had a way of walking. His bell of brown hair was pulled back in a low ponytail and tied with one of Marie's ribbons. Anyone on the street turned to look at him.

Michael Poole came around his house leading two saddle horses. "By the way, that horse of Stuart's showed up. They've got him at the livery. Did you see him?"

"Yes. They showed it to me. Said you had his things. You'll tell me what he had." Robin secured his saddle bags and bedroll with some clothes rolled inside onto the horse Poole lent him. Then he slipped his rifle into the pocket for it. He cinched up the saddle straps himself before telling Poole, "Why do you complain about this horse? She looks fine to me."

"My boy can't ride her. We'll see if you're truly cavalry or not," the constable said.

Robin smiled. "I can ride anything with legs and a mane." He strolled toward the porch where the ladies were waiting. "Mrs. Poole, I thank you for looking after my love Marie."

"Happy for the company, sir," she said. "Well, Marie, he is a beautiful thing to have to wake up to, isn't he? Why haven't I seen him about town?"

"That's why I keep him out in the country," Marie said.

Michael just coughed on his horse. "Come on, man. We can just get there before dark. That horse is yours, Marie."

"I don't want it," Marie said.

"Then, Alice, tell the livery to sell it and give the money to her," Poole called out.

Robin held out a hand to Marie and then kissed her hand. "See you soon, love."

"Be careful." Marie gripped his hand before releasing him.

Robin turned to gracefully mount his horse. He turned the horse about in a circle and tipped his hat to Marie. Then he dug in his heels and the horse took off with the constable having to catch up.

The arrival in the Connecticut town of Norwich, at just before sunset, found them in a seaport town though many miles up the Thames River from Long Island Sound. It was also a rail hub and textile mill town. Cotton arrived on boats. Every manner of textile left on boats. Cabinets and furniture were made there. Silverware was made. Gun factories were springing up. It was the twelfth largest city in New England. Robin held the horses while Poole went inside an inn to secure them a room for the night. As Robin stretched from riding in the saddle for hours, his eyes wandered up the street to the barber shop, the candy store, the jewelry store.

Poole returned. Robin put the reins in his hand. "Wait here a moment."

"But what...."

Van der Kellen walked up the sidewalk and ducked into the jewelry store.

Poole had no choice but to wait. He too looked around but his eyes settled on the tavern.

The store closed up after Robin exited. He met Poole at the horses, pushing something down into his inside coat pocket.

"Let's get these to the livery and then that tavern beckons," the constable said.

"Yes, it does."

"You just ate a sandwich two hours ago. How does your stomach carry on that way?" Poole said.

"That's just the way it goes."

Once they sat down in the tavern, they ordered dinner and a bottle of whiskey.

Robin sat with his back to the dancing girls.

Poole ogled. "What's the matter with you? You aren't going to look?"

Robin glanced over his shoulder. "What is there to see? Legs? I have legs."

"Shit. Not like those," Poole said. "Where've you seen dancing girls with less than that on?"

"Poole." Robin glanced at them again. "I was 16 and the dancers in Amsterdam were topless...and you could fuck them for a dollar."

Poole was speechless. He watched the girls for a while as Robin unwrapped a scarf from around his neck and opened his coat more.

"That damn horse bites me every time I ride her but you...she just purrs and does whatever your knees ask," Poole complained.

Robin laughed. "I have a way with females."

Poole burst out laughing. "I don't know what this way is or you're a wizard on that horse." Poole looked up at the bartender who set a whiskey bottle and two glasses on the table.

Robin laughed harder and poured the whiskey. He then took out of his pocket a tiny box to open it and admire his find at the jewelry store.

"Is it true you're a widower?" Poole asked.

Robin slipped the ring onto his smallest finger to admire it, and then placed it back into the box and inside his jacket pocket. "What did you say?"

"Nothing." Poole spoke louder over the music. "Looks like a nice gift for her."

They ate their meals and each had a few shots of whiskey. The dancing girls and piano player took a break.

"Did you serve in the war, Poole?" Robin asked as they ate.

The constable nodded. "When they called up the militia. Fourth Connecticut Regiment in the war of 1812. What happened in the cavalry? Where did you meet war?"

Robin said, "I fought the British in southern India, among other places, Italy, Germany."

"India? Why that's not even civilized, is it?"

"Dutch colony was revolting against us. The British took advantage," Robin said. "We fought two fronts, three if you include the tigers."

"Lost a lot of men?" Poole asked.

Robin nodded. "Nearly all of us. We lost the colony to the British. I had to escape to sea."

"Lost a lot here too. 1775 to 77. My father's war. You know, they'd have gone a lot easier on you in town if they'd known you fought the British before," Poole said.

"It's nobody's business," Robin said.

"You didn't want to talk about it in front of the girl?"

"No. I won't talk about war in front of my woman. If she knew what I did in war, she'd be terrified of me," Robin said. "And I won't talk about it with anyone who has not survived it themselves."

"Men in town think you're a French sympathizer at best, a pacifist at worst," Poole said. "British spy definitely."

"I couldn't care less," Robin said. "I don't expect to be here long."

"How many men have you killed?"

Robin looked at him across the table. "I lost count. 300."

"How the hell..."

"Averaged three a day, during four months heavy combat. 300? Could be twice that." Robin savored a drink of whiskey. "From the saddle I'm a guaranteed shot. It's almost a curse. On the ground, hand to hand, I'm lucky. I'm not a very big man."

"What was India like?"

"Hot. Horrible insects. Snakes. Tigers. But very enchanting women when you're a very young officer," Robin said.

Poole grinned. "Did you enjoy these women?"

"Well, we heard the British officers had their own harem," Robin said. "Dutch officers, well, we had a few."

"How did you rise to Lieutenant and then Captain?"

Robin did another shot and he wasn't smiling anymore. "Half the company was slaughtered and I led the rest home. My commanding officer and his commanding officer were dead at my feet. Horses blown in half. Boys in the company just standing there in tears. Get everyone back on their mounts, disobey every order they gave me, and get the company the fuck back in retreat. Or there would be nobody left. And that's exactly what I told my colonel."

Michael Poole nodded.

"I got half a dozen medals and a lifetime of nightmares. Next thing I know they want to make me a Major if I go Africa. I had just met this beautiful girl. No way in hell did I want to go to war again in another God forsaken Dutch colony," Robin said.

"So, you are a widower," Poole blurted out.

"We have a lot to do tomorrow because I don't want to be here any longer than we have to," Robin said. "Don't you want to get back to your wife?"

"And three kids? Are you kidding me? I'm in heaven," Michael Poole said. "But you want to get Marie out of there before she sees what all that stuff in bed will get her. I understand."

Their room at the inn had four narrow beds in it. Robin and Michael each took a bed closest to the fireplace and settled in for the night. Robin removed his holster and verified the condition of his pistol.

Poole produced that whiskey bottle and it still had a few shots left in it. He took a drink and offered it to Robin.

Van der Kellen shook his head. "All yours. I don't plan to oversleep in the morning."

"Oh, come on. Live a little."

"This may be a party away from your wife and children but I'm on a serious investigation of why my father, a reputable barrister from Boston and Amsterdam, kept funds recovered during bank robbery prosecutions." Robin pulled off his boots and stood them up right beside the bed.

"So now after clearing all his debt you have to clear his name as well? You don't know he did anything wrong," Poole said.

"Yet."

"You're just going to hand all that gold away and go back to being landed poor but still barely a gentleman?"

"I don't have to justify myself to you." Robin got up and laid out his coat, hat, rifle, holster with his saddle bags on the next empty bed. He slid a chair over to hold his pistol right within his reach for the night.

Poole took another drink. "Just can't figure you. You're not even happy you found a pile of gold in your house. Like you don't want to get used to it being yours."

"It's not yet." Robin laid down on his bed in his trousers and shirt, and pulled the simple wool blanket up over himself.

Poole nodded and then began getting himself ready for bed. "You did say yet. Progress. Good night, Captain."

"Good morning, sir."

"Good morning. I would like to see Mr. John Bradford." Robin entered the Norwich Bank with a letter in his hand.

Poole was seated in the lobby, feet up on a table, lighting a hand rolled tobacco cigarette.

"Who may I tell him is calling, sir?"

"Robin Van der Kellen."

"Yes, sir." The man exited.

Robin glanced at Poole and shook his head.

Poole put his feet down and puffed on his tobacco.

"Right this way, sir."

Robin was shown up the stairs to an office up top, and inside where a man stood up behind a fine oak desk.

"Mr. Van der Kellen, I have received payment from your bank in Boston. To what do I owe this pleasure?" the man said.

Robin flipped the letter up from his pocket and brandished it. "Difficult to make payment when one is dead, sir. You might bear that in mind when calling in a loan."

"Oh? Oh, Mr. Willem Van der Kellen has passed?"

"You know very well my father died. You called at his home just days after when he wasn't yet cold in the ground," Robin said. "I hope you're pleased a grieving son had to read your kind words."

"I am terribly sorry, sir."

Robin paced a moment and repocketed the letter. "What did my father need the loan for?"

"Farming equipment, I believe," John said.

"He hasn't any new farming equipment," Robin said. "Rusted. Plow is dull. What are you talking about?"

"I didn't buy it for him. I only loaned two hundred dollars to him," John said.

"Why did I have to pay you $250?"

"Late fees."

"Late fees? Twenty five percent?" Robin exclaimed. "That's robbery."

John Bradford began to file through contracts in desk drawer and pulled one out. "Here. You want the loan papers. Have them. I want nothing to do with him."

Robin picked up the papers from the desk and met eyes with the banker. "Nothing to do with him? What do you mean, sir?"

"Nothing at all."

"Do you know the banker from across the street? The bank that burned?" Robin asked.

"Robinson. Died in the fire, they say. Burnt so bad they couldn't be sure it was him," Bradford said. "Yes I knew him. Your father met with him right before it burnt to the ground."

"How do you know that?"

"I was watching him from this very window, wondering why he didn't come into my bank and pay me. Figured he was trying to secure a loan from that banker, but he wasn't going to get one. That's for sure. I told him Van der Kellen's word was no better than his money."

Robin reached across the desk and collected the man by his suit collar. He yanked him closer across the desk, knocking some items to the floor. "My father's word was good when he was alive. Where did Robinson live? Where did he keep his records?"

"Kept his records in the bank, like bankers do. Lived on Town Street. Alone. House is empty now," Bradford said. "Are you going to let me go or burn my bank down too?"

Robin released him with a shove that dropped him into his desk chair. "Don't get up." Robin pointed at him.

He looked up at Robin and his mouth fell open.

"What is the date that bank burnt?" Robin said.

"October 1st."

"Anything recovered from inside? What about the safe?"

"Wide open and empty, the safe was. Everything else embers. They just recently cleaned up the ugly site," the man said.

"What about the clerk? The directors of that bank? Who are they?" Robin asked.

"Perhaps the town clerk can tell you."

"Good day, Mr. Bradford." Robin took his papers and paused in the office doorway. "Don't come out of this office with a weapon. I'm not alone."

The man gathered up a few papers and scrambled out the back stairs.

Five of the Norwich bank's directors met with Robin that afternoon, demanding their money. When three of them shoved Robin back into a wall, Michael Poole intervened by firing off a pistol.

That made most of them duck and dive for cover.

"Back away from the lawyer or I'll be reloading real quick," Poole said. "Your bank was robbed. We're the men trying to find the robbers. Remember?"

Robin straightened himself up.

"Besides, that Dutchman over there has killed over 300 British in war in India. If he wanted to, none of you would be going home tonight. Be glad he is patient."

"I'm not so patient. Where's your paperwork? Your proof of investment? I can't do a thing to help you if you won't show me what you are due," Robin said.

"The papers burned in the fire."

"Really? You sir, you say you invested five hundred dollars and kept no receipt?" Robin questioned. "I take a receipt when I buy a train ticket."

The man lunged at him and Poole blocked him, restraining the man by pinning his arms behind his back.

"This meeting is over. Robin, get out the door. I'm right behind you. There is nothing to be gained here," Poole said.

Out on the street Robin looked over at Michael Poole. "You shot a sofa."

"You're welcome."

April 25, 1840

Marie sat at the kitchen table, holding Poole's youngest daughter on her lap. Alice set down a cup of tea for her. Marie told her, "I can help you around here if you just give me something to do."

"You're already doing it. If I have to watch all three of them and get the two off the school, I can't get anything done. You're a surprise my dear. A surprise and delight. I'll get going on that dress of yours shortly."

"I can make the bread then," Marie said.

"What are you going to do with your twenty dollars from the livery?" Alice asked. "Saddle and horse will probably bring that much."

"I don't know. I'll have to think on that," Marie said.

"How did you come to be intimate with Mr. Van der Kellen? If you don't mind my asking, he seems like the gentlemanly sort," Alice said.

"He is. He was always very proper. He was very sick a month ago. The doctor had to visit. He nearly had consumption. I was the only one there to care for him. And I know I fell in love with him then, rocking him in my arms while his fever was so bad he didn't know where he was. He couldn't even speak English for a day," Marie said. "Before that I didn't know him. Didn't know he had a wife once. She died of some illness five years ago."

"Is that what he said? She may have been sick but she died in childbirth, my dear. Child too," Alice said. "Robin's father told Michael once. Said that was why his son didn't come visit. Devastated. He probably can't even face it."

"I have known him to be so honest..."

"Don't hold it against him that he did not tell you yet. I've lost two myself. A man feels so responsible." Alice sat down with her. "He's handsome. Can't blame you for falling for him. He's different, being Dutch."

"It's another language." Marie shrugged.

Alice took a moment to sip her tea. "Mike said he saved you from an attack. Said he almost shot the man's ear off, from quite a distance, intentionally. He protected you. How did you get the gentleman to cross the line?"

Marie smiled. "I spent all my wages on a beef roast for him."

"Really?" Alice laughed. "Smart. Men are always thinking with their stomach."

Robin and Poole rode into Norwichtown on their return to Canterbury. Poole pointed out a house on the left. "Colonel Christopher Leffingwell's house. Supplier of the war. Had five mills in town. Wool, grist, paper, helped us to not be dependent on British imports. George Washington stayed there many times, securing supplies for the army."

Robin said, "Your revolutionary war."

"His father befriended the Mohegan Indians and made agreement with them to found the town of Norwich, where we are heading, giving away Indian land. Leffingwell the elder once slipped food and supplies to the Mohegans one winter when they were at war with the Narraganset Indians and were starving. Uncas, king of the Mohegans never forgot the kindness."

"I thought we were leaving Norwich."

"We did. But the original Norwich was right here, long before the port town sprang up. It was here that Mohegans gave land to the whites first."

"Are they still around? The Indians?" Robin asked as they road past the inn. "Mr. Lee once told me he used Mohegans on his farm seasonally."

"Oh yes. Quite peaceful. Farmers. Fisherman," Michael said. "I need to stop at a silversmith's here. Then we'll stop at a tavern nearby for the local news, if you don't mind."

"I don't mind at all," Robin said.

"That's one tavern that Temperance never took hold in," Poole said. "Court house there on your right."

"I see."

The silversmith's had a front window open, shutter opened straight up above. Poole slid off his horse and handed the reins to Robin who waited on the road with the two horses. Poole stepped up to the window, "Hello in the shop."

"Oh, Michael Poole. Haven't seen you in a while." The man stepped up to the window. "What brings you out this a ways?"

"You got that rifle sight fixed for me?" Poole said.

Robin looked around the town green surrounded by various inns, taverns, a schoolhouse beside the silversmith's. Large, impressive elm trees lined the triangular green on all sides.

Poole paid the man. "Say hello to Captain Robin Van der Kellen. Dutch Cavalry. Served in India."

"Greetings Van der Kellen," the silversmith called out.

Robin tipped his leather hat.

"Speak English does he?"

"Speaks plenty of it after I buy him a drink at Lathrop's," Poole said. "Come on over if you're done."

"Too much work to do. I wish I could. Good day to you both."

Poole put his purchase into his saddle bag and then mounted. "See the red house in the corner there? Tavern we will visit. When the militia was called up we camped right here in the green."

"I see," Robin said.

"The British were never here. We never let them in. They couldn't make it up the Thames because of the forts in New London and Groton. We also have rock barricades in the river to ground their ships. Ours knew the way around them." Poole led him toward the tavern. They tied their horses up outside at watering troughs. "You can leave your rifle. Won't need it in here."

Robin had dismounted and stretched.

Two ladies passing on foot nodded to him. "Hello, sir."

"Good day, ladies." Robin tipped his hat to them.

The ladies giggled as they walked past.

Poole looked at Robin over his horse. "Knock it off."

"What does that mean?"

"Can't take you anywhere. Stagecoach used to run through here, before the railroad." Poole opened the door and led Robin inside where it was dark, lit by candles and lanterns, and there was much laughter.

"There's some men I'd like you to meet," Poole said inside.

"Happy to, as soon as I can see anything," Robin said.

Immediately the bartender picked up a musket and aimed it over the bar at Robin.

Robin drew and cocked his pistol so fast that men parted in between them, knocking over bar stools and chairs as they scrambled aside.

"What are you doing? He's with me! He's Dutch. Not British." Michael Poole ran in between the two men. "I'm Constable Poole of Canterbury. Put 'em down boys!"

"Dutch?" the bartender said.

"Right now! Put 'em down. He's not British. He's a retired Dutch Cavalry officer. Killed over 300 British," Poole urged. "Robin, take it easy."

"I thought you were English. I beg your pardon, sir." The bartender put his weapon down behind the bar and his hands up.

Robin let out a hard breath. "Do you have any idea how close you came to dying? This country is as ignorant as it is large." He finally uncocked his pistol and returned it to his holster.

An elderly man nearby said, "Pour him a drink quick. Best change his opinion of us."

The bartender poured a whiskey and set in out on the edge of the bar, toward Robin. Then he set the bottle there. "You can have the whole bottle, sir. I beg your pardon."

Robin put his forehead in his hand.

The elderly man stepped a little closer. "Constable Poole. I would like an introduction to your friend, a man with a quick draw I haven't seen the likes of very often in my career. I'll venture he has an aim to match, especially since he said he can't see anything in here and his pistol was aimed at Johnson's heart. Small target indeed."

The bar relaxed and chairs were pushed back into place.

"I beg your pardon, sir." Robin smoothed his hands down his coat, covering up his holster.

The elderly man held out a hand. "Son, here the war is over."

"Doesn't look like it," Robin blurted out.

"Will you accept my apology?" The man said, "I am a descendant of Colonel Leffingwell. He was my grandfather."

Robin shook his hand. "I am retired Captain Robin Van der Kellen. Royal Netherland Guard."

"Where did you serve, Captain?"

"In the Dutch colony of southern India, as well as Italy and Germany, sir," Robin said.

The elderly man patted Robin on the back. "Are you hungry? I'd like to buy you supper and hear about affairs overseas."

Robin let out another hard breath.

Chairs were moved back to where they were and the men all took seats again or returned to drinking.

"Drink this and join me then," Leffingwell's descendant said. "This is my son and his companions."

"My apologies, gentlemen." Robin took a seat at their table.

"Damn that was a quick draw," One commented.

Poole pulled in a chair beside him and set Robin's whiskey in front of him. "I know you're gonna drink that."

Robin put that shot back quickly and poured another. Then he passed the bottle. "Perhaps you gentlemen care to help with this."

"You fought the British in India?" A man asked. "Incredible."

"Killed 300 British?" Another asked.

"At least," Poole said. "From the saddle. He's a marksman."

"How do you come to know Captain Van der Kellen then?" The elderly man asked.

The bartender served plates of pot roast to Robin and Michael.

"Constable Poole is assisting me in investigating a series of bank robberies. I am a lawyer trying to wrap up the case," Robin said.

"I was a lawyer myself. Van der Kellen? Son of lawyer Willem Van der Kellen by any chance?" Leffingwell said.

"He was my father," Robin said.

"I knew of him. Can't say I knew him as well as I do his son."

Alice knocked on Marie's bedroom door. "Marie, they're back. Your Robin is back."

Marie threw on a robe borrowed from Alice and hurried with her down to the kitchen.

Michael had an injury to his forearm, and Robin was helping him off with his coat and into a chair. "Water and bandages," he asked for.

Alice kissed her husband and hurried to get these things.

Robin had to keep Poole sitting upright in the chair and bent over him to position his arm out on the table. He tore open the sleeve and examined the arm wound.

"I'll get some hot tea going," Marie offered.

"Thank you, my dear." Alice set the bowl of water, toweling and a roll of bandaging.

Michael moaned as Robin worked on him.

"It went right through. You're very lucky. I don't have to cut it out," Robin told him. "I'll clean it up. Get this bleeding to stop. And you'll see the doctor in the morning."

"You were shot? Who shot at you? Did they follow you?" Alice questioned.

"They didn't follow us. Trust me," Robin said. "Do you need this shirt?"

"Not as much as I need this arm," Poole said. "Robin was the faster rider. Me they got. He came about and finished them off. Hell of a shot, he is. Even with my rifle."

Robin tore the sleeve right off and went to work cleaning the wound and applying pressure.

Poole looked up at him. "You're death with a rifle in your hand. Do you know that?"

Marie set a jar of honey down on the table.

Robin looked at her. "Thank you, Marie. You remembered."

"I remembered everything you said," Marie told him.

"What? He likes honey in his tea? Right now, seriously?" Michael looked up at Robin.

"No, I despise it. But in the jungles of India more men lost arms and legs for simple infections," Robin said. "Their wounds were insignificant compared to yours. Yours needs work and then honey to prevent infection."

Their teenage son appeared in the kitchen then.

"Go get the horses into the barn," Alice said to the boy.

"I'll do that in a moment," Robin told her.

"Travis can do it," Alice assured him.

"Would you bring in my rifle, please." Robin was inspecting the bullet wound in the constable's arm.

"Yes sir." Travis left the house, still trying to glimpse back at the Dutchman. Death with a rifle.

Robin helped Michael up the stairs to his bedroom and only then was able to let out a breath and look to Marie.

"Here you go, sir." Poole's son, 13 years old, handed to Robin his rifle, bed roll, and saddle bags.

Robin thanked him and the boy went downstairs.

Marie clung to Robin and he kissed her mouth with so much hunger.

"Sorry to give you worry. We were delayed," Robin said after.

"Robin," Michael called from his bed. "Keep it down in that room."

"Go to Goddamn sleep." Robin let Marie draw him into her room.

Marie's bedroom in the home belonged to the two daughters, who were sleeping in their son's room for these nights. The two daughters usually slept together in one simple bed that Marie would share with Robin. And the son, who was the eldest, was fine with sleeping on the couch downstairs in the constable's office.

At last, alone with Robin in the small room with one oil lamp to light the space, Marie began to help Robin remove his holster and boots. There wasn't much room between the foot of the bed and the wall. "Who shot at you? How do you know they aren't outside right now?"

Robin took her by the arms and held her close to him to whisper, "Shots were fired. Poole took one in the arm. When I came around, I fired my weapon, then Poole's, and the men backed off. Poole and I got away. We were not followed."

"You are exhausted."

"It's been a long day. Here it is almost dawn. You must have been so worried," Robin admitted. "What's this?"

"One of your suits. The one I first saw you in. White shirt." Marie said. "Travis brought Alice and I back to the estate to get it for you, hoping you would make it back in time."

"Oh, my dear. You thought of everything. That was dangerous. You shouldn't have gone back there. How is your dress?"

"Perfect. Wait 'til you see. Now get out of these pants and into bed." She pulled down the covers on one side of the bed and then reached across to pull them down on the other. "Sleep at least a couple hours."

"Thank you, dear. I'm so tired. Haven't spent that much time in the saddle in years." He pulled down his trousers and sat down on the bed. He unbuttoned his shirt and tossed that onto his pants and boots.

Once he was lying down, Marie blew out the lamp. She laid her robe across the foot of the bed and slid beneath the covers with Robin. He lay on his back and she aligned alongside him, her head on his shoulder. Robin wrapped his arms around her. And he was very soon asleep. She rested her hand on his chest, soothed by his breathing and his warmth.

Chapter Ten Wedding Day

April 15, 1840

When Marie awoke, she found a cat standing on Robin's chest and Robin was petting it. The small animal was purring loudly.

"Oh, the little girl's cat must have been in here with us."

Robin returned his hand to Marie's arm. "Just came to wish us well, on this our wedding day."

"I will now ask you to stay on and welcome a new member of our community, a gentleman who has served bravely in the Dutch cavalry, where he fought against England in the far-off land of India, braving such horrific creatures as elephants and tigers and red coats."

Robin shot a look at Constable Poole who was sitting on the aisle of his row in the church. Poole was just grinning.

"Stay on and witness the wedding of retired Captain Robin Van der Kellen of Amsterdam, Netherlands to Miss Marie Longuiel of Bridgeport."

Poole stood up in the aisle and took Alice's arm. He gestured for Robin to come to him.

The Poole's children looked on with excitement from beside Marie.

Behind them, Jennifer and Joseph Lee stood up also. Their children were beside them. Joseph patted Robin on the shoulder. At that point everyone rose.

Robin finally stood up and took Marie's hand. Once she stood up in her lovely pale blue gown, the congregation applauded. Robin drew her through the pew into the aisle with Poole. Marie, with her long dark hair in ringlets to her waist, really had ever been seen in town before. Her gown barely fit between the pews and rustled as she squeezed it through.

In the aisle, Robin took her arm onto his and couldn't help but gleam at her. He led her forward to the Reverend. Constable Poole and his wife Alice followed them and stood on either side of them for the ceremony. Robin wore that fine black suit that he had on when Marie first saw him. To many in town who had not seen him before, he looked European, wealthy, and handsome. He removed his top hat and held it in hand.

And when the time came for the ring, Michael Poole opened the little velvet box from Norwich, and Robin took out the small diamond wedding ring to place it on Marie's finger.

They were pronounced man and wife. Robin could at last kiss her. And then they both signed the register.

"I present to you Captain and Mrs. Robin Van der Kellen."

Outside the church, the banker and several men from the fort were gathered. Poole remained close at Robin's side. "It's going to be just fine around here now, Dutchman. I told them what a shot you are."

Immediately the banker said, "Why didn't you tell us you fought the British? We've all fought them. We were afraid you were one of them, frankly."

"I can appreciate that but I simply do not talk about war," Robin replied.

Mr. and Mrs. Lee came forward to shake hands with Robin. "Congratulations Mr. and Mrs. Van der Kellen."

Mrs. Lee took Marie's hand. "I can't wait to have you both over for supper together, Marie. I'm so happy for you."

June and Marta stepped in, to hug Marie. Even Rachel and Louise hugged her too.

"Alice, did you make this gown for her? She is beautiful," the banker's wife said.

"I did. And I made her pantalettes and corset. She asked for extra laces," Alice said, making everyone around them laugh.

Robin looked at Marie with his mouth open and when he blushed all of the men around laughed.

"I'll loan you some scissors." Poole handed him the box for the ring.

Marie clung to Robin, laughing.

"It's all right. A cavalryman always has a knife in his boot," Robin quipped.

Robin and Marie walked back to Poole's house. "I know you want to get home alone but I've made you a special lunch first. And for you, Marie, I made you a pot roast to take home for supper tonight. You just have to heat it over the fire while you are…."

"While he's figuring out those laces," Michael interrupted.

"Thank you, very much. May I have just one moment with her?" Robin said on the porch, taking Marie by the hand.

"It's cold out. Go into his office," Alice told them. "Go on."

Robin leaned in and stole a kiss from Marie before agreeing. Marie's hand was cold.

Inside from the porch to the left was the constable's office. To the right was the sitting room where the Poole's and their children went.

Robin drew Marie into the office and just immediately kissed her.

Alice hurried her children into the kitchen. "Isn't that so sweet. He just had to kiss his wife."

"Yes. I'm sure that's all he is thinking about," Michael Poole said.

"But he is kissing her," the 9-year-old daughter said. "They're newlyweds all right. She looks like a princess."

Marie giggled and had to break off their kiss.

Robin hugged her up off the floor. "Are you happy, my love? Do you like your ring?"

"I love my ring. What a wonderful surprise. I had no idea you were getting me a ring." Marie hugged him about the neck. "I can't stop looking at it."

"I am also going to give you my mother's ring, but I wanted you to have one all your own. Does it fit?" Robin let her down and took her left hand into his to see it.

"Yes. It is perfect. How did you do that?"

"Look, my little finger is the same size. See? I thought so," Robin said. "I need to be alone with you."

"We will be. We do have a long ride home. You must be starving," Marie told him.

"I am. Is that chicken?" Robin said. "Marie, you and I must make a trip to New York. I need to meet with Albertson's partner. I have a really good lead on the...French things we found. And I believe the East Fourteenth Street Bank is long gone. I need to be certain."

"Gone? Do you mean?"

"It's looking as if he left it for me, at least some of it. I just have to be certain," Robin said. "Poole can't go with me, but he said he'd drive us to the train station in New Haven."

"We're going to New York City?"

"Does Alice have any dresses in her shop you can use?"

"Well, yes."

"At least for two days on the train. You'll get more in the city. You need gloves. White gloves," Robin told her.

"I've never had white gloves."

"Come on. It won't be all work in New York. We can also make it a…."

"Honeymoon?" Marie barely managed to say. "I never dreamed of."

Robin smiled and kissed her. "I am starving. Come on."

"Oh Robin! We're going to New York!" She hugged him about the neck.

Robin and Marie sat down at the table with the Poole family and found Travis staring at him. "You fought the British in India? We just learned about India in school. It's where all the tea comes from."

Robin nodded. "Yes, and all the spices from the Far East. Curry, Cinnamon, Paprika, Turmeric…"

"Pa says you have a British pistol. Can I see it?"

"After he's eaten, Travis. Not at the table," Alice said.

"Did you kill a British soldier to get it?" Travis went on. "How did you get it?"

"No talk of killing at the table," Alice scolded.

"I agree with your mother. It is not proper conversation for the table or in front of ladies. I'll show it to you after," Robin said. "Ahm, Michael, we leave for New York day after tomorrow, if that is agreeable with you."

"Day after tomorrow," Michael said. "We'll take your wagon and I'll bring your horses back here while you're gone."

"Thank you. Alice, we are going to need some travel clothing for Marie," Robin said.

"I have the perfect thing," Alice said. "This is so exciting. Going to New York for your honeymoon."

"And business," Michael added.

"About that, I need to speak to you after we eat and they go to the dress shop," Robin said.

"Starting to learn the word 'mine' are you?" Michael grinned.

"Does he always eat that way?" Alice teased.

Marie laughed. "Yes, unless he is sick. Although I don't know where he puts it. He eats like a horse and stays so thin."

"Before you are my age you better stop eating like that," Michael told him.

Robin laughed. "I'm sorry. This is so good. For some reason, I'm starving."

"Good. You need your strength for tonight," Alice teased him.

"And this is fit conversation for ladies?" Michael asked, to much laughter.

"This is a wonderful gown," Robin said to Alice. "And so kind of you to get my suit. All joking aside, as Marie and I had no family to share it with, you really made this a wonderful day for us to remember."

After the lunch, they packed Marie's bag and the pot roast into the carriage. Marie and Alice walked across to the dress shop.

Travis tugged on Robin's jacket. "Sir, do you have the gun on you?"

Robin shook his head. "Not to get married. It's here in the carriage." He reached over and pulled it out to show the boy.

"So that lion there means British East India Company?" Travis said.

"Yes it does. This weapon was only issued to British officers. I had to kill the man who owned this. He had it pointed at my head, you see?" Robin told him. "I had no choice."

"Well how did you do it, sir?"

"Already fired my rifle and pistol and no time to reload. I used my bayonet," Robin said.

"And ran him through to claim the gun from his lifeless hand?" Travis said, looking up at Robin.

"Something a bit less romantic than that, but yes," Robin told him. "Now I must speak to your father alone, if you would please."

Travis stalked off into the house, still glancing back at Van der Kellen.

Constable Poole leaned against the carriage and folded his arms. "Now you've done it. That boy will never look up to me."

"Ah he's only just learned about India. It's an exotic far off land to him. Not a graveyard as it is to me. Poole...."

"You have to keep the money, Robin. The three banks, none of them had French money. In fact, I should probably give it back to you. It was probably your father's."

"You'll keep that 10% as well as 10% of all the rest of it," Robin said. "There's a lot more than you know."

"You found the 103?"

"There is more in three locations in a note from my father. I haven't even tried those places but I will tomorrow. As soon as I talk to Albertson's partner and try to find the bank in New York, I should know the rightful owners of all of it," Robin said. "I'll post you a letter from New York just in case I don't make it back. And you're to see Marie gets 90%. That was our deal."

"You just watch your back. That's all you think about. We were followed from Norwich. You might be followed to New York," Poole said.

"I'll be giving you some money to cover expenses until I return. Did you tell Alice about... the feathers?" Robin asked.

Poole fidgeted.

"Poole!"

"I had to! I was so damn happy she thought I had another woman," Poole said.

That made Robin double over laughing.

"Shut up." Poole shoved him. "She's a constable's wife. Hears all sorts of confessions out of that office."

"Over a bottle of whiskey no doubt," Robin said, wiping his eyes.

Poole laughed. "Be careful in the city, Robin. You are coming back, right?"

"This is where I live now." Robin nodded. "I'll take the last two journals with me to read on the train. Maybe I can figure this out."

"You're a smart one, Dutchman. Except for one thing." Poole pointed toward the dress shop. "You let two ladies go shopping on your pocketbook."

The just wedded Van der Kellens arrived back at the estate. Robin set the brake and climbed down. He held both hands up to Marie.

She slid across the seat and reached for Robin's shoulders.

He hoisted her down against his body and pinned her to the carriage for their first married kiss at home. Marie wrapped her arms around his waist and Robin pressed against her as his kiss became deeper and hungrier.

Klootzak grunted.

Robin stepped back from Marie and drew her clear of the wagon. "I need to be with you."

"Well, I'll just get this roast into a pot over the fire." Marie smoothed a hand up his chest.

"I have to unhitch these horses," Robin said.

"Then...race you upstairs."

That evening, Robin knelt at the chest at the foot of his bed and unlocked it with a brass key.

Marie looked on. "What is that symbol?" The front of the wooden chest had a symbol painted in gold, a large 'V' with an O intertwined on the left and a C on the right side of it.

"Vereenigde Oostindische Compagnie," Robin said. "The Dutch East India Company. It was a trading company, colonization company much like the British version. It is time I walked you back through my life. Would you like that?"

"Very much. Is that your uniform?" As the lid was raised, Marie caught sight of a blue jacket with gold cording. There were swords and Dutch naval pistol. "Oh, please let me see that."

"Oh. Yes, we should start with that." Robin moved some maps aside and pulled out the blue Dutch Cavalry Captain's jacket. This one had gold shoulder boards and gold cording with red trim around the two rows of buttons that ran up either side of the chest. "This was for riding. With this lovely helmet. But the one you want to see is the dress uniform. This one." He laid the blue and red one on the bed and pulled out another blue one from the chest. This was a longer finer blue coat with white lining inside and white lapels that folded back on both sides with polished brass buttons. He pulled that one on over his shirt. "And of course…." He pulled out the big black hat and put that on as well. The hat was tall and narrow, coming to a point in the front and back. "This was worn with white shirt and the white trousers. My tassel needs to be ironed. It's supposed to stand straight up."

"If I hadn't lost my heart already, Robin, the sight of you in uniform would have surely done it." Marie touched his lapels and his shiny buttons.

He smiled and removed his giant hat. He set it aside and pulled out the two swords. "My cavalry sword. And this one, a ceremonial Mughal sword with ivory handle. That is from the tusk of an elephant."

"An elephant?" Marie was amazed, looking on and into the chest with wonder. "You can fight with a sword too then?"

"Ahm, yes. With either hand. Here, you may have this silk scarf from India." Robin knelt down before the open chest and handed her the blue silk with gold tassel trim.

"Robin," she sighed, feeling the silk in her hand and holding it against her cheek. "What is this called? The shine to it...."

"Silk. From the Orient to India and made into things like the lining of my coat." He went back to looking inside the chest for something, beneath other shirts and ties he would need for New York. He found a small jewelry box. Now he opened it to remove a gold cross pendant with a diamond in the middle. He placed this about Marie's neck. And then there was a ring. This ring had one large diamond and two smaller ones on either side.

"Are these...are these real?" Marie asked.

"These were my mother's. I remember them well. She was never without the cross pendant. My mother was very devout." Robin placed the diamond ring onto the middle finger of Marie's hand, beside her own wedding ring. "Your fingers are much more delicate and tiny. We can get this adjusted to fit any finger you wish. But I want you to wear these."

"But, but, Robin...are these diamonds?"

"Yes of course."

"You didn't sell them when you needed money?" Marie asked.

"My mother's jewelry stays in the family. I'd...eat one of those horses before I sold these," Robin said. "Klootzak first."

That made Marie laugh. "That tough bastard?"

Robin burst out laughing.

She admired the ring then. "Well, I can barely get a white glove on over this. But I suppose maybe I can pass for a lady."

"You've always been a lady," Robin said.

"What...what is this worth? I can't imagine." Marie sighed.

"Priceless, to me. If you are washing laundry you had better put it back in this box and keep it safe somewhere. In the nightstand perhaps," Robin said. "You can keep it in the safe."

"We should take the money and run away to Amsterdam," Marie blurted out.

"I'd be lying if I said I didn't dream about this."

"What is it like? Amsterdam?"

"It is a city of islands and canals. Here is a small painting of it. Fishing is the big industry. Banking center of Europe. Descendants of the Vikings you know? That's me." Robin pulled some things aside in the chest to reveal all the weapons lining the bottom. "My collection."

Mr. and Mrs. Van der Kellen walked out along the rock wall, leaving the house and courtyard behind, and walking out toward the rear of the estate. A rock wall divided one field from another. Robin carried over his shoulder a shovel and a rifle.

"Does this go all the way back to the family plot?" Robin asked.

"Yes. All the way even past that to the river," Marie told him. "You were at the Lees?"

"They're taking the cow while we are gone. Their bull will give her another calf. She will continue to give us milk when she comes back home to us."

"Oh. What did the note say?"

"Along the rock wall North to the star. When the star meets the wall and buried right below that," Robin said. "What do you suppose the star means?"

"I don't know." Marie laid her hand on Robin's back.

"That way is North. This is the only rock wall going North."

"It does go a long way. Maybe a mile or more," Marie said.

"Fine land for growing hay. Alfalfa it looks like." Robin noted. "If someone had the men to work it."

"Why would he hide anything out here?"

Robin turned and looked back at the house in the distance. "If the house burnt down, I suppose. He'd have to find a place where the stock men wouldn't have seen him burying something."

"And out here, it would seem he was walking back to your mother's grave," Marie said. "I'm sorry."

Robin nodded. "I saw their graves when I arrived in November, when I got us our first turkey. I just have not been back since. Looks like an old orchard."

"Yes. I picked apples last fall. Lots of them," Marie said. "That was the pie when you arrived."

"Great pie." Robin reached back to take her hand momentarily and then had to balance the rifle and shovel with both hands. "Watch yourself along these rocks. Rattlesnakes out here."

"Oh really?"

"With spring coming, they can lie among the rocks to warm up. Just watch every step, my love." Robin told her.

"Robin, the star!" Marie pointed.

Robin looked.

A revolutionary war star from the distant cemetery lined up directly over the corner of the rock wall.

"Along the rock wall North to the star and buried right below that," Robin said aloud.

They both looked at the ground in the corner of the wall and all of the leaves piled up there by the wind.

"Stand back. Watch for snakes. Just hold this. Don't shoot at any snakes or you'll shoot your husband." Robin handed the rifle to Marie and used the shovel to pull the leaves out, as she laughed. Once he'd cleared it, the corner had only bare ground and nothing growing in it, as if it had been dug out last summer. Robin began digging there. On his second push with the shovel, they heard the clunk of metal on wood. There were no trees overhead. It couldn't be tree roots. Robin kept digging until he uncovered the top of an ornate wooden box. He kept digging carefully to free it.

And when he pulled out the box, it was nearly a foot square and four inches deep. "I know this. The family bible was in this. I found the bible in the library and wondered why it was out of its box. Marie, you see your cross pendant fits into the cover, right here."

"It does." Marie knelt down beside him on the ground.

"The key!" Robin suddenly realized he had the mysterious key from the safe in his holster. "Now I know what it goes to." Robin opened the latch and raised the lid. The box was full of gold and silver coins. He pulled out a handful. "Dutch."

"This is a US dollar." Marie grabbed one coin. "More dollars. And this." She held out a gold pocket watch.

Robin took the watch. "This is my father's. I do believe he hid some of his own things in here. I was starting to think he was buried with this."

"I guess he didn't trust us to give it to you. How did you get your mother's ring and the cross?"

"He had them delivered to me in Boston, years ago. Her wishes, I imagine," Robin said. "Well, let's search the ballroom and find the last one."

Chapter Eleven Cabin 12

April 27, 1840

The train arrived, belching smoke and steam so loudly that Marie covered her ears with both hands. Robin put an arm around her. Passengers disembarked and porters hopped down. Robin and Marie waited, standing beside four bags and a trunk of theirs, not his VOC trunk but another. "Stay calm darling. We'll be attended."

They were in an area of the platform exclusively for well-dressed passengers and their baggage. The men all had black top hats, overcoats and suits. The women had wide skirts of various colors and furs. Some women had fur shawls and muffs. Marie saw the glint of white gloves on these women around her.

Further down the train platform, Marie could see women dressed more like she had been in the kitchen, in gray broadcloth skirts and knit shawls, holding hands with children or carrying babies on their hips. The men down there wore hats of all sorts but not like Robin's black silk top hat.

Soon a porter stepped up to them. "Your name sir?"

"Van der Kellen."

"Ah yes. I have you right here. I'll take your bags. It will be a few moments. If you want to get a coffee inside, I will come round you up."

"You'll remember who we are?" Robin put a tip into his hand.

"Oh yes sir. I'll remember her."

Robin grinned. "Come on, Marie. We have time for a coffee."

"Well, what did he mean by that?" Marie whispered into Robin's shoulder, following him through the crowd of black suits and top hats and the wide skirts of women passengers.

Robin escorted Marie into the train station and into the café.

"Yes, sir. What can I do for you? Are you on that ten o-clock train?" the host asked.

"Yes. We were told to wait here," Robin said.

"It's running late. Right this way to a first-class table, sir and madame. Would you like coffee or tea while you wait? Totally complementary. The train will be a bit late as she must take on water before she leaves for New York. Going to New York are you? Never been there myself."

Robin and Marie were seated at a white linen table near the windows, in the sunlight. "Coffee. Would you have any sandwiches?"

A waiter quickly served them coffee and cookies. "Coming right up, sir."

Marie looked about. They were surrounded on this level by the fancy dressed people while clearly separated by a division and on a lower level were the regular people, as Marie decided to call them. "People are looking at us."

"No, they're not. They're looking at me. It's the hat," Robin said.

"Robin, every man here has the same hat."

"You are gorgeous. Stop worrying darlin." Robin sat back in his top hat and picked up his china cup of coffee. "It will be a long time until lunch. You need to eat something here."

"I fit in all right?" Marie asked him.

"No, you don't," Robin said.

"What? They can tell?"

Robin crossed his legs beside the small table and sat back with a wry smirk. "You stand out among all these mules in corsets. I'll keep saying it all day, if I must."

She finally laughed. "You can't possibly be hungry already."

Robin, in his fine black suit and silk top hat, held onto Marie's hand as she stepped up onto the luxury sleeper car. Marie pulled up her skirts with her other hand. She had to release Robin's to take the handrail and climb up in her new boots, navy blue dress, and Robin's mother's coat with fur collar.

Inside, a rail porter took Marie's hand and assisted her on board.

Robin bounded up the steps to join her.

"Right this way, Mr. and Mrs. Van der Kellen. Your luggage is already in your cabin." The porter led them down the carpeted hallway along one side of the train car. To their left were the private cabins of the guests. He led them down to #12 and pulled back the wooden pocket door. "Number 12 will be yours for the two-day journey to New York and I will be your porter. The dining car is right forward of this one. Gentleman's smoking car is two cars behind this one. Lady's water closet is in the front of each car and gentlemen's is in the back. Your champagne is chilling on ice for you. Would you like me to open it for you, sir?"

"Yes, thank you very much." Robin slipped him another silver coin. Robin removed his top hat and gloves. The porter hung his topcoat on a hook beside the pocket door and then the fine silk top hat beside it.

"Thank you, sir. I will open the bottle now then. The train shall be leaving the station shortly. Please use care when stepping across to the next car."

Marie entered the cabin to find a built-in couch to the left and to the right bunk beds, larger one below and narrower one above. Their luggage was visible beneath the couch and in the small closet at the far end of the bunk beds. Marie judged that the lower bed was probably large enough for the two of them to snuggle up in. The upper bunk could be folded up and stored away. Above that was a row of narrow windows and above that a curved lime green ceiling. Woodwork was a glossy dark oak. She strolled over to look inside the closet at her gowns already hanging with Robin's suits. Toiletries were provided along with towels, robes, and extra blankets. Three large windows lined their cabin, one along the lower bunk, one at the couch, and one in between. The carpet was a lush dark green. Cushions were green.

Robin helped her off with her fur collar coat and the porter hung this beside Robin's.

Along the windows of the seating area at their own private bar, the champagne was opened and poured into two glasses. "Lunch will be at 1:00 today. Dinner will be served at eight. I will come around with a knock to announce it. My cabin is in the rear of this car should you need anything at any hour, Mr. Van der Kellen. Thank you." The porter bowed and exited, closing their pocket door.

Marie gleamed at him. "I never saw such a thing. I feel like I'll be thrown off the train as a stow away."

"Nonsense, Mrs. Van der Kellen. I've only spent my own money on this. Nothing from the treasury yet." Robin looked around and drew his pistol from the coat pocket and laid it on the bar.

"Treasury?" Marie strolled toward him.

Robin offered a short flat champagne glass to her.

Marie removed her white gloves and laid them on the bar. "Look at this. Actual ice. I never saw that except for in the winter, and in places you don't want it." She accepted the glass and a kiss on the mouth from him.

Robin unbuttoned his jacket and picked up his glass. He pulled out his gold pocket watch and checked the time.

"You looked just like this when you arrived back in November," Marie suddenly realized. "I could barely speak to you. You were so handsome, almost unreal, and I don't think you even noticed me."

"Oh, I noticed you." Robin tapped his glass lightly to hers, making them ring. "The girl with authority."

"The kitchen witch." Marie held her glass up to him. "Robin, something is wrong with this wine. It is boiling."

"Oh darlin, this wine has a second fermentation. It bubbles. It's nice and cold, I assure you," Robin explained. "It was on ice."

"Well, I don't know what any of that means."

"It means those bubbles will go straight to your head if you don't drink it slowly. It's a delicacy from France."

Robin stepped across the gap between train cars and turned to find Marie backed against the other car, looking down at the gap and rushing tracks beneath them. He extended his hand to her. "Marie, take my hand, look at me and just step across."

It was windy and loud between cars. Marie was hesitant to let go of the door behind her.

"Trust me again. I won't let you fall," Robin said. "Lift your skirts so I can see your feet. Higher. No, higher."

"Robin!"

He laughed.

Marie put her hand in his. Her other hand gripped her skirts out of the way.

Robin pulled her across as she shrieked into his arms, making him laugh.

She clung to him. "Stop laughing. I've never been on a train before."

"Lots of firsts this week." Robin grinned.

"More than I care to tell you."

Robin laughed and opened the door to the dining car. "You're very brave, darling." He and Marie entered laughing, drawing glances from other passengers. He offered his arm to steady her on the moving train.

"Right this way, Mr. and Mrs. Van der Kellen." The server showed them to a table for two.

Robin let Marie take the seat facing forward on the train. He was perfectly content to sit backwards.

As Marie looked around, they may have actually been better dressed than most. She saw other ladies remove their white gloves. So, she pulled off hers and put them in her lap. The couple at the next table were drinking wine already at lunch. All of the gentlemen wore top hats similar to Robin's. It was the first time she noticed Robin's hat had a tiny gold VOC pin in the band.

Marie smiled. "Is that a hat pin? Your Dutch East India Company pin?"

Robin sat back and his knee met hers beneath the table. He smiled. "It is a cuff link which I lost the mate to."

"Very clever use of it then," Marie said. "Wait a minute. You lost a gold cuff link? It is gold isn't it?"

"I wasn't always mindful of such things."

The train came to a stop then.

The dining car was lushly appointed in velvet curtains, tapestry on the ceiling, built in tables draped in fine white linens. The tables were set with gold trimmed china, polished silverware, and short flower vases. The glassware, most of it not stemware, but if it had a stem it had a wide base to hold it steady on a moving train. Small silver salt and pepper shakers were on each table. And the tables were a mix of seating for two or four depending on which side of the train they were on.

"Why have we stopped, Robin?" Marie asked softly.

"To take on more water and coal for the engines. They time the meals to occur when we're stopped. It's no doubt easier to transport meals from the kitchen car," Robin said.

Robin and Marie were served chilled white wine and several courses of lunch. Marie was looking to Robin for which piece of silverware to use for each course. Soup. Salad. Braised beef and vegetables. But by the time she finished her small glass of wine, after the champagne in their cabin, her cheeks were flushed and she giggled at everything he said. Then their glasses were refilled.

Before she touched her glass, Robin put his hand over the rim of hers. "Slow it down, love. I'll be carrying you back to our cabin."

Marie nodded. "Robin, this is what you were accustomed to? No wonder my cooking and my table was such a disappointment."

Robin reached across and took her hand into his. "I couldn't afford this lifestyle then. My disappointment was no reflection on you, darlin. Are you all right? The motion of the train does not bother you?"

"No. I'm fine," she said.

"You tell me if it does." Robin crossed his legs beneath the table and sat back, sipping his wine. "If this whole trip does not make you feel sick, then we can think about a trip to Amsterdam."

"Really?"

"Six weeks at sea. It's a long time," Robin said.

"How often does your sister write?"

"My sister Mila writes a couple times a year. She tells me that Robert and his wife have two children. She has three. Our younger sister Tess has one," Robin said. "They don't know our father has passed yet. I wrote them as soon as I was notified, but it will take at least three months for my letter to reach them and Mila to write back."

"Do you think any of them will come to see you in America?"

Robin shook his head. "The only one who could, would be Robert and he is a doctor. Amsterdam civilization would collapse without the good Doctor Van der Kellen."

"Robin, there is nothing keeping me here, you know?"

Robin looked down at the table, thoughtfully.

"My place is wherever you go. Robin, how did you know what the ancient Egyptians used honey for? In school in the Netherlands?"

Robin shook his head. "In the infirmary in India, trying to save my friend. He'd been attacked by a tiger. He didn't last more than four days. There was an Egyptian doctor."

"Your friend, what was his name, dear?"

"Liam. He died at 21 years old. Eight in the morning. October the first, 1824. We enlisted together."'

"I'm terribly sorry."

"Anyway, let's change the subject."

"Sir, Mr. Van der Kellen, would you care to join us in the smoking car?" One of the other gentlemen offered after dinner.

"I appreciate the offer but I do not smoke," Robin said.

"Then come along for the brandy."

"That I would enjoy, however, my wife and I have only been married for three days," Robin said.

After a moment, the dining car cheered and laughed. "We have newlyweds among us."

Robin and Marie blushed.

"You'll be wanting to get back to your cabin then," the gentleman said.

"We'll have a drink to you sir."

"You'll be having a better night than us."

"Not much room to maneuver in these bunks. Watch your head, young man."

"We'll have extra coffee for you in the morning."

"Don't embarrass the young lady," one of the wives scolded.

They had half a bottle of champagne to enjoy back in their cabin. And they enjoyed it, curled up in the bed together in blissful post-intimacy. "Is the window cold?"

"Not with all the wine I've had." Marie slid her bare legs beneath the blanket and quilt anyway, and pulled the sheet up over her sleeping gown.

Robin was sitting up against the headboard, shirtless, in only just his undergarment. He sipped his champagne and rested his head back. It was dark out as the train traveled along. Few if any lights from passing streets could be seen. One oil lamp was lit in their cabin and it was affixed on the bar.

"Are you? What are you looking at?" Marie quickly closed up the neck of her gown. "My chest?"

Robin smiled. "I'm satiated not blind. You wish me to climb up above to sleep? I'm perfectly willing to do so."

"Not on your life." Marie giggled into her glass. "Don't make me climb up there with you."

There wasn't a lot of room for them. Their hips were almost side by side. The bunk was just barely long enough for Robin to stretch out and that was only because he was not a tall man.

"Unless you need to roll around to sleep," Marie added.

"Are you saying I roll around a lot?"

"You don't know? Robin, you wake up on the opposite side of the bed, don't you?"

He laughed. "Maybe you climbed over me. I don't know."

Marie stroked a hand down his bare chest.

"Where am I going to put my gun? It's always to my left beside the bed," Robin said. "I have nothing but aisle here."

"Put it right above you on the bunk, perhaps."

"I suppose that is the best option," Robin said. "Marie, I need to teach you about weapons. You are not to ever touch that gun until I do teach you. It is loaded, you know? It is deadly."

"I would never."

"Pick it up wrong and you could fire it."

"I won't touch it."

April 28. 1840

"Won't you join us, young newlyweds? You must be due for conversation with someone other than yourselves," An older gentleman said, making the dining car laugh.

Though there were empty tables beaconing them, Robin nodded. "Thank you, sir."

A server held out the chair beside the window, across from the young woman for Marie.

Marie sat and was pushed forward.

Robin sat beside her, across from the older gentleman.

The woman and Marie looked to be about the same age.

Tea was served to them with biscuits and fruit.

Marie looked for a moment at all of the silverware with a bit of a panic. Which spoon to sugar her tea?

The woman across from her laughed. "I'm Elizabeth. I had to learn all those quickly or my husband would slap my hand at the table." She demonstrated which spoon with her own tea.

Marie smiled shyly.

Robin examined the man, who was probably sixty or more in age. "I am Robin Van der Kellen and this is my wife, Marie."

"Fine pleasure to meet you. Edward Miller and my wife Elizabeth," the man said.

Robin perfectly buried his surprise at their obscene age difference. "The pleasure is ours."

"And what brings you to New York? Is it business then? Or do you reside there, Mr. Van der Kellen?" Edward questioned.

"Ahm, business. I am a barrister in Boston. And I thought Marie would enjoy her first trip to New York," Robin said.

"Oh, how wonderful. You shall love all the shops and the theater and the museums," Elizabeth said enthusiastically. "All though of course Boston has all of those as well. These will be different."

"Barrister? A lawyer then. Do you research or argue cases in court?" Edward asked.

"Both, I'm afraid. I'm not part of a large firm but rather independent," Robin said.

"I suppose that gives you autonomy then, doesn't it?" Edward said. "Your accent would have you originating abroad."

"Amsterdam."

"And how long have you been in the new world?"

"Five years," Robin said.

"Edward, stop interrogating him. His tea is getting cold." Elizabeth and Marie giggled quietly.

Robin smiled and sampled his tea.

"Robin is an unusual name," Elizabeth said. "How did you meet your husband, Marie?"

Robin inhaled.

Marie took a moment to unfold her napkin in her lap. "He rescued me from a thief. Robin was once a soldier."

Elizabeth sighed.

"Where did you serve then Robin?" Edward asked.

"In the Royal Dutch cavalry, from the age of 18 to 23," Robin said.

Marie tried some of the fruit, blue berries, and candied pears. She couldn't contain a look of excitement at Robin.

She felt his hand on her thigh beneath the table, tapping on her.

His hand being absent from the tabletop was of notice to Edward, highly improper, and amusing.

"Dutch cavalry. You would know horses so well then. Was it horses that drew you into the cavalry or weaponry?" Edward asked.

"Both, I confess. I grew up on a horse farm," Robin said. "Competition rider in my formative years."

"You're traveling from Boston to New York? How did you get here then?" Edward asked. "You were not on the Worchester train."

"Oh, I moved from Boston to Canterbury this past fall," Robin explained. "We boarded in New Haven."

"That explained why we did not see you on the Norwich and Worcester Rail," Edward said. "We have made our way from Boston like grasshoppers. Norwich to Lyme. Stagecoach to New Haven. Avoiding the steamer ships, you know? Trying out the new form of transportation. Do you have a place to stay in New York?"

"I thought I would get a hotel near the station," Robin said.

Elizabeth looked urgently at her husband, tugging on his coat.

"I won't hear of it. You must stay with us. We can't have newlyweds staying in a hotel, and by the train station no less. Trains will keep you up all night and the smoke will permeate your room," Edward said. "Elizabeth would very much enjoy Marie's company."

"I would very much love to converse with a woman my own…age," Elizabeth said cautiously. "And you'll have all the privacy you wish in our guest wing. Come and go as you wish or join us for supper. When Robin is working we can get our hair done and go to the theater together."

Marie was smiling.

"Well, there you have it. It seems the ladies have decided it," Edward said. "What say you, sir?"

"I don't wish to impose," Robin said. "I am very flattered by such a generous invitation."

"No imposition whatsoever," Edward said. "When we depart the train you shall be our guests. It will be very amusing to me to hear about your campaigns in the Dutch cavalry, and equally delightful to send Beth out of the house with someone her own age."

"I will accept your generous invitation if only to keep Marie safe and accompanied while I investigate my case," Robin said. "I was afraid to leave her alone in the hotel."

"Oh, she won't be alone," Elizabeth said. "She will be with me the whole time."

"I would love that," Marie said. "If I must be apart from him for even a moment."

The girls giggled.

Robin raised an eyebrow and all of that made Edward laugh.

Marie was invited into Edward and Elizabeth's cabin, # 9, with the young Mrs. Miller while all the gentlemen retreated to the smoking car.

Elizabeth poured them glasses of wine.

Marie sat on their sofa, noticing both of their bunks had blankets turned down.

"Marie, tell me how Robin rescued you? Was it very dangerous?" Elizabeth questioned.

"Oh. Robin pulled him off me and tossed him away. Then he disarmed him and ran him off by pistol," Marie said. "I was in great danger."

"Off of you? How did you not faint?"

"Well Robin returned to me and I just threw myself into his arms. I never felt so safe in my life as in his arms," Marie said.

"I'm certain of it. He is so handsome, Marie. You are a lovely couple."

"How did you come to be married to Edward?"

"You mean because he's so much older than I? It was arranged. I was to inherit quite a lot and my parents feared a young man would squander the family fortune. Edward is a very smart banker. Very kind and well meaning. I just tire him with my childish chatter, as he calls it. I am so delighted to talk with a woman my own age," Elizabeth said. "Do you know much about your husband's business?"

"No. He's sworn to secrecy on his cases."

"How exciting. And is he passionate? Have you yet? Or is he being patient?"

Surprised, Marie sipped her wine first. "Elizabeth, you know, we could not wait. He is very passionate."

Elizabeth said, "Call me Beth. I'm afraid I've never known what it's like with a young man. I won't tell anyone. How does he make it known to you that he wants it?"

Marie blushed. "I'm afraid I may need to finish this glass to be bold enough to say."

Beth brought the bottle over. "Please do, Marie. I do hunger for details. Was he your first? I'll bet you didn't know *that* was going to happen, did you? I sure didn't. Was he gentle enough? I'll bet he was so romantic."

That evening late, Robin slid open their pocket door and fell in, spilling onto the floor.

Marie got up from their bed and hurried to him. "Robin, are you all right?"

He sat up, leaning on his hand. "The train jolted there. No, that's … not quite right. I'm afraid they've gotten me a bit drunk though I tried to stop them."

"You didn't try very hard." Marie laughed then. She pulled his boots in and shut the door. "You smell like smoke. Were you smoking too?"

"No, of course not. Well, perhaps a little."

Marie took him by the arm and pulled him up onto the sofa. "Did they know you were this drunk?"

"I dare say the old married men thought it amusing to intoxicate the newlywed," Robin blurted out. "They just kept pouring."

"And it would be rude not to drink it, I suppose." Marie laughed. "Here. Get out of your jacket."

"Well, it would be. I'm sorry, darling. I just haven't been a real gentleman in so long. I suppose I needed that," Robin admitted as she pulled his jacket down off his shoulders and freed his arms. "Where is my coat going? Marie, my gun is in the…"

"I can hang this on the door and they will clean the smoke out of it by morning," Marie said. "You're sitting on it. Raise up that backside of yours."

Robin did so and she took the coat. She carefully removed the pistol with two fingers by the handle and carried it to the upper bunk. Then she hung the jacket on a hanger outside the pocket door.

"Hope we didn't get him in too much trouble with the wife," said a gentlemen in passing.

Robin laid back on the sofa, laughing.

She closed it again.

She pulled off his boots and he curled up there on his side. Marie got a blanket from the upper bunk, beside the pistol, and covered him with it where he was. She brought him a pillow and Robin kissed her, giggling.

April 29, 1840

"Whatever did you discuss with Elizabeth all evening?" Robin shook a packet of hangover remedy into his tea the next morning. He stirred it in and shaded his eyes from the window as he drank it. "And how the hell did I get across two train cars last night? They must have carried me."

Marie giggled.

"What?" Robin asked.

"She wanted to know what you're like in bed. Were you being patient or had we been together yet."

Robin coughed on his tea and brought a napkin to his mouth. "Females."

"What did you talk about over brandy and cigars?"

"War in India and all the exotic scantily dressed prostitutes that hung around the troops," Robin replied.

"Prosti…." Marie brought a hand to her mouth.

"Never touched one. Don't worry," Robin assured her. "Syphilis was never anything I wanted. She asked what I am like in bed?"

"She's married to a man who could be her grandfather. Can't blame her for curiosity."

"Has she done it with him? Poor girl," Robin said. "How am I to make eye contact with this girl now?"

"I only told her romantic things, not what you have in your trousers," Marie said. "Not that she didn't want to know. Trust me you can meet her eyes today."

"That is a relief."

"The wealthy are so very blunt, Robin. Far more so than we are," Marie said.

"Yes, they are. You almost have to be just to fit in. You know we never rehearsed what we would say when asked how we met. You did a very fine job on the spot there," Robin told her. "You're a very quick thinker, and a bit of a cool liar. I shall have to mind that in the future."

Marie smiled. "I'm a terrible liar. That's why I told the truth. I only omitted everything I had to."

Robin grinned. "Is that the trick to it? I shall make note of that, when my head stops splitting."

"Are you certain you want to stay with the Millers? You're not doing this just for me?" Marie questioned.

"I am doing it for you but I had a long talk with Edward last night, before I got drunk. And I may need to talk with some of his contacts in the banking industry. Depends on where my case leads me. There is ah…a gentleman's agreement that it would be rude of me to refuse such a generous invitation."

"So how…how do we handle this? How do I behave?" Marie asked.

"No doubt, many things will surprise us both in the Miller's house. They're very wealthy. Don't comment on it. Just go along. Be yourself, of course. Have a wonderful time with Elizabeth."

Adam Hudson

Chapter Twelve Cursed Money

April 29, 1840

Edward Miller's carriage was a large elaborate black brougham with two Percheron draught horses, two drivers, and seating inside the carriage for six people. That made plenty of room for trunks and bags up top and in the boot and a few inside on the floor. Edward and Elizabeth sat backwards, allowing their guests to sit facing them and take in the city view through the windows.

While Elizabeth and Marie chatted, Edward asked, "Is this your first visit to New York, Robin?"

"No, I have tried some cases here," Robin said. "Half a dozen times perhaps. Different courts. Traveled by steamer though."

"I stopped taking the steamer after what happened to the Lexington. Besides now the train goes all the way through to Boston," Edward said. "Almost."

"What is the Lexington?" Robin glanced out the windows as the tall buildings passed and carriages passed.

"Steamer boat out to Boston. It burned and sunk recently. Only six people survived. I won't get on one of those death traps ever again," Edward said. "I was fortunate the fire of '35 didn't burn down my house. It took most of the financial district. You will find everything new down there."

"I was there a year after. There was much rebuilding still going on." Robin nodded.

"Is the language ever a problem for you? You seem quite fluent."

"Some phrases catch me up. I might take a moment to do the translation. I still think in Dutch. Customs are different. I find that more of a problem." Robin crossed his legs comfortably and found Elizabeth looking at him.

"I do too, even going to Boston or Philadelphia. They don't like a tall hat in Philadelphia. It's a smaller one I wear there," Edward said. "Your suits are from Amsterdam then? Very fine tailoring."

"Not all of them. Some I had made in Boston. But this one is one of my favorites from overseas," Robin said.

The carriage entered through an ornate iron gate and beneath a stone arch to park in the courtyard of a New York marble mansion. It was nearing sunset and the courtyard was lit with gaslights. Windows surrounding the courtyard were welcoming with lamplit rooms inside.

A butler came down the steps to meet the carriage. "Welcome home, sir."

"Run inside and tell them to open the guest wing. We have brought friends from Connecticut."

"Oh delightful. How many rooms, sir?"

"Just the one on the corner and tell the cook as well," Edward said out the open carriage door.

"And tell the maid they are newlyweds. Make it extra special," Elizabeth called.

Other staff members came out to collect bags and trunks. They immediately recognized and sorted which belonged in the mansion and which were new.

Edward stepped out first and held out his hand for his wife. Elizabeth gathered her skirt tight and climbed down. Then Edward said, "Marie, take my hand. Watch your step here."

Robin picked up his top hat and put it on his head. He also grabbed his briefcase.

Marie was assisted to the cobblestone entry to five steps up to the entrance of the Miller's three-story wrap around mansion. She looked up at the wrought iron and glass portico above her head and the gaslights on either side of the stairs.

Elizabeth took Marie's hand even as she gave instructions to the staff. But she paused verbally and physically to watch Robin emerge from the carriage, ducking his hat out the door as he stepped down, and then standing up straight beside Edward. Robin moved with such balance, confidence, and athleticism. He stood there, as tall as Edward, sporting the three-piece black European suit with tails.

"We'll have your room ready for you momentarily, as soon as we get your things upstairs," Jonas, the butler said.

"Marie, would you like them to prepare a hot bath for you before dinner? I always love that following travel. It's so dusty on the road,"

Elizabeth said. "We can set you up in a guest room beside mine for that."

"Robin, a few drinks in the parlor while they prepare your room?" Edward offered.

"I would be delighted." Robin held out his arm for Marie and she linked onto him to climb the stairs together. "Go ahead, Marie. Indulge yourself."

Two grand iron and glass doors were opened and guests passed into the marble entry. Robin gave Marie a kiss on the mouth before she hurried off with Elizabeth up the winding stairway, leaving a crew of household staff to swoon.

Edward led Robin down the hall, around a corner and into a pre-Victorian parlor. "I've never seen Beth so happy. She really enjoys the friendship with your wife, young man."

"I'm delighted they have made friends." Robin removed his hat and ran a hand up through his hair.

The valet, a young man of Marie's age, held out both hands to take Robin's coat and hat. He gathered the wool coat over his arm and held the silk top hat. "Thank you, sir." He turned to collect Edwards, but watched Robin unbuttoning his suit jacket.

"This is Adam, my valet. Let him be of service to you, Robin." Edward then followed the butler Jonas toward into the salon, giving a few instructions to him before pouring glasses of liquor for Robin and himself. "Adam, give your special attention to our guest."

"Yes, sir," Adam said.

"Thank you." Robin accepted the glass. He sniffed it. He tasted it. "Aren't you afraid to have this in your possession?"

Edward looked at him.

Robin tasted it once more. "Isn't this illegal?"

Edward burst out laughing. "Hush. Yes, I do have a stash of illegal scotch. I didn't think you were a prohibitionist. How did you know?"

"I know something aged in a charred oak wine barrel," Robin said. "It does not come from Kentucky."

Edward laughed. "In my defense, I purchased a supply of it in France. I bring it out for special occasions."

"Thank you for reminding me the British make two exceptional things," Robin said.

"Scotch and…what, sir?" Edward asked.

Robin set his briefcase down beside a mahogany sofa and matching table, out of the way. "Weapons."

Edward tapped his glass to Robin's. "Your wife will be upstairs for a while. At last, you can tell me something about British weapons, such as that fine pistol that stuck out of your pocket on the train perhaps?"

"Would you like to see it?" Robin asked.

"I would be thrilled to perhaps even hold it in my hand," Edward admitted.

Robin picked up the briefcase and opened it on the chair. He drew out the pistol with care. "Do you know pistols, Edward?"

"I have a lovely collection of dueling pistols and I recently acquired a Colt revolver," Edward said.

"A revolver? I would love to see that some time." Robin held out his pistol in both hands. "This is loaded, Edward. I would caution you not to pull the hammer back or place a finger into the trigger just in case. And never point a pistol in any direction where a person is standing, even through a wall."

Edward only looked at the weapon. "You are speaking to a man who did plenty of hunting in his younger years."

"I meant no offence. That was my military training spilling out, I assure you." Robin said and they both laughed together. "Feel the spectacular balance of it."

The pistol was placed into Edward's open hands and he marveled over it. "Tell me, how did you get a British pistol?"

Robin lowered his voice. "I had fired my rifle and pistol already. This was aimed at my face. The colonel did not expect me to attack him, as if all that gold cording and brass would dissuade me. I cut his throat with my bayonet and collected this pistol fast, before he hit the ground even. There can be a trigger reflex with death."

"Please take this back. My palms are sweating now," Edward urged.

Robin had the weapon then.

Edward patted him on the back. "I can't wait to get your opinion of my collection, Robin. What is it like to kill a man? Is it thrilling?"

"Thrilling? No. It's terrifying every time." Robin returned the pistol to his briefcase and set it on the floor again, between sofa and table where it could not fall over or be kicked. "Forgive me." Robin picked up his scotch and downed the whole thing.

"Oh, I'm right behind you." Edward guzzled his. "Another round?"

"Let us see that revolver?"

Robin was introduced to the corner guest bedroom while Marie was off in the other wing with Elizabeth. The luxury of the room was overwhelmingly like the home he grew up in. Pale blue flowers danced on wallpaper, curtains, and the bed covers. A royal blue carpet encircled the canopy bed. Sofas and fainting couches were either royal blue or pale gold. Gold framed paintings depicted pastoral lake scenes. The sounds of carriages and horses on the cobblestone street below were very faint and unobtrusive.

The formality of procedures flooded back to him just as the hot water filled a porcelain tub in the next room. And then the valet entered the bedroom.

He observed Robin Van der Kellen taking that pistol from his brief case and placing it on the left side nightstand beside the bed. The weapon was pointed away toward the window, lying on a white doily beneath a vase of cut yellow roses.

"My name is Adam. I shall quickly press a fresh suit for you, Mr. Van der Kellen. Would your suits be in the trunk then? I can do the unpacking and ironing." The valet was about twenty years of age and immaculately trimmed and dressed. His cheeks were flushed pink.

"No. Marie's dresses are in there. These bags have the suits. Prepare the black one and a white shirt, if you would please," Robin said. "It's in here, I believe."

"Right away, sir. Would you care for a haircut and shave?"

"Ahm…" Robin turned and considered the young man for a moment. "If you…if you gave me a haircut, what would you suggest?"

"Oh." Adam stepped around him to observe and even touch Robin's hair from behind. "Trim a couple inches off. Get it out of your eyes. Free up these curls and let it still long enough to be tied with a ribbon as it was when you arrived."

"You…saw when I arrived? I did have it tied back."

"That is the latest fashion. We don't want to ruin that." Adam's voice was a bit deep for one so young and waif-like in appearance. He spoke with an imposed professionalism that his blush contradicted. "Your sideburns are perfect. They just need a tiny trim but they perfectly frame such a handsome face, sir."

"Very well then. I'm afraid I have not had a proper haircut since I left Boston," Robin said. "I probably look as if I've been running with wolves."

"Oh. Six months at least, I would say. Has your valet left you?" And then Adam gave him a doubletake when the wolves comment sunk in. "Wolves?"

"You could say that. Yes."

"No valet? Well. Who prepares your suits? Polishes your boots?" Adam prepared his iron in the fireplace.

"Well, between myself and the maid...." Robin stammered.

"Maid? How can a woman know a thing about dressing a gentleman? After your bath then, I'll fix you right up. You'll be delighted. Wash your hair and I will cut it wet," Adam said. "Do you have shoes for dinner or want me to polish these boots?"

"You'll find shoes in with the suit."

"Very well then, sir. With pleasure, sir. I have some blacking for those boots as well."

Robin stepped into the adjoining bathroom and closed the door. Looking at the steaming warm tub, he unbuttoned his shirt down from the collar. There were towels, robes, slippers, shaving supplies. He undressed fully, placing his clothes on the dresser by the door. Then he stepped carefully down into the tub. On a table beside the tub, he found shampoo and soaps, and a vase with a pink rose in it. The soaps were arranged on a silver dish.

Robin ducked beneath the surface to wet down his hair. He then shampooed and rinsed. And he sat back in the hot water to wash his face and use a hand towel.

A knock on the door and then the valet reached in to take Robin's clothing and replace it with the black suit, white shirt, stockings, undergarment, and necktie. "Do you have enough towels, sir? Can I get anything else for you? Glass of wine perhaps? Whiskey?"

"No, thank you."

The valet shut the door and went back to unpacking and pressing the rest of Robin's clothing. Two maids began doing the same for Marie's, with one of them rushing off to bring the light blue dress and underthings over to the room where Marie would be dressing.

Robin enjoyed his hot bath for a while and then toweled dry and got dressed in everything but the jacket before he opened the door.

"Ready, sir?"

"Yes, please," Robin said, still buttoning his vest.

The valet happily entered with scissors and comb. "Sit in the chair, please, sir. This is my specialty. You shall be pleased, I think."

"I'm sure of it." Robin sat.

"My uncle was a barber. Trained me well. Would you like me to dry your hair after the trim? Straighten it or let it curl?" Adam offered a fresh towel to him and draping it about his shoulders. He began combing Robin's hair out over the towel. "You have very thick hair, Mr. Van der Kellen. Wonderful. Let me trim your sideburns as well."

"Whatever you think is best. How long until we are due downstairs?"

"An hour, sir. Plenty of time."

"Thank you, Adam. I apologize for how much work I've given you." Robin closed his eyes as the young man combed through his hair.

"My pleasure, sir. I haven't had this much fun in ages. Mr. Miller does not have much hair."

Robin laughed outright.

When Marie was brought to the guest room for the first time, she was wearing her light blue wedding gown, the nicest gown she had. Robin emerged from the bathroom in his black trousers and white shirt, his hair neatly trimmed to just his shoulders and bangs trimmed with a left side part. The valet lifted a jacket onto Robin and slid the necktie on beneath Robin's collar and began to tie it for him.

"Thank you, very much." Robin put a gentle tap to the valet's shoulder, and the young man backed off. Robin went to Marie in her wedding gown and took both her hands into his until the valet and two maids left them alone and closed their double doors.

Robin smiled warmly. "Good evening, Mrs. Van der Kellen."

Marie hugged him about the neck. "Robin this home is so beautiful. I love your hair, darling."

Robin embraced her. "Customs will no doubt be as strange to me as they may be to you. Just go along with it. Whisper into my ear if you have any trouble with anything, my dear."

"I've never had two maids tend to me in the bath before. One washed my hair for me. The other brought be wine. They did up my corset for me. And look, they pressed my dress already," Marie said into his ear.

"Excuse me. Did you say two maids helped you in the bath?" Robin said. "Did they…I mean, bathe you? Towel your body? Perfume you?"

She looked up at him. "I had no idea men thought such things."

"Good thing you cannot hear my unexpressed thoughts." Robin said. "Are you all right with everything?"

"I'm loving everything." Marie looked around the room. She noticed his pistol beside the bed. "I see you unpacked."

"You know what I find surprising? They gave us one room. I suppose it is because they know we are newlyweds," Robin said softly. "Unusual. Scandalous I should think."

"Oh? Elizabeth and Edward do have their own rooms," Marie said. "Hers is the most beautiful bedroom I have ever seen. She has a dressing room. She has a whole room of gowns and shoes alone. She said I may borrow whatever I like."

"I expected to have to sneak into my own wife's bed." Robin leaned in and kissed Marie on the mouth. "I suppose the entire house anticipates us conducting ourselves as newlyweds. Mmmm. You smell so lovely. Let us not disappoint."

"Robin, it took me ten minutes to get into this." Marie giggled, pushing his hands away from her buttons in the back.

"Really? Take me one minute to free you of it."

Robin took Marie's white gloved hand onto his arm and walked down the hallway toward the grand staircase.

"Which way?" Marie whispered, glancing at closed doors, paintings on the walls, Oriental vases on tables.

"I saw the dining room near the parlor."

"You forgot your hat," Marie said.

"No top hats at the table in a residence. I'm not sure about your gloves. Just do what Elizabeth does," Robin whispered. "Sorry, it was never lady's hands I was looking at."

"No doubt what you were looking at," Marie said.

Down the curved marble staircase they went.

They could hear activity below, staff setting up for dinner.

The butler was in the hallway, shooing the valet to leave them. "Ah, Mr. and Mrs. Van der Kellen. Allow me to show you to the dining room."

Adam lingered for a glimpse at Van der Kellen before retreating to the back rooms off the kitchen.

A grand table was set with linens, crystal, silver, and flower arrangements. A great fireplace was lit. Edward was pacing with glass of scotch in his hand. Servers were placing things on the table.

The walls were white with several lace covered windows, pastoral paintings, and wall sconces with lit oil lamps. The table had seating for 6 with extra chairs lining the room. An oriental rug covered most of the floor in the room.

Edward said, "Go up and tell Mrs. Miller to hurry it up. Come on in Marie and Robin. How is your room? Is there anything that you need?"

"Everything is wonderful," Robin said.

"Cocktail, sir?" the butler asked. He instructed a maid to send for Elizabeth.

"Ahm, scotch or brandy would be wonderful," Robin said. "Thank you."

The butler held out a chair at the table for Marie and she took her seat. "And may I get you a glass of wine, Mrs. Van der Kellen?"

"Yes, please."

Edward strolled over and took the head of the table.

The butler held out the other chair to Edward's left for Robin.

Robin sat down where instructed, across from Marie. "Thank you again, Edward, for accommodating us. This is most generous."

"My pleasure, dear Robin. I do apologize though for my wife's tardiness to dinner. It's her forte'."

Robin smiled.

Marie looked down the table to the other end, set obviously for Elizabeth but with an empty chair between them. She would seem to be so far away.

The butler served a crystal goblet of red wine to Marie and then a crystal and gold rimmed scotch glass to Robin. Then he stood back behind Edward awaiting instructions.

Edward sat back. "It is good to not be moving anymore. The train, you know?"

"Very much so."

Elizabeth made her entrance in a vibrant lemon yellow gown and diamonds about her neck. "I just couldn't make up my mind what to wear tonight."

"This is lovely," Marie told her, removing her gloves beneath the table when she saw Beth did not have any on. She pocketed hers.

The butler held the chair at the end for Elizabeth. "I'll get a glass of wine for you, Mrs. Miller."

"I'll have what Marie is having, Jonas." Elizabeth selected the chair next to Marie instead and pulled it out for herself. "Robin has had a haircut. Very handsome. Was everything to your liking then? Did Adam look after you?"

"Very much so," Robin said.

The maids rushed to gather Mrs. Miller's place setting and move it to where she was now seated.

Elizabeth smiled warmly at Robin and then at Marie. "You are the most lovely newlywed couple. We must drink a toast to you immediately and welcome you to our home."

Edward and Jonas exchanged a look.

Marie tried but did not enjoy an oyster. Robin enjoyed his with a horseradish sauce on them. Clam chowder was served in pewter crocks. Fresh peas from the South were bright green and crisp and drizzled with melted butter. French roasted duck was served with wild mushrooms, herbed mashed potatoes and gravy. When everyone was already stuffed, hot apple tarts with maple syrup and tiny assorted cakes were served for dessert.

The first morning in New York

Thursday, April 30, 1840

They toweled each other off from a shared bath and dressed together. Robin unfolded into Marie's hand thirty more dollars, in gold ten-dollar coins.

"And who am I supposed to murder?" Marie looked up at him.

Robin burst out laughing. "Dresses. Buy some dresses. At least three more and make certain one is an evening gown with shoes. You're going to need one tonight for dinner. He's inviting guests. Ask Elizabeth to take you. And Marie, keep your purse beneath your coat. You're in the big city. You and Elizabeth together look very wealthy. There are pick pockets even in the fine neighborhoods."

Marie slipped the money into her purse. "I will. I think that butler will be with us all day. You know I've never been to a city bigger than New Haven."

"You will have a wonderful time, I'm certain. Just don't ever say anything about my purpose here or how we really met. Not a word. Do you understand?" Robin said.

Marie nodded. "I won't betray us."

"It would all change if they knew. She may be your friend now, but she wouldn't if she knew. It's just the way they are. See how they treat their own maids and cooks. And don't challenge it," Robin said. "They may not even know their names. Please."

Marie wrapped her arms up about his neck. "I promise to be careful. And you be careful."

Robin slipped that gun into his briefcase before hugging her. "I'm always careful."

"Just like Edward. You talk as if the conversations of females simply doesn't interest you," Elizabeth said at breakfast downstairs.

"On the contrary," Robin said. "I'd much rather stay and hear about how good I am in bed."

Everyone laughed, especially Edward. Jonas, behind Edward burst out laughing.

"But one of us must go to work," Robin added, eyebrows raised.

"You must make use of my carriage and driver. He knows the city. He will take you to conduct your business," Edward said at breakfast. "I won't be needing it. My bank manager is taking me to see his accounts today."

"You are too kind, sir."

"Nonsense. You don't know how happy Elizabeth is," Edward said. "One thing you must learn, young man, is that if the wife is happy your life is in peace."

"I whole heartedly take your advice then, and your carriage." Robin folded up his napkin and set it on the table.

"He'll have you back here by five to get ready for dinner," Edward said.

Robin rose from the table. "Thank you ever so much."

"My pleasure."

Robin bent beside Marie to kiss her hand. "Have a wonderful day my love."

"Then let's be off, Marie. We will shop and have lunch and just enough time to catch a matinee at the theater. My yellow carriage will take us."

Robin was helped on with his overcoat at the door. He picked up his briefcase carrying the British pistol, put on his top hat, and left for the black brougham.

Stopping at Beth's home with their dresses and shoes, Beth handed to Marie a bottle of perfume. "For tonight, my dear."

"I couldn't."

"I bought it for you. You will melt his heart tonight with this," Beth told her. "And then you must tell me details. Is he working to make you with child? You know what I mean."

"Oh. Is there a way not to?"

"Of course. Do it with a man who is too old," Beth said. "How much I wanted children."

"I do not believe there is an age limit for a man," Marie said. "Tell me, how do I...prolong our times together?"

"Because you enjoy them?" Beth grabbed hands with her and whispered, "Are you as pleased as he ?"

"I could be if he could last just a little more," Marie whispered.

"Get on top."

"You're joking."

"Ride him like a stallion. He'll last longer," Beth said. "And when you've done it, let him."

Marie blushed. "I don't know if I'm so bold. It would shock him."

"In a good way."

"You're quite the match maker."

"Oh, on the way from the theater we shall stop in the lingerie shop. Then I am a match maker."

"That's not going to make him last longer."

"Is Mr. McCoy in? Do you hold the insurance policy for the East Fourteenth Street bank?" Robin asked.

"We used to. Who's asking?" A man behind a desk stood up.

"I'm Robin Van der Kellen." Robin removed his top hat and held it with his briefcase down in front of him.

"Good lord. You must be joking."

"Excuse me."

The man hurried to an office behind him, knocked and burst inside. In a moment another man emerged and walked up to Robin, looking him up and down. He extended a hand. "You're a relative of Willem Van der Kellen?"

"He was my father," Robin said, moving the briefcase to his left hand with the hat, and shaking the man's hand with his right.

"Come away from the windows. I mean, come into my office, sir."

Robin followed him into the office and the door was shut on them by the other man.

"Tea, sir? Whiskey?" The man's hands were shaking such that he had to put them into his pockets. "Absinthe? I know that's what I need right now," McCoy mumbled.

"I'd much rather get to the point. Absinthe? Seriously?"

"Sit." The man sat behind his desk. "I mean, please have a seat. I'm James McCoy. I met your father once. He was prosecuting attorney for the robber who cleaned that bank out and set it to fire."

"Yes, I know. I saw the location this morning. I was not aware it burned so thoroughly," Robin said.

"What can I do for you, sir?" McCoy said.

"I was hoping to see any bank records, such as what kind of currency it contained at the time of the robbery. Who invested in the bank? Who did the money belong to?" Robin said.

"I'm afraid all of that burned in the fire," McCoy said. "It cleared them right off the books with me, I'm afraid. Gone as if they never existed. Had hundreds of people here trying to trade in their bank notes. Half of them were obviously counterfeit, not even the right size and shape. One fellow had bank notes misspelled the bank's name. One had a note written for $5,000, as if anyone would believe that. I wrote your father about it. Gave out $72 in total to those who kept their broken bank notes. Other than that, I couldn't tell you who the investors were if I had to. Of course, you could run an advertisement in the paper. Every citizen in New York would suddenly have a fortune invested in the place or print counterfeit notes."

Robin nodded. "I'm certain. I read your letter to my father. That is how I found you."

"What is your interest, sir?"

"I have taken over my father's practice. I'm just wrapping up loose ends," Robin said. "What was my father's business here with you?"

"Looking for the same things you are. He was about to go to the jail and interview the robber. Pascal, I think his name was. He was just fishing for anything and I have no documents from the bank. I merely insured the business against a failure in the bond market. In fact, the bank had quite a lot invested in bonds on Wall Street. But the owner died in the fire."

"In the fire? I did not know that."

"Who do I give these bonds to?"

"I suppose I'll have to take them, until I find the rightful owners. Did he have any family?"

McCoy dug through his desk for a key to a safe behind him. Then he produced a dozen or so papers from a file inside it and they shook in his hand. He had to lay them on the table for Robin to pick them up. Robin studied McCoy before glancing over the bonds and dropping them into his briefcase.

"You might want to talk to the police. But the owner was inside during the robbery. I believe he was shot dead long before the fire. He was a Jew. You know, a Hebrew. Had no family here apparently."

Robin sat back and thought a moment. "Where did he live?"

McCoy began gathering other documents and items into a briefcase of his own, behind the desk. "Maybe they can tell you at the police station. I don't know what else I can tell you. When that bank burned, and Pascal died in jail, your firm's business ended here."

"So it seems." Robin stood up.

"I'm sorry I couldn't be more helpful." The man stuffed items from a desk drawer into his bag and closed it up as he stood.

"You have been very helpful. I thank you very much."

"Good day, sir."

Robin paused and really studied the man. "What are you withholding from me?"

"Nothing, sir. Of course, nothing."

"You seem about to flee, honestly. What is it?" Robin said.

"It's just that, sir, you have a lot of nerve coming in here this way, right through the front door and all."

"Excuse me?" Robin shot back.

"Well, you have all the money. I don't want to be seen meeting with you," McCoy said.

"What makes you say this?" Robin asked.

McCoy looked down and opened a desk drawer. He selected a folded newspaper and then handed it across the desk to Van der Kellen. "When Pascal the robber died, he said he gave all the money to your father. If I were you, I'd be catching a boat to Australia right now."

"Mr. McCoy, I have a legal obligation to return all of the bank money to the rightful owners. I'm merely trying to ascertain who they might be," Robin explained.

McCoy picked up his hat and coat. "Get the hell out of town, buddy. I know I am." He turned and hurried out the back door of his office, leaving Robin shaking his head.

Robin met his driver at the curb. "Take me to the nearest police station."

"Immediately, sir. Is there trouble?"

Robin patted him on the arm. "Of course not. I'm just investigating a crime.

Robin sat down in the back of the carriage, crossed his legs, and read the newspaper from some time ago. Then he exhaled, "Verdomd."

MORNING HERALD.

Cursed Money   November 4th, 1839, New York

Bank Robber Christian Pascal disclosed to lawyers' location of $2 million and all died suddenly.

On his death bed in jail, trial about to commence, Pascal confessed to the robberies and fires at three banks. Two banks were in the city and one in Norwich, Connecticut. His court appointed defender Thomas Albertson immediately was joined at the cell by prosecutor Willem Van der Kellen of Canterbury, Connecticut. Confession was heard by both. The sum from the three banks estimated to be in great excess of $2 million in total and location of which was divulged to both lawyers. Before Pascal could name his accomplices, he passed away from his gunshot wound. The trial would not resume.

Lawyer Thomas Albertson was shot dead in the street outside his home. It has recently been learned that Willem Van der Kellen also passed away in

Canterbury. It is not known his cause of death or if the money has been in fact, found.

By Susan Eddy

"Here you are, sir. The police station. It's very busy I can't stay here long," the driver called down to Robin, who was stepping out of the carriage already.

"Meet me round the corner then. Up there," Robin said and was suddenly knocked flat on the sidewalk by a man. He grabbed up Robin's briefcase and took off running. Fortunately for Robin, he ran directly into two policemen.

Robin was helped to his feet by the officer with his case. His hat was handed to him.

Robin's driver was out of his carriage immediately to offer assistance.

Robin brushed off his pants and jacket. "I'm fine. Thank you." He accepted the briefcase back.

They could see the officer hand cuffing and bringing the assailant back toward them.

"Do you wish to press charges, sir? We saw the whole thing."

"Of course, I do. I won't stand for this sort of thievery," Robin said. "I want to know who he is and what he's after."

The man was dragged up to him and held there in front of Robin.

"We are going forward with robbery and assault charges," one cop said to the other.

"Well arrest him then for robbing a bank," the man said, pointing at Robin.

The police looked at Van der Kellen in his three-piece tailored suit and silk top hat and laughed out loud. "Get on inside then you thief. Log him in. Sir, please come along and we'll get you cleaned up."

Robin was ushered into an office and handed a cup of tea while the other man was locked into a holding cell and searched.

"Are you all right, sir?" A secretary offered him a napkin and dabbed it to his chin.

Robin didn't realize he'd scraped his chin on the stone walk. He padded it and saw a bit of blood on the napkin. "Thank you. I'm all right." He sat down and held the cloth to his chin. He drank some of his tea before the two officers came into the room with him and sat down.

"How are you, sir?"

"I'm fine, yes. Thank you. Who is he?"

"What is your name, sir?"

"Robin Van der Kellen. Barrister at law," Robin said. "State of Massachusetts in the US and in Amsterdam, the Netherlands. I am legal in New York."

One of the cops nodded. "You're in danger sir. Are you working for your father, I assume, Willem Van der Kellen?"

"In a way. My father has died and I am wrapping up his cases," Robin said.

"What is in the bag there? The one this man tried to steal?"

"Documents involving a bank robbery, the East Fourteenth Street Bank. My father prosecuted the bank robber a Mr. Pascal, who died before his trial. I was hoping to discuss the case and testimony with you," Robin said.

"We know the fellow who flattened you on the street. We've been after him for some time," The cop said. "He is Pascal's partner. A Malcom Benedetti."

"I've never heard of him. Pascal had a partner? Even my father didn't know," Robin said.

"Benedetti said you have all the money from the robbery, all $2 million worth."

Robin nearly spilled the last of his tea. He rattled the cup down into the saucer onto their desk. "What? If I had that would I be here?"

They laughed. "If there was that much involved, we'd be searching for it ourselves."

"There wasn't that much in a dozen New York banks. Don't be ridiculous," Robin said.

The cops laughed. "So true, sir. May we have your signature on these arrest forms? We're going to escort you home and post a guard watch."

"One more thing." Robin pulled out that newspaper and slapped it down on the desk. "How did a confession to one's attorney end up on the front page of a newspaper? Did your guard sell the story? They did everything but print my address with a map and a big X to mark the location of two million dollars."

"Oh. Saw that did you?"

"Yes, I bloody well saw it. Thanks, a fucking lot. Where can I find the partner of barrister, excuse me, lawyer Thomas Albertson? They were the defending law firm who got the confession."

"Certainly. I can get you that."

Marie walked out of art store with Elizabeth and the butler trailing behind them. "Beth, I don't know what to do."

"About what, darling?" Elizabeth joined arms with her as they walked along the sidewalk.

"Robin gave me money for the dresses but your butler paid for everything. Now, what do I do?" Marie whispered. "He even paid for the cartography tools."

"Don't give it a thought. I never do." Elizabeth shrugged. "When Jonas comes along, he pays. Keep the money. Besides, every wife needs a secret stash her husband knows nothing about. Believe me, it comes in handy."

"You cannot go in there alone, sir."

"I will be just fine. Stay in the carriage."

Robin Van der Kellen strolled into a neighborhood while his carriage and driver waited on the main street. He glanced at an address on a paper in his hand. Then he walked deeper into the alley, past carts and vendors and hookah cafés. The smells of curried lamb filled the air and Robin's stomach growled. The languages around him included Hebrew, Arab, and ah, at last...Hindi. Robin said to the man in Hindi, "I beg your pardon, sir. I am looking for an address."

The young Indian immigrant got up and went to stand before the much taller Dutchman. "How is it you speak Hindi, sir?"

"I lived in Pulicat, for a time," Robin said.

"I am from Bombay."

"Ah. British colony."

"You are not British, sir?"

"I am Dutch."

"Then I will show you the way. Are you hungry, sir?"

"That curry smells wonderful," Robin replied. "I should purchase some on the way out."

"This way. This way. I'm sorry, sir. They appear to have left the apartment. No one has seen them," the man said after speaking with some others in the alley.

Robin let out a long breath.

The man looked up at him, and the scrape on his chin, the fine suit and briefcase. "Would you care to come back to the food stand with me?"

"I could not be a bother to you."

"Please. It honors me so that you speak our language. I cannot understand why you were in Pulicat."

Robin removed his fine top hat and said gently, "I served in the Dutch cavalry stationed in Pulicat for two years."

The young Indian man doubled over. And he sobbed.

Robin bent and put a hand on his shoulder.

The man stood up. "Come for tea. All of my family died in Pulicat."

Robin took the man under his arm as they strolled back toward the alley with the food vendors. "We tried so to save them. So many of us died trying to save them from the British."

The man nodded. "I know."

Back at the food cart, the man dished out a bowl of curried lamb and rice with a spoon to Robin.

Robin took paper money from his pocketbook and tucked these into the man's hand. "I wish you well in the new world."

"Namaste. Namaste. God bless you."

Robin walked back to his carriage, devouring the spicy lamb. How strange he must have looked, a Dutchman in black top hat, briefcase under his arm, eating a bowl of curry as he walked by. He was the only white man on this street and yet he was stared at almost the same way in Canterbury.

Robin now walked up to an address in a wealthy neighborhood, though his driver looked on just as nervously. Robin climbed five steps and knocked on a door. He waited, looking about.

In a moment a butler opened the door. "Hello sir."

"Hello. Would this be the home of Mr. Mika Raikonen?" Robin removed his top hat and held it with his briefcase.

"Yes, it is. Come in please." The butler stepped back.

Robin walked into the entry hall and grand stairway where a black bunting was draped all the way up. As his eyes followed it up, he anticipated already what he was about to be told, and he frowned.

"I regret to inform you, Mr. Raikonen died yesterday. Would you wish to speak to Mrs. Raikonen or the eldest son, perhaps? What is your business, if I may?" the butler asked.

Robin let out a breath. "No. I do not wish to bother them at such a time. If you could convey that Mr. Willem Van der Kellen's son and partner came calling."

"You need to wait here, sir." The butler pointed right at the floor and scurried back into the house.

"Oh no." Robin sighed. He straightened his ascot and vest. He fiddled with his briefcase as he waited. "Here it comes."

The butler returned gesturing for Robin. "Come along. Hurry."

Robin was shown into a parlor where the widow, family members, and two police officers were waiting. The body of their loved one was laid out in front of the fireplace. Robin kept his hat in hand politely.

It was the policemen who went to him and they escorted him from the grieving room with the butler across the hall into a dining room where he shut them in with double doors.

"Your name is Van der Kellen?" the officer said.

"Robin Van der Kellen."

"He's too young to be him," the other officer said.

"Willem Van der Kellen was my father," Robin clarified. "I was hoping to talk to Thomas Albertson's partner, Mr. Raikonen. But I see I am too late."

"Raikonen was shot dead yesterday, right out front. Can you tell me anything about that?" the officer said.

"Given that Albertson was shot dead over two months ago, I should think you could tell me about any of this," Robin replied.

"What is your business here, sir?" the policeman asked.

"I am a Barrister at Law. Lawyer as you call them. Out of Boston. I am wrapping up my father's cases as he has died as well," Robin explained. "As far as I know, Albertson and Raikonen were defending a bank robber who died in jail, a Christian Pascal. My father was the prosecutor. Pascal's partner a Mr. Benedetti just did this to me trying to rob me of bank bonds. He is now in custody. If you question him, you may find he's your killer."

"When was Benedetti taken into custody?"

"About three hours ago," Robin said.

"Did these bank robbers kill your father?" the policeman asked.

"About half a dozen cigars a day did," Robin replied. "Heart condition. But I appreciate your condolences."

The two cops looked at each other. One finally said to Robin, "I don't like lawyers, and you in particular, Dutchman. But I am forced to do my job and warn you there were more than two bank robbers. You best get your fancy suit out of this city before they put bloody holes in it."

"What do you know about more bank robbers?" Robin's eyes narrowed.

"There were four men seen here when Raikonen was shot. I'll be questioning your Benedetti."

"I insist on being present for that."

"You'll have to get a judge to order me. You've got no client here. Mind your own damn business."

Robin stepped back, lifting his chin.

"Don't be bothering this widow and get on your way, sir." The officer opened the door.

The butler was waiting in the hall.

"Show this blood sucking lawyer out."

Robin looking worried

Chapter Thirteen Dinner Party with the Dutchman

Thursday, April 30, 1840 continued

Edward Miller reached out and took him by the arm. "Robin, my friend, are you all right, sir?"

Robin smiled, nodding. "I'm quite well."

The girls scrambled into the entry and immediately saw the mark on his chin.

"We were told about your assault. You must let my physician see you. I would certainly like to be certain," Edward said.

"I am quite all right. That is really not necessary but I do thank you. I can assure you we are safe as the police insisted on a guard to the house. For that I do apologize," Robin said. "I would understand if you ejected us immediately."

"Nonsense my thrilling friend." Edward waved the butler into the entry with a silver tray and a glass of fine scotch on it. "Quickly now. Serve it to him. Brace up and come on inside. Do tell about your adventures. I hear you were in China Town and everything."

Forced by the offer, naturally, Robin accepted the drink and downed a good gulp of it. His coat was taken from him. His brief case taken and set on the couch nearby. It was the removal of the coat that made him realize his shoulder, knee, and hip were a bit sore.

Marie went to Robin and embraced him. Robin hugged her. "I'm fine."

"Do tell, what assault you were party to and why?" Edward asked.

"Let him sit, darling," Elizabeth insisted. "He was accosted. Hit in the face, oh poor Robin."

"Sort of my typical day at work," Robin said.

Edward drew Robin with the ladies into the sitting room right beside the entry. Robin and Marie were sat together on a love seat with Edward and Elizabeth across from them.

"What happened, sir? Do tell."

Robin slid his arm about Marie. "Ahm, one of the bank robbers knocked me flat in front of the police station and took my bag but he ran right into two officers leaving the building. So, he was caught. My property returned to me. There is not much more to tell than that."

"Extraordinary excitement. What an amazing barrister you are, sir," Edward said. "Part lawman and part soldier indeed."

"Hardly. I didn't see him waiting for me. Caught off guard," Robin said. "Didn't expect that in front of a police station. Hard to tell if you're being followed when everyone has a black carriage and black Percherons."

They stared at him.

"Then I went looking for the defending lawyer's partner only to find he'd been shot dead yesterday. They had police shove me out the door like a vulture circling the grieving family. I had no intention of bothering them. There he was laid out in the parlor," Robin said casually. "I also tried to find the dead banker's family down in Chinatown but they were all moved out. Long gone."

"You went into Chinatown alone?" Edward questioned. "How did you manage in there?"

"I don't speak any Chinese, or Arabic, or any of the other languages there except Hindi. I picked up some Hindi living in India for two years. I did have a good lunch down there."

"That shall make exciting conversation for the party tonight," Edward said. "Say something in the language of India."

Robin appeased Edward with a phrase in Hindi.

"And what does that mean?"

"Would you have any black pepper?" Robin said.

"I should have known," Marie said.

"I think. Or I may have asked for a cold remedy," Robin said, to their laughter. "They might actually be the same word."

"Go now, get cleaned up for supper," Edward said. "And drink that up. You'll feel better."

Robin glanced at Marie and downed the scotch at once. And it did brace him up. "I need to talk to you. My words, is this your new gown? Good lord."

"You did well to notice a woman's new gown," Elizabeth coaxed.

"Good lord, girl." Robin pulled her up off the seat and held her up by the hand, taking in the cobalt blue evening gown and heels. "You are a stunning woman."

"You're hurt, my dear." She kissed a finger and touched it to his chin so gently.

He leaned his forehead to hers. "I'm all right now. Let me look again."

"Darling, I have a surprise for you. Elizabeth and Jonas helped me find some surprises for you." Marie smiled warmly at him.

"More surprise than this beautiful wife of mine?" Robin grinned.

"I can't wait 'til you show him," Elizabeth declared.

"Come this way." Marie took his hand and drew him to the other side of the room to a card table.

Edward held Elizabeth back where she was.

Robin looked at the items on the table and his hand immediately was drawn to the roll of white parchment paper.

"These are all for you. For your cartography," Marie said.

"Oh Marie…" Robin picked up the paper roll to examine it up close. Then he observed the jars of ink, pens, ruler, a device, and a wooden arm rest. "Marie, these are wonderful."

"And Elizabeth got you these maps of Massachusetts, New York, and Connecticut for study," Marie said.

Robin picked up the device. the quill and pen holder.

"I have no idea what that is for," Marie admitted.

Robin demonstrated. "You stick this end and in the other put an inked pen or graphite and draw a circle or arc of whatever size you desire. I've always wanted one. I can also measure distances on my practice maps to transfer it exactly to the white parchment. Oh Marie. I love you so much, my darling." Robin kissed her mouth quickly and looked to Elizabeth. "Thank you so much for the maps, Mrs. Miller."

"You must start calling me Elizabeth at least," She declared, to everyone's laughter.

"And what is this for?" Marie indicated the fine wooden arm rest.

"For writing or drawing details in the center of the map, without smudging everything else with my arm. Like this, you see." He picked up a pen and demonstrated, resting his wrist on the wooden bridge piece. That had him bent a bit over the table.

Elizabeth put a hand to her mouth.

"Well, good job Jonas, locating these stores for Marie," Edward said.

"I see the gentleman is pleased with these tools. I'll admit, I had never been in that particular shop before. We'll have to take Mr. Van der Kellen there to see if there is anything else he needs," Jonas said.

"Thank you ever so much," Robin said.

"Bring everything up to his room. Guests will be arriving soon, Jonas," Edward said.

Marie gleamed as she looked up at Robin. "Surprises for tonight have only begun."

"My good friends, I invited you here to welcome young newlyweds that we met on the train. And I do wish you to welcome the young lovers. But as you are all the leading bankers of New York, I must inform you that Mr. Van der Kellen is also a fine barrister fighting bank robbers, in fact today he got one arrested. Welcome, Robin and Marie Van der Kellen."

Robin exacted a formal bow and drew Marie to the table. Elizabeth drew Marie beside her. Robin took the seat beside Miller at the head of the table. There was much applause from ten couples Edward had invited to his dining table.

"What would you say, Robin?" Edward asked before they would sit.

The applause subsided and they looked on with great interest.

Robin just tenderly brought fingertips to his scraped chin. "I beg your pardon for my appearance, but the brick ways of New York are not very forgiving when one is attacked by a bank robber."

That made the bankers and their wives raise wine glasses and cheer.

Everyone sat at last.

"I do apologize for surrounding you with so many bankers," Edward said to much laughter.

"Not 'tall, Edward. Where I am from in Amsterdam it is the banking center of Europe. Many of my friends went into banking. One of my sisters even married a bank owner. I'm quite at home among the species," Robin said.

That made them laugh again.

"More at home it seems than we are with a celebrity," one of the bankers said.

In the silence that followed and everyone looking to Van der Kellen, he said, "I...beg your pardon?"

"You are quite famous in the papers, Mr. Van der Kellen. A famous lawyer putting an end to bank robbery."

"Tell us about it, will you, sir?"

Robin sipped some scotch before saying, "Officially my father was the prosecuting attorney of a bank robber but the defendant died of a gunshot wound during the trial. I have just been following up on loose ends in the case."

"You speak modestly, Robin," Edward said. "Unless by loose ends you mean the other loose robbers, such as the one you got arrested today."

"Well, I find lawyers in America are treated much differently than they are in the Netherlands. It seems bank robbers are more revered," Robin said. "And lawyers reviled."

"You may feel differently tomorrow, sir, when you see the headlines," one of the men said. "Dutchman catches bank robber right in front of Police Station."

Robin looked at him down the table. "Oh no. I do hope not. This notoriety I do not seek."

"I'm told the banking news the day before it prints," the man said. "My inside sources tell me you are about to be made a hero on Manhattan Island."

"Already a hero in war," Elizabeth spoke up.

Van der Kellen wet his lips. He set his hands on the arms of his chair, elbows up.

Jonas stepped in behind Edward and whispered to him. "He's about to leave the table."

"Dinner is to be served now," Edward said. "And I'm told dessert will be all the confectionaries from the Dutch side of town, in honor of our guest. Jonas, have them serve the first course now."

"With pleasure, sir," Jonas said.

Robin sat back and relaxed his arms. He looked to Edward.

During the fourth course of dinner, Robin asked the party of bankers, "How rare is French currency?"

"In New York banks? About as rare as an Arabian knight," one banker said, to much laughter.

"Would there be record of it then, in an exchange perhaps?" Robin asked after.

"Of course, there would be record. You must go to the central exchange office up town where any bank would have exchanged it for the dollar," Another banker said. "Have you found some then? How intriguing."

"One of the banks robbed contained some foreign currency. I was curious to see if any of it turned up in town," Robin said.

"I'll leave you the address," the banker said.

"Thank you, sir," Robin said. "Can you tell me, what happens to the currency when a bank goes out of business? Each of your banks issue your own currency, in paper or coins, is that correct?"

Edward answered, "Yes. We each issue our own currency and it backed up with the deposits in our vault. We then purchase Government Treasury Notes, from the US or the state, or make investments. Interest charged on loans is how we make money for the bank."

Another banker spoke up, "So in the case of these burnt down banks, their notes devalue immediately with no vault to support the notes."

"All the people and the businesses or shops with East Street Bank notes are simply out of the money?" Robin questioned. "They can't deposit those notes at one of your banks?"

"We won't accept worthless paper," another replied.

"Same as if they printed the notes in their basement," another said.

"Would people hold onto these broken bank notes?" Robin asked.

"Throw them in their fireplace in anger, most likely," Edward said. "Are you thinking of opening your own bank?"

Robin shot him a look.

"That's a no," The other bankers laughed. "Don't do it, young man!"

Robin lowered his eyes to his vest.

Marie looked at Robin across the table from her, in his tuxedo. His white shirt had at least fifty pearl buttons from collar to belt. Robin didn't even unbutton half of them when he'd pulled the shirt on over his head.

"All this banking talk. Pray tell, Robin, are you sore at all from your fall?" Elizabeth questioned.

Robin nodded. "A few places, yes. Now that time and excitement have subsided."

"What hurts?" Elizabeth asked.

"Ahm, just my knee and shoulder a little," Robin said. "Thank you for asking. I'll be fine."

"Tell me, Mr. Van der Kellen, are there a great many bank robberies to keep you busy or do you run other legal cases?"

"My father's expertise was in financial crime. A great many of his cases were far less exciting than bank robbery. My interest was always in defending the unfortunate," Robin said.

"I dare say, listening to his accent is almost as fascinating as looking at him," One of the wives said, making them all laugh again. The ladies all drank to that.

"Almost but not quite," another wife said.

"I dare say a little scrape on his chin only adds to his character," another said.

"I could have a hatchet stuck in my back and my wife wouldn't notice," her husband said.

"How long have the newlyweds been married?"

"Six days." Marie and Robin said in unison.

"Six days? Not even a week yet? We are keeping these young lovers from getting to know each other."

The gathering moved into the adjoining salon for desserts and drinks. Robin at last, was standing close beside Marie, with his hand on her lower back, admiring her cobalt blue silk gown. His mother's diamond cross hung about her neck and just above her cleavage. "Where did you get the ear bobs?"

Marie looked up at him. "They're Beth's. She loaned them to me."

"You like blue, don't you? I think it might be your favorite color," Robin told her.

"Yes especially this blue," Marie told him.

"What did you do today?" Robin whispered to her.

"Shopped. Bought beautiful things. Then we had the most marvelous lunch and we saw a play. It was in Italian. I have no idea what it was about but I loved it," Marie enthused, gleaming in her smile up at him.

Robin inched closer until he was leaning against her. "I'm so delighted."

"Must you work again tomorrow?" Marie held onto his vest with two fingers through where it buttoned.

"Yes. I'll go to this currency exchange. Marie, I found out the most wonderful thing today. My father was honest," Robin said. "I am following his footsteps here. He did exactly as I am doing, searching for the records."

"Robin, that's wonderful."

He stole a kiss. And then he couldn't resist a longer kiss which drew applause from the room and spoons jingled against crystal glasses. Robin raised his head from hers and took in the room.

"They are newlyweds," Elizabeth declared.

"And marvelously so," one of the wives said.

"I beg your pardon." Robin gave a nod to the room.

"Carry on, young man," Edward advised, handing a scotch to Robin. "How long were you in India?"

"He served in India?" a banker asked, stepping closer.

"I said that before. He fought the British in the Dutch colony of India," Edward said.

"Did you see an elephant?" one of the wives asked.

Robin smiled. "Had the great displeasure of riding them many times, yes."

"Oh Robin, do tell," Elizabeth urged.

"The mangrove swamps, our horses cannot get through and if they did the tigers would get them. If we had to enter, three or four of us together would ride on the back of an elephant and take him through with a native driver of course," Robin said.

"So, elephants are real?" Elizabeth asked.

"Well, of course they are," Robin said. "And there are monkeys, little monkeys that are fond of picking pockets. They can open a saddlebag too. Steal your canteen and then you have a very hot long ride back with no water. They can undo knots as well."

"How do you ride an elephant? Is there a saddle?"

"No saddle. There is a sort of a matt with handles around the outside. This is on the animal's back. Four of us could sit up there and hold on with the handles. The driver sits on the elephant's neck with one bare foot behind each giant ear. This is how he steers it," Robin explained. "Pushes his toes against the ear."

"Fascinating. And did you see a wild tiger?" Elizabeth asked.

Robin finished his drink and found Edward refilling his scotch. "Ahm, yes one of my good friends was killed by one. We saw tigers many times. I had to shoot one in a hallway once. They are beautiful but deadly creatures."

"Robin, you tell the most spectacular and chilling stories," Edward said. "You make it sound as if the British were not the deadliest adversary there, but India itself."

"Almost, sir," Robin said.

"There must have been something wonderful about India?" Marie questioned. "Tea maybe?"

"Those exotic young Hindi maidens with their veils and not much else...." Edward began to tease him.

Robin raised one finger. "I never saw any of those."

That broke up the room laughing.

"Dance with me?" Robin said to Marie as the other couples began to dance in the ball room.

Marie pressed her mouth to Robin's ear. "I do not know how."

"Just follow my lead." Robin took her hand and drew her along with him.

Marie saw no other person in the room from then on as she went with Robin into the ball room. She let him take one of her hands and placed her other on his shoulder where he set it. And then she looked up at him as they danced to the fine music of instruments played in the corner of the room, a piano, a cello, and violins. She felt only his shoulder in her hand and his hip against hers. She tried not to step on his feet too much, but for the most part her wide skirt prevented such an intrusion on the fantasy, or perhaps it was his skill as a dancer.

House keepers and the valet stole glances at them dancing, from the side rooms.

In between songs Robin would kiss her on the mouth and the other guests would applaud. She would stroke his hair and the ladies would giggle. And Marie could not help but imagine the laundry she had hung in Robin's ballroom. "I thank you for this. I never imagined I would ever."

May 1, 1840 Friday morning

After Marie and Robin enjoyed breakfast in a Dutch café, a musket shot rang out and Robin dropped in the street. People screamed and ran. But one man was running right for him, reloading.

Marie dove for Robin's briefcase, unclasped it open and drew out his British pistol. She placed it in Robin's hand.

And Robin, lying flat on his back, his right shoulder bleeding heavily, cocked and aimed that pistol up at the man standing over him and fired. It was the loudest thing Marie ever heard.

Police blew their whistles and came running.

Marie knelt, leaning over Robin, shielding his head in the street.

Robin's driver skidded down beside Marie.

Robin urged Marie up into the driver's hands. "Take her. Look after her."

The shooter had dropped right on Robin, and he kicked him off with both boots and then collapsed on his back in the cobblestone street.

The policeman split up between Robin and the assailant. "This one's dead."

The cop over Robin picked up that British pistol and felt it burning hot in his hand. He took in Robin's fine suit and the dress on Marie. "What happened here, sir?"

"Open your eyes man! He just shot me!" Robin yelled.

"I need the ambulance here," Robin's policeman ordered to the other. "We are getting you to the hospital, sir. Can you tell me your name? Is there any reason he'd want to shoot you or was it robbery?"

"I'm barrister Robin Van der Kellen. I'm investigating bank robberies," Robin said between gasps. "Marie, are you all right?"

"He's a what?" One policeman said.

"He's a lawyer," the other answered. "They call them a barrister in England."

Marie took off her shawl and pressed it against Robin's bleeding shoulder. "This is awful, Robin. You're bleeding so much. I can't stop it."

"This is a British gun. Are you an Englishman?" the policeman asked.

"No. I am Dutch. I went to war against them. Dutch cavalry."

"I'm going to need to impound this weapon. But you'll get it back, if it's not illegal to carry."

Robin grabbed onto Marie by the arm. "Marie, don't let them take off my arm. Promise me."

"Oh, Robin I promise."

"Look after my wife. I'm afraid I must pass out now."

The driver picked up Robin's bag and set his hand on Marie's shoulder. He squatted beside her telling the police, "Get him up into my carriage. I can get him fast to the hospital."

"We can run sirens for you," the policeman said. "You two, help me lift this gentleman into his carriage. Be careful. He's been shot."

The driver helped Marie to her feet as several men lifted Robin up into the floor of the carriage.

"You're the wife? Come along ma'am."

Marie was helped up inside to kneel with Robin.

Two policeman road with them inside and two up top.

A police wagon lead them quickly away, sirens blearing. The two men held Robin down while Marie kept pressure on his shoulder.

In a private hospital room, Robin was lying flat on a bed, his shirt off and right shoulder wrapped in thick bandaging and padding. Robin was pale and breathing hard. The nurse was taking away instruments in a bowl and a blood-soaked towel.

The policeman brought Marie into the room.

"Oh, Marie, are you hurt?" Robin looked up.

She grabbed his left hand into both of hers. "I'm fine. Are you in much pain?" She leaned in and kissed him.

"Marie, listen to me. I don't have long. They're coming back with a surgeon to cut out the lead ball. Marie, get Elizabeth and Edward here to sit with you. It's going to be a while, hours probably. And don't let them take off my arm. My arm is fine. Tell them I said that." Robin gasped for breath. "Stay with Elizabeth. And Marie, you take all this money. Give Poole his share. Get the money and live here near Elizabeth, if I don't survive."

"Robin, darling, don't say such things. You're going to be fine. Oh Robin." She smoothed her hand on his forehead. "Robin, darling?" She leaned in and kissed him. "I will be close by."

The door banged open and a flurry of doctors and nurses entered. "Ma'am, we will need you to wait in the reception. It's going to be a while. Lead ball is deep inside his shoulder. I could feel it with the probe."

Marie kissed him again. "He said to tell you his arm is fine. Do not do anything to his arm."

"I shouldn't be needing to do anything to his arm. Please ma'am. I don't have long to work while he is out on laudanum. I must get started."

Robin's eyes opened and he moaned. "Stoppen. Stoppen. Laat het stoppen." Make it stop.

"Oh my. Oh...dear Robin. You woke up." Elizabeth leaned over him in the bed.

"Ik kan je niet horen," Robin whispered. I can't hear you.

"English, Robin. Tell me what to do," Elizabeth said instinctively louder and more clearly.

"Waar is Marie?" Robin asked.

"She went downstairs for something to eat. I'll get the doctor. Hold on, Robin." Elizabeth hurried out of the hospital room.

For a moment, Robin was alone, looking up at the ceiling. He lay there, trying to get his left hand free of the blanket.

And then Elizabeth was back over him.

"The doctor is coming. Marie will be back in just a few minutes. They're getting her." When Elizabeth put her hand on his left arm, he held up his hand reaching. She freed his hand from the blanket and held hands with him. "They're coming. Are you in much pain?"

"Beth...Beth, you must tell them...too much laudanum," Robin whispered.

"Robin? Robin?" Elizabeth gripped his hand.

In rushed the doctor and two nurses. "You said he was awake."

"He was. He said to tell you too much laudanum," Elizabeth said.

"Sir? Sir, can you hear me?" The doctor raised Robin's eyelid. "He is heavily sedated. No more laudanum until I order more. Let him wake up fully. He has been out far too long."

Several hours later, Robin saw the ceiling of the room again. Light came in from the left side across the ceiling. Suddenly a shadow blocked it. His chest felt as if an elephant was sitting on him. He tried to sit up but could not. And he cried out. "Laat het stoppen." Make it stop.

"Robin." Marie hurried to his side. "Robin, can you hear me?"

"Marie…."

"I will get the doctor."

"Ga niet. No don't go," Robin whispered. "Don't go. Don't go. Don't go."

Elizabeth bolted out of her chair to the nurses' station.

Marie held his left hand and leaned close. "I'm right here darling. I'm not going anywhere."

"Oh, mijn God."

"Robin, you're all right. The surgery went just fine. You are all right," Marie told him.

"I thought…Did they take off my arm?" Robin said.

"No." Marie gripped his left and his right hand. "Feel that. I'm holding both your hands, darling."

Robin raised his head to see his arm, gripping her hands. "I'm all…together?"

Elizabeth returned and leaned on Marie's shoulder. "Doctor is coming."

The doctor and a nurse hurried in to see that his eyes were open. "Raise him up there. Sit him up enough to drink some water. Mr. Van der Kellen, can you hear me?"

"Wat?" Robin said softly. "Waarom heb ik zoveel pijn?" Why do I hurt so much?

"He's speaking Dutch," Marie spoke up. "Give him a moment."

"Dutch? You have been out for many hours. We need you to drink water, all that you can. All right, sir? How is the pain? Do we have a Dutch doctor or nurse here?"

Robin looked at him for a moment. "Chest pain, a lot. Not so much damn laudanum. You nearly killed me. Don't give that much to a horse."

Shocked, the doctor just looked at him. "I...was told you struggled during surgery and they had to give you more."

Marie and Elizabeth let the nurse in to crank up the head of the bed. Marie took the glass of water from her. "I will get him to drink this."

"No more laudanum. Not for me," Robin declared. "I'd rather it just hurt."

"You will require laudanum for several days. The pain is severe. What you're feeling right now is while you are on laudanum," the doctor said. "But we'll lessen the doses. Ladies, you will need to leave the room." The doctor began to open Robin's bandaging.

"I'm getting my husband to drink this water," Marie insisted.

"And I'm helping her," Elizabeth vowed, clinging behind Marie, shaking.

The nurse had the head of the bed raised just over halfway and stepped back.

Robin drank some of the water for Marie. And he put one knee up beneath the blanket. "How long was I out? I feel like I died."

"Nearly a day, sir." The doctor got the bandaging open and padded a bit with some fresh cotton. "This is looking very good."

Elizabeth had to turn away. His wound was stitched, jagged, and bloody.

"A day?" Robin said.

"He needs something to eat. He's fainting." Marie found Robin's forehead was wet and clammy to her touch. "It has been nearly two days since he ate anything. He eats all the time."

"I will bring him something right away." The nurse exited the room.

"Sir, this wound is looking good. Let's get all the water and food into you we can tonight," the doctor said. "And I will need all the ladies out of the room because the next thing he's going to need to do is relieve himself. He hasn't yet."

"Well now that you mentioned it," Robin said.

Elizabeth actually turned red and grabbed onto Marie's arm. "Let's wait in the hall."

"We'll be right back." Marie set his glass down on the table. She waited in the hall with her arm linked with Elizabeth's.

Beth let out a long breath. "Did you see that wound? I've never seen anything so horrible."

"Still bleeding. I would have thought if they stitched him up it would stop," Marie said. "I've never seen anyone shot before. But he's awake and thinking all right. The worst is over."

"Yes, it is. Now he can heal." Beth sobbed into Marie's shoulder.

The doctor walked out and shut the door behind him. "Mrs. Vander Kellen, he needs to eat something and drink all the water he can. He's very weak. The surgery was hard on him. He's healthy and strong but make no mistake, he lost a lot of blood. Infection is still a concern."

"I will see to it, Doctor," Marie insisted.

"I will see if there is a Dutch doctor or nurse on staff," the doctor said.

"He speaks English. Give him time. He's just come out of sedation," Marie reminded.

"Of course, madam. This is no place for ladies."

"This is exactly the place for his wife," Marie insisted.

Elizabeth remained with an arm linked with Marie's.

"I do expect him to recover well. But he will need a lot of care and time." The doctor moved on to the next room.

Marie opened the door and led Elizabeth back into Robin's hospital room. Her husband was lying back on the raised bed, his eyes staring at the opposite wall. He had no shirt on and the thick cotton bandaging wrapped around beneath his arm and around his neck to hold it in place. "Are you cold, darling?" She reached to pull up his sheet and blankets.

"No." Robin held them down. He was breathing hard. And he moaned a bit when he swallowed. "I'm so hot. Just leave it."

"Can you drink this? They are bringing you something to eat. I do hope it's easy to eat." Marie held the water glass for him and helped him drink it.

Elizabeth was gripping the rail at the foot of his bed. "Edward and I will bring whatever you want to eat tomorrow. Anything. Anything at all. A great assortment."

The nurse entered with a tray containing a small bowl of soup, some bread, and a tea pot with three cups. She set it down on the table behind Marie. "I thought perhaps you ladies would like the tea, if he doesn't. I can feed him if you need to go home."

"I'll see that my husband eats something before I even think about going home," Marie said.

"Yes ma'am." The nurse left.

Marie examined the tray. "The soup is very hot." She brought him the bread and broke off a piece. "Can you eat this?"

"No."

"Yes, you can." Marie held the piece of bread to his mouth.

Robin brought his left hand up to take the bread. He ate some.

Elizabeth found a pitcher of water and a bowl. She dampened a cloth and stepped up the other side of the bed, his wounded side. She used the cloth to wipe up some blood from Robin's right arm and his chest.

"I apologize for this, Elizabeth," Robin whispered.

"No need. Just rest, dear Robin," Elizabeth said. "You said you were hot." She wiped the damp cloth down his arms and wrists, and the center of his bare chest to cool him. "I am a married woman. I know what I'm doing." She wiped it across his bare abdomen and the line of hair down the middle to his navel.

"Thank you for staying with me. You must be tired." Marie was fixated on Robin and the water glass.

"No more than you. I'll stay until I can escort you home for sleep, when Robin is stable enough," Elizabeth said.

"When I eat something, I would have you take Marie home and see that she rests," Robin said. "I'll be all right now."

"I will."

"I promise." Marie fed him more bread and then checked the temperature of the soup.

Elizabeth refreshed the cloth with cold water and gently dabbed it to Robin's throat and forehead, watching him close his eyes. "We can bring him some clothes and better food in the morning."

"I can't believe how long he slept," Marie said. "Robin, remember how we did this when you were sick?" She set a napkin on his chest and sat down on his bed, facing him. She held the soup bowl for him and offered the spoon to him. "Can you take the spoon or...."

"I cannot," Robin said.

Elizabeth took the water bowl away.

"Let's get some of this into you. You need it for your strength." Marie fed him a little soup with the spoon. "Your cheeks are nice and cool. No fever, darling. You just think you're hot then."

Elizabeth walked out to the nurse's station. It was nearly ten o-clock at night.

"Mrs. Miller?" A nurse looked up at her from behind the desk.

Elizabeth opened her purse and showed a few gold dollars to the woman. "I want someone in the room with Mr. Van der Kellen all night until I bring his wife back. Do you understand?"

"We have other patients here, Madam."

Elizabeth doubled the coins in her hand. "One person in the room with him all through the night."

The nurse was met by another. They looked at each other.

The first held out her hand for the money. "We can take turns watching Mr. Van der Kellen."

"Split it. Take turns. Whatever it takes. That man's a very important lawyer and he's just been shot," Elizabeth insisted.

"One of us will be in his room all night," the nurse said.

"He'll tell me if not." Mrs. Miller released the money to them, picked up two cookies off their desk, and returned into Robin's room, where she handed the cookies to Marie. "Maybe he'll eat these."

Chapter Fourteen Boring Little Barrister

May 2, 1840 Saturday

In the morning Edward brought the two ladies back to Robin's room with their butler Jonas carrying a basket of food. Marie carried clothes for Robin.

A policeman was standing guard at the door.

The doctor was just leaving and paused in the hall to tell them, "He's a little better today. Resting. He was able to stand up and walk a bit. No sign of fever yet. We would like to watch him for a few days. Please try to get him to eat and drink all he can."

"Yes, I will. Thank you, Doctor," Marie said.

The policeman asked, "Which one of you is Mrs. Van der Kellen?"

"I am."

"And who do you have with you?" the policeman said.

"I am Edward Miller and this is my wife," Miller said. "The Van der Kellens are guests in my home."

"I am to make sure nobody but you three enters, unless a doctor or nurse." The policeman nodded to them. "His orders. War hero, you know? Magnificent pistol he's got."

"Thank you, officer," Miller said.

The cop held the door open for them, glancing inside.

Robin was reclining in the bed, on pillows and with the head raised halfway again. He had a white hospital shirt on, open down the front, and blankets covering him up to his chest. His eyes opened.

A nurse rose from a chair beside him. "Good morning, Mrs. Van der Kellen. He's a little better."

Marie went up close to his side and took his hand into both of hers. "Robin darling. Are you okay?"

He let out a breath. "Not quite. Did you get some sleep?"

"A little," Marie said. "Edward and Elizabeth brought you some breakfast and lunch. I brought you some clothes for whenever you want them. We brought you a nice soft sleep shirt, one of your favorites."

"It is just as well I'm wearing one of their shirts. I'm bleeding on everything for now," Robin said.

Edward and Elizabeth stood at the foot of the bed together. Edward said, "Robin, if there is anything we can do for you, just say so."

"Thank you. Look after Marie, is all I beg of you." Robin was still breathing in sudden short breaths.

"Do you think you could eat something?" Marie asked.

Elizabeth took the clothing from her and set them into the top dresser drawer in the corner of the room. Robin's riding boots were in the corner there. "Jonas, you can set up the food on the top here."

The butler got to work, removing the breakfast from the basket. He had blueberry muffins, scrambled eggs with ham in it, fresh biscuits, and other things for Robin.

Elizabeth slipped another dollar into the nurse's hand as she left the room.

Marie sat on the edge of Robin's bed, facing him. "Does it hurt much?"

Robin nodded. "You know what? Third time I've been shot. This better be the last."

"Good Lord," Edward said.

Jonas brought an assortment of breakfast on a plate with a folded napkin and spoon up to the bedside where Marie sat. "Here you are, sir. If there is anything else I can get you, I will go anywhere in the city for it. In fact, I'm told there is a Dutch side of town. I'll be going there to see what I may find for you right after I leave here today."

Marie set a tray table over Robin's lap.

Robin looked up at them and his eyes rolled toward Jonas. "Dutch side of town? Bitterballen. You must find that."

"Bitterballen?" Jonas repeated. "I shall hunt that down, sir."

"Or apple tart. Or Dutch pea soup. I don't know what I can manage to eat and keep down. I threw up that soup last night. Didn't make the nurse very happy." Robin looked down at his blankets as he tried to get his hands free of them. "Luckily there was one here all night to look after me. It was not a good night for any of them."

Marie unfolded the napkin on Robin's chest and took the plate from Jonas onto the tray. "Try this then." She broke off part of the blueberry muffin and fed it to him. "Was the nurse mean to you?"

"No, of course not. Three of them got me a new pillow, new sheets, cleaned up the floor."

Elizabeth turned to look out the window, masking her smile.

Jonas stepped back to the far end of the room to await instructions.

Edward pulled up a chair to the other side of Robin's bed and sat down. "Does it hurt you to talk, Robin?"

"No." Robin had another bite of muffin. "Hurts to breathe."

"Can you eat this?" Marie asked him.

Robin nodded. "I like it, very much. Thank you."

Jonas let out an audible sigh of relief.

Elizabeth gripped the rail at the foot of the bed. "You must feel awful, dear Robin. I don't know how you managed to stand up, as the doctor said you did."

"Said you even walked a bit," Edward added. "You are a strong man, Robin."

"Ah. He made me walk to the vanity closet over there," Robin said. "I have bled a lot. I want to faint when I stand up."

"I have something for you, when you're feeling up to it." Edward showed him a flask.

Elizabeth walked over from the window and folded her arms. "Edward."

That made Robin smile. "What are you waiting for?"

"Robin. You can't have that with your breakfast," Marie exclaimed.

"I'm the one shot. I'll have whatever I want," Robin declared.

Edward and Jonas laughed.

Jonas brought two small glasses to Edward.

"It will settle your stomach, I'm certain." Edward poured a shot for Robin and one for himself. "As no man should drink alone I shall be forced to drink with you."

"Forced?" Elizabeth said.

Robin took the glass in his left hand and drank a sip.

"Well, anything to get you to eat," Marie told him.

Edward drank an equal portion. "To your health, Robin. Such as it is."

"Such as it is." Robin laughed and then winced as the brandy hit his stomach. He pulled his knees up beneath the blankets. "Now the eggs look good."

May 3, 1840

The following day Edward brought a young man with him to Robin's hospital room where Marie and Elizabeth were already sitting with him.

"Robin, this is my personal physician. He's not a surgeon but he's going to look after you when you come home. This is Dr. Ian Van Allen. Ian, this is the famous bank robber catcher, Robin Van der Kellen."

The man held his black physician's bag in both hands and moved around the bedside to be up by Robin's right side. "Pleasure to meet you sir. Read about you in the papers. How are you feeling today?"

Robin met eyes with Edward at the foot of the bed. "Papers? Verdomd."

"What did your surgeon say? May I? Any fever?" Ian put a hand on Robin's forehead.

"Danish?" Robin asked.

"On my father's side. German on my mother's," Ian Van Allen said.

"I don't know what I can tell you except that the ball missed everything important and got lodged in my shoulder blade," Robin said. "It was at almost the end of the weapons' range or it would have gone right through me. That would have destroyed my shoulder blade."

"Yes. May I take a look?" Ian asked.

Elizabeth and Marie stood on Robin's left side.

"Of course."

"Ladies may wish to avert your eyes." Van Allen opened Robin's shirt, folding it back off his shoulder. He raised the padding to peek beneath. "Missed your clavicle. Missed your lung. Injured a rib perhaps. Missed major blood vessels to your arm it appears. All good news, sir. You're very lucky."

"I am. But not lucky enough to not get shot," Robin said.

That made them all laugh except the young doctor. "I am going to speak to your surgeon. I think you lost a lot of blood. You're quite pale and weak." He buttoned Robin's shirt back up. "Take in all the food and water you can. Rest. I'll look after you when you are released. I'll coordinate your recovery with your surgeon. Any questions for me?"

"How long have you been a doctor?" Robin asked. "Two weeks?"

"Two years."

"Harvard medical school. Top of his class," Edward added.

Robin laid his head back and let out a breath. "It's something when your doctors are younger than you are."

"Get used to it," Edward said.

"Robin, are you all right? Darling?" She smoothed her hand on his forehead and cheek. He was pale. His eyes closed. "Okay, just rest then. Hardly a boring little barrister."

May 4, 1840

"Jonas, get his arm there. Help him up the steps." Edward Miller said from his front door and his butler hurried forward to assist Robin Van der Kellen up the front steps. Jonas had to take Robin's left arm over his shoulders as Robin was quite weak by that late hour.

"I'm terribly sorry for all the trouble," Robin said.

Edward took Robin's right side, not touching that sling, but held onto Robin by the waist to steady him. "Nonsense, Robin. I fear we have not provided you with the honeymoon we had promised."

"You have no idea how much humor pains me at this moment," Robin said, as the two men assisted him up the steps.

"Upstairs to bed now." Edward urged.

Adam the valet held open the front doors. "What can I do? What can I do, sir?"

"May I just sit down for a rest?" Robin asked. "Immediately."

"Into the parlor then. Put him on the big sofa," Edward said. "Adam, we are not to touch his right arm. Prepare some pillows there for him."

The policeman entered the room as well, looking about behind them.

"Your wife probably saved your life, sir, handing you that gun," the policeman said. "Do you mind if I have a look around the place, Mr. Miller?"

"Please do, good officer," Edward said.

Robin and Marie looked at each other. "So glad you are out of the hospital."

Edward, Jonas the butler, a couple maids were all waiting for instruction. And the police officer was walking throughout the lower level of the house.

Adam slid throw pillows in beneath Robin's right elbow and the sling.

A maid swooped forward and pushed a foot stool up in front of Robin and then unfolded a wool throw blanket over his lap. "May I get you anything, sir? Are you hungry at all?"

"I'm actually starving. I'm sorry to be so blunt. It's the laudanum," Robin said.

"We will prepare supper right away sir." She bowed and hurried to the kitchen with another maid.

"Can I get you a drink, Robin?" Edward asked.

Robin shook his head. "I'm on too much medication right now. Thank you. Edward, I apologize again for…"

Marie sat beside him and adjusted the blanket over his lap.

"No, Robin. I won't accept it. You are a most worthy guest." Edward sat down across from him. "What a cool head you have, to take aim and shoot an attacker who has just shot you down in the street. He was a bank robber wasn't he? You put away two in as many days."

Robin held his left hand to his chest and let out a breath. "I need a holiday."

Jonas burst out laughing and then Edward did too. And they didn't realize Adam was still there until he made an inhalation.

Van der Kellen looked down at his own sling and arm, adjusting it with his left hand. He found a bit of blood coming through yet another shirt.

"Adam?" Jonas said.

Adam had his hand to his mouth. He looked pale himself.

"Get out. Go to the kitchen. Check on dinner, would you?" Jonas urged the valet.

"Yes, sir." Adam made his way out.

Jonas stepped forward and offered a handkerchief for the blood. At a nod from Robin, he tucked it in between shirt and bandages for him.

"Robin, I would like to offer my summer home to you. It is on Long Island, on the beach. If you would like to hide out there with Marie for a time, I will send staff to open the place up. It is starting to get warm enough to enjoy the place," Edward said. "Elizabeth could go with you, or not, if you wish to be alone. Just consider it. You and Marie have been though a week that I'm certain was as terrifying as it was wonderful. You did just get married. And you are young and in love."

"I appreciate your offer." Robin let out a hard breath. "But, I need to see the papers found on this shooter. I need to go to Boston now."

"You need to rest. You need to spend time with your wife. Change your priorities," Edward advised. "Your work ethic is admirable. But you've just been shot, Robin. You are done working for a few months."

Robin held onto his sling with his other hand. "I suppose so. I can't even hold pen to paper right now."

"You must recuperate here of course. You do not have to decide anything now."

"But I am endangering your family just by being here," Robin said. "My own home is probably being ransacked by thieves as we speak. Anyone I am with is in danger."

Edward and Jonas looked at each other.

"With all those police out front? They assure me we are safe," Edward said. "And I am quite famous with my neighbors now, for sheltering a famous barrister in my home. My next dinner party will be the most popular in New York." Edward smiled warmly at him. He got up and patted Robin on the knee. "You are not going anywhere until you are well enough to do so. Jonas will send a letter to that constable friend of yours to check on your home. Constable Poole of Canterbury."

"No, please. I will write him. Edward, you have been most kind. And I have not been able to fully disclose to you my purpose with these bank robberies," Robin said.

"You can't write now. Your business is your own," Edward said.

"But not when it endangers your household," Robin said. "These bank robbers think I have the money. They think I have two million dollars."

Edward stood up. "Leave us. Please. See that supper is being served out there on the table. I'll bring him along. He can't eat anything here with only one hand."

The staff left and closed the folding double doors.

Edward paced to say quietly, "Have you? Sorry, what a leading question. Two million dollars.... Robin, I've been a banker for thirty years. There is an accounting of every dollar put in my bank. And I can tell you, the East Fourteenth Street bank had similar records. But my Dutchman, it burnt to the ground with the owner inside it. If the money stolen from it came to be in your possession by way of Albertson to your father and then to you, well who do you plan to return it to? The robbers? Keep it. They should have secured their vault better."

"There were three such banks. I just found out two of them burned," Robin said softly. "The third just folded up and disappeared from Norwich, Connecticut. How does a bank up and disappear?"

"Take the money and return to Amsterdam with your lovely wife, a rich man," Edward whispered to him. "You're a war hero. You deserve it. You don't have it on you, do you?"

Robin shook his head.

"But you do have it?" Edward asked.

Robin only made eye contact.

"You've done all anyone could to return it, nickel and dime, to the original owners. If the documents no longer exist and the bank no longer exists, son, you're at the end of the line," Edward said. "What exactly is troubling you about it? Your conscience?"

"French francs," Robin whispered. "I cannot account for where they came from."

"I haven't seen any around here since they all pulled out, twenty years ago," Edward said. "Let me inquire with the exchange in Boston and save you a trip. I'm sure they haven't either."

"It's too dangerous."

"My office does similar inquiries all the time. I will merely ask if there is a sum of Francs available for purchase and if it resides in a bank for me to exchange with," Edward said. "Will that serve your purpose?"

Robin nodded. "It will indeed. I am not...I am not what you think I am." The Dutchman lowered his chin and pulled his sling closer to his heart. Marie held his left hand in hers.

Edward looked kindly on him. "Are you a barrister? Are you following up on your father's cases? Are you formerly of the Dutch Cavalry? Then you are exactly who I think you are."

"I'm not an aristocrat."

"Neither am I. I'm a banker. I work for a living. I made all of my money, and well married into it. Now let's get some supper into you both. Come along now."

"She hasn't had anything to eat either." Robin stood up and let Marie take the blanket. "I can't even take care for her because I've been..."

"You've been shot, my friend. We are going to look after Marie. Don't you worry." Edward extended a hand and got around on his left side. "If you're dizzy at all, you just grab hold of my arm. Come on, son. We must get some good food into you."

Robin was seated with was a cup of tea and biscuits as the table was being set with plates of food. His eyes went up to Marie with a look of exhaustion.

Marie took the seat on Robin's left. "Let me help you."

Elizabeth sat across from Robin. "Are you in much pain? You look so pale, dear Robin."

"The carriage ride did me in. But if my arm is still, it is not so bad," Robin said.

"Are you cold? Get this fire really going, please," Edward told the server. "And get his going upstairs in their room. Make it warm up there."

The butler Jonas came in and set Robin's briefcase down behind him. "The driver brought Mr. Van der Kellen's bag in."

"You did get your pistol back?" Marie asked.

Robin nodded. "Yes."

The police officer entered the room. "Everything appears secure, Mr. Miller. And Mr. Van der Kellen, I will get you access to those papers tomorrow, sir. Have a good night, sirs and ladies. There will be two officers outside all through the night."

"Good night, Officer Richards," Robin said.

He exited.

Marie cut up braised pork and roasted root vegetables for Robin, who shrunk at being unable to do it himself.

"She's practicing for when you have children," Elizabeth said.

"There. What do you need?" Marie told him.

"Marie, ahm…." Robin looked at her.

"It's okay." Marie put her hand on his shoulder and toyed with his hair a bit. "You're tired and in pain."

He eventually nodded and picked up his two-pronged fork with his left hand.

Marie moved his teacup within his reach. And then she started to eat her own meal. She watched him using the fork and struggling a bit. She pushed a spoon over to him. "Use this, darling. It will be easier."

Robin set down the fork and tried the spoon instead. "Better with a sword, believe it or not."

"Well let me remove all of the crystal before you try that," Edward declared.

Robin managed a brief smile and a bit of a laugh. "Thank you."

Edward and Elizabeth let them eat in peace for a while, without further questions. They were talking about their other relatives.

And in time, Robin leaned his forehead to Marie and laid his hand on her thigh beneath the table.

Marie kissed his cheek and his pout. "You need to eat something. You'll feel better when you do." She smoothed his hair back and tucked it behind his ear. "It was a long ride from the hospital. And you need to lay down."

Ian van Allen came skidding into the room. "I beg your pardon. I just found out you were released from the hospital, sir."

Robin looked up at him. "You haven't missed anything. I'm still shot, man."

"Ian, have a seat. Have you eaten? Bring him a place setting," Edward said.

Ian sat down across from Robin, watching him learning to eat with his other hand. "You are better at that than most."

"I might be better at trimming the garden than cutting this meal," Robin explained.

Ian stared at him while the others laughed.

Robin let out a sigh. "Oh. All those stairs. I did not think my manhood could diminish such that stairs are my greatest challenge."

"Don't worry. We'll help you. Get that valet in here to help us," Ian said.

"Getting Adam," Jonas said.

Ian helped slide Robin's chair back and steadied him to stand up. Marie got up and circled around him.

"Anything we can do?" Edward asked, worried. "We can carry him up. He's a slender fellow."

"I'll manage. I'll just pass out when I reach the bed," Robin insisted.

"The exercise will be good for you. We will just make certain you can't further injure yourself," Ian said.

"Such as falling and breaking my neck?" Robin said. "Ian, you must lighten up. Did they drain your sense of humor away at Harvard?"

Ian finally laughed. "I'm sorry. The partner in my firm has a lot of pressure on me to do well here."

As they started down the hall, Robin said, "Don't worry. Edward and I are going to give a very high reference for you. You have no such pressure here."

Adam, the young valet hurried out from the servant's kitchen. "Sirs, at last I can be of assistance?"

Jonas grabbed Adam and moved him forward. "Just tell us what you want us to do, Dr. Van Allen. We're getting Mr. Van der Kellen up to bed."

"Adam get under Mr. Van der Kellen's left arm and let him hold onto you. I will guide him and protect his right side should he fall down. And Jonas, follow behind Mr. Van der Kellen to keep him from falling down the stairs," Ian directed. "Marie, just hurry up to his room with the maids to get the bed turned down."

Robin looked up at the grand staircase and estimated twenty-five steps between him and the second floor where their bedroom awaited.

"Adam," Ian urged. "Gently. Let him set the pace."

The twenty-year old let Robin put an arm around his shoulders and then wrapped his arm about Robin's waist, beneath his jacket. "Is this okay, sir? Forgive me. Lean on me if you please."

"Yes." Robin nodded. "Sorry for this."

They started to climb the stairs. Adam kept one hand on the rail and the other supportively about Robin's waist.

As these stairs were very wide, two maids hurried past and up with trays of supplies.

Adam took more and more of Robin's weight as they climbed together. He stooped a bit, being a couple inches taller but just as slender as Robin.

Marie waited at the top, her hand over her mouth as she looked on. "He's getting faint."

Jonas stepped up and put both hands on Robin's lower back.

When he could, Robin made the last two steps to the top.

"Very good. Not much further," Ian said. "Let's walk nice and slow to the bedroom. Marie, tell them to turn down the left side of the bed."

Marie met eyes with Robin and then hurried into the bedroom.

The two maids set up a tray of brandy and cookies on the table. They stoked up the fireplace. And one turned down the blankets as Marie instructed. Then they stood in the hall awaiting instructions.

Adam helped Robin walk around the bed to the left side and sat down with him on it.

"Let him rest," Ian said.

Adam slid carefully out from beneath Robin's arm and stooped down at his feet, unbuttoning his ankle boots. "Whenever you are ready, sir. I can't believe someone shot you. I just can't believe it."

Robin held his hands, both of them to his chest. For a few moments it was all he could do to breathe. "Mijn God, that hurts."

"We'll get some laudanum into you so you can sleep. Let's get him into bed. Ladies, leave us please." Ian opened his medical bag to search for the medicine and a spoon. "Mrs. Van der Kellen, give us a moment please. It just makes this easier."

"Very well then." Marie exited to the hall with the maids and shut the door.

Adam removed Robin's boots and set them aside. He removed stockings.

"I'll get you a brandy to help this go down." Ian walked over to the table and chairs at the foot of the bed.

Adam gently untied Robin's sling. "Are you all right, sir?"

Robin nodded. "Just in a lot of pain. Thank you for your help, Adam." He let the valet ease the jacket off of him. "You're already better at that than any nurse in the hospital."

"I will get you a sleep shirt. Just one moment." Adam scurried to the dresser where he had unpacked Robin's things, and located one.

Ian brought the medicine and a glass of brandy to the bedside. "Here. The sooner the better." He poured a spoon of it and fed it to Robin over the brandy glass.

Robin took the glass with his left hand and downed all of it at once.

"Oh my. I thought you might just wash the taste away." Ian collected the empty glass in shock.

"You thought wrong. I'd bring that bottle over here if I were you," Robin said.

Adam did so, delivering the bottle to the nightstand, and bringing the night shirt.

Ian just stepped aside then. "I don't think you're supposed to drink while in your condition."

"Laudanum is about ninety percent alcohol, isn't it?" Robin asked, looking away as Adam unbuttoned his shirt down from the top.

"I suppose it is."

"Then how can a bit more alcohol be my problem?" Robin asked.

"Oh, if you're bleeding I may pass out myself." Adam opened the shirt to reveal bandaging around and under Robin's arm, around his neck, with thick padding over the wound.

Robin glanced down at the white cotton and linen bandages. "Better let Ian redo this then."

There was blood soaking through and a bit onto Robin's shirt.

"Oh my. I think I can collect this." Adam bristled as he removed Robin's shirt. "How will we do the trousers?"

"I'll stand up and you pull them off my feet when I sit down," Robin said. "How do you suppose Elizabeth does Edward's?"

Adam looked at him and then to Jonas and Ian. Jonas burst out laughing while Ian said, "I'm afraid the Dutch sense of humor evades me."

"I never understood the Danish humor," Robin replied.

Finally, Ian laughed.

The maids and Marie stopped Adam when he came out with his arms around Robin's clothing.

Adam gave a little bow. "Mrs. Van der Kellen, he asks that you convince the doctor to let him have more brandy." He was distracted by the shell buttons on the shirt and hurried down the stairs then.

The maids giggled.

"Sounds urgent," Marie told them. "Thank you and good night."

"Ring if you need us, mum."

Robin rested back against pillows for a while, sipping his brandy, talking with Ian as Marie paced back and forth at the foot of the bed. "Ian, is there any way I can lay on my side to sleep?"

"There might be. You're not going to like the process," Ian said.

"He's so exhausted. If there is any way to help him," Marie said.

"Let's get you on your left side with a pillow to rest your injured arm on," Ian said. "Show her how to do this for when you go home. You can't do this on your own."

"You don't know what those words do to me."

"Ah, we are learning how to work together." Ian got him rolled into the new position and pulled the sheet and blankets over him. "Now, how is that?"

Robin took time to slow his breathing. Then he said one word into Ian's shoulder, "Heaven."

Ian looked at Marie. "Sarcasm?"

"No, he's serious," Marie said.

"Wonderful. Wonderful, sir. Madam, I will be in the next room. If he needs anything just knock on my door. I'm a very light sleeper when on duty." Ian eased Robin's right arm down onto the pillows and stood up.

"What if I'm making love to my wife? Am I to do it quietly?" Robin asked.

Ian looked horrified. "I beg your pardon."

"That was sarcasm," Marie told him. "I probably will come knocking when he bleeds all over these sheets."

"Oh. Oh, he is bleeding again. I can fix that." Ian quickly rummaged through his medical bag. "I can fix that. Avert your eyes, madam."

Marie shrugged. "Relax, doctor, and stuff another bandage in there. He's so tired, doctor. He needs to sleep badly."

Ian pulled out fresh padding and bandages which he very gently slid into the attached bandages. "How is the pain, sir?"

"Tolerable. Thank you, Ian." Robin just gripped onto Ian's jacket for a bit and clenched his eyes shut.

The young doctor sighed with relief. He laid his hand lightly on Robin's injured shoulder. "That laudanum will put you to sleep soon. Send for me if you need anything, sir. Sleep well for as long as you can and then let me come help you onto your back again." He exited toward the door and whispered to Marie, "Wake me." He left the room and closed the door softly.

She sat down on her side of the bed. "I think I shall sleep on the couch and let you rest."

"No. Please," Robin whispered. "Please lie behind me, so that I know you're there."

Marie changed into her night gown and blew out the lamps. By the light of the fireplace, she gently crawled onto the bed with Robin, and beneath the sheets. "Are you cold?"

"No. Very hot. Can't do a thing about it."

Marie eased the covers down off Robin's right shoulder. "Just tell me. And when you get cool later, tell me to pull them back up. I'm afraid to touch you."

"Please put your hands on me. Just don't push on my shoulder."

Marie laid down behind him with her head on the next pillow. She put her right hand on the back of his neck and smoothed his hair out on the pillow. "I like your haircut very much. I'm glad it is still long though. How is this? Does this hurt you?"

"It's wonderful."

She leaned closer and kissed the base of his neck. "I love you so, darling."

"Oh God, Marie. I love you. I long to wrap my arms around you again. I'm sorry. This is going to be a bad night."

"Then I'm in it with you. Let us pretend, we are home, lying on the hill, looking up at the sky," Marie whispered. "What planets do you see?"

Robin whispered. "Venus and Mars, near the moon there."

"Then it is summer. We are on a red picnic blanket with a bottle of wine. What falling stars are these?"

"The Perseids. It's mid-August."

"Then we hear the crickets. And an owl," Marie whispered. "How many falling stars did you see?"

"None. Just looking at your eyes." He sounded as if the laudanum was taking him.

"I see dozens of fireflies as you make love to me."

After only four hours Marie had to knock on the doctor's door. He opened it a bit. "I'll be right there."

He grabbed a robe to pull on and slippers and then entered Robin's room.

Marie held her robe closed. "He needs to get onto his back and I tried to help him but he had terrible pain. I thought I should get you."

"Rightly so." Ian rounded the bed to check on his patient. "Robin, I'm going to sit you up so you can take some laudanum. Then we'll lay you on your back for a time. Did you sleep well on your side?"

"Yes, until I moved," Robin admitted.

"Good. Here is the way we can do this…"

May 5, 1840

"The tavern on the corner near the Oyster Pub. That was my favorite."

"Yes, it is right near Harvard. I'm sure all of the students went there. My home was just four blocks the other way."

"And you lived there for five years? What made you leave all that and move to Connecticut?"

"Ahm, my father passed and I had to settle things there."

Edward looked inside to find Ian and Robin talking. Robin was sitting up in the bed and Ian had pulled up a chair alongside.

317   The Dutchman   By Susan Eddy

"Edward, come in," Robin said.

Ian looked up.

Edward strolled up to the foot of the bed. "How are you today, Robin?"

"Finally had some sleep, thanks to Ian. But I feel like I've been thrown under a stampede," Robin said.

"I believe he is suffering from contusions as well as from blood loss. He's drinking all the water he can," Ian reported. "If possible I believe it will help him to eat red beef."

"Thank you, Ian. I do hope you are getting enough rest here, Robin. I came up to make sure Elizabeth isn't too much of a distraction from your resting, but I see she is not even here," Edward said.

"She took Marie with her to the bakery, I believe," Robin said.

"They are out of the house? It is good for Marie to get out. Shouldn't we leave Robin so he can sleep?" Edward asked.

"No, I've slept enough. We were just reminiscing about Boston," Robin said.

"Which parts? You know my brother lives on Garden Street. He's a physician at the General Hospital," Edward said. "We were coming back from visiting him when we met you on the train."

"Garden Street? I used to live on Myrtle, just a block from there," Robin said.

"And what a lovely neighborhood it is there," Edward said.

That evening

"Marie, I haven't even made a home for you yet and we carry on at night as if there is no care in the world," Robin said. "You could already be with child and I know better than that. We can't keep doing it that way. I've been selfish. I've needed you so much." He lowered his chin and was so beautiful in his misery with the flush of his cheeks and reddening of his lips. "I have desired you so much."

Marie held onto his lapels firmly. "Robin, I am young and healthy. I'm certain Adrianna was too. But if she traveled on that long ocean voyage, sick and with child...it is not anyone's fault what happened."

Robin tried to get up and she restrained him there.

"Awful as it was, it was not your fault. And it won't happen again," Marie told him.

"She was terribly ill and...and gave birth two months too early. They both died. I held him...my son," he whispered, his eyes tearing so. "And for many years I thought I can't be with any woman ever again."

That broke Marie's resolve and she sobbed.

Robin stood up and pulled her to him with his arm in the sling like a barrier between them. But his other arm wrapped about her neck. "And to think I had good news to bring you today."

"Good news? You have some good news? Don't tell me yet. Not this way." Marie sat up. "I must wash my face, before I look puffy all day tomorrow."

She went to the pitcher and bowl on the table nearby and poured the cool water into it for splashing on her face. Then she dabbed with the towel.

Robin slid his boots off and began unbuttoning his shirt.

Marie said, "You didn't want that valet Adam to undress you?"

Robin smiled a bit and shook his head. "He seemed a bit too eager."

Marie smiled. "And you are shy." She finished unbuttoning the shirt for him and as it was not tucked into his trousers, she opened it back off his chest. "I'll have to carefully remove this sling to get the shirt off you." She used both hands to unbuckle his belt. She pulled the belt through the buckle and began unbuttoning his trousers. "When you are feeling well again, I don't want you to make love to me any differently than we have been. You do have a house we can live in. Although, I concede that you cannot seem to earn a living there."

Robin laughed out loud. "The money is ours. I can't find a single damn person alive to give it to, except us. And I'll give another ten percent of the rest to Michael and Alice, of course. The French coins, I still don't know who they belong to or where they came from but the $103 have lost all their records in two bank fires. The French gold I'd imagine to be worth another $50,000. The Norwich bank money is another $200. And now I have bonds that I have no idea how much they are worth."

Marie examined his sling and untied it. He winced as his arm moved. He took in a sharp breath as she eased his shirt down and off. And then she retied the sling into place. There was some bleeding through his bandage, but not as much. Marie kissed his bare shoulder. "You are supposed to have more laudanum now."

"May I trouble you instead for a glass of that brandy?"

"In the middle of the night you'll regret your choice." Marie moved to the table nearby and poured two glasses of brandy and set several cookies onto a sliver plate. She brought one brandy and the plate of cookies to Robin in the bed. And he got to sip brandy while he watched her undress, slip out of her corset, and into a silk night gown. She took down her hair and began brushing it. "Robin, I would have married you on my income."

"In the past six months, you've earned more than I have."

"Do you have any idea how fine you look on a horse?" Marie asked.

"Of course. Why do you think I didn't join the artillery?" he said.

Marie refilled his brandy already. "I'll get you laudanum in the middle of the night. Skirt chaser."

Robin Map Making

By Susan Eddy

Chapter Fifteen Offended Gentleman

May 6, 1840

"My manager has to fire someone today. I may have to do it for him. He has no guts at all for this sort of thing," Edward said. "I'll be out for the morning."

Edward made his exit.

They heard him from the hallway saying, "Adam, get me my rain boots, will you? It looks cloudy out there."

"Elizabeth, by any chance do you write?" Robin was finishing his breakfast of pastries, eggs, and sausages, sitting up at the dining room table.

"I do. In two languages. English and French," she said.

"Marie writes in French as well. You can pass notes, but be wary...I read it very well," Robin said.

"Do you wish me to write a letter for you?" Elizabeth asked.

"I need to let Constable Poole and his wife know we are all right," Robin said. "And they only speak English."

"Why don't I dictate a letter to Alice then?" Marie suggested. "Unless you need to send any details of the case to the constable?"

Robin shook his head. "I like your plan better. Don't mention I've been shot. He'll give me hell for it soon enough."

"Language," Marie whispered to him.

Robin rolled his eyes. "My apologies ladies."

"We'll do that today," Elizabeth assured. "Have you talked about our summer home?"

Robin shook his head again.

"If you want me to drop it, I shall," Elizabeth told him.

"I was just too tired to discuss it. You may tell Marie about it," Robin said.

"Oh Marie, we want to lend you our summer home on the beach, complete with staff, just so you will have your honeymoon and be safe away from the city," Elizabeth said. "It's beautiful there. Stay a few weeks or a few months. Robin can heal. You can be alone together."

"You didn't want to come with us?" Robin asked her.

"Oh. I would love to. I didn't want to impose. I want you to be happy and alone together. You don't want to bring me along," Elizabeth said.

Marie and Robin glanced at each other.

"I wouldn't feel right going without you," Marie said to her.

"Of course, you can feel right there without me. You can finally be alone together. If however, you want me to go, if I can make it easier for you. I will allow you plenty of time alone together. I have friends out there and I love to walk on the beach for hours. You can do whatever you like there," Elizabeth said. "The drawback is, that it will be a train ride followed by a two-hour carriage ride to get there. I don't think Robin is able to do that yet."

"We have...imposed on both of you so much already," Robin said. "I'm inclined to think when I'm healed enough we will go home."

"But write to you and visit again some time," Marie said. "Right, Robin?"

"Of course. Elizabeth, I do not wish to part you from Marie. I'm sorry, I just do not see another way forward," Robin said.

"I'm hoping you will move to New York. But of course, if you move to Boston, we can visit you," Elizabeth said. "If you are going home from here, then I do hope you will stay and recover a good long while."

Dr. Ian Van Allen entered the dining room and sat down at the table with them. "How are you today, Mr. Van der Kellen?"

"I am better. Thanks very much to you. I slept much better," Robin said.

"I will caution you on the use of laudanum. There is some talk in the medical community that it may be habit forming. It also has other unpleasant effects," Van Allen said.

"I have used it before. It's terrible what it does to my sleep habits," Robin said.

"Yes. That is one of them. You should use as little as possible and wean yourself from it," Van Allen said.

"What are the other side effects?" Marie asked.

"Oh? Well, no marital benefits until that heals and you're off laudanum," Van Allen said, shyly.

"Why is that?" Robin questioned.

"You won't be able to, sir. He won't be able to," Van Allen said to Robin, avoiding eye contact with Marie or Elizabeth. "Not on laudanum. But that will pass when you stop taking it."

"Excuse me, marital benefits?" Marie questioned.

That made Robin burst out laughing and Elizabeth giggled.

Even the doctor laughed. "Do you have enough laudanum from the hospital?"

"Yes. Though you've given me no incentive to take it now."

At midday, Jonas entered the dining room and set down a large bowl in the center of the table, in front of Robin. "Ladies and gentlemen, I give you Dutch bitterballen."

Robin gleamed and looked up at him. "It looks wonderful."

"I shall serve you first then." Jonas spooned one deep fried crispy ball into Robin's bowl. And then another. "What are these, sir?"

"Usually, beef stew inside a bread ball," Robin explained.

"And I also have Dutch pea soup, just as you asked, followed by all manner of sweet treats," Jonas said.

Robin sat in the main salon, reading one of his father's journals in his lap. His feet were up on a stool and a blanket across his lap. To his left immediately was a table and his teacup, which the maids kept refilling. His back was to the front window of the home, giving him plenty of reading light. He flipped another page and then just dropped the leather-bound book when he jolted. A folded letter then fell out of it.

The maid heard the book hit the floor.

Robin sat forward to reach for it but couldn't.

The maid hurried back to pick it up for him. "Here you are, sir." She handed him the letter too. "There are more letters for you in the den."

"There are?"

"Yes. I'll bring them right away, sir."

"Thank you. Do you know where Mrs. Van der Kellen is?"

"In the conservatory, I believe. Would you like me to get her, sir?"

"Yes please." Robin was turning pages to get back to where he was.

"Shall I fetch the doctor?"

"No. I'm all right." The letter was addressed to Mr. Van der Kellen. It was sealed. Robin broke the seal and unfolded the paper.

Robin had his left hand to his forehead when Marie entered the salon.

"Robin? I thought she said you were all right." Marie moved closer to him and sat down on the sofa on his injured side.

"I've just found something." Robin wet his lips. "I will now read to you the words of my father."

To my son Robin,

As the fine barrister you have become, I know you will one day find this. If you have not already found four stashes of currency, I will now list where they are below and how I came by them. I'm certain you have begun to question my integrity and no doubt your own as I have now put you in my exact position. I wish I had lasted to see you again and inform you myself that there is no way to return this money and you must now keep it with a clear conscience. Unlikely anyone else in the region can read this except you. Take this money and live well. Send some to your brother and sisters if you wish. Return to Amsterdam if you wish. Live up to your fairy tale name, as was your mother's wish. It is my deepest regret that I was not more openly supportive in the loss of your wife and son. I was deeply wounded by it, as I am in no doubt certain you were. You must start life over once again and take a new wife. I fear I pushed you to joining the cavalry. It was always my wish that after Robert went into the medical profession that you would follow me into my profession. I was always uncertain that the gentlest of my two sons would prosper in a military career. To me you were still the boy with the rabbits in his

328   The Dutchman   By Susan Eddy

pockets. When you arrived in America, a barrister in your own right, and remained aloof of me, even after your losses, I realized I had been the cause of this rift. I would have you know that I was always proud of your rank and medals in the service. Your experience in war, no doubt, will get you through the dangers that you are now about to inherit. You have received the $200 have you not? You are in great danger, my son.

East 14th Street Bank, New York $18000 Treasury Notes, Gold, Silver, Massachusetts State Bank Notes -Pascal

High Street Bank, New York 289000 in US Treasury Notes and Gold - Pascal

Norwich Bank and Trust, Norwich Connecticut territory $185000 in Connecticut State Notes and Continental - Pascal and Robinson

French traders F8000 - Robinson and Stuart

Ontario territory French traders F2000 -Robinson Stuart

"French forts?" Marie questioned. "I thought they left the new world many years ago."

"They did here but not to the North. Robinson. Possibly Albertson's partner? The man who shot me was older than I am, by ten years perhaps. Old enough to have fought the French or fought with them. I need to see those papers the shooter had in his possession. I need to see troop rosters from twenty years ago when it would have been the New York militia, the Connecticut militia such as Michael Poole, and others. Stuart was too young to have been in that war."

"Yes. I don't think he was much older than I am," Marie said.

Robin shook his head. "Father hated me then. He made that very clear...to an eighteen-year-old boy. Said it was foolish to waste an intellect like I had on the cavalry."

"Why did you join?"

"Glory. Of all stupid things. And to avoid marriage."

The maid knocked, entered and delivered four letters to Robin. "Excuse me, sir. These are for you."

Robin opened and read letters of invitation from Edwards banking friends. And there was another letter.

Mr. Van der Kellen,

Sir, I realize how inappropriate this inquiry for employment is, given that I am employed by such a good friend of yours. But if I may be so bold, when you and your wife leave for Connecticut, I would very much like to work as your most devoted valet and aspiring butler. I am at your service.

Adam Hudson.

Edward Miller hurried in that evening and went into the salon where Robin was asleep sitting up on the sofa and Marie was chatting with Beth.

"Did Ian come? How is he?"

That woke Robin and he looked about.

Edward removed his hat and pulled up a chair in front of Robin. "How are you, my friend?"

"Tired, but all right." Robin closed up the journal on his lap. Four folded letters were beside it.

"The doctor was here wasn't he?"

Robin smiled painfully. "Yes. He's been in a few times and still seeing other patients."

"Tonight, I have all six bankers that would very much like to come to dinner again tonight to make a proposition to you. You need only to hear them out, have your dinner, and get upstairs to bed," Edward told him.

"I cannot be obligated to your friends. About them…"

"You should hear them out. They don't consider it an obligation at all. They would like to offer you a position as a bank security consultant. Given your expertise in bank robbery, there is no one better suited for the job. I'm one of them, dying for any advice you have on the matter," Edward said.

"I have legal expertise. I do not see how any opinion I have would qualify as bank security," Robin said.

"You have far more expertise than you know, sir. You know intimate details in the cases of multiple bank robberies." Edward patted him on the knee. "I told them you would be hard to convince, that you are independently wealthy and do not need to work at all. You are catching bank robbers because you are good at it. I'm afraid, that only spurred them on."

Robin only opened his mouth.

"The wives are not coming. It's not a party. Just dinner and a discussion with you before you need to rest tonight. They all know you were shot down and so bravely killed your attacker. Do not give your advice freely. They need to hire you to get it."

"I thought you wanted me to holiday at the beach. Now you want me to save every bank on Manhattan."

Edward burst out laughing. "You are the most witty and entertaining of friends."

"Yes. Apparently." Robin indicated the small pile of letters. "Your friends are most generous, inviting me to convalesce at their homes too. I shall have to thank them in person, and kindly refuse. I hope they understand that I can't write them a letter myself."

"I'll have Jonas write them on your behalf. Give me these letters. Oh Gregory, Markus, Victor, and Enri. You don't want to stay with Enri. It was his wife found you so handsome with your scraped chin." Edward made him laugh and hold his chest tightly. "Vulnerable such as you are, she'll never let you rest. Look at them trying to steal away my house guest! And that letter? You missed one."

Robin looked down the letter from Adam Hudson. "Oh this is personal."

May 7, 1840

The following day, at last he could rest comfortably in that canopy bed with several pillows, soft blankets over him, and good food. Marie and Elizabeth were immediately with him, getting him anything he needed, fluffing pillows, and commenting that it was a good thing Marie could sleep with him at night to make sure he was all right.

"Where's Edward?" Robin asked.

"He went to the bank today. He should be back soon for dinner," Elizabeth said.

The two women sat on the bed with him, Marie up by the pillows with him and Elizabeth at her feet.

Robin's pants were folded up on the chair beside him. His boots stood next to the chair.

"So, tell me, what are the concerns of ladies today?" Robin mused. "Are you doing each other's hair now? You both look so lovely."

"We did, actually," Marie told him.

"She knows different styles than I do," Elizabeth said.

Robin picked up his teacup from the table on his left. "Did you write to Alice yet?"

"I did. It was posted this morning," Marie told him. "I told her we were staying with wonderful new friends, everything was going well, and we thought we would stay on a bit longer."

Elizabeth got up and crossed the room to close the bedroom door. Then she returned to sit where she was at Marie's feet. "I wish to ask both of you something. And you are not to speak of this to anyone."

"What is bothering you?" Marie asked.

"I will have your word first. You will not speak of this to anyone, especially Edward," Elizabeth said.

"Yes, I give my word," Robin said.

"And so do I," Marie said.

"First of all, I adore both of you so much. I would never do anything to come between you. I want you both to know that," Elizabeth said. "And if you refuse, I will always understand and think no ill will of you. I only hope that just by asking you this, you will not hate me forever."

"I couldn't possibly hate you, Beth," Marie said.

"I am telling you this now in broad daylight, to demonstrate that I have thought this through with a clear mind. And this is an ask out of my friendship for you. You love each other very much. I can see this." Elizabeth then found it uncomfortable to look at either of them. "My greatest fear is that you will leave after I ask you and I will never see you again."

"That will not happen," Marie told her. "What is it?"

"I should go with you to the summer home and open it up for you. Robin can rest and heal. And then… For three years I have been married to Edward and still no child," Elizabeth said. "I think you know what desperate thing I would ask."

"Stop," Robin said gently. "Beth, I cannot allow you to ask this."

"I meant no disrespect to either of you. Marie is like a sister to me and you not quite like a brother because you are so very handsome," Elizabeth said softly. "You would make such beautiful children, Robin."

"Elizabeth, I understand your impatience. But you must open that door now," Robin said. "You are young and have every chance of having children with your husband if you are patient."

"If I was to share him with anybody," Marie said softly.

"I cannot betray my vows and my heart. You do not know what you are asking. And I beg of you to open that bedroom door before anyone in the house becomes suspicious. You don't know what a dishonor it would be," Robin implored softly. "Marie, open the door or I shall have to."

Elizabeth got up, opened the door, and walked out through it.

Marie put her hand on Robin's sling, gripping his forearm a bit. "I'd better go talk to her."

"Was I too cruel?" Robin whispered.

"No. But I think if you agreed, I would have agreed," Marie said.

"No. You are too young to know what you are saying. Years later you would regret this. Marie, please tell her what happened with

Adrianna. Perhaps that will ease her mind," Robin said. "And explain I am afraid to do it even to you."

"I got my monthly. I'll go tell her what you said." Marie patted his arm.

"Marie." Robin asked for her to come closer. "Our children are for us to have. If we are so lucky."

She leaned in and kissed his mouth. "I'll send the valet in to look after you."

Robin shook his head. "You will not."

"I swear I will." Marie left to search for Elizabeth.

Robin sat back, finished his tea. He looked longingly at the carafe of brandy on the table, so far away at the end of the bed. He let out a long slow breath and laid his head back on the pillows.

Jonas the butler looked into the room. Then he entered with a tray of tiny sandwiches and more tea. His boots made the floor squeak.

Robin opened his eyes.

"How are you, sir?" Jonas brought the tray over to set things on Robin's night table. "I thought this would be easy for you to eat when you wanted them."

"Thank you. That was so thoughtful," Robin said. "Would you bring me that brandy and ahm, don't tell my wife?"

"Of course, sir."

Robin picked up a sandwich. Some of them had roast beef, some had ham, all of them had cheese.

Jonas poured a brandy for him and set the carafe beside the tray. "How is that, sir?"

"Wonderful. Thank you. Can you tell me, where is my pistol? It is usually here on the table."

Jonas pulled out the drawer to demonstrate the weapon was right there.

"Oh. Thank you," Robin said.

"Feel better knowing where it is then?" Jonas closed the drawer again.

"Ah. Yes." Robin smoothed his left hand up on his right shoulder. "Given the circumstances."

"How many times has it saved your life, sir?" Jonas handed him the brandy glass.

"Fourteen, by my count," Robin said.

"Traveled much of the world, have you? I traveled to Europe once with Edward, many years ago. Went to France to visit his relatives there," Jonas said.

"Relatives in France? My mother was French also," Robin said. "I shall have to ask him where from."

"The Rhone valley, I believe."

Robin nodded. "Wonderful wine there."

"Yes." Jonas nodded.

"Jonas, how did Adam come to be employed here?" Robin asked quietly.

"Adam? His is a sad story. Almost seven years ago we found him shining shoes on a street corner for pennies," Jonas said. "He was just a teenage boy. Orphan."

"He told me his uncle was a barber," Robin said.

"I think he was, though why he was not living with him, I do not know," Jonas said. "Said his parents died of the yellow fever. He was living under an awning behind a store. Edward took him in. Put him to work with odd jobs about the house. Sent him to school. And he had a talent for tailoring and barbering it turned out. He did a fine job on your haircut. The ladies seem to think so anyway."

Robin smiled. "Yes. He did a fine job. You must tell him for me, after I've left, that I could use such a talent at home but circumstances don't permit it, with him working for Edward. My situation in Connecticut is evolving and to where it will lead, I do not know."

Marie blew out the lamp beside her and snuggled down into bed with Robin, mindful that his right shoulder was not for resting her head upon that night or any night in the near future.

"Marie?" he whispered. "I fear we did her a disservice by allowing her into our bedroom. I suppose it began in the hospital and we just thought little of it once we came back here. We have overstayed our welcome."

"Once I told her what you said I may, she had such terrible regret for asking. I tried to reassure her we were all right," Marie whispered. "How soon will we be leaving?"

"Tomorrow I will send Jonas or Ian to the train station and arrange our return trip as soon as it is available," Robin said. "I will conclude my business here with the documents from the police station."

"They will be shocked. Edward will be."

"I have thought of my way to repay him for all his kindness, to spite my refusal of his colleagues offer of employment," Robin said. "And declined visiting with them."

"Has something changed between us? Why are you speaking so formally to me?"

"Marie, no, my love. It's just being in this house. The damned formality of it all. Writing thank you letters to everyone for everything and I can't even feed myself with this hand. I want to hold you. I need to hold you now more than ever," Robin said.

Marie slid closer to him, up against his body beneath the blankets. She followed his sling with her hand, seeking his, and linked fingers with him on his stomach.

"Are you disappointed that you are not with child already?" he whispered, his mouth on her temple.

"Not at all. We are barely able to be two people much less three."

May 10, 1840

Robin set pen, ink well, and paper down on the table. "Jonas, take notes if you would please. And thank you for writing those letters on my behalf."

The butler sat down at the paper. "My pleasure, sir."

"What is it?" Edward questioned.

"I'm about to disclose how to secure your banks from anything such as the robbers my father and I have put away for good," Robin declared.

"What fine entertainment this shall be," Edward said, as they were still clearing away the dinner plates.

Elizabeth and Marie were enjoying another glass of wine each, watching Robin Van der Kellen pace to the end of the table and back, his posture so formal and regal, his left hand adjusting his tie and his vest.

Edward pushed his dish toward the kitchen maids and stood up at the head of the table. "Do tell, Robin. Don't keep me in suspense."

"In both cases of the two banks that burnt, there was a young lady working as receptionist and Paul Stuart engaged them in some false romance. Instead of bringing them lunch he brought them lamp oil and hid it beneath their desks. He learned bank schedules, where the keys were, even the combination to the safe. He learned on which night only the owner would be inside the place. It was that night that he entered by key, killed the owner, entered the vault and safe. He and his partner collected all the money, covered the bank with a splattering of lamp oil and lit the place," Robin said. "Are you getting that down, Jonas? Receptionist, lamp oil, keys, combinations, and schedules. You must keep the first two out of the bank and the last three a secret and keep changing them often."

"Only married receptionists then," Edward declared.

"No, don't fire the ladies. Do not let them have knowledge of combinations and access to keys," Robin said. "And the other thing, your records. Duplicate them and keep a copy in another location, here at home for example. Not all of the daily records need duplication but who has deposited what money must be kept in a second location. After all the building next door can burn down spread fire to your bank."

"And what of the Norwich bank that disappeared?" Edward asked.

"Robinson was the owner himself. Using the name Roberts in Norwich, he partnered with Pascal to steal all the currency from his own bank and disappear to New York." Robin paused behind his own dinner chair and picked up his wine glass for another sip. "Hire security officers and do not ever allow any one person alone inside the bank. Someone must be watching what enters and leaves the bank, particularly parcels, packages, anything large enough to contain an explosive or flammable liquid."

"Explosive?"

"A small keg of black powder with a long wick will certainly finish off bank records and cover up a murder, and far more expediently than any fire will," Robin said. "And open a vault."

"Have any of these banks exploded?" Edward asked.

"Not yet, but I certainly would be evolving that direction if I was a bank robber. You wouldn't even have to murder the owner, just leave him inside. In another moment, all the money is yours and all evidence blown to the next territory."

"My dear, Robin, you are a genius," Edward declared. "May I share this information with my friends?"

"It is your information to do with as you please," Robin said.

Edward stepped closer to Robin then, looking him in the eyes. "I will be sorry to see you off in the morning. I am sorry to hear that your business draws you elsewhere. I'm certain Elizabeth will very much miss Marie's company."

Robin lowered his eyes.

"Have we offended you in some way?" Edward asked.

"No. Certainly not. It is I who have committed the offence. I have stayed here in your company for days and days, endangering you and your home, allowing your friends to finance my hospital care. If I remain any longer I am going against my good conscience," Robin said.

"Then...your business does not call you away, but rather your pride?" Edward said.

"I...."

"Robin, if I am to call you friend and I definitely intend to, I must insist that you stay until you are mended and able to travel home without suffering at every jolt of that train," Edward said.

Robin shook his head ever so slightly, looking to Marie.

Edward met eyes with Elizabeth and his mouth fell open in shock. "Everyone else leave this room at once. I apologize Jonas. I would speak to Elizabeth, Robin and Marie alone."

The maids and butler scrambled to exit and close the doors.

"And no listening from over there," Edward called after them.

Robin turned to face Edward with rigid military posture.

"Beth, surely you did not ask him?"

Elizabeth began to cry.

"Beth? Are you out of your mind?" Edward turned to Robin then. "Good sir, you must not be so offended by the insane suggestion of an extremely young girl. I see by your very being that she has offended you and impertinently imposed herself into your very marriage. You cannot hold such offence that you would leave the entire city and go home at once?"

"I am not offended, sir. It is my business that calls me away."

"A man who holds a sack of gold in his hands and seeks to find its owner makes for a terrible liar," Edward said. "I've never seen a gentleman more offended in my life. I most sincerely apologize. Madam Marie, I apologize to you as well. I regret very much that your friendship with Beth may be irrevocably spoiled."

"Oh, I do hope it is not," Marie said.

"I shall see you to the train station in the morning and hope that you find better company on your return voyage than we turned out to be," Edward said.

Robin reached up behind his head to undo his sling. He was then able to extend his right hand to Edward. "I hope you accept my apology for leaving so suddenly. Your hospitality and friendship have been very dear to me, to us both. I have brought you nothing but trouble."

Edward carefully grasped hands with him, taking Robin's hand gently between both of his. "It has been an extraordinary, great pleasure knowing you, Robin Van der Kellen. You are an extraordinary Dutchman, indeed."

Robin met eyes with Marie and she exited with him from the room and up the stairs.

Chapter Sixteen Parlor Trick

May 11, 1840

Standing on the rail platform together, the Van der Kellens watched Edward's carriage leaving. Marie wore a lush green velvet gown and matching coat. She had an enormous green velvet hat with the plume of a black feather. And the gentleman Robin, in a fine charcoal suit, Kelly green shirt, and top hat had a fluffy ponytail of light brown curly hair, and his right arm was in a blue silk scarf sling. A porter went right to them to draw them to their sleeper car and assure them their luggage was already aboard.

Marie did not remove her hat until inside the car. She looked down at Robin who was staring intensely down the length of the train. "What is it, darling?"

He looked up at her. "Thought I recognized someone getting on in third class."

The porter stepped in beside Robin. "May I assist you, sir? You can't grab the bar, can you?"

"Just let me hold your arm, if you would." Robin put his left hand on the porter's forearm and made the first step up onto the train. Then he took Marie's hand and climbed the next steps up.

"Are you all right, sir?" The porter bounded up beside him. "You are in cabin #5. Right ahead, Mr. and Mrs. Van der Kellen."

At last, they stood alone together inside their cabin on a train bound back for New Haven, Connecticut. Marie took the top hat from Robin and hung it on the hook behind the door. She reached up behind him, beneath his ponytail to untie his sling.

Robin caught the sling and straightened his right arm for the removal of his topcoat.

Marie hung the coat near the hat. "I can help you put that back on."

"I will leave it off for a while," Robin said and sat down on the sofa. He lowered his chin, breathing hard for a few moments.

Marie poured a glass of brandy and offered it to Robin. "Cheer up, darling. Neither of us could have predicted the wealthy would be that blunt."

Hesitantly, Robin took the brandy glass with his right hand, as if experimentally. But it made him wince. He had to steady it with his left hand quickly. "I'm so sorry, Marie. How my fear of leaving you alone in a hotel turned into all of that?"

Marie sat down beside him and began to reapply the sling to his right arm. "I should never have told her how passionate you were."

Robin looked at her.

Marie smiled warmly at him. "They are still our friends. She meant no harm, did not wish to take you from me. Desired you, obviously."

He sipped his brandy at ten o-clock in the morning.

"How lovely your sighs are when you…."

He looked at her again. He smiled just a bit. "Well, I shouldn't have told Poole I took your virginity before we married."

"You bragged to him?"

"He's such an ass, I couldn't help it." Robin looked down at his briefcase and opened it to extract one of two pistols inside it. "Edward's revolver. I think may give it to Michael."

"You don't want to keep such an invention?"

"I prefer a more elegant weapon that actually requires skill."

Robin sat down to lunch in the dining car, seated across from Marie. He began rearranging his silverware and location of the teacup to suit his left hand. The train proceeded backwards for him and forward for

Marie. Their sever brought them tea, lemonade, biscuits and soup of the day to start.

"Marie, were you happy when it was just us in the house and we had bread and your vegetable soup?" He asked softly.

"Of course, I was," Marie said. "Especially once we…were together."

Robin took out his gold pocket watch to check the time.

A man paused in the aisle, beside Robin's table, overhearing them.

Robin looked up at him.

"Sir, that is an unusual style of suit and manner of speech. What's an Englishman doing here?" the man said with a bit of hostility.

Others looked on from tables around them. All conversations stopped.

Robin set his napkin on the table as he stood up. He showed the gold cover of his watch to the man. "Do you recognize that?"

"I do not, sir. European crown of some sort."

"Yes it is. Royal Netherlandian Crown."

"Where is that?" the man said. "Sounds English."

Robin's eyes narrowed. His left hand felt for his left pocket but found it empty.

Another man stood up from the next table. "The Netherlands. He's Dutch. Not British, you fool. Pour him a drink later because you definitely owe him one. The Dutch were on our side." He took a look at the watch in Robin's hand just before Robin put it away.

"Why do I owe this little man a drink?"

"He's Dutch cavalry. He's killed more Red Coats than you ever will."

"How do you know that?"

"Those are riding boots, worn a bit from the stirrup. His palm is scarred from the reins. The suit is from Europe. He's about thirty. I'd say he probably fought in the Anglo Dutch Wars."

"That's a very skilled parlor trick, sir," Robin said. "You have me at a disadvantage."

The man showed his own scarred palms to Robin. "US Infantry. I know another horseman when I see one."

"Indeed. I would like you to join us," Robin offered.

"I would be pleased, sir." To the other man in the aisle, he said, "Move along, would you? I hate to see any cavalryman harassed, except a British one of course."

He turned to Robin and took in Marie in her green velvet then.

"Owen Abrams, sir. I'd shake your hand but I see that would be an unnecessary cruelty."

"Indeed, it would, Mr. Abrams. I am Robin Van der Kellen. This is my wife, Marie." Robin sat. "Have a seat, please."

Abrams sat beside Marie but with acceptable distance. "My pleasure, Marie. You didn't fall off a horse, did you?"

Robin laughed. "No. Never have. May I ask what was your rank, sir?"

"Colonel. I am still in the service, on my way up to Quebec for a meeting. Taking civilian transportation, I do like to blend in."

"Colonel Abrams, you are off to meet with the French?" Robin questioned. "What a coincidence that I run into you, sir."

"Really? How so? And what was your rank, sir? If I may ask."

"Captain when I retired. I served in India, Germany, and Italy," Robin said. "I am now barrister at law, State of Massachusetts and the Netherlands," Robin said. "Trying to prosecute some bank robbers but they keep...getting shot, and so do their lawyers."

Abrams' eyebrows rose.

They both paused speaking as the first course was served to all three of them and more tea.

After the server left, Abrams said, "Is that how you got shot, Captain?"

"I fell out of a carriage."

"A cavalryman does not just fall down," Abrams said. "Unless shot."

"Would you be traveling to Fort Senneville?" Robin asked.

"How did you know that?"

"You said Quebec." Robin looked down at his steak.

Marie reached across to cut it up for him.

That make Abrams smile.

Robin sat back and smiled as well. "Thank you, my love."

"Been married long?"

"Not two weeks," Robin said.

"Good Lord. Has that put your honeymoon to an end?"

Marie giggled.

"Apparently not. Just delayed." Robin smiled.

"Robin, you should rest," Marie insisted.

"I just want to see If Abrams is there. If so, I'll have a couple drinks with him. That's all," Robin said.

"You're still trying to give away money that is yours," Marie told him.

"The French Fort's money," Robin said. "It's one thing to keep bank money with no records. To keep money from the French treasury is an act of war. This went missing over a decade ago. Do they even know it is missing? That's what I want to find out."

"The French pulled out. They want nothing to do with our war with England," Marie said.

"I won't give away anything. I just want to ask him a few more questions," Robin said. "Trust me, darling."

"Be careful. He's cunning."

"Am I not?" Robin slipped his pistol into his belt beneath his jacket. "Not forgetting this again."

"With your left hand?"

Robin met her eyes and said, "With a gun, yes."

"Against a Colonel?"

"It was a Colonel I took this from," Robin said. "He's not my enemy. And even if he's not there, I will not be intimidated on this train because I am Dutch. I'll have a couple drinks and return to you."

"Robin, you can't even eat soup with your left hand."

"I can shoot straight, if I don't have to shoot too far."

Van der Kellen would have attracted attention in the smoking car even without his arm in a sling. He was about average in height with the other men and many of them had long hair as well. But his charcoal suit was tailored in a European fashion, lined in black satin, and had a bit of a tail. His green shirt was from New York. Something about him was unusual.

The bar tender handed a glass of brandy to him and four men gathered around him.

"Got shot, I'll bet," one said. "Did you?"

"Who's asking?" Robin said.

"Are you a police officer then?"

Robin shook his head. "I'm a barrister."

"A what?"

"A lawyer. An advocate."

"Does it offend you, sir, to be mistaken for British?"

"Humph. Shouldn't it?" Robin replied and sipped his brandy.

The men all laughed.

Another asked him though, "Why the pistol, Dutchman?"

Robin set down his drink and turned to face the man. The man was just smoking and waiting. "I'm going home. I don't want any trouble."

"I don't mean you trouble, sir. Did you fight in this English Dutch war?"

Robin picked up his brandy and had another sip. "I'm trying to enjoy a drink here. An interrogation typically begins with introductions."

The gentlemen broke up laughing.

"The Dutchman is clever."

"Can I get you another brandy, sir? And let us have those introductions."

Colonel Abrams entered to find Robin entertaining this group of Americans with a story about meeting a tiger in a hallway. Someone had slid a rifle along the floor to him just in time. He swooped it up, dropped on his ass, and fired at the great beast. Still has a fang on a leather string. Abrams got himself a drink and lit a cigar, listening. And he waited for Robin to come across and sit down with him.

"You said it was a coincidence to run into me," Abrams said. "Seemed as if you wanted to know something about the French."

Robin nodded. "In a way. I think one of my bank robbers may have served in the militia in the Fort Senneville or Michilimackinac regions about ten years ago. His name was Christian Pascal. I do not even know if he was American or French. I wonder if you might look into that and write me what you find out. I suspect French."

"I will see what I can do," Abrams said. "Is this bank robber on the loose?"

Robin shook his head.

Abrams pointed to Robin's sling. "Did he do that?"

"No. His friend Robinson did and I shot him in the face," Robin said. "Pascal is already dead so I won't be able to convict him for the treason I may have evidence he committed."

"What treason is that?"

Robin sipped his brandy for a moment. "Pillage. If Pascal was ever assigned to one of those forts, it might give him motive to commit this treason, that of robbing the French treasury."

"Good lord," Abrams blurted out. "I don't think they'd even know they are missing any money. Senneville, that is. Negotiations with them are so confusing that I've been sent to talk in French to them face to face. If they do not know where their own troops are, I can pretty much guarantee they do not know where their treasury is either."

"I see. I do wish you would inquire about Pascal and is there a sum of Francs they are missing," Robin said. "I would go with you as I am a Dutch citizen and therefore an impartial negotiator. But I'm not certain I can make the journey just now."

Abrams smoked and thought for a few moments. "I will inquire about Christian Pascal and write you. I will try to find out if the Fort is missing some money and if so how much. Do you know where it is?"

Robin nodded.

"We could return it?" Abrams asked.

"We could."

"I may send for you," Abrams said. "You won't disclose the amount?"

"No. I'd like to see if the amounts are similar."

"Understood. They may be satisfied with knowing Pascal is dead. War with the British in the North is diminishing. We need our French allies up there, if we're to get the British finally off this continent," Abrams said. "If war came to Connecticut, could we count on you to you enlist?"

Robin frowned. "I have no more stomach for war."

Abrams indicated Robin's sling. "Were you shot?"

Robin just made eye contact.

"Be sure to give me where to write you before we depart the train. I surmise you are departing your own little war in New York City."

"There's something else," Robin said. "Unrelated to the case. And this is not for my wife's ears. If you should encounter a French soldier, about the age of fifty, by the name of Jean LaPierre Longuiel, will you let me know where to find him?"

"Not for your wife's ears?" Abrams jotted down a few notes with a handmade version of a pencil, into a small notebook.

"She only reads and writes in French. Write to me in English, if you would," Robin said. "I wish I would be accompanying you to Senneville. The blackard should be my father-in-law. Abandoned her mother well before Marie was born."

"Well. Feel sorry for him if you ever find him." Abrams poured more brandy for the both of them. "All soldiers tend to seek company when they can find it. Even the French. Are you so certain you didn't leave any half white children behind in India?"

At that Robin stood up, collected his hat. "Good night, Colonel." And Robin left.

Marie handed Robin another glass of brandy and then crawled over his feet into the bunk with him. She slid beneath the covers and pulled them up over them.

Robin's sling had his right arm tight to his body between them.

He sipped his brandy and leaned his head back.

"How is that? Are you comfortable?"

"No."

"You didn't take any laudanum yet."

"If I must, I'll get some myself tonight," Robin said.

"Robin?" Marie put her hand on his upper right arm. "Perhaps I can distract you. When we are…together, what do you say to me in Dutch?"

He laughed out loud.

"What?" She smiled.

He took another drink. "You caught me."

"How so exactly?"

He laughed. "I do not know those words in English, though I do now add that I love you." And he followed that with the Dutch translation.

"What are you saying? Something…inappropriate?"

"No. It's very appropriate. They do not teach those words in school." He was smiling.

"Where did you learn them in Dutch then? A tavern?" Marie teased him.

"Tavern. Barracks."

"Why would you say such a thing to your wife?" Marie said.

"Because it is necessary to tell you that…and I think you know what I am telling you even if you do not speak Dutch, that the conclusion is inevitable at that point."

"The conclusion?"

"I only know those words in Dutch," he insisted.

Marie laughed. "You are saying that you must conclude it and can't stop it?"

"Precisely." Robin nodded.

"Does it hurt?"

"Oh God no," he said.

"Do you suppose poor Edward is too old to conclude it?" Marie asked.

"That must be possible."

"So, if you and I do not want to have a child too soon, we would have to not be together?"

"We can do this together. I just cannot finish it this way," Robin whispered. "And that is very hard to resist. Impossible maybe. I'm so sorry that there is not a married woman with whom you can ask these things. I'm just a man. I don't have all the answers. I have only spoken about these things with one other woman my whole life."

"Alice. I can ask Alice feminine things."

"Yes. I'm sure you can. Just don't tell her how passionate I am or how nicely I sigh. You know what that got us last time."

Marie burst out laughing. "Would you like your glass refilled? I think I deserve one myself."

"Indeed, you do."

Marie crawled out of the bunk again, in her night gown.

Robin laughed and handed his empty glass to her.

"I'll get you a tiny amount of laudanum too." Marie kissed his forehead and his mouth. "I can't believe you say naughty things to me in Dutch, and I thought it was so romantic. How do you say I love you?"

"Ik hou van jou."

May 12, 1840

Colonel Abrams approached them at their dinner table. "Mr. Van der Kellen?"

"Abrams?" Robin looked up at him coolly.

"I am sorry to intrude," Abrams said. "I did not see you at lunch."

"We took lunch in our cabin. I am not feeling well," Robin said.

"Sorry to hear that. Is there anything I can do for you?" Abrams asked. "Have I angered you?"

"Please sit down," Robin said.

Abrams took the seat beside Robin this time and studied the lovely face of Marie across from him. The daughter of a French soldier. After war of 1812. Quite possible.

It's just...I can't seem to find an amount of laudanum that relieves the pain but does not make me sleep for hours...and hours," Robin said. "Not a restful sleep though."

"Well, I can't think of anything that works better than that. Whiskey perhaps," Abrams said. "The train jolting around can't feel very good."

Robin shook his head. "Can't wait to get off this thing. Slightly less jerking than an elephant."

"You are getting off in New Haven? I hope you can rest there before continuing home." Abrams received his meal too, to catch up with Robin and Marie. "I am not trying to discern where you live. You did ask me to post you a letter."

"Yes I did."

"You can trust a Colonel of the United States."

"I beg your pardon. Of course, I can."

"As an immigrant here, easily mistaken for English, and recently shot, I don't wonder you are cautious," Abrams said. "I can't answer your questions and write you if I don't know where to send the letter."

"Canterbury, Connecticut," Robin said. "We may be moving to Boston this summer. I'll leave word at the post to forward any letters to me."

Abrams nodded. "Is that it? There's no one following you on this train? No one from New York?"

"No of course not. I ran into that fellow again and he apologized," Robin said.

"Just making sure," Abrams said. "What makes you move to Boston? Your work then?"

Robin nodded. "I'm staying at my father's home in Connecticut. He passed away months ago and I will sell off his estate and return to Boston. Met Marie in Connecticut."

She smiled.

"My wife is in West Pointe. I am based there, if you ever need to reach me," Abrams said.

Robin, before Marie was drawn

By Susan Eddy

Chapter Seventeen Carriage Accident

May 13, 1840

Robin was just about to step down from the train onto the platform when a hand was extended offering assistance. Robin was startled to find Adam Hudson standing before him. "May I help you, Mr. Van der Kellen?"

"Adam? What are you doing in New Haven?" Robin held onto Adam's arm and stepped down from the train. "Oh. I see. That was you I saw getting on the train."

Marie hurried down beside him. "Does Edward know you're here?"

"No, ma'am. Not exactly," Adam said.

Hotel porters gathered around, shouting out the names of their hotels or the names of their expected guests. A barrage of them spread across the train platform, their parked carriages had the hotel names painted on the sides. And Robin recognized the name of one hotel downtown. "Get that fellow's attention." He pointed the porter out to Adam.

Adam quickly collected the man and brought him to Robin.

"Yes, sir. We have a fine suite available for you. Are these your bags? We can transport you and all of the bags. We have a carriage right over here," the porter said.

"We'll need a suite and another guest room nearby," Robin said, meeting eyes with the young valet.

"For your valet? Of course, sir. Would you like him in the servant wing or a guest room on the top floor with yours?" the porter asked, picking up suitcases.

"With us, please," Robin said.

Adam gave him a doubletake and carried his own two bags.

Two other porters picked up Robin's trunk and everything was brought to a waiting carriage with the words, "New Haven Green Hotel" painted on the carriage doors.

Adam assisted Marie up into the covered brougham and then Robin paused with him outside to whisper, "Do not use my name. The name is not safe here."

"Yes, sir. Is it all right?"

"Yes." Robin made his way into the carriage, his right arm in a sling. His top hat just fit as he sat beside Marie, facing forward.

Adam made a quick look at the boot to be sure all luggage was aboard. He handed them his own two small cases. Then he climbed inside and sat facing Robin with a terrified smile.

Marie smiled back. "Adam, how did you get here?"

"I was on your train. I have resigned from the Millers. I confess I have followed you with the hope of becoming your valet and aspiring butler. Is that okay, sir?" Adam blurted out.

"You are most welcome," Robin said.

"I feel sorry for Edward, though. What made you do such a thing?" Marie asked. "What if Robin turned you down?"

"I gambled that I would not be accepted in New York but here, I might have a chance," Adam said. "I do not expect to be paid what I was in the city. I understand you live in the country and I have never been outside of New York city, but I do hope to be the very best that I...."

"Adam, you sold me. Relax," Robin said. "I can afford you."

"How are you, sir? You look...terrible, if I may say," Adam said. "You really do need help."

Robin sat back and held his sling closely. "I didn't sleep on that train. I can't wait really to lay down in a real bed."

"We will be staying in New Haven a few nights until our friend Constable Poole comes for us. It will let Robin recover a bit before a long carriage ride home," Marie said. "I need to do some shopping."

"I would be delighted to assist with shopping. Anything that you need," Adam said.

"We need quite a lot if we are to return the house to entertaining," Marie said. "There's not a full set of china to serve your dining room table, Robin. Not ten place settings that match anyway."

"Go right ahead, darlin. Get whatever you wish and let Adam arrange things," Robin agreed.

"A full service of china. Wonderful. What about silver and linens and glassware?" Adam urged.

"We need the whole thing. I don't believe Robin's father ever kept up the house to that level. There once was a full set but as dishes got broken over the years, since Robin's mother passed, they were never replaced. And there is only a set of six fine silver pieces anyway," Marie said.

"I can't wait to see your home. I'm so excited."

"Prepare yourself. It will be quite rustic to your eyes. We can use your help to modernize and open up the second wing. Let Marie pick out the china and glassware," Robin said.

"And if you have any decorating ideas while we are in town, I would like to know them," Marie encouraged.

"I'm so excited. Here I thought at best I would be valet to Mr..."

"Shhhh," Robin interjected.

"Are you all right, Adam? You look a bit faint yourself." Marie reached forward and tapped on Adam's knee. "You can tell us."

"I'm just a bit hungry, is all," Adam admitted.

"We'll be ordering up dinner just as soon as we get to the hotel. For now..." Marie passed him a tin of cookies from her travel bag.

"Oh no. I couldn't."

"Yes you could," Marie told him. "Please."

Adam looked down at the cookies and then ate one.

"You should have sent word to us you were on the train. You would have taken meals in our cabin," Robin said. "Are you all right?"

Adam nodded. "I was terrified to ask you. Are you really rich from those bank robberies?"

"Well...In a word, yes."

Then Adam sat back and ate a cookie with a smile.

Two hotel porters just finished transporting all of Robin and Marie's luggage from the depot up to their suite on the top floor. Robin paid them each a tip and they left.

Alone at last in a luxurious hotel suite, Robin faltered.

Marie hurried to him, taking his left arm. "Oh my. Robin?"

"I'm sorry. I..."

She helped him into the bedroom where he sat on the foot of a grand canopy bed and collapsed back. "Darling, what can I do? What do you need?"

"I'm so exhausted. I couldn't rest much on that train, even if I drugged myself to sleep." Robin laid his head back and held his right arm in his left. "Tormented with bad dreams even if I did sleep. My chest was hurting and now it's my back."

Marie smoothed his hair back gently from his cheek and his ear. "I'll order supper up here. You can rest. Go to sleep if you can. I think you're safe here."

He looked up at her. "I'm so sorry, my love. I would like to have taken you to a nice supper downstairs."

She undid the ribbon that held his locks back in a ponytail, releasing his light brown curls and letting his head rest back comfortably. "I have had many nice suppers with you on this trip. I'd like nothing better than to put you to bed."

"Wish I felt up to that."

Marie smiled.

"I will just lay down for a while."

"Adam can go down and order our supper to be sent up to us," Marie said.

"Are you okay with him working for us?"

"We need the help. He's adorable. I'll have him order you a nice bottle of brandy to help you sleep."

"Thank you, dear," Robin said.

"Can I get your boots off first?" Marie asked.

"Please." Robin pulled his pistol from his coat pocket and laid on the bed beside him.

"Do I still dress you or does he now?" Marie looked at him, pulling off his boots for him and setting them upright beside the bed as he would have.

"I think you know the answer to that."

There was a knock on the door already.

"Will he do my ironing for me?" Marie stood up after removing Robin's boots.

"He will do whatever you want him to."

Marie went to the door and asked, "Who is it?"

"It is Adam, ma 'damme."

She opened and let him enter the salon and dining room of their suite.

Adam looked around. "This is lovely. May I do the unpacking for you?"

"You may, but first I need you to order up dinner for us all to be served in here. And get a bottle of brandy for Robin. Put it all on the room. Remember our room number is 12," Marie said. "You need to eat before you do anymore work. I'm sure you did not have much on the train."

Adam tried to see into the open bedroom door but all he could make out beyond was a bed post and a settee beside it. "Shall I bring up a menu for you first?"

"No. You can choose. I trust you." Marie patted him on the arm.

Adam straightened up. "My first assignment. Do you fancy dessert?"

"Of course. Don't you?"

"Is there anything you or Mr. Van der Kellen do not like?" Adam asked.

"Him? I haven't seen him not eat anything," Marie said. "Just get whatever's best."

Adam didn't return until he was accompanied by three maids carrying meal trays.

Marie opened the door for them and let the maids set up on the table, with Adam nervously overseeing. Marie prepared a tip for each maid and put coins into their hands at the door as they left, her own heart racing such that her hand almost shook.

Adam ventured boldly to look into the bedroom and found Robin laying back on the bed in his clothing. His sling, coat, and jacket were on the settee. His feet were on the floor. That British pistol was beside him on the nightstand.

Marie entered the bedroom past Adam, to lean over Robin and lay a hand gently on his chest. "Robin?"

"Did you enjoy that?" he asked.

Marie giggled. "I gave them each a dime. Was that too much?"

"You would know better than I. I was thinking I didn't know if you still had money on you. Take more from my coat, would you?" Robin said. "Marie, you'll be wonderful at running your own home."

"May I help you to the table, sir?" Adam asked from the doorway.

"Yes, please. And when we're alone, call me Robin. Help me sit up, would you?"

Robin was seated at the head of the table and Marie on his left side.

Adam was about to slide his place setting down to the far side, when Robin said, "Stop. Just sit right here with us. I know you are used to dining in the kitchen and not with the people you serve, but we are not that formal in Connecticut."

Adam took his seat at Robin's right, across from Marie. "This is okay?"

"Absolutely," Robin said. "Join us."

"I think it's time we all told everybody the truth," Marie said, as she began raising lids off the plates before them.

Adam helped her with the lids.

"You mean everything?" Robin asked.

"The whole thing. My secret. Your secret. And any secrets why Adam left the Millers to work for us. And then we can all be friends with nothing between us," Marie said.

"Great idea. Pour me that brandy then," Robin said. "What exactly is my secret? I have a secret?"

Adam laughed at that, and served brandy to him. To Marie he poured a glass of red wine.

"You know. Why we left the Miller's."

"Oh. Oh shit."

"Language, Robin. I'll start," Marie said. "I can go first. I'm not ashamed of it. I was Robin's maid in Canterbury. I used to work for his father. I was the cook really. And Robin and I, well, we fell in love and married."

Adam looked from one to the other. "Oh, that is so romantic. And you were not married long before traveling to New York. This has just happened. I am overwhelmed."

Robin smiled. "So you can see why we did not tell anyone at the Miller's. Marie is my wife and will be treated as such and I know that won't be any problem with you."

"Your secret now then?" Marie asked Robin.

"Mine shall come last. I'm fairly certain it wins the prize as most shocking. But go ahead Adam, and let's see what you can do," Robin encouraged. "If you're comfortable with telling us why you followed us here."

"I was homeless when Mr. Miller and Jonas found me. I was considerably younger than I am now. They took me in and sent me to school. And I became his valet. My uncle was a barber and I learned a bit from him before both my parents died of the fever," Adam said softly. "I would have stayed with Edward of course, but then you came. A brilliant lawyer, a brave soldier, so admirable, I just couldn't bear the thought of never seeing you again. Never knowing what adventures you have next, I mean. What is the situation like in your home? Do you have many servants? You said you did not have a valet since you lived in Boston months ago. That led me to hope that you might have work for me."

Robin looked down at a fine plate of beef roast, potatoes, and roasted root vegetables. There was a fine gravy on it, and four pieces of silverware beside the plate. There was a bowl of fruit and biscuits. "When I arrived in Boston five years ago, my wife and child died. I..."

Adam gasped. "Oh my, sir."

"I was alone in Boston then, taking over my father's law firm there while he practiced some law in Canterbury. When he passed, I was given notice that a bank in Boston would claim his estate if I did not pay off his debt. The estate and land that he owned in Canterbury were worth more than my law practice and small townhome in Boston. I sold those off and moved to the country. Looking back, I was quite low and very poor by my own standards. I was not sure I made the right choice, especially having to let ten staff go in Boston and then to fire four more in Canterbury. I needed to keep a cook. I could look after my own horses. I'd have to do a lot of work around the house, but I could do it," Robin said softly. "I became very ill with fever and Marie tended me through it. I was in love with her before then, but I was raised that I could not take advantage of Marie and her circumstances. She worked for me. She was quite dependent on me. And it was just the two of us."

Adam smiled warmly, shyly. And he saw them holding hands on the table. "I was with Edward for two years before he married Elizabeth. If he ever told her of my past, she never let on. She took such a liking to you, Ma'am. You were wise not to tell her you were a maid and cook. She had them crying on many occasions. Everything had to be perfect when she came into the house. No offence. Was there some argument at the table when everyone was asked to leave the room? Was Mrs. Miller...caught alone with you, sir?"

"Caught alone with me?" Robin asked.

"There was some talk, in the house. Nothing improper about you, sir. Besides, mostly it was after you were shot," Adam said.

Robin sipped his brandy.

"She made an advance at him," Marie spoke up. "In her defense though, I must say, she just really wanted children with Edward and wasn't having any. She was desperate to have a child."

Adam raised his eyebrows and sat back. "That is not all she wanted."

"Say nothing to them," Marie told him. "The Millers are still our dear friends."

"We just felt, I felt it proper that we go home," Robin said.

"The way she looked at him." Adam met eyes with Marie. "How do you stay friends with her?"

"A lot of women look at him that way. Doesn't mean he'll sleep with them."

"I only have eyes for you, darlin," Robin said to her.

Adam smiled warmly. "Wonderful. I am delighted to serve happy newlyweds. Who is this constable?"

Marie gathered her things and left with two maids to take a hot bath down the hall. That left Robin with Adam in the hotel suite.

Robin poured two glasses of brandy and offered one to the valet.

"Thank you, sir," Adam said. "I just want to say that I appreciate so much that you hired me."

Robin sipped his brandy. "I do hope you understand what you are getting yourself into. That estate in Canterbury is a hay farm."

"Wherever you go, sir."

"Did Elizabeth ever carry on like that with other men?" Robin asked.

"All of Mr. Miller's friends are his age. You met them at the dinner party," Adam said. "There have been a few delivery men she had opportunity with."

Robin almost choked. "Okay. The other thing you need to be aware of is that there may be robbers out there looking to kill me or follow me back to my home and kill me. They may want to search the place for the money. This may be a bit dangerous for you."

"I...I can be another set of eyes for you. I will alert you of any suspicious characters," Adam vowed.

"You must be as tired as I am. You may retire to your room, Adam, when you finish your drink."

"What time shall I come round in the morning to help you?" Adam sipped the brandy. "You look tired, if I may say."

"I'm so exhausted. But I doubt I will sleep here."

Robin awoke, as Marie crawled into bed with him by the light of the fireplace in their room. Marie wore her new black silk night gown. Marie snuggled up to him. "Robin, I must tell you something about money. I'm sorry. I didn't know what to do."

"What happened?" Robin reached for her with his left hand.

"The money you gave me for dresses..."

"Yes?"

"I spent some on lingerie, shoes, and getting my hair styled," Marie said.

"How did you buy the dresses then?"

"It all happened so fast. Beth was buying dresses too and the shop just gave the whole bill to the butler. He paid it before I even knew," Marie said. "I feel terrible. I want to do what you say, but I was caught up. I was too embarrassed to tell you. I tried to give it to Beth. She told me to keep it."

"Oh. Well. Edward paid Ian a lot more than that. His friends paid my hospital bill. I don't know what happened. Did we look like we needed charity?" Robin wondered. "Compared to their wealth? Perhaps. You didn't buy those ear bobs? We must get you some."

"I didn't know you brought any of the treasury with you. I didn't want to spend all your money. I still have ten dollars," Marie said. "Oh, and I still have that horse money in my stockings."

"You... Well, next time you can just tell me. I'll understand. We both got caught up." He kissed her forehead. "Keep it, darling. Just keep it safe."

May 14, 1840

Marie awoke in bed, hearing Robin speaking softly in the next room.

"...a pot of coffee please."

"Yes, sir. Of course. Are you all right, sir?"

After a pause Robin said, "Ahm, I just, I just got out of the hospital a few days ago."

"Oh, sir, let me bring you breakfast up here for you and your wife. It's no trouble at all. I'll bring an assortment."

"Thank you. That would be very kind. Breakfast for three. My valet, of course. Just put it on the room."

"I'll be back up shortly. I'll have the coffee up first immediately, Mr. Longuiel."

Marie slid out of bed and pulled on the hotel robe. She drew it about her and tied the belt as she walked to peek around into the sitting room of their suite.

Robin was just closing the door. He had pulled on his sling over his sleep shirt and wrapped his robe about himself. He looked at Marie shyly, sliding his left hand up through his messy hair. "I must have been a sight. Frightened the poor girl. Thought I'd get some coffee up here before you woke, love."

Marie went to him and took his good arm. "You didn't sleep but a few hours, Robin. What are you doing up?"

"My back hurts too much to lie down in any way possible. What am I to do?"

"Come back to bed, darling. I'll quickly dress," Marie said.

"Just help me get trousers on. I'll see to the maid and the breakfast," Robin said.

"No. Robin. Sit down in the bedroom for a few minutes. You look faint." Marie moved him to the couch in the bedroom but she did retrieve his trousers for him and start his feet into them. She pulled them up to his knees. "Just sit. You're pale as a ghost."

Robin nodded. "Quite right."

Then Marie went to the armoire to select a shirt for Robin and dress for herself. She stepped out of her robe and night gown and quickly into pantalettes and corset.

"Come here, I can help you," Robin told her.

Marie did so and let Robin pull her stays and she reached back to tie her corset. "That's good. Easy." She stepped into her dress and pulled it up.

"I'm sorry. I can't do buttons with one hand," Robin told her.

There was a knock on the door already.

"Stay right there," Marie told him. She went to the door and opened it to find the maid with a coffee pot and tray of cups, cream, and sugar. "Do come in and set that on the table. Please."

"Yes, mum." The young woman, a bit younger than Marie set the tray on the dining table, then the coffee pot. "Allow me, mum." She did up the buttons on the back of Marie's dress. "I'll fetch the breakfast now. Was there anything special for your husband, Mrs. Longuiel?"

"Whatever you think is best. You'll be back with it?"

"Oh yes, mum."

"Okay. Let me get a tip for you when you return."

"Mum, if I may be so bold, what happened to your husband? He said he was in the hospital."

Robin appeared in the doorway, still partly dressed in trousers and bathrobe. "Carriage accident."

The maid looked to him. "Sir, is there anything I can do? Help with your shirt? Boots? Pour the coffee?"

Marie smiled. "Just the breakfast for three please. I can manage his shirt for him."

"Of course, Mrs. Longuiel."

The maid exited and Marie poured two cups of coffee. "Darling, you'll have to stop answering the door without being dressed. We can't have fifteen maids in here trying to help you."

"Are we certain?" He sat down at the table and poured cream into his coffee cup. Then he pacified himself with the cup to his mouth. And his dark eyes looked up at Marie in exhaustion.

"All right. Stay right there. Maybe it's food that you need." Marie went back into the bedroom to retrieve some coins into her pocket for a tip. Then she had just returned and sat down with her coffee when there was a knock on the door.

Robin made a panicked look toward the bedroom. "My gun is...."

"Easy." Marie patted him on the hand. She called to the hallway, "Is that you, miss?"

"Mrs. Longuiel, yes. I have your breakfast, mum."

"It's her, Robin. It's all right." Marie opened the door and indeed the maid carried in a tray of covered dishes and silverware.

Robin rattled his cup down into the saucer. Then he just held his hand to his mouth.

The maid set up his service and Marie's across from him. She set out his plate of eggs, biscuits, sausages and bowl of canned fruit. Then the same for Marie. Another setting for Adam. And she refilled Robin's coffee cup. "Mum, shall I fetch the doctor? We have one just around the corner."

"I'm all right. Thank you," Robin said.

"He's okay. We're just making our way home, resting here a few nights." Marie slipped a sliver dollar into the maid's hand. "Thank you, dear. Keep this our secret, all right? I'm not actually Mrs. Longuiel, you see?"

"They never are, mum. I won't tell anybody. I understand. I'll be working this floor, mum. Just ring the call bell there if you need anything."

Marie locked the door after the maid and sat down at the table. "Carriage accident?"

"I don't want to be caught out here with my gun in there again. That can't happen again," Robin whispered harshly. "And nobody is to know I got shot. Can't have somebody on the street asking around if they've seen anybody recently shot. I'll feel better once Poole gets here. Course… then he'll catch me with my mistress."

Marie looked at him.

"I do believe you're starting to enjoy lying."

Robin Van der Kellen walked Adam Hudson into a tailor's shop. Robin removed his top hat. "I would like you to set Adam up with two new three-piece suits, please."

Adam looked at him with round eyes and tried not let his eyebrows give away absolute surprise.

"And with those, he will need four shirts, under clothing, shoes, and anything else that goes with them," Robin said. "We are leaving town tomorrow. Is that a problem?"

"Oh no sir. We have some lovely suits here that we can tailor to fit your son perfectly."

Adam had to turn away, as if to look at the suits.

"Yes. He's been off at school and I can't believe how much taller he is. We need a couple new suits for him. Hat too. And a warm coat." Robin started toward the door but paused to say, "Meet us at the café on the corner when you're done here. We'll be on this street shopping. Will fifty dollars cover it?"

"My sir! Yes we will get him everything he needs. Can we have over night for the tailoring?"

"Absolutely." Robin handed the money to the tailor. "Adam, don't be shy. Work with the tailor and meet us for lunch."

"Yes, father." Adam tucked his chin down with a smirk.

Robin met Marie out on the sidewalk and they walked away. She wrapped her arms around Robin's left arm and strolled with him down the block. "What's that look for?"

Robin finally burst out laughing. "They think he's my son."

Marie laughed. "Good thing I didn't go in with you. What on earth would I be?"

Robin halted her at a crossing as there were carriages approaching. "It won't do us any good to be in an actual carriage accident now."

Marie giggled and hugged closer to him. "Sorry. I was looking at you. Trying to figure out how you have a son almost my age."

"Yes, well, I would have been fifteen when I had him." When it was clear Robin led her across the intersection. "I'm not saying it wasn't possible."

"We'll meet up with Adam after he's done with the tailor, won't we?" Marie asked.

"Of course. He only had two suits to his name," Robin said. "I'm surprised. He will meet us for lunch."

"Robin there's something about him I think you must know," Marie said.

They stopped walking and Robin waited for her to say more.

"I think he was very unhappy at the Millers. I saw Jonas tell him several times to get out. I thought that was so rude," Marie said.

"I saw it. I agree. I thought you were going to mention the other thing," Robin said.

"Oh, that he's infatuated with you? Don't let it go to your head," Marie said. "Oh Robin, look at the goblets in that window!"

Robin laughed. "All right. Try not to look as if you've never seen a wine glass before."

"Oh, just shut up and buy them, Robin." Marie pulled him up to the shop window.

"You are the lady with money. Why don't you buy them?" Robin said.

"And embarrass you? I wouldn't do that to you." Marie looked up at him.

Robin laughed and drew her into the shop.

No less than four ladies looked at them, three were shopping and one working behind the counter.

Marie moved closer to study the wine glasses in the window of blown blue glass. "Do you think there is any way we can get them home without breaking them?"

The shop lady hurried from behind the counter. "Where is home, Madam? I can wrap them very well for you. They don't have to make it to San Francisco, I hope."

"No, not that far. Just a few hours by carriage," Marie said. "How many should I get?"

Robin shrugged. "How many do you want, darlin?"

"Four. No, make it six," Marie said. "Eight. Do you know how wonderful they will look with your plates from India?"

Robin smiled. "A dozen, then. Can you wrap them and send them to the hotel across the street please?"

"My pleasure. We have more over here if you would like to look at those as well," she said.

Marie noticed the two other shoppers taking Robin in, all head to toe of him.

Robin was struggling to unbutton his jacket beneath the sling his right arm was in, to get his pocketbook out.

"Your name, sir, so I can send it to the right room?" The shop lady was watching his left hand undoing the buttons.

"Longuiel." Robin opened his pocketbook. "How much do I owe you?"

"One dollar, sir. How did you break your arm?" She began wrapping Marie's glasses in paper.

"Told my wife to buy her own damn glassware," Robin said seriously.

Marie burst out laughing.

Then Robin smiled and blushed.

The other women in the shop laughed.

The sales lady giggled. She held out her hand for his payment and then wrote out a receipt to give him, with a note on the back that said, "I love you."

Robin glanced at the note, smiled and pocketed it with his money. "Is there a wine shop nearby? She's going to want to drink something out of these lovely glasses."

One of the shopping ladies spoke up, "We saw a wonderful wine shop just a block that way."

"Thank you," Marie told her.

"Past the bakery."

They sat down together in a café at the front of the bakery, for some coffee and treats. "Dutch," Robin said, holding his hand to his full mouth for a moment. "Did not expect to find this in a bakery here."

"How wonderful. A little bit of home for you," Marie said.

"A little bit of Amsterdam for me. Home is wherever you are," Robin said.

"Robin," Marie said softly. "Everything you say is so kind. Except that comment about me breaking your arm."

He smiled warmly. "Thank God. Here comes Adam."

Robin paused on the sidewalk as Marie went into a linen store. As she was buying a few things, he was watching a black horse toss its rider to the ground. It caused a gathering of gentlemen along the fence, blocking his view. When Marie emerged she said to him, "New sheets and towels being delivered to our hotel too. The front desk is going to hate us." She turned to see where he was looking.

"Would you mind if have a look at a horse over there?" Robin asked. "You can go into the next shop if you like."

"I'll go with you. I don't know how steady you are crossing the street." Marie took his left arm and let him balance with her as they walked.

Some gentlemen in the crowd turned and walked away.

The black horse was riderless and circling in the pen, shaking its head. Its muzzle was down at its left shoulder.

Robin stepped up to the rail of the pen, studying the horse.

The man that was thrown limped toward him as other people walked away. He put a hand on the fence and cursed.

"You need to loosen that bit," Robin said.

"What do you mean? On the horse?" The limping young man met eyes with Robin.

"When a horse shakes his head that way it means the bit is too tight. He can't even raise his head," Robin said.

"I know that. If I let him raise his head he'll leap right out of here and take off again. Spent two days catching him already."

"Is he for sale?" Robin asked.

"You don't want that horse. You want those."

"Bring him over here. I would look at his teeth. His conformation is excellent," Robin said.

Another man came over as the one in the pen walked toward the black horse. "Excuse me, sir. I own the livery. Did I hear you're in the market for a horse? We have…."

"That's the one I'm interested in," Robin said.

"I'm not sure you understand. That horse just threw every rider that got on him all day."

"The bit's too tight. The saddle is too tight. You never let him run off his steam. If you ran him, he wouldn't mind someone sitting on him in the pen," Robin said. "The power in those back legs. He's a jumper, isn't he?"

"I hate to tell you this, especially a potential buyer, but this bastard can jump this fence at a standing start," the owner said. "Like a dammed explosion went off underneath him."

The horse was led partway up to Robin and then closed the distance rapidly itself. It put its head up to the fence but could not raise it over the top. One brown eye looked at Robin.

Robin reached in and loosened the bit, allowing the horse to raise his head over and it nuzzled Robin knocking him back a step.

"Well, I never saw." The thrown rider put hands on his hips.

Robin petted the horse and held onto the bit to open the mouth and examine teeth. "Three years old?"

"Just barely. How do you know horses?" the man in the pen asked.

"Six years in the Dutch cavalry," Robin said. "How did you come by this horse? Did you breed him?"

"We bought him before we knew he'd throw every man who sits on him," the owner said. "I don't know what you can do with him. Look at him I suppose. I'm not entirely sure he's broken. I was told he was."

The horse nuzzled Robin again.

"He likes you a damn lot better than he does me." The man in the pen wiped dirt off his pants.

"What did you pay for him?" Robin asked.

"I want $200 for him, US," the owner said.

Robin laughed out loud. "You think I'm joking."

"I think a gentleman like you would like one of these other horses over here," the owner said.

"Why? Do I look elderly? It's only a broken arm." Robin said. "What did you pay for him?"

Marie looked up at Robin unsurely.

"Paid a hundred for him," the owner said. "That don't come with no saddle."

"I don't want that saddle and neither does the horse. I'll pay you $110 for him. Hold him until tomorrow midday for me." Robin glanced at the barn behind the owner for a moment. "Ahm, hold this my dear." He handed his pistol to Marie.

She took the pistol and looked up at him, confused.

"Just by the handle and point it down, darling." Robin reached into his inside jacket pocket for his leather pocketbook. "Take that saddle off him. Let him run his ass off out there in the corral. Brush him down and feed him. I'll come for him tomorrow midday." Robin counted out the paper money. "A bill of sale, if you don't mind."

"All right sir. I'll be needing your name for that paper." The owner took the money. "How do we shake on this with your arm broken there?"

Robin painfully removed his arm from his sling and shook the man's hand. "Robin Van der Kellen. Three words."

"Three words, sir?"

"Van der Kellen. With a K."

"Ah. Mr. Van der Kellen, do my conscience some good and don't let that horse kill you." The owner said. "You sure you can handle him? Not a good practice to take advantage of a gentleman."

Robin showed his scarred palms to the man. "Six years on horses crazier than that one. And running from tigers in India? You should see how high they jump. Pistol back, darlin.'"

Marie returned the weapon to Robin and he pocket it.

Others looking on, moved away.

Robin signed for the horse, kept his bill of sale, and told the man, "Don't let my horse run away." He and Marie returned to the other side of the street. The horse paced the fence line behind him, snorting loudly. "I'll be back to spring you tomorrow."

Marie clung to him. "What was the pistol about?"

"A casual way to drive off the two pick pockets that were watching me from the barn."

"Are you sure? No Van der Kellen on your books?" Michael Poole said at the hotel desk. It was then that he saw Robin leaving the hotel restaurant and looking right at him. "Never mind. I had the wrong name." Poole walked to him, taking in the blue silk sling on Robin's shooting arm. "What is this? This is not you being careful, is it?"

"Come in. I will explain." Robin led him into the dining room where Marie and Adam were waiting. But he pulled Poole aside near the doorway and said quietly, "I do have good news for you. But we'll have to talk about that privately. We're not starting back today."

"This is your shooting arm. Why is it in a sling?" Poole whispered urgently.

"Because I got shot." Robin started into the dining room.

Poole caught him by the jacket and halted him, making Robin cry out in a bit of pain. "You what?"

"If you don't mind, my shoulder is in quite a lot in pain from surgery," Robin said.

"Surgery? To remove a lead ball?" Poole walked around to the front of him to look him over. "Where?"

"In New York." Robin winced.

"Klootzak."

Robin drew his chin back. "You're speaking Dutch now?"

"Picked up a word or two. Is he following you?" Poole urged.

"No but there are three more out there in New York," Robin said. "Robinson, Albertson's associate shot me."

"Did you question him?"

"A dead man tells no tales," Robin said. "But when he lived, he owned the Norwich bank. Roberts and Robinson were the same man. He was stealing from his own bank. Albertson was in on it, hooked him up with Pascal and Stuart, and another one Benedetti."

"You do not look well enough to travel." Poole said.

"I've had two days rest here, waiting for you. I don't see how I can look any better than this. Marie and I can leave tomorrow. Oh, and we must collect my horse. I bought a riding horse while we were here."

"You did?"

"Come on and eat. I'll tell you about the rest in private," Robin said. "I have hired a valet in New York. He worked for friends of ours. He's quite young and impressionable."

"Valet? What did you hire that for? You need farm hands." Poole looked over at the young man sitting with Marie. "He looks terrified."

"Marie must have told him all about you."

At the table, Adam rose to shake hands with Constable Poole. He wore one of the new suits, charcoal with a brocade vest and white shirt with a tall collar. Around the collar he had tied a brocade ascot that matched his vest.

They shook hands and though Adam gave a firm handshake, Poole still hurt him with his.

They sat down with Marie.

"Can you still shoot?" Poole still questioned.

"Ask Robinson," Robin said. "Though I can't raise a rifle yet."

Poole looked from him to Marie and finally said, "Good day, Mrs. Van der Kellen. Hasn't been much of a honeymoon for you, I expect."

"That's Mrs. Longuiel here," Marie said.

Poole looked from her to Robin. "Oh, that explains it."

Robin looked at Adam. "Nice. I like that suit. Looks good on you. Did you get the other?"

"In the morning. And the other shirts that they had to take in," Adam said. "I had to get some sleep shirts and other things to use up all the money. I hope that was your intention."

"Yes it was. Very good," Robin said. "Before we go, I want to pick up more grain for the horses. It's a better price here. And Marie wants to get supplies at the mercantile too. Probably better that we leave tomorrow midday then after we get supplies. We'll get you a room, Poole."

"You want to save a few bits on grain but pay it for a hotel room? Alice's maiden name was Pullings."

"What?" Robin said.

"Wouldn't I be Mr. Pullings in New Haven?" Poole smirked. "For the room?"

Adam burst out laughing.

Robin slapped Poole on the shoulder. "Shut up. It's rather more than that. It's the supplies the lady wants," Robin said. "And she's in charge now."

Marie laughed.

"Ah hah. That didn't take long," Poole said. "Nice dress, madam. I see you have been shopping in New York. You do have good news for me, right?"

"I do. Yes. Not here. We need to not discuss it here."

"I have to wait until tomorrow?"

"No. You will help me get upstairs after and I will tell you," Robin said. "It's all good news."

Michael leaned forward to Robin. "You can't get up the stairs by yourself?"

The waiter came and took their dinner order, recommending the beef tenderloin, which Robin and Michael accepted. Marie chose the duck. Adam chose the chicken and dumplings. Robin ordered a bottle of French red wine for the table. And then he quickly ordered another bottle of white Cotes du-Rhone, telling Marie that this wine was from the region in France where Edward Miller had family. The waiter left them, pleased.

"Well, good thing I'm here to guard you now. You shouldn't have gone to New York without me. We're going to have a discussion about your arrogance," Michael said. "I'll get some more black powder today. What ammunition do you need?"

"Mine are both .62 caliber. You have my rifle in the wagon?"

Poole nodded. "That is convenient. Is that intentional?"

"Of course. The British don't fuck around," Robin said. "Oh. My apologies, Marie."

Poole laughed. "You are relaxing, finally."

"If I'm reloading on horseback, I can't bother to load two different weapons with different shot."

The waiter returned with the two bottles of wine to demonstrate the labels to Robin and offer to him the first taste of the red. Robin delegated the first taste of the white to Marie. Servers delivered the first course to each person at the table while the waiter offered the red or the white French wines in accordance with the entre they had preferred. It was red wine to Robin and Michael and the chilled white to Marie and Adam.

Poole shoveled food into his mouth. "Damn this is good."

"Another holiday away from your family?" Robin squinted as if annoyed. Poole was sitting across from him. "If you scrape that knife on that china once more, I'm going to impale you with it."

"Get me a room. I can't wait to see dessert here. Do you mind if I scape my fork on the plate?" Poole pointed his fork over at the valet. "Does this kid carry a pistol?"

Adam pulled his chin back from that fork.

"No. Well I haven't shaken him down or anything." Robin undid his sling to cut up his own steak.

"No. Certainly not," Adam reached to help cut the steak and so did Marie. Their hands met over his plate.

Robin waved them both off. "I can do it."

"You're getting better," Marie remarked to him.

"When did this happen? After you posted the letter to Alice and me?" Michael asked.

"Before. Almost two weeks since," Robin said softly.

"I should have gone with you. You're not safe on your own," Michael said. "How did this happen? Dark alley? Out alone at midnight? Something an arrogant lawyer like you would do?"

"Ten-o-clock in the morning, right in front of the exchange. Right in front of Marie at the carriage. If she didn't hand me my pistol I'd be buried by now." Robin put a bite of steak into his mouth.

"Don't say such things," Marie scolded him.

"Sorry, love. He was at a run when he fired, precisely why he couldn't deliver a fatal blow. Still, it knocked me flat in the street." Robin paused to try another bite of his steak. "The surgery would not have been bad had they not nearly killed me with laudanum. Was it a day before I woke up?"

"A dreadful day. Intolerable day," Marie said.

"Yes it was," Adam agreed.

All three of them looked at him.

Adam just quietly continued eating, cutting his dumplings into bite sized pieces.

"So, who were these friends you stayed with? The Millers?" Poole asked.

Robin and Marie looked at each other and Robin said, "We acquired Adam from them. Met them originally on the train."

"You met them on the train? And then were guests at their home?" Poole asked.

"True." Robin nodded. "An older man of about sixty years and his young wife Marie's age. They became fond of us when they found out we had just been married. Marie and the girl, Elizabeth became good friends. The man, Edward, is a banker. He and his banking friends took some fascination in my profession and my catching bank robbers."

Following the dinner, Adam imposed himself between Poole and Robin to gather Robin's arm about his shoulders. He helped him climb two flights of stairs to their top floor hotel suite. He helped Robin to sit on the sofa, while Poole paced about inside and Marie shut the door.

"What is the good news? Does this kid know?" Poole said.

Between deep breaths that obviously hurt him, Robin said, "The money is ours. Still unsure about the French Francs, but the rest of it..."

"Well hallelujah. You're rich, Robin. And you finally bought yourself a horse." Poole glanced at Marie and nodded. "Listen, Robin. You look beat to shit. You're not putting me in another hotel room. I'm spending this night right there where you're sitting. You stand down.

Take your damn laudanum and get some sleep tonight. I got you covered."

Robin looked up at him.

Adam almost shook.

"Seriously," Poole said. "I have the watch tonight."

"I look that bad?" Robin questioned.

"Yes, you do. I've seen this look after combat many times," Poole said. "So, you're going to rest tonight before that long ride home tomorrow. That ain't gonna' go easy on you."

"You best ask Marie's permission. It is her privacy you are invading." Robin looked from one to the other. "Oh. I see you already have."

Marie sat down beside Robin and wrapped her hands around his upper arm. "I'm so worried about you. You hardly sleep. You wake at every sound in the hallway. You were so nervous about the maid setting up breakfast in here. Michael is here to help now. Let him do his job."

Poole sat down in the armchair across from them. "I'll get my bag and rifle from the carriage. It's out back in the barn. I'll check on your draughts. I'm sure they're eating their way out of the barn by now."

Robin looked at Michael unsurely.

"I'll be back in just a few minutes. And then you stand down, Captain." Michael stood up. "And don't you blame her for telling me you need help. We all know you're not accustomed to needing it. When I come back here, you'll take my orders for the night. And that's just the way it is."

Robin just nodded.

"Sir?" Adam questioned.

"It's all right. Michael is a very good friend of ours. We can trust him," Robin said. "He's here to protect us."

Michael indicated the valet. "Can you trust this kid? Does he know how rich you are?"

"We can trust Adam. He actually sent me a letter of inquiry when we were still at the Miller's, before he knew about the money. Marie, the day I found my father's message in the journal."

"Message? What message from your father?" Poole asked.

"He listed all the robberies and where the money was and who stole it," Robin said. "And a few words for me."

"So, what exactly is Adam going to be doing for you? Hands as soft as Marie's. He's not going to chop any wood for you and these guns scare the hell out of him." Poole pushed his rifle into Adam's hands and the valet had no idea how to hold it. He nearly pointed it at the hallway and Poole pushed the barrel up against Adam's shoulder. He positioned his hands to safe places on the barrel and butt of the gun.

"Adam, you must forgive Constable Poole. He doesn't have a clue what a valet or butler does," Robin snapped. "Don't grab him like that, Michael. He's hired and he knows his job. It's not security."

Poole took his rifle back. "No, it is not."

Adam deepened his voice. "I prepare his suits, cut hair, give shaves. You don't know what those are, obviously. I prepare the dining room service, serve meals, handle correspondence, answer the door..."

"Answer the door. You don't open his door to nobody you don't know. You got that? Crooks out there think he's got their money, and he does. They already shot him once. Flashing a lot of money around shopping, he's going to attract more crooks. You can put suits on him. Fine. I can keep him from getting holes in them, if you know what I mean." Poole stepped back from Adam and toward the door. He met eyes with Robin. Then he left their suite.

Adam sunk into a chair.

Marie put a hand on the valet's shoulder. "Don't you let him frighten you. He's rough as a bear, but he means well. You can help me get Robin into bed and take his laudanum."

"Bring the brandy?" Adam questioned.

"See? He's fitting right in," Robin said. "You don't know what those are...." Robin laughed heartily. "You really must give Michael Poole some shit or he won't ever respect you. You're off to a splendid start, Adam."

May 15, 1840

Poole returned with a maid who set up coffee and light breakfast on the table.

Robin walked out in his robe and sat down with him. "Well thank you, Michael."

"No, thank you. I put it on your room," Poole said with a grin.

"You remembered what name my room is under?"

"No. But that cute maid sure did. How is Mr. Longuiel? Isn't it awful? A carriage accident? How did it happen? Did he fall off?" Poole said. "I told her I ran you over."

Robin nodded. "I meant thank you for standing guard last night. Pour me a cup of that, would you?"

Poole leaned forward to reach the coffee pot. "You know, I'm not your servant. I am in fact a very wealthy man right now."

"Yes. Yes you are. And you're soon to be a very dead man if you go home without a very expensive gift for your wife." Robin poured fresh cream into his coffee and stirred with a fine silver spoon.

"Oh my God. I have to get her something. Give me a hundred dollars," Poole said.

"Is that...is that the going rate? For the mother of your children? For the woman who puts up with you night after night?" Robin sat back and sipped his coffee.

"Marie? Marie, I need your help out here," Michael called.

Robin laughed. "Fill this up again. It's a small cup."

"Marie?"

She opened the bedroom door and came out in one of her new gowns. "Give him a hundred dollars, Robin. You have it. I saw your purse."

"See?" Poole said.

"Now what are you going to bring her?" Robin said. "I'll bet you have no clue."

"What did you buy Marie?" Poole looked up at her.

Marie put her hands on her hips.

"Michael, you see all those packages over there that you will have to carry down to the carriage?" Robin said. "You're the one who reprimanded me for shopping."

Poole looked over at the packages. "Oh. I see. I thought you were in bed recovering, mostly."

"I was. But we also were buying new glassware, china, new linens, shoes, earbobs, a sapphire necklace, gowns...." Robin said.

"Sapphire necklace? We didn't buy any necklace," Marie said.

Robin pulled a box out of his robe pocket and opened it. "You love blue, don't you?"

Marie shrieked and took the box. "When did you get this? When I was picking out the earbobs?"

"The earbobs that match that necklace, yes." Robin returned his eyes to Poole across the table.

"I hate you," Michael said.

Robin produced another box from his pocket and held it out. "Here. Give this to Alice."

Michael leaned in and took the jewelry box. He opened it to find a gold heart pendant with a diamond in it.

"Marie picked it out for her. Don't tell her that," Robin said.

"You two rehearsed that whole damn thing," Michael complained.

Adam knocked on the door.

Poole barked at the door. "Who is it?"

"It is Adam Hudson, Constable."

Poole opened the door, let him in, looked about in the hallway and then entered and shut the door again. "He can stay with you while I get the carriage ready."

"I shall get to your packing right away," Adam said.

"Have some breakfast first." Robin handed twenty dollars to Adam. "You may need a few things from town. You won't find much in Canterbury so get it now."

"Thank you, sir." Adam pocketed without counting. "But you already bought me so much."

"Well, you won't find any of that aftershave lotion in Canterbury," Robin said.

"Really? What sort of town doesn't have aftershave lotion?" Adam sat down at the table and poured coffee for himself.

"Canterbury," Robin said.

"Careful. Town I was born in," Poole said.

"Obviously," Robin said. "How many cases of brandy and wine did you get?"

"Four each," Adam said.

"Are you opening your own tavern?" Poole asked.

"I see a celebration in the future. I must stock up," Robin said.

Chapter Eighteen Home

May 15, 1840

Poole and Robin rode home in the carriage seat, Poole driving on the left, while Marie reclined on new blankets in the back. Adam sat on the crates of wine, holding on with both hands. Robin cradled his sling in his left arm on his lap, wincing occasionally.

"Lay down in the back," Poole told him.

"With the women?" Robin said. When Poole laughed he added, "And Adam."

"How much money are we talking about here? All together? What have you found? You said there were three more stashes of it and it's all ours," Poole said.

"Very well. You are entitled to know. You seem to be the only man I can trust in this country." Robin looked back at Marie again. "First of all, I know there is no one to return the US Treasury notes and state currency to, that we have no choice but to keep. The only money in question is the French which, if stolen from the French treasury, is in fact, an act of war to have in our possession," Robin said. "And I know this because I've sent a fellow to jail for just such an offence."

"Robin, you do speak eloquently. But I'm still going to split your lip if you won't just give me a figure," Poole said.

Adam almost got to his feet but Marie urged him down.

"Five hundred and forty-eight thousand not including the Francs," Robin said. "Or the bonds."

Poole stopped the horses immediately.

Adam let out a shriek, being thrown into the back of the front seat.

Robin grabbed on to keep from falling off with so sudden a stop. "What? Did you see something?"

"Yeah. I did. I'm rich. Fifty-four thousand dollars is my cut?" Poole grabbed onto Robin's forearm, his uninjured one. "If I'm rich, you are filthy rich. Are you out of your Dutch fucking mind? You are right now easily the wealthiest man in Connecticut. Go buy a mansion in Boston. Plan a trip to Amsterdam to let your family meet your wife. Buy your own ship. Get out of here."

Marie tugged on Robin's coat from behind. "Robin, you're in no condition to go anywhere. In the past two months you've almost died twice."

Robin looked back at her.

"Please stay home and rest," Marie urged him.

"Marie, you're right, of course. I'll be on alert, Michael." Robin cradled his right arm in his left. "The two women you worked with before, would you want us to hire them back? Would they still be around?"

"Yes. Both of them were very nice. They're working at the Inn," Marie said.

Poole started the horses moving again. "She needs help there in that big house. And more help than the boy can do. You need stockmen, farm hands. You crazy ass Dutchman."

"Let us gather the two women in town while we are there," Robin said.

"You need a milk cow too. And some hired guns," Poole said.

"Marie, they're to work for you. Will they do that?" Robin asked.

"Yes. They will be fine. I'll just cook," Marie said.

"And sleep with him," Poole said.

Adam and Marie both burst out laughing.

Robin rolled his eyes.

"Oh, come on. You've missed my sense of humor, Captain."

"Barely." Robin glanced back at Marie. "Teach the women to help you in the kitchen. At least, have them do anything you do not want to. Chances of finding more help out here are slim."

"You have just been shot, Robin. You need to sit on your ass at home and recover. I'm sending Travis out to help you. You put him to work outside," Michael said. "The boy is almost 13 now. He can chop a cord of wood for you, shovel stalls, get your garden ready for planting. He can even hunt you some pheasant or turkey. He'd do the whole thing just for a chance to see you shoot that pistol."

"I'll teach him to shoot the pistol. I had 14-year-olds in my regiment. If he can shoot a pheasant he can learn to fire and reload a pistol," Robin said.

"You do that and you may never get rid of the boy."

Adam stood up beside Marie, looking about at the town of Canterbury, as Alice Poole walked toward them with June and Marta.

"I think you're safe at your house now that you shot two bank robbers and got the other arrested. There aren't any others that we know of, right?" Poole asked, setting buckets of water down for each of the two Friesians.

"There are three in New York," Robin said.

Travis led Robin's saddle horse over to the trough for his drink and tethered him there.

"They don't know you live here, do they?" Poole asked.

"Only if they can read the papers." Robin moved to intercept the three women.

"What?" Michael said.

Marie was standing in the bed of the wagon with Adam. "Robin lift me down."

"Stay right there. We'll be on our way shortly." Robin held his sling in his other arm.

June and Marta looked excitedly up at Marie in the wagon. They each set down a couple bags.

Robin took a breath. "Ladies, I do apologize for having to end your employment last fall. If you are not in objection, Marie and I would love to have you back."

"Love to!" Marta cried out.

"Very delighted to," June added.

"Oh yes, hurry and climb up here. I have so much to tell you." Marie reached out for their bags.

Robin bent to pick up a case and Poole blocked him. "Don't you be doing that. Get up in the wagon."

"Are you all right, Mr. Van der Kellen?" June questioned.

"Get into the wagon and sit your ass down. I'm sending Travis out to help you. He can chop wood and tend horses, all the chores you can't do." Poole picked up the bags instead and handed them up to Adam.

"This is Adam Hudson, my new valet and butler," Robin said.

"Welcome, ladies." Adam extended a hand to Marta.

"Marta Johnson." The young strawberry haired maid clambered up and hugged Marie in the bed of the wagon.

"June Taylor," June said and climbed up after her. "Pleasure to meet you, Adam."

Marie hugged her too.

Travis brought Robin's new gelding back to the wagon. "Wow, I never saw such a great horse. He must have cost a fortune. Have you ridden him yet, Mr. Van der Kellen?"

Robin looked back at the black horse and the boy. "No, I have not. I saw him...demonstrated. Don't try to ride him yourself. He's barely three years old and still...really angry about being gelded. You might say."

Poole laughed.

"Demonstrated?" Marie looked down at Robin.

He grinned and gestured to be quiet, with one finger to his lips.

That made Adam laugh. He sat down again with his elbows on his knees and looked about at the town of Canterbury. "This isn't main street is it? Is this the whole town? I can see the whole thing from end to end."

Marie sat up front beside Robin and they started the last of the journey toward home. Robin put the reins in Marie's hands. "You drive. I'll talk you through it. Nothing really to do until we need to turn."

"I...I've never driven a team in my life," Marie said.

Adam sat on the crate behind her. "Should I be worried?"

"Prepare to dive out on my signal," Robin said.

"Robin," Marie scolded.

"Did you manage to honeymoon before Mr. Van der Kellen got shot?" June blurted out, sitting on wine crates.

"June, really," Marta said.

"You know you're wondering the same thing," June said. "I'm betting they did before that wedding."

They heard a rider come up behind them and it was Travis on his own horse. He slowed and road up alongside the carriage, on Robin's side of it. "Here I am sir. Ready for orders."

Robin smiled. "Here is my first command. Away from town you are to call us Robin and Marie. And this is Adam, June, and Marta."

"Oh, my pa would whip me if I did."

"Well then I suggest you don't tell him," Robin said. "I said to him you were almost as old as the men under my command. No need to treat you like a boy anymore."

Marie smiled, stifling a giggle.

"What can I do for you when we get to your place? I can unhitch these horses and put them up," Travis offered.

"Can you? Do be careful with this one." Robin pointed at the draught horse on the left. "I call him asshole in Dutch. Klootzak. Be careful. Your father knows what that word means."

Travis laughed. "Klootzak. And what is the other one named?"

"Genie, that's Dutch for genius. Because he's dumb as a rock," Robin explained. "It's meant to be encouragement."

"Okay. Klootzak and Genie. Can't wait to see what you name the gelding." Travis laughed hard.

"I don't know that one yet. I'll think of something the first time he launches me into a tree, probably," Robin said.

"After being in the cavalry, I'll bet you can ride any horse on earth," Travis said. "You road that one pa got me and neither of us can ride her."

"I'll teach you how. Now this one, that I just bought? I'd rather have that kind of horse than any other. He's brilliant, a pain in the ass, and I know when he learns I can ride him through fire and back, he will start to do what I need him to do before I even ask. Try not to make eye contact with him because that fires him up," Robin said. "I'll teach you how to ride your mare. She needs a commander on board."

Marie and the women burst out laughing.

"I'm perfectly serious."

Adam doubled over laughing.

At the stone archway into Robin's estate he said, "Pull back on the right-hand reins and say, het recht."

"Het recht?" Marie said, pulling the right on mostly Genie.

The horses turned into the driveway and pulled them through the archway.

"How…how will I get them to stop?" Marie worried.

"Can't tell you now or they will. Just wait," Robin said.

Travis laughed, riding his horse behind them, alongside Robin's new black horse.

"Het recht," Robin said, getting the team to turn toward the house in the circle drive. "Now pull back on all reins and say, stoppen."

She pulled back as he said it. And she added, "Stoppen. Oh, very good. Good boys."

Robin reached down with his left hand and set the brake. "Good job, darling." He climbed down and had to hold onto the rail for a moment.

"Are you all right?" Marie asked him.

"Oh my God that hurt." Robin leaned his head to the wagon and held onto it.

"Stay up here, girls, and help pass things to the back, would you?" Marie said.

"Robin, are you all right?" Adam scrambled over to him.

Travis dismounted behind Robin. "Pa said you're not to be lifting nothing."

"Did he? I don't think I could lift a cat," Robin said. "Why don't you carry supplies into the kitchen and then luggage up the stairs? The horses can wait a few minutes. Here's the key to the house."

Travis, almost as tall as Robin, took the key and opened up the house. Then he returned the key to Robin and began carrying in their groceries. Adam followed him with a crate of preserves and jarred fruits.

Marie climbed down to Robin's. "Go in and sit down, Robin. You look pale."

"I've been sitting for days. I'm just a bit dizzy." Robin walked back to his magnificent new horse, who was looking at him with muzzle down. The horse sniffed at him. "This is your new home, my friend. Can't wait to put my Dutch saddle on you, though that won't be for a while." As he petted the horse on the nose, it nuzzled toward him.

"He likes you so much," Marie said.

"Yes. For some reason he does. Maybe he knows I understand him."

Adam emerged from the kitchen, looking at the red painted manor home, the barn and the outbuildings. To his credit, his expression did not give away his shock at just how rustic it really was. Dirt driveway. No outdoor lighting. Very little brick or stone on the house. But he turned carrying luggage and packages that the women pushed toward the back of the wagon.

Travis and Adam made several trips.

"Travis, you must choose a room upstairs for yourself. Just pick one. Some of my things are in the small room so choose one of the others. Adam will be in the room by the stairs on the right." Marie carried a smaller bag in. "The women in the middle rooms."

"Yes, Mrs. Van der Kellen. I mean, Marie." Travis set crates of groceries on the kitchen table.

Adam followed Marie into the house and sorted the crates on the floor. Then he stood and looked at the primitive kitchen table, hearth and the worktables. He turned around, looking up at baskets of basil and rosemary. He seemed confused by the candles hanging by conjoined wicks from nails in the beams.

Marie glanced at him. "Your room will be at the top of the stairs on the right. You can look about if you like."

"I think I had better help you unpack the food first. Here are the preserves and the meats."

"The girls can do that. Are you all right? Adam?"

He nodded and forced a bit of a smile. Then he strolled closer to her in the kitchen and asked, "Is it all right with you if I'm here?"

Marie put a hand on each of his upper arms. "I'm delighted to have you here. Robin needs your help very much. If you need anything, you tell me." She felt him trembling. "What is it?"

"I'm...I'm a little nervous, I suppose."

Marie pulled him into a quick hug. "You will be just fine here."

He actually clung to her a bit.

Marie let him go with a pat to his shoulder. "Now have a look at your room. Top of the stairs on the right. Tell me if you need anything."

"Where is the um...water closet?"

"Down the hall here to the right or upstairs in the middle room. I'll get you a pitcher and bowl if you want to wash up," Marie told him. "Unless you're looking for the outhouse."

Adam blushed.

She went to the cabinets and took out a pitcher and bowl. The pitcher she filled in the water barrel beside the pantry and then she filled Adam's arms with them. "Anything else, Adam?"

"That should do it. Top of the stairs on the right." Adam nodded and left for the stairway.

"I'm so tired. I just think I should lay down a bit before dinner. I don't want to be so far away from all the activity," Robin said.

"Well, I can fix that. Why don't I pull one of those couches in here along this wall?" Travis asked.

"I like the way you think, Travis." Robin met eyes with Marie and smiled.

Travis went into the parlor and pulled a sofa into the kitchen and between the table and the wall. "How is this, sir? I mean Robin?" He turned it facing Marie's kitchen.

Robin made his way to sit down on the couch. "This is excellent, Travis."

"These are china and glassware. They stay down here." Adam pointed to crates that June and Marta were picking through.

"I will bring the luggage upstairs." Travis grabbed two and went at it.

"Boundless energy at that age." Robin reclined down on the sofa and wrapped his right arm in his left.

Marie went to him and kissed his mouth. "Rest, darling."

Adam wandered down the hallway, looking into the dining room.

Travis walked in then. "Oops. Ma warned me you might be newlyweds again."

"You are quite all right Travis," Marie said. "I'll get to cooking."

"Let me do something." June joined Marie being the worktables. "I'll get some supper going. Just tell me what you have here."

Travis grabbed two more bags. "Can I take the end one on the left? With all the windows?"

"Take it. Enjoy the windows," Robin told him.

"Oh boy." Travis disappeared up the stairs again. "I don't even have a window at home."

"You're so good with a young man like that." Marie brought a blanket from the laundry over and laid it out over Robin. "Take a nap, darling. I'll wake you when it is time to eat."

"Could I trouble you for a brandy? I'm so used to the bar on the train."

"I am too. I'm glad we bought wine."

"You bought wine. I'm glad I bought brandy," Robin said.

June was pulling jars of beets and pickles from the crates. "Look at these. My word."

Marie pointed to the beets. "Let's have those, the brisket, and get some potatoes boiling."

"I'll do the potatoes," June said. "Look at those pickles. Can we open the pickles?"

"Yes, of course," Marie said.

Adam returned from the dining room and sat down at the table. He turned his chair to face Robin. "You do not use the dining room? It has sat cold for many months."

"No. This past winter we were eating in here," Robin said. "But now with you and all the new dishware, feel free to open the dining room as you like. Just not tonight. Don't worry about it tonight. We'll all eat in here and enjoy the heat from the hearth." Robin reclined back on the sofa with his brandy glass.

"I shall get settled into my room then." Adam took his two bags up the stairs and met Travis on the way up.

"What can I do?" Adam returned to the kitchen.

June brought plates and silverware to the table. "Set that end of the table."

"Where does your rifle go?" Travis asked Robin.

"Put the rifle up on the mantel." Robin sipped brandy from his sofa, legs crossed beneath his blanket.

"Yes, sir." Travis set the rifle up over the fireplace. And he returned to look at the pistol on the end of the table. "What a fine pistol. Where does that go?" Travis offered his arm to Robin for standing up.

Robin used him to get up from the couch. "Stays right where I put it."

"You're here, Robin. Then Marie, Travis, and I'm over here." Adam designated the end of the table was for Robin, head of the household, Captain of the Guard.

"As you wish," Robin said.

All six of them sat down and passed beef brisket, pickled beets, mixed beans, and herbed potatoes around. And many of them watched Robin trying to manage with one hand.

"I would like to thank everyone," Robin said. "I appreciate all of you. I must say a few words. Marta and June, please be aware of perhaps the obvious. I was shot by bank robbers who know I have their money. There were three more after me in New York. Should they find their way here, they will find me. I would gather us all up and go to Boston if only I could. We must be on alert. You must notify me of any men on the property, immediately."

"I'll be working outside mostly. I'll be on guard," Travis offered. "My pa will be visiting."

"Does Adam shoot?" June questioned.

"Ah, no. Sorry," Adam said shyly.

"If you give me musket, I can hit a rattlesnake at twenty feet," June said.

"Is that right?" Robin said. "I could use you and Travis to reload for me then. I figure we have a few days head start, maybe a week. But do not let your guard down. If we have trouble, I am the one to be shooting anything. I was a cavalry officer. Six years of war. I will put to an end quickly any sortie by these bank robbers. I won't have that on my property."

After a moment, June said, "Amen."

Some let out a breath and returned to dishing out food.

"Are you rich, Robin?" Travis said. "I overheard Ma and Pa talking about gold coins."

Robin inhaled deeply. He sat back in his chair. "I am sorry about the talk of war. We will have a talk about the money and the banks. I'm too tired tonight and it's a very long story, including the part where I got shot. I won't be surprised like that again."

After dinner, Robin moved back to the couch and reclined back, holding his sling with his left hand, and put his feet up with boots off the end of the cushion. He picked up his letters from the post.

Travis passed him a glass of brandy from Marie.

Marta and June cleared away the dishes.

"Oh. Thank you." Robin took a sip.

"Does it hurt, where you were shot? Where at exactly?" Travis asked.

"Yes. It's right here." Robin touched his right shoulder with his left forefinger. "I still can't lift a rifle yet. I'll try that when we go hunting in a few days."

"Did they have to cut out the ball?" Travis asked.

Robin nodded.

"Was it very painful? I think you must be very brave to get through all that," Travis said. "I want to see it, what it did to you."

The women looked over.

"Oh?" Robin glanced up at Marie and Adam. "Well, I'll have to change bandages at some point. I'm afraid it will leave a bad scar. I have two others. I was shot in the leg once and once right through my side over here. Both of those had an entry and exit wound. This is actually the first time that the shot didn't go all the way through."

"What was worse?" Travis asked.

"Oh, this one. For certain," Robin said. "Did Klootzak give you any trouble, putting him in his stall?"

Travis laughed suddenly. "You didn't tell me he goes in the first stall. I figured he would be on the left of Genie. But he's not. He sure explained that to me."

"Oh no. Did he hurt you?"

"No. Just knocked me flat is all." Travis laughed.

"Yeah? Did that to me 14 times one day," Robin said and they all laughed. "Adam, you see what I meant by rustic? Are you wanting for anything in your room?"

"I borrowed a lamp from another, and I am quite all right in there. It is comfortable," Adam said. "If you don't mind, I had a look at your room too. I do believe it suits you."

"Really? How so?"

"Grand four poster bed. Trunk at the foot with gold lettering on it. Two swords crossed over the fireplace. Lovely balcony for seating out there in the hot weather," Adam said. "Not elaborate. Not overly lush. But comfortable."

"It does suit him," June agreed. "Especially the weapons."

"Where did you get them swords?" Travis asked.

"One is from the Dutch Navy, and the other a gift from an Indian Moghul." Robin opened the first letter from a law firm in Boston. He quickly glanced through it and then opened the next one. "Well."

"What is it?" Travis asked him. "Letters from family?"

"From law firms." He met eyes with Marie then. "It is a good thing I don't need a job. Surprising how bad that makes me feel, that I'm not wanted."

"Well, they're foolish, sir," Adam said.

They said good night to everyone, and then closed their bedroom door to finally be home in their own room at last. Robin sat on the edge of the bed and laid his pistol on the nightstand.

Marie began undoing his sling and found Robin was holding onto her skirt, pulling her close. She kissed his forehead. "You must be exhausted. Let's get you into bed now."

"Are you sorry we're not alone?" he whispered.

She eased the sling down and off his arm. He still wore his fine new suit from New York and needed help to remove the jacket. "We need the help. You need to rest."

"Marie, do you want to stay here then? Hire a staff to do all the work here. Or do we still move to Boston even if I do not need to find work?" Robin asked.

She unbuttoned his shirt. "Home is wherever you are."

"Did he light that fire in here, for us?" Robin asked.

"Yes, Travis did. Quite helpful, isn't he?" Marie smiled. "Lit one in his room too. I think he's quite enjoying that big room on the end. Living like a king in there."

"Should we have given it to Adam?" Robin stood up and let her ease down his jacket and shirt. His shoulder was bandaged, with lengths of wrapping going around his under arm and around his neck to keep it from slipping down. He looked down at his arm as he flexed his fingers. "Well, you run the house. Would you rather live in New York?"

"I could see Beth. But Robin, we don't have to decide now, do we? Wouldn't you want to go back to work some day? Maybe you would want to take me to meet your family and then you decided where to live and work." Marie pulled back the covers on the left side of the bed for him. She collected his suit and laid it over the chest at the foot of the bed. "You don't have to decide anything now."

"We do not have to decide now," Robin realized. "I value your opinion." Marie pulled off his boots, and he handed his trousers to her. Then he climbed into the bed and grimaced at how bad his shoulder hurt when he put weight on that arm.

"Do you want a shirt to wear?"

"No. I just want to lay down in my bed."

Marie pulled the covers up over him and then began to undo her hair, brush it out, and changed into her night gown behind a screen. "I think I'll have Adam and Travis help me turn one of these little rooms into my walk-in closet, just like Elizabeth has."

"Yes, absolutely."

"I have such wonderful clothes to unpack. I can't wait to do that tomorrow."

Robin laid back and was soon asleep, even before Marie blew out the lamp.

Adam Hudson, however, sat up in his new bed, staring at the oil lamp beside him on the table. There were no sounds in the house, no sounds of horse's hooves on cobblestones, no distant sirens. It was dark without city gaslights. He heard Travis moving about in the room across the hall from him. And then it became all quiet over there.

Wearing a new sleep shirt made of white cotton, in a double bed clothed in new linens that had never been slept on before, he reclined back and smiled. Tomorrow he would begin working to make Robin more comfortable, his home more welcoming, and his attire absolute perfection.

May 16, 1840

It was hot that morning as Marie came downstairs, finding June and Marta already at work. "Morning ladies."

"Marie, good morning, Mrs. Van der Kellen." June poured a cup of coffee for her and set it on the table. "Are you going to tell us how your first time was?"

"I only just got up." Marie laughed.

June laughed. "Come on. How was the magnificent Mr. Van der Kellen?"

"Wonderful." Marie smiled.

Travis bounded into the kitchen, rifle in hand. "The door was open so I looked in on him. He's still asleep."

"Good morning, Travis. Robin really needs to rest. He's still having a lot of pain." Marie sat with her coffee and looked about the kitchen. "Are you making bread?"

"I'm going to check on the horses first. I do that at home you know?" Travis put his rifle strap up over his shoulder.

"Will you check for eggs out there? Bring some in would you?" Marta said. "Trying to make bread but it's fighting me."

"I'll be right back then."

"Travis, wait." June put a slice of brisket with a slice of cheese into his hands.

"Thank you. So much." He went out the kitchen door.

Adam entered, straightening his vest and jacket. "Good morning, ladies."

"Morning Adam. Did you sleep well?" Marie said.

"Coffee or tea for you?" Marta asked.

"Coffee. I'll get it myself. I know my way around a kitchen." Adam accepted a cup from her and used the towel to lift the hot coffee pot to pour. "It is so quiet here. I'm afraid I awoke frightened at every hoot."

Marta handed him a plate of brisket and potatoes. "Nothing's gonna get you up in your room, silly."

"Thank you. This still feels...unusual." Adam brought his meal to the table and sat down. "How is Mr. Van der Kellen this morning?"

"Sleeping," Marie said.

"What do you need me to do today?"

"Settle in. Unpack the dishware. Oh, the pieces in the sideboard, be very careful with them. I'll show them to you. Robin sent them to his mother when he was stationed in India and then she brought them with her to America. The teapot has a crack. But they are very important to Robin."

"I will be very gentle with them. I look forward to seeing these pieces. What is this VOC on all of his belongings?" Adam asked.

"I can't pronounce it but it means Dutch East India Company. Wait until you see Robin in his uniform coat. Oh my. He is the most handsome thing," Marie said.

"Yes indeed. I don't think my heart could take that," Adam said and then met eyes with the women. "I mean the surprise of the lawyer in a uniform."

"I know what you mean," Marie said.

"So how was he, your first time?" June questioned.

"Or the second or third?" Adam added, to much laughter.

"I'm not telling any of you!" Marie said. "At least...not 'til I've had my coffee."

"I want to completely wash down that dining room and mop it today, if that is all right." Adam sipped his coffee. "What is in the closed off portion of the house?"

"You're welcome to go in and look about. Robin wants it all reopened. There is a ballroom on this floor and I've been drying laundry in there all winter. I'll need to make another room for that. And upstairs are smaller bedrooms," Marie said.

"We should probably move to one of those once it is opened and refreshed," Adam said. "We are in your guest rooms. Is it safe to walk about outside? Without a gun, I mean."

"Well yes, unless we have bank robbers. You can walk down to the river. It's very nice. You can even swim in the river, which is what I plan to do this afternoon," Marie told him. "Did the talk about bank robbers frighten you? We just have to keep our eyes open."

Robin didn't come down until almost ten o-clock, dressed in casual trousers and shirt, but not shaven. He set his pistol on the end of the kitchen table and sat down near the hearth.

"I was about to check on you. Did you sleep all this time?" Marie brought him a cup of coffee.

"This morning I slept. Last night, not so much. Don't have to tell you this." Robin took the coffee and asked, "Where is Travis?"

"He watered the horses, brought in eggs, ate his breakfast. Now he is chopping wood," Marie said. "He was worried about you this morning. He'll be glad to see you up at lunch then."

Adam appeared in the hall.

"I'm starving. Can I trouble you for..." Robin looked up at her.

Marie kissed him. "You are no trouble at all. Brisket and eggs the way you like them, with pepper."

He smiled. "The laudanum finally put me out this morning. My whole arm and back hurt me so."

"You buttoned your shirt by yourself."

"Major accomplishment of the day," Robin said. "Trousers too."

Marta and Marie giggled.

"Morning, Adam," Robin said.

Adam entered and sat at the table too. "Morning, father." He was wearing his new suit.

Robin laughed. "I am not old enough to be your father."

"Then you must stop calling me kid," Adam remarked.

"Touché. How long has Travis been out there?" Robin asked.

"Not even an hour," Marie said.

"Go look at him. Make sure he's alive. He's using an axe you know?"

"I can do that." June disappeared down the hall.

"Adam, you used to give Edward a massage?" Robin said.

"Oh yes. I would be very careful not to hurt you. I'll go very easy. Mr. Miller would drink heavily and fall asleep with his pillows in a terrible way. His neck would go stiff," Adam explained. "What else can I do for you today?"

"Settle in. Get settled in. Please bear in mind Travis is only twelve years old. He says what he thinks," Robin said. "He'll be here about a week perhaps."

"It is overwhelming how much work there is for a man to do here. You've been doing it all by yourself for months. Even a simple thing like moving some furniture for Marie will take both Travis and myself to do. How did you manage so?" Adam sipped a coffee.

June returned. "He's fine. Still chopping the wood."

"I was hoping to get the china unpacked and the dining room set up for dinner tonight. I've mopped it and wiped down the entire furniture in there. I stocked the fireplace with wood," Adam said. "The six of us will have a finely set meal tonight."

"Then we will make something special," Marie said. "Be careful of my new blue wine glasses. I can't wait to use them."

"I found them. They are in wonderful condition. Very lovely choice." Then Adam looked at Robin. "You will let me give you a shave after breakfast, sir, and that massage."

Robin's eyes met Marie's. "Very well then, Mr. Hudson. If you insist."

"Where is your jacket and vest? Shall I get them for you?" Adam asked.

"I couldn't get them on myself and who's going to see me out here?" Robin said.

Adam folded his arms. "After your massage and shave, I will get your jacket and vest onto you properly. I'm sure you will feel better when you are dressed better."

"I am way too hot for jacket and vest," Robin protested.

"You are too hot," Marta blurted out. To her horror, everyone burst out laughing.

May 17, 1840
419   The Dutchman   By Susan Eddy

Robin and Travis walked into the kitchen that afternoon. "My dear, we are pleased to announce that it will be the men doing the cooking this evening,"

"I thought you didn't know how to cook?" Marie looked over from washing laundry in the corner.

"I know how to cook this."

"What did you shoot?" Marie asked. "Travis got a pheasant?"

"Bigger."

"Turkey?" Marie asked.

"Bigger," Robin said.

"Robin shot a deer," Travis said. "I chickened out."

"Deer? We have venison?" Marie stopped and walked over to them. "I can make that pot roast but with venison, you know?"

"And you can make that tomorrow. Tonight, I will pan sear venison steaks for supper. Learned that in India." Robin rummaged in the kitchen for a good knife. "Make something nice to go with it."

"We can salt some of it. I have a keg ready," Marie said.

"I'll handle that." June pulled out a few large pots.

Robin selected the right knife and took her biggest pot. "We'll be back. Travis, you have the stomach for this?"

"I'll manage." Travis trotted out after him. "They have deer in India?"

"Keep Adam inside the house and far away from these windows."

"Oh my. I never thought I would ever be...dining with you." Marta danced into the dining room and spun about in a pale pink satin evening gown.

June stopped her with both hands. "Don't knock the table over, girl." June wore an evening gown of burgundy and velvet.

Robin stood up at the table. "Please, join us, ladies. Everyone can start their new work tomorrow."

Adam held the chair for Marta and then the next for June, seating them across from Marie and himself. "Welcome ladies. It would be rather self-serving to say how lovely you both look this evening, but I shall say it anyway. You both look very lovely indeed."

Marta giggled. "This is the most magnificent gown I have ever seen. Thank you so much Adam, and Marie."

"Adam, you are a genius with thread. I'll give you that," June said. "I'm very thankful today."

Adam strolled around the table set formally with white linen cloth and the new dishware. Wine already filled the blue glasses of Marie's and the new silverware was set at each plate.

"Thank you, Adam," Robin said.

"The table looks lovely, Adam," Marie said. "You did such a fine job at everything."

"I only wish I had flowers to set the table with. Candlesticks with blue candles will have to do," Adam said.

They passed plates of venison steak and bowls of mashed potatoes, gravy, peas, and beets around the table.

Travis tasted his wine, wearing one of Robin's dinner jackets. "This is fun. Like a costume party."

"Which is an excellent idea. We should do a costume party some time," Adam enthused. "I can make anything out of cloth. Medieval princesses and knights. You name it. At the very least, we could get to see Robin in his cavalry uniform."

"Rather be a Mughal Emperor, myself," Robin said.

"I'm not being one of your Hindi maidens," Marie teased him.

June looked down at her plate and smiled. "I just want to say how grateful I am to be here. Grateful for this meal and the very nice new room upstairs. Grateful for the gown. I've worked for a lot of families and never…never have I been treated so well."

"Yes thank you, Robin. I'm so happy I could jump around," Marta said.

"And you did," June reminded her.

That made Adam smile. "I feel the same way. It is difficult to sit still."

Robin smiled. "I would be happy if we all ate in here every meal. We all have our jobs. I will need to hire a stock man and bring some more animals back to the farm. But for now, we are all right."

"Is it true then? About the bank money?" Marta questioned. "The rumors in town…say that you are rich."

"The way I want you to answer those rumors is this," Robin said. "My father left me a fortune. He lived like a miser here and…left it to me."

"And we will be improving things here. Possibly selling this and moving to Boston. He hasn't decided yet," Marie said. "You can come with us of course."

"So…you are rich?" June questioned cautiously.

Marie looked to Robin.

"My father and I both tried every way possible to return this money to the people but there are no bank records left, from three banks. And these robbers also stole from the French in the north. It was all here. This is why, beside each of your plates is an envelope containing a bonus for you. Things are going to be a great deal better here going forward," Robin said. "Just be vigilant as there may still be bank robbers out there who know where this house is. Alert me if you see anyone. Don't let on that you are suspicious of them, just let me handle it."

"And...how are you feeling? Robin?" June questioned.

Robin sipped his wine, using his left hand. He set the goblet down beside his plate. "I'm still having a lot of pain. Shoulder blade hurts quite a lot. There is no comfortable way to sleep. I'm quite tired a lot."

Marie put her hand on his on the table. "You'll be all right."

Robin linked fingers with her and nodded.

"You were in the cavalry?" June asked. "They say you're a marksman."

"A captain. He served in India, fighting the British," Travis spoke up. "They want to make him a Colonel here."

"Let's hope there is no more war here, and I won't have to," Robin said.

"Will you tell us about India?" Marta asked.

"I will. All in good time," Robin said.

"You need to eat something," Marie told him. "Shut up and eat. I'll tell them about New York."

Robin was sitting at his desk in the office, entering into a ledger with quill and ink. "Please have a seat, Adam."

Adam entered and sat in front of the desk, looking about.

"May I inquire what do you anticipate being paid?"

"Oh. I expect salaries would be less here than in New York city. I do not know what a butler makes in Connecticut," Adam said.

"May I ask what you earned in New York?"

"I do not wish to outprice myself. I simply want to work for you. I admire you greatly, sir. Your catching of the bank robbers and how dignified you handled the whole being shot situation," Adam said.

"No need to be evasive, Adam. At least when we are alone, speak your mind to me. Why do you want to work for me, for less money that you were making and so far away from any of your friends?" Robin asked.

"I didn't have any friends there. Didn't have any close ones. I do admire you so." The young man lowered his eyes. "They were mean to me."

"Who were mean to you?" Robin sat forward then.

"I'm not an orphan. I ran away." Adam paused to wipe his eyes. "But even in the Miller's staff there were those who were mean to me."

"I can assure you, no one is going to be mean to you here," Robin said firmly but gently. "Your own family was cruel to you?"

"My father beat me so bad that I...I never went back," Adam said softly, still with eyes down on the floor.

"How old are you, Adam?" Robin asked.

"Twenty-four," Adam said.

"How old are you really?"

Adam shot eyes at him, blue eyes. He barely whispered, "Twenty."

"Adam, I've been all around the world. I have known all manner of people, of men. I have known that a certain kind of men existed in the cavalry, who were like you. Do not be frightened. I think I am right about you. I think you know that I am not that way. Are you going to accept that and be all right with that?" Robin said gently.

Adam put a hand to his mouth.

"If I have made the wrong assumption, just tell me I'm wrong," Robin said.

"Will you send me away? Just away or to...to an asylum?"

"No. Absolutely not," Robin insisted firmly. "Your place is here now. People love who they love. I may be forward in my thinking about that. But it is what I believe."

Adam wept a little bit. He drew out a handkerchief and wiped his eyes with it.

"Your father beat you for this? Was there a final straw?" Robin questioned.

"He caught me with another boy," Adam whispered.

Robin let out a long hard breath. "Okay. Relax. You are safe here, just as you are." Robin pulled a brandy bottle out of his desk and poured two shot glasses. He slid one across the desk toward Adam. "Don't tell my wife I keep this in here. She thinks more than two glasses of this is an addiction."

Adam smiled. "Anything you tell me is a confidence, Robin."

"And the same to you. Have a drink and then I will ask you something." Robin drank his. He watched Adam sip his rather than down the whole thing. "Have you ever been with a woman?"

Adam shook his head.

"Are you sure you don't want to? I will take you to Norwich. Turn those blue eyes on them and you'll have your choice." Robin grinned. "I must have gotten away with saying it was my first for years."

Adam laughed out loud.

Robin grinned for a moment longer. "You are safe here. You are also going to be paid an awful lot more than my former valet or butler in Boston were. As long as you promise me you won't save it up and run away again."

"I'm not leaving. You must keep the fortune," Adam blurted out. "Oh! I'm so sorry. It's the alcohol making me blunt."

"That brandy hasn't yet hit your stomach, kid." He laughed. "If you help me improve this house to almost New York standards, you'll be paid very well. Afterall, you are both valet and butler here. You should be paid more. You must be aware of what you are getting into, Adam. I want to double the size of this home. I want to open the closed wing. And for a time, Marie and I will make a trip to Amsterdam to visit my family. We will be gone for several months. June is in charge when I am gone. Can you take orders from a woman?"

"Of course, sir. I mean Robin. I see the possibilities in this home. I see what can become."

"Well, you have better vision than I do if you see possibilities in this home. It is a crude country farm to me. It needs work," Robin said.

"Let us see what we can do with it then. Perhaps you will buy homes in Boston and Amsterdam then. You actually like to drink this brandy?" Adam hiccupped.

"Hudson is not your last name. Is it? I couldn't help but notice the Hudson River runs right by there."

Adam looked at him.

"Was your father wealthy?"

Adam nodded.

"Any brothers or sisters?" Robin asked.

"Sisters, why?" Adam asked.

"Did your parents die of yellow fever or did you just tell Jonas that?" Robin asked.

"Why do you ask me this?"

"Sorry but I can't help being a lawyer. You are legally entitled to everything your father had. Who did it go to?" Robin asked.

"He still has it," Adam said.

"Someday it would give me great pleasure to set this right for you. Then you can look after your sisters, your mother too. I would like to know your real last name," Robin said.

"You are too good a lawyer. You will find them. And I do not want to see any of them until he is dead. Or I will kill him."

Robin tapped on the desk to get Adam's full attention. "Don't do that. Don't go to jail when he was the one in the wrong those years ago. All right? I like that you were honest with me. But I don't like that you lied to me about your name and your age. Is there anything else I need to know about?"

"I'm so sorry. I am so sorry. When I am here for one year, on that very day, I will tell you my name."

Robin looked at him across the desk.

"Give me one year of peace and not fearing for my life. Please, sir. Can I legally change my name to Hudson then?"

"I can do that for you. You best tell me your name so that I can file papers with the court. That way, if anything should happen to your father, you can inherit."

"My uncle would inherit it. He'd look after my sisters."

"When you're ready, you tell me. Whatever your father had is yours when he passes, if he likes it or not. Adam, how much education have you had? Do you read and write?"

"I do. Yes. I finished the eighth grade." Adam sat back and crossed his legs. He sipped more brandy.

"I could make you a legal assistant. It would pay much more than a butler's salary. You give it some thought."

Chapter Nineteen Birthday Party

May 18, 1840

The following day, Travis came in from his work outdoors in the late afternoon and set a basket of eggs on the kitchen table. He took in Robin sleeping on the couch and Marie checking the venison pot roast over the fire. Quietly he said, "Is he supposed to sleep so much?"

"He needs the rest," Marie said. "Do you hear that?"

"Yes." Travis went to the window to look out. "It's Pa." He went back outside.

Robin was awakened. He clutched his sore arm to his stomach with the left hand. "Is someone here?"

"Michael Poole, apparently," Marie said. "Travis went out to him."

Robin sat up and pulled his blanket up into a cushion for his arm. "Is that your venison roast? It smells almost as good as the beef did."

Marie went to Robin and kissed him.

"I'm glad he came by. I separated out more of his share. I wanted to give it to him," Robin said. "Help me up."

"I'm sure he'll stay for supper. You'll get your chance." Marie held an arm out for him to hold onto.

The door opened. Poole and his son entered. "Robin, how are you? Good to see you, Marie."

"Hello Michael," Marie said.

"I'm all right. Thanks," Robin said.

"How's the boy doing for you? He showed me his cord of wood already," Michael said.

"I couldn't have gotten by without him," Robin said. "Travis is a great help to us. You're staying for supper, aren't you?"

"Happy to. I just came out to bring you this package." Michael sat in a kitchen chair across from him. He set a thick envelope on the table and pushed it toward Robin. "Looks like it went to Boston and they forwarded it out to Canterbury. Lucky it found its way here at all."

Travis went to wash up.

"You could post some letters for me. They're just to my brother and sister, and the Millers." Robin slid the package toward himself, sat down, and began working to open it.

"Sure will. How is that arm?" Michael asked.

"Oh, it is impossible to do anything. And if I take laudanum to sleep at night, I sleep all day," Robin said. "Michael, I want to give more of the money to you."

"I wanted to talk to you about something too. I'm thinking about staying here a while, keeping watch."

Marie brought both men a cup of tea.

Robin looked up at her. "We're being cautious."

"And I need to know if you are just packing up and leaving for Europe," Poole said.

"I don't think so." Robin met eyes with Marie. "Has something happened?"

"Alice and I were thinking if we moved to Boston we could send the children to better school. We were just more inclined to do it if we had friends there," Poole said. "And I don't need to be a constable anymore."

"Well, yes it would be nice to have friends in Boston, as it is here," Robin said. "We should visit my family in Amsterdam. Then I would like to return to Boston and do some work as a barrister for the poor."

"You could definitely have a home in both countries," Michael said.

"What is this?" Marie indicated the package.

Robin broke the seal and opened it to let spill out a bundle of cash. He began reading the letter.

Poole grabbed the cash. "Two hundred dollars here."

Robin put the letter down and his face turned grey.

Marie slid her hand onto his shoulder.

Poole grabbed the letter from him and saw Dutch. He handed it to Robin.

To my son, Robin.

I could think of no other way to get you to come to Canterbury. Forgive me. Here is the loan money. Do be careful. These bank robbers are dangerous. I hope this explains everything and you have by now found my journals and the bank money. I can find no bank records for the three robberies and no way to return the money to the people. Consider this my last will. The fortune is yours. Return to Amsterdam and live the life I wished for you. Your loving father, Willem.

Robin dropped his chin down.

Poole took the letter from him to set it on the table with the money.

Robin cleared his throat. "I was waiting to hear from Edward Miller about French francs in Boston, and then to hear from Colonel Abrams about the French treasury. Once I do, then I would buy back the francs from you and I'll just take them to Amsterdam. Take Marie to see Paris." He met eyes with her and smiled. "Michael, you and I can work together, in Boston. Only cases we want to take, to help the poor."

"I would be very interested in that. Alice and I were just afraid that with all you went through, you would just pack up and never come back. I could understand that. I really could. You made it clear this is not your country."

"However, Marie and I have friends here. And we don't in Europe," Robin said.

"What about your family?" Marie asked him.

Robin rolled his eyes. "My brother...well he's not like me. He's a good surgeon but he's the one you don't want, if you must talk to him at all."

Poole laughed.

"My sisters, I would like to visit," Robin said. "I wrote them that I have married Marie and I would write again should we start a voyage back to Amsterdam."

"Are you going to give them a share of the money?" Poole asked.

"My father left that up to me. I expect to bring them each an equal share," Robin said.

"Equal with you? You solved the case. You found the money. You got shot for it. You put away two bank robbers," Michael Poole said. "Don't you dare split your money with three siblings."

"Oh. Equal with me? No," Robin said. "Equal with each other. I have no intention of telling them how much I kept, or you kept for that matter. They didn't offer to help me pay off Fathers' debt, now did they? Not even my brother who inherited his horse farm."

"They didn't offer to come help you when your wife and child died," Marie said.

That made Poole look at her.

"I could have used any help then but Marie does not know what a grueling trip it is to cross the Atlantic," Robin said. "Not one of them even cared to urge me to move back to Europe, given that I had nothing here."

"I saw the deer out there. A rare thing around here. Did you show Travis how to shoot that?" Poole asked.

Travis returned to the table, looking from his father to Robin.

"I showed him how, yes," Robin said.

"Travis got his first deer?" Poole brightened.

"I was expecting a turkey," Travis said.

"Ahm." Robin looked at the boy. "I shot the deer. He watched how I did it."

Robin met Adam at the door to the upstairs second wing. "Adam, you can keep the room you have or take first choice of these other rooms. But let's get this opened for the two maids to take rooms in here."

"I'll stay wherever you put me." Adam followed Robin up the eight steps and into the hallway.

Robin entered the first bedroom and examined the fireplace that it shared with the second bedroom. He leaned to put his head inside the fireplace and look up.

Adam ran forward. "Careful. You don't know what's up there."

"A nest. That's what's up there." Robin backed out. "I'll have to get a chimney sweep out here before this one is used."

Adam examined the bed and pushed on the mattress. "It's not bad. Just hasn't been used in years. What sort of nest? Bees?"

"I'm thinking squirrel, actually." Robin moved on to look inside the other rooms, six all together.

Adam wandered into another room. He found one on the farthest corner with windows on two sides. It had a fireplace on the outside wall and he tried to look inside like Robin had. He soon ran back to the hallway as fast as he could, shrieking. "There's something in there."

Robin caught him. "What? A rat?"

"Bigger. Very big." Adam clung onto Robin's arm.

"How big? Do I need my rifle?" Robin asked, half laughing.

"I don't know. It moved."

"Where?" Robin entered the room and looked around. Something ran as fast as it could from the fireplace to beneath the bed. Robin ducked down to look beneath the bed and met eyes with the creature.

"Robin, what is it?" Adam urged, shaking in the doorway.

"It's a cat, Adam. It's one of the cats." Robin stood up with hands on his hips.

"It was huge. There's no way that was a cat," Adam insisted. "I was thinking small bear."

Robin grinned. "Cat."

Adam held a hand to his heart and caught his breath. "Are you sure?"

"We have cats in Europe. I grew up with kittens in my pockets. I ought to know," Robin said. "Anyway, this fireplace looks fine. It's right above the one at the end of the ball room. Same chimney, most likely. This is a nicer room than the one you have. Why don't you take this one? Unless it's the bear you don't want to live with?"

Adam lowered his chin and then looked at Robin again.

Robin examined the windows. "These are in good shape. Which room do you want?"

"Well, there is no fireplace in the room I have. Could I move the dresser and the chair down here?" Adam asked.

"Yes of course. I'll help you," Robin said.

"You can't help me. You have one arm. Travis will help me." Adam looked about in the room. "It has more windows than I had in the Millers."

"Whichever you want. But I'm sure if you don't take this room now, one of the women will," Robin said. "You'll have to decide before they do."

"How did the cat get in?" Adam eventually looked beneath the bed at the black cat.

"Keep looking. It takes a decent size opening for that cat to get through. Let's check the other rooms. Maybe there is an open window," Robin said.

"What do we do about the cat?" Adam followed him.

"Name it Bear and give it something to eat," Robin said. "You won't have any mice."

"I would rather have a cat than mice," Adam agreed. "You likely want the rooms in your wing for guests. These rooms are too small for guests. I will take this one, if I can use the fireplace."

"Of course, you can. Let's find two other rooms for June and Marta. I'd really like the women to have the rooms on either side of this fireplace."

"Perhaps Travis can climb a ladder up there and get the nest out. He is quite small and tall," Adam said. "I can't do ladders or small spaces either."

"It's possible I can free it up with a broom handle," Robin said. "I'll go get Travis. You can go ahead and set that room up for yourself. Bring in some firewood for it. You'll need a lamp or two."

"And an offering of food to make peace with my roommate," Adam said.

May 20, 1840

"I posted your letters," Michael told Robin. "I brought the French francs like you asked."

"I'm going to exchange them one for one then," Robin said. "What do you plan to do?"

"Well, about that." Poole followed him into the house. "Alice and I were thinking of leaving Travis with you for a bit and we'll take the two girls with us to Boston to look around. Think about living there."

"Excellent. Before you do, let me give you a letter to drop off at the newspaper. I want to post this estate for sale, and start working on that," Robin said.

"You know, Robin, we will buy it from you if you do plan to go away to Europe and never come back. If you went to Europe, nobody would ever know Marie worked for you. It might go easier on you both," Poole said quietly. "Not that I would like to see you go."

"I think the same is true of Boston." Robin let out a long sigh. "It seems we both have options. And that is a good thing. I might not go to Boston at all. I haven't decided."

May 21, 1840

Robin put his finest Dutch saddle on the back of his new horse and began cinching it up in the stall. Travis looked on through the stall gate. "There's no saddle horn on that? It's so thin. How do you ride with that?"

"Less leather between the horse and myself means I can feel him better. The horn's for working cattle, which I have no intention to do. I have direct contact with his mouth from each rein and I hold one in each hand. He will quickly learn what I want him to do from the reins and my knees. Now, this fellow has never had this kind of saddle on him before." Robin looked at Travis through the stall. "So, I'm going to mount him the first time right here. Make sure he's calm with it."

"Are you sure you should be on a horse already?" Travis asked.

Robin pulled off his sling and handed it through the gate. "Hold this for me."

Travis did so. "Oh boy. I'm in deep shit if you get hurt."

Robin moved around to the left side of the horse, slid his boot up into the stirrup and hoisted himself up onto the horses' back. "Don't talk like that in front of your father." He pulled back on both reins, tucking the horses' chin down.

Travis just looked up at him. "Well how do I say that in Dutch?"

"In diepe shit." Robin released the reins, letting the horse relax. He patted it on the neck. "Easy. Easy boy. Travis, is your horse saddled and ready?"

"Yes, sir, Robin," Travis said. "You won't tell me?"

"I want you and your horse to walk right beside me on my left. Don't grab my reins. But pace your horse close to my side. Open this stall and go mount up." Robin sat comfortably on his new horse. "I just told you, in diepe shit. It's spelled different."

"Oh lord." Travis did so, opening the stall gate and then mounted his own horse. He walked his up in front of Robin's.

Robin walked his new horse out of the barn, alongside Travis. But once out in the sunlight, the new horse started to buck.

Robin held on and cranked the horses' head down and to the side. "No. No. If you do not walk nice and easy, I'm holding you down."

Travis kept his horse close on the left.

Robin let the head up and they walked forward into the courtyard. "Let's circle the courtyard. Nice and easy. There." He patted the horse again.

After a complete circle, Robin said, "Now let's go the other direction. Easy."

The horse turned for Robin. And it bucked again. Robin cranked his head down again. "No. We are not running yet. Easy. Easy now."

He let its head come up again and they walked in the other direction, with Travis still on the left side.

"Does he hate it?" Travis asked.

"He wants to run. That's all. I need him to learn the new tack before we do," Robin said gently. "And he needs to learn Dutch."

"He can do that?"

"Oh yes. I know in an emergency I won't remember to translate," Robin said. "But if he learns the reins and my knees, he can learn the Dutch later."

439   The Dutchman   By Susan Eddy

When Robin let his head up this time, the horse bolted down the driveway toward the gate. Robin let him go and eased back on the reins saying, "Hou op."

Travis caught up and road alongside. "Jesus he's fast."

Robin laughed. "Shit he's fast! He has more to give." He brought the horse to a stop, patted him on the neck and turned him around toward the barn again. "What a spectacular beast. Let's tell Marie we're going for a ride down the road a bit."

In the courtyard, Marie was standing with her arms folded.

Robin road his beautiful black gelding around her and to a stop in front of her. "Yes Madame?"

"Are you out of your mind?" Marie asked.

"I'm fine. We're going for a short ride. He's taking to me. He just has a lot of energy to burn off," Robin said.

"Well don't go far and Travis stay with him," Marie called.

Robin and Travis took off down the driveway.

May 22, 1840

Robin had been out riding his new horse with Travis when they heard gunshots at the estate. "Whoa. Hold up." Robin drew his rifle and cocked it. "Travis you've got your rifle? Is it loaded?"

"Yes, sir. Yes."

"You duck down and stay behind me. Don't shoot it. You hand that rifle to me when I fire mine. Then you stay back and reload mine then yours when I drop it."

"I hope it's not Adam," Travis urged. "He wanted to know about shooting."

"No. That's not any of my weapons. When I take your rifle you stay back and be on your guard. You'll hand me mine when I come back or wave you in," Robin told him. "You have your orders."

"Yes sir."

Robin road cross country from the Lee farm next door toward his estate, making a shortcut while Travis went for the driveway. Robin could see a man in the courtyard reloading a rifle.

And the man turned to see Robin jump the rock wall with his horse.

A second man ran for Marie and took her down in the dirt.

"Robin, three men..." Maire screamed out before the man got his hand over her mouth and held her by knife on the ground.

As the man began to finish loading his rifle and aimed it, Van der Kellen shot him in the chest from full charge on horseback. Then Robin pulled his horse to a stop in front of Marie. He dropped the rifle and pointed his pistol.

Travis peeked around the house on his horse.

"You drop that gun, or I'll cut her throat!" The man howled, lying on the ground with Marie.

Marie tried to pull back but couldn't.

"You're dead if you don't release her." Robin dismounted.

Travis dismounted and ducked against the corner of the house, rifle in hands.

Robin had that pistol pointed at the man's head, but he had to use both hands to steady it. He quickly glanced around but could not see any others.

"Get up girl." The man stood up with his arm around Marie and a knife still at her throat. "You're going to give me that horse, mister. Bring it here."

"You give me the girl and you can take the horse," Robin said.

"Robin, they know the money is in the root cellar," Marie called out.

Robin said to her, "Quiet. Girl. Get ready to het recht."

"Give me that horse. I'm not kidding," the man said.

"Take the horse. I just want the girl." Robin aimed the pistol. "Het recht!"

Marie dove down to her right and the man ran to Robin's horse, mounting it from the wrong side.

Robin collected Marie in his arms. "Run to Travis around the house. Go."

"One in the house I think," Marie warned him. "Adam is hurt…."

Robin's new horse circled and circled, and finally bucked the man right off his back. Robin shot him on the ground. Robin now grabbed his rifle off the ground, his reloading kit from his horse and slapped the horse to run it off. Then he and Marie ran for the corner of the house, where young Travis was covering them with a rifle.

"There's another in the house." Marie skidded down against the house between Robin and Travis.

"Reload my rifle, Travis." Robin immediately began reloading his pistol. "Where's Adam and the women?"

"They think the money is in the root cellar. I had to tell them it was somewhere," Marie said. "The others are all in the house somewhere. They went after Adam. He was the only man here."

"I want you and Travis to get on his horse and ride to the Lee's. Go."

Once Travis handed Robin's Baker back to him, he mounted his horse and held out a hand to Marie. "Should I get my pa?"

"No. Get Marie out of here. Where are Marta and June?"

"Upstairs, hiding I think," Marie said. "Adam ran for the library."

Robin made a stirrup of his hands and helped Marie mount the back of the horse with Travis. "Go Travis."

Travis handed his loaded gun to Robin too.

Van der Kellen, well-armed, crept around the front of the house and in through the window to the library. He could see blood on the floor. "Adam?" Robin crept around the desk.

 He found Adam unconscious on the floor beside the desk. His forehead was bleeding but he was breathing. "Adam? Shhh."

Hudson looked up at him and reached to wrap his arms around Robin's neck.

"Are you all right?" Robin whispered.

"Yes."

"Listen to me. They think you're dead. You get under this desk and don't move until someone comes for you. Stay there."

Robin moved past him.

Adam crawled around the desk and beneath it to curl up inside the knee hole.

"Van der Kellen."

The man lunged for Robin and they wrestled for the pistol. Robin was thrown into the wall and dragged the man down to the kitchen floor with him where they both fell down the pantry stairs. Robin threw a sack of potatoes on the man and then dove on top to plunge his boot knife into the man's throat. When Robin stood up, he saw June in the pantry door, musket in her hands.

"Don't shoot."

"No sir." June lowered the musket. "Is he dead?"

"Dead." Robin pulled the potato sack aside as he retrieved his pistol. "Adam is hurt in the library. You take him and Marta and hide out in the quarters in the dark all night until somebody comes for you."

"Yes, sir."

Robin grabbed his sword off the kitchen table and ran out the back door to find his horse waiting for him.

"Robin, I'm so sorry. He took her. One of them jumped me and took my horse with Marie." Travis was crying, walking up the road toward him.

"One of them took Marie on horseback?" Robin was reloading quickly in the saddle. "Which way did he go?"

"Toward Norwich. Up the road," Travis said.

"I want you to catch one of their horses out there and go get your pa. I'm going for Marie," Robin said. "He won't get far on your horse with Marie struggling."

Robin came on the man who was riding with Marie and when he did, the man pushed Marie to the ground. He spun his horse around and struggled to raise his weapon. Marie screamed, trying to get out of the way of the horse.

Robin fired a shot at a near gallop and struck the man in the arm, knocking him from his horse.

Marie scrambled back as he scurried to catch her. She screamed and picked up a rock but dropped it when he spun her around.

Robin dove from his horse right onto the man, knocking him away from Marie. And the two men fought hard on the ground, rolling from the force of Robin's landing. They pounded each other repeatedly, rolling in the field. The man secured both hands on Robin's throat as Robin drove his sword right through the man. Then he stood up and slit the man's throat with one swift stroke.

A single gunshot rang out.

"Robin!" Marie shrieked.

Van der Kellen pulled Marie behind him to see another man riding in fast. "Marie, run! Get out of here."

The man approaching held up his smoking weapon. "Van der Kellen?"

"Who is it?" Robin brandished that sword. "Get off that horse and face me!"

"Colonel Abrams." He walked his horse in and dismounted. He inspected the man Robin had killed. "Are you both all right? Miss Marie?"

Marie wrapped her arms around Robin from behind him, shaking.

Robin glanced down at the bloody sword in his right hand. His right shoulder hurt him such that he doubled over and cried out in pain, with Marie nearly holding him up.

Abrams began reloading his rifle. "Are there any more men?"

"Got this one. I got two at my house," Robin said between breaths.

"Are you shot? Stabbed?" Abrams asked him.

"No. Just...hurting. Marie, are you injured?" Robin stood up and took her under his left arm.

She embraced him. "I don't know. No. I can't stop shaking. I saw what you did to that man."

Abrams searched the attacker and found documents, a map, coins, which he just pocketed. Then he looked at them. He picked up Robin's Baker and carried it over.

"Can you walk, Marie?" Robin asked.

"I don't...think I can ride anymore. But I can walk," Marie admitted.

"We've run the shit out of these horses. We can't ride them until they have a rest anyway. Rain coming in. We will ahm... walk back to those cliffs. Take some shelter," Robin said.

Abrams gathered the reins of Robin's and Travis's horses. He brought them to Robin.

"You're certain there were three all together?" Robin asked Marie.

"I only saw three."

Robin cleaned off his sword in the grass and sheathed it on his hip, opposite the pistol. "Knew they were coming for me."

Abrams met eyes with Robin. "Best get to some shelter. I saw lightening on the ride in. I'll take two horses. You take yours." He put Robin's rifle into its pocket on Robin's saddle.

They lead the horses back across the field, back tracking in the horse prints. It was almost dark out.

"June and Marta all right?" Marie clung to Robin's right injured arm, supporting it.

"They're all right. Hiding in the quarters while Travis brings out Constable Poole," Robin said. "Adam was hit in the head. I found him, knocked out on the floor. But he wasn't shot."

"You must hurt so bad," Marie said.

"I'm not thinking about that yet." Robin looked to Abrams.

"I saw what you did to that man, Robin." Marie looked up at him. After a few steps she took Robin's arm around her shoulders to help him walk.

Robin found them a ravine with a ledge overhang for shelter. He tied the horses to a tree not far from them. Then he set his guns down on the ground, beneath the ledge. "Marie, sit down here." He removed his overcoat, his right shoulder hurting badly as he did so, and he put his coat on her. "Just sit. I will get a fire going."

"Is that wise? Will they see it?"

"Who's going to see it out here?" Robin smiled a bit at the familiar phrase. "Poole and Travis will get back to the estate to look after the women. They will make sure home is clear. And we will return in the morning."

"Spending the night here?" Marie asked.

They heard thunder.

"That's it for tonight. Yes." Robin started collecting firewood nearby.

Abrams tied his horse up with theirs and removed items from his saddle.

Robin came back to Marie and assembled his firewood with a pile of dry pinecones and pine needles. Then from his saddle bag he had a flint and a flask of black powder.

"Isn't that gun powder?" Marie was alarmed.

Abrams watched him for a moment and smiled a bit. He picked up some firewood for them.

"Yes. Just stand back a bit." He struck the flint with his knife and on the second try, a spark lit the pile of black powder with a tiny explosion that lit the pine.

"Well, I never knew you could do that," Marie said. "I wish I knew that in the kitchen years ago."

Robin smiled. "I don't think we want you lighting kitchen fires with black powder, my dear. Might blow up the house."

"Just a tiny bit like that?"

"It must be just a tiny bit and it's damp out here. That is a factor as well. I'll gather more wood." Robin got up and met Abrams at the horses.

Abrams put a hand on his shoulder. "I followed these men down here. Coming for you. Two of them were enlisted men. Are you injured?"

"Aside from getting the fuck beat out of me, no." Robin checked on the horses, who were also under the ledge, and then collected more fallen wood to burn.

Marie edged some of his kindling into the fire to keep it going.

"I'll get the firewood. You guard your wife there," Adams said.

Robin set more into the fire and laid a collection of wood beside it. He went for more. "We'd better gather enough for the night. It will all get wet shortly."

"Did you know your horse would throw that man like that?" Marie asked.

"Oh, he mounted on the wrong side. Of course. And I don't think he'll let anybody but me ride him. He circled and wouldn't let Travis mount him." Robin eventually gathered a large pile of wood for their fire and then he returned to the horses to check Travis's saddlebags. He came back with two canteens and four apples.

"You don't have to take their saddles off, do you?" Marie accepted the apples from him.

"I should. But I'm figuring we'll only be here four or five hours until it's light enough to go home. They'll rest as they are."

"Sit down, darling. Where are you hurt?" Marie urged him.

Robin sat down beside her, leaning back against the rock wall. "My shoulder is really bad. That's all. And how was your day, love?"

Marie laughed at the way he asked that. "I am so sore all over. I could hardly get my legs around that big horse."

"Better around me." Robin arranged the wood on the fire and then set his weapons easily within reach. "Get some rest then. I'll be on guard."

"We must remember to thank Travis for always being hungry and having apples in his saddlebags," Marie said.

Abrams was listening. He squatted down with them and shared some jerky. He accepted an apple in exchange.

Robin had the Baker and the pistol reloaded.

"Will you now tell me about war, that I've seen you kill five men?" Marie asked.

"I can't remember the face of my first wife but I surely remember the man I took this pistol from. He haunts me," Robin said. "No, I'm not telling you what I've done in war. If there is a hell, I'm surely bound for it."

"My wife once said, there's no hell for a war hero but war itself," Abrams said.

"I saw you so bravely defend me, even when your guns were empty. That's what I saw," Marie said.

"You're a strong woman, Marie," Abrams spoke up. "You and my wife have that in common."

"Oh Robin." Marie squirmed into his arms. "My Dutchman."

Robin leaned his head back against the rock. "Marie, you can't hug a warrior when he's on guard. You're cracking me out of it."

Abrams chuckled quietly. "Women will do that."

The rain came down. The sound of it on the ledge above and the rock underfoot made hearing if anyone was coming impossible. As Marie curled up in Robin's coat and slept beside the fire, Robin got up, pistol in his hand and stood beside the horses, listening. He reassured his new horse with a hand on his snout.

"Robin?"

Robin hurried back to Marie's side. "I'm right here. You're safe."

"Oh Robin." She sat up, cold and sore, and looked up at him in the light of the campfire. The rain was still coming down out beyond their shelter.

Robin sat down beside her and let her curl up against him. "You're okay, Marie. I'm right here."

She clung to him. "Where were you?"

"Just standing guard."

Abrams was sitting up against the wall, alert.

"Actually standing? Aren't you tired?"

"If I sit for too long, I might fall asleep and I don't intend to." Robin embraced her. "Abrams is here too."

"But I have your coat and I'm the one by the fire. That isn't right," Marie said.

"Of course, it is. I'm fine." Robin looked at the man beside him. "You collected papers off that man. What did he carry?"

"Oh, I forgot all about that." Abrams opened his jacket to find the papers folded up in his pocket.

Marie sat back beside him and then reached to put another piece of wood on the fire.

Abrams handed a map to Robin.

"My house. Got the distance from town wrong. Not even the right street name. Directions out from New London. Surprised they found it at all." He passed that to Owen Abrams and accepted others. "French. A letter from Christian Pascal."

"I tracked the men right to your estate. Two women said you went out in this direction. Two men were dead in your driveway," Abrams said.

"Marta and June, were they all, right?" Marie urged. "And Travis? Did you see a boy? And Adam?"

"Just two women. They were fine. They told me what happened," Abrams said. "Had to show the one with the musket my insignia first."

Robin smoothed his wet hair back from his face. "How long ago were you there?"

"Not two hours ago, at a ride in the dark," Abrams said. "Sorry for the approach. No time to waste."

"Quite right," Robin said. "The last one took Marie captive."

"You got all the others?" Abrams said.

"Yes. Who were they?" Robin asked. "They knew Christian Pascal, the one I asked you to look into."

"Well, two of them were US Army. Served with Pascal. Not exactly honorably discharged. Stole from French traders up in Mackinac territory. Were arrested for a time. Those were the two in your driveway." Abrams shook water from his hat and coat before tossing more wood onto the fire. "Anything else in those papers?"

He dug out the papers from his pocket again to give them another look over.

"Robin, I don't know how to tell you this," Abrams said. "The French forts aren't missing any money, that they know of. All in order, they assured me. The French francs must have come from French traders. This might ease your pain a bit. I do believe you're filthy rich."

May 23, 1840

"I've raised the stirrups for you, Marie. It will be easier on your legs, but harder to mount." Robin steadied Travis's horse and held out his hand to Marie. She could barely get her foot into the stirrup and reach the saddle horn to pull herself up into the saddle. Then she had to arrange her skirt around and beneath her. She still had Robin's over coat on too.

Robin was looking up at her. He laid his hand on her thigh. "All right, darling?"

"I'm so glad it's only a couple hours until home," Marie sighed. "Yes."

"And you'll take some of that laudanum and sleep, after you eat something of course." Robin handed the reins to her. He turned to his own horse which nudged him.

"Robin, I don't know how to ride," Marie said. "You said this one needs a commander on board."

"He'll follow this one or I'll tie him to it." He moved around to the horse's left side to mount up. "Easy, Springen. We're not going to run like hell this time. We must look after Marie." He patted the horse on the neck.

"Springen?"

"It means Jumper in Dutch," Robin said.

Abrams mounted his horse and pulled it up beside Robin. "Fine looking animal there. It suits you."

"This horse reads my mind. If not for Marie, I'd be in love with this horse," Robin said.

Abrams laughed while Marie eyed her husband.

The three of them road up Robin's driveway into the estate and were met in the courtyard by Constable and Travis Poole.

"Well thank God, you found them." Michael Poole grabbed the reins of Marie's horse. "You must be Colonel Abrams."

"And you must be Constable Poole." Abrams dismounted and shook hands with Michael. "Good to meet you."

"Pleasure, Colonel. Marie, may I lift you down?" Poole asked.

Travis had the reins of Robin's horse. "Are you okay, Robin? You look beat to shit, man."

"Don't you address him that way," Michael scolded Travis.

"It's quite all right." Robin dismounted. "We've fought side by side. He's earned the right to speak to me common." He held onto Travis's shoulder.

Marie let Poole help her dismount and then she folded into Robin's arms.

Marta and June came out of the house then. "Oh, thank God you're all right."

"Look after Marie, please." Robin passed Marie into the women. "Is Adam all right?"

"He's laying down. Got quite a head wound but talking to us. Says he's okay. You must be exhausted," June said. "We made plenty of food for everyone. Come inside and get warm."

Robin and the men remained outside. Robin held his right arm in his left and met eyes with each of them.

"Well...bout time you invited us in for a drink," Colonel Abrams said.

Robin burst out laughing. "Inside for a drink then. Yes."

"Travis and I will unsaddle these horses and get them fed. We'll be in shortly," Michael said.

"We'll hold off on the brandy until you join us. Both of you," Robin said. "I suppose we have some men to bury after that, but not with my family. These will go out in the field."

Robin and Abrams both collected their weapons off their horses.

The horses were led toward the barn and Robin opened the door for Abrams.

Colonel Abrams entered the kitchen and stood warming by the fire.

"Would you like to take a room upstairs and get into some dry clothing? I can get you some things to wear if...." Robin said to him.

"Thank you. I have some things I can change into." Abrams indicated his saddle bags. "God that food smells good. I could eat a horse."

"Help yourself." Robin indicated the biscuits on the table. "And let's hope it didn't come to that."

They each grabbed a biscuit and started up the stairs. "Travis has claimed this room. I don't know which room Michael has chosen but if you don't see anything in there, take it. How about this one?" Robin gestured into a third room.

"Thank you. Wonderful. I'll be down to the table shortly." Abrams went inside and Robin shut his door.

Robin walked down the hall to Adam's room and found him sitting up on the bed, about to get up. "Stay right there. Everyone's home now. We're all right. How are you?"

Adam held onto his head and started to weep. "I'm okay, I think."

Robin went to him and sat down on the bed facing him. He let Adam wrap his arms around his neck. Robin patted him on the back. "I'm so sorry, Adam. I want you to take it easy for the next few days. And someone must check on you every few hours. You can't sleep for very long with a head wound like that. Are you dizzy? Trouble seeing?"

"No. No. It just hurts so."

"A little laudanum and some food is what you need. Let me get out of these wet clothes and I'll be back. You lay down and rest." Robin deposited him back onto his pillows and headed toward his own room. Then he knocked on the closed door.

Marie opened it. "Come on in, sweetheart." She was changed into a dry blue broad cloth.

Robin entered and the two maids were ready to make a quick exit. Each one giving a bit of a nod and a, "Mr. Van der Kellen."

They hurried out.

"Check on Adam. Bring him some food and this laudanum. One spoon of it for him," Robin told them.

June picked up the medicine and they left together.

Robin closed the door and hugged Marie to him.

"Home safe at last." Marie sighed.

"With a house full of friends, it seems." Robin released her. "I am soaked through. I need to change. I need this arm in a sling again."

"I can help you with that. Give me this jacket."

She helped Robin undress, revealing bruises and cuts all over him. His wound in the upper chest was bruised as if it bled again. His throat had bruises from the man's fingers. As Robin sat on the edge of the bed and she eased clean trousers up his legs, he said, "I'm sorry you must see me this way. I'll be so bruised up for a while, after a battle. There were many months in India that I was always bruised, always hurting when I walked."

Marie let him rise and pull up the pants. "Well, you don't want to see what my hip or my knee looks like right now. I did take a tiny bit of laudanum. I feel better that you have help here. You can rest while Poole and Abrams look after us."

Robin started his sore arm into a shirt and she helped him on with the rest of it. "Darling, I never meant for you to know what war is like. Now you have lived it."

She kissed him. "You'll teach me to shoot and reload. Next week."

"Next week?"

"After I'm not so sore. I'm not afraid of your guns. I just don't know how to use them," Marie said.

He buttoned his shirt. "For most people I would say that it is choosing when to and when not to use a gun. But you can handle yourself. You have the mental strength that can't be taught. Weaponry is easy enough to learn."

"So, you'll teach me?"

"Teach you and do more than that. The next time I go to Norwich I'll buy you a small little pistol for your very own," Robin said. "Perhaps then you'll never be attacked again."

By Susan Eddy

In a few moments Robin and Marie were the last to enter the kitchen.

Marta and June were ready to serve a big lunch to them. "Do you wish to eat in here or the dining room, sir?"

"Here of course. It's where the big fire is." Robin moved through the gathering, setting a hand on Adam's shoulder. "Are you all right, kid?"

Adam nodded. "I'm fine, really. And you, Robin?"

"Sore all over." Robin moved into the kitchen to retrieve one of the bottles of brandy and five glasses.

"Marie, sit down. We'll take care of everything," Marta told her. "I'll get you some tea."

Marie sat beside the head of the table. Travis sat beside her.

Adam was sitting across from them with a bandage about his forehead.

Robin set the five glasses on the table and poured brandy into each. He set one before Abrams, Michael, Adam, and Travis too. Then he picked up his own glass. "Thank you, gentlemen. Wouldn't be here without each and every one of you."

The men raised their glasses and clinked them together. Adam was smiling, thinking he'd always wanted to do that.

After they drank, Michael said to his son, "He's got you drinking brandy now?"

"Sorry pa," Travis said.

"He's earned it," Robin insisted. "Brave as any cadet. As a matter of fact, June with that musket should be downing a brandy as well."

"Well fill it up." June pushed her teacup toward the bottle.

Robin grinned as he filled up her cup.

"Robin, the way you jumped that stone wall and then shot that man at a full charge...Never seen anything like it." Travis sighed.

"Travis, no talk of war at my table," Robin corrected. "Even if I do come off rather well in it." He took a good drink while the other laughed.

"I could make you a Colonel in the infantry, Robin. You should consider it. A man with your skills is hard to find," Abrams said. "What are your plans for the future?"

"Yes. What do you plan to do with the money?" Michael asked.

Robin took his seat at the head of the table. "Well, Marie and I would like to visit Amsterdam. And then maybe build this place up, improve it. Maybe build an all-new stone mansion."

Marta and June began setting plates, silverware, and dishes of food on the table.

"Like that idea," Adam remarked.

"Have a seat here with us, when you have it all on the table," Marie told them.

"Thank you, mum." Marta smiled.

May 25, 1840

Michael and Alice Poole arrived with Mr. Lee and his eldest son, and more than a dozen men from surrounding farms, with their horse drawn sickle mowers and horse teams, with their wives and food. Along with them were six Mohegans on horseback.

Robin and Marie went out to the courtyard in surprise.

"What is all this? What's going on?" Robin asked.

Mr. Lee got down off his wagon. "Mr. Van der Kellen, we your neighbors have come to get your hay fields harvested. It's time. You have no help here. Your horses are going to need it. Hell, our horses are going to need it as we used to buy it from your father twice a year. Our thought was, we help you get it in the barn, you'll give us a deal. If you are agreeable?"

Robin put his left hand to his mouth. His right was still in a sling.

Marie reached her arm around his waist.

"I...I didn't know it was ready to harvest," Robin stammered. "I can't charge you for hay you harvested. You're welcome to take it."

"We'll leave you plenty for your own horses, sir," Another neighbor said. "Fill your barn first."

"And what about the Mohegans?" One of the men asked.

"Oh, I'm paying them for their day's work," Mr. Lee spoke up.

"Paying them for an Indian's day's work?" Robin questioned. "I'll pay them a white man's share and they're entitled to some of the hay."

"You're going to give these Indians some of the hay?" one man asked.

"They road in on horses, didn't they? They'll bring a wagon next time and take home some shares of hay," Robin said. "If you don't mind. On this farm, a man's work is the same, no matter the color of his skin, or what country he comes from. This all used to be their land."

"Mr. Van der Kellen, I'm your neighbor on the other side, Tom Sharp. Deeply regret not stopping by sooner given the loss of your father. We're just all so grateful to you catching bank robbers and killing that horrible rapist. We come to help."

Mrs. Sharp stood up on their wagon. "And we brung the food. Your Mrs. can tell us where to set it up."

Robin looked to Marie. "We'll have to get the laundry out of the ball room. We'll be needing the space for the party when the work is done."

"Mohegans too?" Mr. Lee indicated the six Indians. "They'll be eating outside."

"They'll be eating wherever we do," Robin said.

One of the Mohegans dismounted and walked forward to Robin.

Robin offered a handshake to the Indian.

"Blacksmith in town said you got shot. Need help." He shook Robin's hand very gently, given the sling on his arm. "My relation."

"Oh, he is? Thank you. Your help is most welcome," Robin said.

"And guess what, everyone, today is Robin's birthday!" Marie announced.

The visitors cheered and began to get off wagons and unload food.

"Right this way, ladies," Marie told them. "Let's set up for the party."

Marta and June hurried to help. Adam helped to carry food inside the house.

Robin looked at the men. "You are most welcome. I haven't the first idea what's to be done when it comes to hay."

"Hay needs to be cut, stacked, dried. Then in a few weeks we return to bale it. It grows again and we do it all over again in the fall. Don't you worry. I'll be taking charge of that," Tom Sharp said. "You just rest that shooting arm and be a lawyer if we ever need one."

"Or a marksman," Constable Poole said.

"Or a Colonel," Abrams said.

"My pleasure," Robin said.

Tom began shouting orders to the farmers. Everyone began unloading food from wagons and then the horse teams were organized.

Abrams and Poole stood on either side of Robin Van der Kellen.

Robin looked from one to the other. To Michael he said, "You wanted to send your children to school in Boston."

"I still can, when they're old enough for boarding school," Michael said. "Get them out of the damn house finally."

Robin and Abrams laughed.

"So, your plans, Captain?" Abrams asked. "Colonel? I heard you were offered a commission."

"Starting to like Connecticut. So many friends here. I think I'll stay a while and hire some more help for Marie. Visit Amsterdam and return here. Have some children perhaps. Defend this territory if it comes to it," Robin said.

"You might make an American yet."

By Susan Eddy

Made in the USA
Middletown, DE
20 June 2023

32979294R00258